THE STRANGE DEATH OF FIONA GRIFFITHS

HARRY BINGHAM

An Orion paperback

First published in Great Britain in 2014
by Orion Books.
This paperback edition published in 2015
by Orion Books,
an imprint of The Orion Publishing Group Ltd.
Orion House, 5 Upper St Martin's Lane,
London WC2H 9EA

An Hachette UK company

1 3 5 7 9 10 8 6 4 2

ISBN 978-1-4091-3724-5

Typeset by Input Data Services Ltd, Bridgwater, Somerset

Printed and bound by CPI Group (UK) Ltd, Croydon CR0 4YY

The Orion Publishing Group's policy is to use papers that
are natural, renewable and recyclable products and
made from wood grown in sustainable forests. The logging
and manufacturing processes are expected to conform to
the environmental regulations of the country of origin.

www.orionbooks.co.uk

To my beloved N.

'The universe is full of magical things patiently waiting for
our wits to grow sharper.'
Eden Phillpotts, *A Shadow Passes*

Praise for The Strange Death of Fiona Griffiths

'Confronts the reader with profound questions about human nature in the midst of a fast-paced plot' *Sunday Times*

'DC Fiona Griffiths is small, bullish and psychologically fragile

... than the

... read'

... Lady

... Telegraph

... most

... freak-

... ell and

... Mail

... erantly

... sbeth

... and a

... top

... rotic

... eview

Harry Bingham is a successful author. He also runs The Writers' Workshop, an editorial consultancy for first-time writers, and organises the York Festival of Writing. He lives near Oxford.

By Harry Bingham

FIONA GRIFFITHS NOVELS

Talking to the Dead
Love Story, With Murders
The Strange Death of Fiona Griffiths

OTHER NOVELS

The Money Makers
Sweet Talking Money
The Sons of Adam
Glory Boys
The Lieutenant's Lover

NON-FICTION

This Little Britain
Stuff Matters
Getting Published
How to Write

1

September 2011

I like the police force. I like its rules, its structures. I like the fact that, most of the time, we are on the side of ordinary people. Sorting out their road accidents and petty thefts. Preventing violence, keeping order. In the words of our bland but truthful corporate slogan, we're Keeping South Wales Safe. That's a task worth doing and one I enjoy. Only, *Gott im Himmel*, the job can be tedious.

Right now, I'm sitting in a cramped little office above the stockroom at a furniture superstore on the Newport Road. I'm here with a DS, Huw Bowen, recently transferred from Swansea. A finance guy from Swindon is shoving spreadsheets at me and looking at me with pained, watery eyes. We have been here forty minutes.

Bowen takes the topmost spreadsheet and runs a thick finger across it. It comprises a column of names, a row of months, a block of numbers.

'So these are the payments?' says Bowen.

'*Correct.*'

The finance guy from Swindon wears a plastic security pass clipped to his jacket pocket. Kevin Tildesley.

'So all these people have been paid all these amounts?'

'*Correct.*'

'Tax deducted, national insurance, everything?'

'Yes. *Exactly.*'

The only window in the office looks out over the shop floor itself. We're up on the top storey, so we're on a level with the fluorescent lighting and what seems like miles of silver ducting. The superstore version of heaven.

Bowen still hasn't got it. He's a nice guy, but he's as good with numbers as I am at singing opera.

I bite down onto my thumb, hard enough to give myself a little blue ledge of pain. I let my mind rest on that ledge, while the scenario in front of me plays itself out. I'm theoretically here to take notes, but my pad is mostly blank.

'And these are all employees? Contracts in place? Bank accounts in order? Anything else, I don't know . . . pension plans and all that?'

'Yes. They are all contracted employees. We have their contracts. Their bank details. Their addresses. Everything. But two of the people – these two,' he says, circling two names on the spreadsheet, 'these two don't actually exist.'

Bowen stares at him.

His mouth says nothing. His eyes say, 'So *why*. The *fuck*. Were you *paying* them?'

Kevin starts to get into the detail. Again.

He tries to puff his chest out to take control of this interview, but he doesn't have much chest to puff. The room smells of body odour.

Anyway. We go round again. The Kevin and Huw show.

Payroll is handled centrally but data is entered locally. Head office routinely 'audits' local payroll data, but what Kevin means by that is simply that the entire company's data is fed into a computer program that looks for implausible or impossible results. The two phantom names – Adele Gibson and Hayley Morgan – didn't ring any alarm bells.

'So, for example,' Kevin tells us, 'if we find multiple payroll entries that share the same address or the same bank account, we'd be very suspicious. Ditto, if there are no deductions being made for tax or if overtime claims seem unnaturally high. So basically, we've *done* an audit-quality data check.'

His voice is high and pressured. I realise that he's worried about his own job. He's the Head Office guy who was meant to make sure this kind of thing didn't happen. And here it is: having happened. The fraud only came to light when the superstore got an enquiry from the bank of one of the recipients.

I ask how much money has been lost.

Kevin starts to answer. His voice catches. He drinks water from a bottle. Then, 'Thirty-eight thousand pounds. Over two financial years.'

Bowen and I look at each other. Steal £38,000 and you're looking at a two-year prison sentence, give or take. It's too big a fraud for us to ignore, but I can already see Bowen wondering how he can dodge this one. Give him a good bit of GBH or assault with intent, and Bowen is your man. Give him an investigation full of spreadsheets and people with plastic badges called Kevin from Swindon and Bowen, big man that he is, looks pale with fear. This shouldn't really even be our case. Huw and I are both attached to Major Crimes, and this case is strictly Fraud Squad. Only there's a sad lack of violent death in South Wales at the moment, while our colleagues in Fraud keep on getting sick or taking jobs in the private sector.

So we're here, with Kevin. A stack of manila folders sits on the desk in front of him. The personnel files for this branch. All of them. Current employees, past employees, temporary and part-time staff. Everyone.

Bowen looks at them. He looks at me.

Kevin looks at us both and says, 'These are copies. For you.'

2

Bowen and I fight. I lose.

Neither of us wanted to take the case. Bowen, because he's terrified someone will ask him to add up. Me, because people always want to chuck the paperwork-heavy cases my way and I spend my life trying to avoid them.

I'd hoped that because Bowen was, in Cardiff terms, a newbie, I might just have the edge in this particular turf war. Shows how little I know. Bowen is older than me, senior to me, is a man, drinks beer and used to play rugby, and all those things count for more than anything I can muster. Bowen is assigned to a simple little manslaughter case – no investigative depth, the likely perpetrator already in custody, but still: a proper crime and a proper corpse – and I get to play with Kevin from Swindon.

When I complained, DI Owen Dunwoody, who gave me the assignment, told me to think of it as a good career-case. 'Not particularly fun, but very solvable. Good promotion fodder.'

When I complained again, Dunwoody said, 'We all have to do things we don't enjoy.'

When I complained again, Dunwoody said, 'Fiona, just do your bloody job.'

So here I am, up on Fairoak Road, doing my bloody job. A brisk day with a shiver of rain.

The place I need, a brick-built block of flats, lies opposite the cemetery. Would offer one of the best views in Cardiff except that the houses here choose to turn their backs on the dead, offering up garages and back gardens to the graveyard, instead of facing it front on.

I park off-street, in a resident's bay. A cluster of grey plastic bins watches disapprovingly.

Flat 2E. Mrs Adele Gibson.

Kevin isn't quite right to say that Adele Gibson doesn't exist. She does. She may or may not have helped sell cut-price faux-leather sofas in a superstore on the Newport Road, but she exists all right. Council tax. Electoral roll. Phone.

I ring her bell.

Nothing.

Ring it again. Keep the buzzer pressed down for twenty seconds, but nada, nothing.

I'm about to start trying other bells in the block, when a car enters the car park and stops. A blue Citroën Berlingo, with its nearside trim missing. A man gets out, opens the back and starts fussing with a ramp. An electric wheelchair hums out backwards. Cerebral palsy, I guess, seeing the woman in the chair. Fortyish. Clean hair.

The man closes the car. The pair approach the house.

'Adele Gibson?' I ask the woman. 'I'm looking for a Mrs Gibson.'

'Not me,' says the woman.

The man opens the front door, but doesn't want to let me inside. 'A security thing,' he says.

I show him my warrant card. 'A police thing,' I say.

The woman who isn't Adele Gibson enjoys her minder's comeuppance.

The corridors inside are wide and there's a lift, even though the block is only three storeys high. Laminated fire notices in large text and bright colours.

'This is sheltered housing, is it?' I ask. 'Are there staff on site?'

The man gives me the answers. Yes and no respectively. It's a council-owned facility designed to be disability friendly, but intended for residents who can live semi-independently.

The woman hums off down the corridor, the man following on behind. A smell of curry.

Upstairs. Knock on the door at 2E. Nothing.

I call Jon Breakell in the office. He's the other poor sod who's been lumbered with this case. I ask him to contact social services, find out what the deal is with Adele Gibson. He says OK and asks if I'm coming back for lunch.

I'm not. The furniture company's other phantom lives up in Blaengwynfi, in the country above Aberkenfig. Jon says he'll call me when he gets something.

I'm in a bad mood as I start the drive, but the miles and the mountains start to soften my ill temper. There's something about these mining towns – the cramped valleys and injured mountains – which feels truthful to me, more truthful than anything you can find in Cardiff.

Bracken on the hills. Water flashing white and silver in the streams.

Buzzards.

The cottage in Blaengwynfi stands above the main village, up on the hill. A metalled road runs as far as a small line of four new brick houses, then gives up. A cattle grid marks the boundary to the open hill and an unmetalled driveway runs the remaining two hundred yards to the cottage. Crushed rock for the tyre tracks, grass growing freely in between. Sheep wander across the road.

I drive up to the cottage.

It's small. Probably just two bedrooms. Green painted front door. A modest effort at a garden. Low stone wall keeping the sheep off. No lights.

A red Toyota Corolla sits outside a wooden garage next to the house. Water butt. Log store.

There's no bell so I knock at the door. Wait long enough that I'm within my rights to peer through all the windows, but I don't see anything much. Net curtains in what I think must be the kitchen. There's a smell, like that of a manure heap, only not as sweet, not as grassy.

Drive back to the little group of four houses lower down the hill. Knock on a couple of doors until I find a neighbour. Ask about Hayley Morgan. The woman I ask looks blank, until I point up at the cottage, then says what people say when they don't know the people they live next to. 'Oh, Mrs Morgan, keeps herself to herself really. Doesn't cause any trouble.'

I can feel her curiosity tugging at me, like a kite on a string.

I don't give her what she wants. Knock on the two other doors. Get another don't-know-don't-care from a mother who has a fag in her mouth and a TV on loud in the front room.

I'm just heading back into the valley when my phone bleeps with a text. I was probably out of signal higher up. Jon Breakell. BIT WEIRD. CALL ME.

I call him.

'Oh hey, Fi. Look, I just got off the phone with social services. There's been some problem with Adele Gibson's bank account. Money's been going into it from the furniture place but it's gone straight out again. That's been going on for a while apparently, some sort of bank cock-up, but just recently, the last eight weeks, *all* the money has gone out. Social security money. Disability living allowance. Whatever. Anything that's been paid into the account has gone straight out again.'

'Gone where?'

'Don't know. The payments are made out to a T.M. Baron. I'm trying to trace him now.'

Jon starts telling me what he's doing with social services and how he's going to trace T.M. Baron, but I cut him off. 'Later.'

Drive back up the hill. Fast, springs protesting at the potholes.

I'm a city girl but I've spent enough time on my Aunt Gwyn's farm to know the smell of manure, and that wasn't manure. At the cottage I knock again for form's sake but I'm already looking for a rock. Try to slide one out from the garden wall. I don't manage but I do find one erupting, like an oversized molar, from the muddy verge beyond.

Wrench it out. Heave it through the living room window. Reach through the broken glass for the catch. Open the window, sweep the worst of the glass off the shelf and slide myself inside, taking a pair of latex gloves from the car before I do.

The smell is stronger here. Definite. It's like the smell you get from chicken left too long in the fridge. A smell that combines the damp meatiness of mushrooms, the gamey quality of hung fowl, the choking quality of ammonia. All that, only intensified. Compacted.

The living room has two armchairs – blue, velvet covered, old – and some thin cotton curtains. Some books. A TV. Fireplace.

The standby lamp on the TV is not illuminated. Gloves on, I flick a light switch. Nothing happens. An old-fashioned phone on a side table, but no dialling tone when I lift the receiver.

Go through to the kitchen, passing a tiny hall, flagstones on the floor, wooden stairs leading up. Mail, too much of it, by the door.

The whole house is cold.

Hayley Morgan lies in her kitchen.

She looks tiny, frail. Like a thing flung, not a person fallen.

8

She's dressed – grey skirt, blue top, cardigan, fur-lined boots – and wears some make-up. Mid-fifties, at a guess.

She's been dead a while: body flaccid, no lividity. But the smell is the strongest indicator. This kitchen feels no more than ten or twelve degrees now, and it's the middle of the day. Decomposition doesn't happen fast at these low temperatures, but it's already extensive. The smell isn't even just a smell. It has a more physical presence than that. A scent that climbs into your nostrils, occupies your sinuses. It's like a ball of cotton wool, dense and damp, that makes breathing difficult.

I push a window open, though crime-scene procedure would have me touch nothing.

Morgan is terribly thin. There's a sharpness about the way her bones poke from her skin that's somehow agonising. Like an African famine repainted in Welsh colours.

Some sign of a head injury. Nothing much. I guess she fell, hurt herself, and never got up again.

I start to explore the kitchen.

Look inside the fridge, swing the cupboards open, look in every drawer. The kitchen sink doesn't have cupboards beneath it, just a red gingham curtain on a piece of clothes line.

Cutlery, crockery, pots and pans.

Cling film, sandwich bags, old boiler manuals, oven racks.

Kitchen cleaner, rat poison, dustpan and brush.

But no food. None. Not anywhere.

Not a spillage of breakfast cereal. No tin of fish, no box of catfood, no place where some dried fruit has spilled and never been cleared up. In the dustbin, I find a packet of sugar that has been torn open. Usually with sugar, when you shake an empty packet, it rustles with the glassy tinkle of sugar crystals caught in the folds at the bottom. When you think about it, in fact, it's rare for any packaging to be completely empty.

There's always a little ketchup left in the bottle, a little sauce left in the can.

Not here. The sugar packet looks as if it's been sucked or licked clean. The paper's smooth texture has become fibrous and uneven. Something similar is true of any other food waste I can find.

I shake the packet of rat poison.

It doesn't rattle. It's completely empty.

I leave the house, putting the front door on the latch, and drive down the hill until I get a signal. Call Dunwoody.

'Keeping out of trouble, are you?' he asks.

I don't know what the answer to that is. I'm standing by my car, just below the cattle grid, watching a buzzard test its weight on the winds blowing up from Aberkenfig. Its armaments seem tactless somehow. Excessive.

The bird hovers overhead as Dunwoody repeats his question.

I still don't know how to answer, so I just say 'Yes.'

3

The next thirty minutes are spent with the logistics of death. Get a duty officer up from Neath, SOCOs from Swansea, the divisional surgeon from Cardiff. It's Dunwoody's job to do those things really, but I find myself doing most of it. I keep him in the loop, more or less. He promises to come over 'soon as I can'. I ask him to get a full set of phone records from the phone provider. Also bank records. Also any medical and social services records. I'd do it myself except those things are easier to do from the office.

I also speak to Jon Breakell, who says T.M. Baron has been traced to an address in Leicester.

'And you're going to tell me that Dunwoody has got some uniforms kicking down the doors.'

'Not exactly, but this kind of changes things, I guess.'

'Just a bit.'

I hang up.

I'm parked just below the cattle grid, but within sight of the open moorland. From where I am, I can count six sheep, but there will be dozens more, roaming the hill, cropping the grass, disturbing the grouse and the pipits, the skylarks and the plovers. There are enough sheep on this hill to feed a family for years. Hayley Morgan died as next season's roast dinner grazed the verge beyond her kitchen window.

There's only one road up to the cottage and when a clean blue Passat noses its way up the road, I travel with it. The

Passat discharges one SOCO, Gavin Jones, and a plump DS, who turns out to be Bob Shilton, the duty officer from Neath. Jones has a porn star moustache, sprinkled with grey.

I say, 'You're it? This is the team?'

Jones the SOCO, who clearly knows his colleague socially not just professionally, says, 'Yes, love, this isn't *CSI*.'

I'm thrilled to be called 'love' by anyone with a porn star moustache, but can't help pointing out that the woman inside died via a combination of starvation and poisoning. That we believe her to have been the unwitting accomplice of a complex fraud. And that, actually, crime scene investigation is precisely what this is.

The two men roll their eyes at each other over my head. I'm too prettily feminine to be offended. Just say, 'She's in the kitchen. You can view her from that window.'

Jones looks through the window. Clocks the sight, the smell. And, when it comes to the point, seems reasonably professional. Suits up properly. Gloves and mask. Steps into the house. Doesn't go in far, just enough to view the corpse.

I ask him if he has a spare suit in his car. He does. It's ridiculously large – a man's size, XL – but I put it on anyway. By the time I'm ready to re-enter the house, the fat DS is sitting on the garden wall about to light up.

I say, 'If you're going to have a cigarette, you are not having it there. You haven't secured the back of the house. You haven't checked the garage and parking area. Given that any third party would have arrived by car, those areas form part of the crime scene. DI Dunwoody is on his way over here now and he will expect me to report to him when he gets here.'

I tie off my charm-package with a neat little smile and head on into the house. Jones hasn't moved far. The little front hall commands the living room on the left, the kitchen on the right. He's checking both rooms with a high power ALS lamp, swapping filters to check for biological traces.

'No blood that I can see. Plenty of fingerprints, of course. No drugs showing up. Let's try bright white.'

He removes the filter and swipes the torch around the floors. The cottage isn't the cleanest, and the living room has an open fire which looks like it provided the only heating for that part of the house. Under the torch's glare, every footprint shows up precisely in the dust. The scatter of glass crystals gleams like diamonds.

'That's you?' says Jones, pointing at the footprints which lead from the living room window to the kitchen.

'Yes.'

There are other prints, but small ones, belonging either to a woman or a child. Hayley Morgan, whom we haven't yet approached, was no bigger than me. Jones assesses the dead woman's feet from a distance and looks at the pattern of marks on the living room floor.

'I don't see anything,' he says, meaning male footprints.

'Me neither.'

We both assume any fraudster is a man, though we have no particular reason to think so.

In the corner by the TV, there's a bundle of papers, down with the firelighters and matches. Most of the paper looks like it's there to start a fire with, but there are a couple of soft cardboard document wallets.

'I'd like those, when you can.'

Jones nods and asks me to pass him his camera. He photographs the scene, wide-angle and close up. Photographs the floor. Moves over to the document wallets. Checks them, close up, for biological traces, and nods to indicate that they're clear, as far as he can see.

He gives them to me.

As all that is happening, I'm looking into the kitchen. The smell is still intense, though there's air moving through the house now and I'm standing in the hall by an open door. The more light and air there is in this house, the smaller Morgan seems. A minor detail. A styling accessory.

I take the document wallets, but say, 'What's that?'

The kitchen has a rough, textured plaster. On the wall above an electric night storage heater, someone has scratched away at the plaster, wearing a hole right through to the old-fashioned breeze blocks beneath. There are grooves left in the soft plaster. Jones focuses his torch beam on the area. It's hard to be sure, but the grooves look like toothmarks.

Jones doesn't say anything direct, just, 'We'll know when we examine her mouth.'

'Yes.'

'Those things.' He nods at the exposed block wall. 'They're made of compacted coal ash. Waste materials from a blast furnace. God knows what kind of chemicals in there.'

'Yes.'

He shines the lamp on Morgan's face. Her personality somehow shrinks away under the illumination. Simplifying, reducing. There is dust on her face. The dust might be a combination of plaster and coal ash or it might not. He moves his lamp away and there is something reverential in the way he does it.

I have my documents. He has his camera.

'I'll get on then,' he says.

I don't know how to answer that either, so I just say 'Yes.'

4

Later that evening. We're in an evil little pub near Blaen-gwynfi. A red carpet, darkly patterned to compete with the beer stains and the ground-in food. Stone benches beneath the windows and a smell of damp. There are four drinkers here apart from us, all men. They attack their pints the way infantrymen march: slowly, knowing that the road ahead is long.

I'm here with Dunwoody, Jon Breakell and Buzz. Buzz – DS David Brydon, as far as my colleagues are concerned – isn't on the inquiry team, but when he was done for the day he cadged a lift out here with a scientific officer from Cathays. He'll drive back into town with me later.

Brydon and I are a fairly public couple now, treated by a unit as our colleagues. We're careful to be properly professional while at the office, but out here, at the end of the day, in a time which might be an after-hours social or might, if Dunwoody is feeling generous, count as formal overtime, those rules are more relaxed. Buzz and I sit side by side on one of the stone benches. He had his arm around me earlier, as a way of showing that he was relaxed. He's removed it now, but I can still feel its phantom weight across my shoulders, the warmth of him down my side.

The table is littered. Bank statements. Phone bills. Water bills. Electricity. Correspondence. Everyone leaves the paperwork to me. Fi Griffiths, the paperwork kid. I don't mind, except when Dunwoody puts his beer down on one of the phone bills, creating a ringmark.

'That's Exhibit A under your beer glass,' I say.

He moves the paper, not the beer.

With Hayley Morgan, it's the same deal as it was with Adele Gibson. For eighteen months she received money from the superstore, but that money vanished again, almost immediately, to an account operated by T.M. Baron. For most of that period, the rest of Morgan's finances were untouched. She had a tiny income, tiny expenses, but she got by. Lived as she chose. Then twelve weeks ago, her account was drained. Every penny that came in was instantly taken. At the end of every day, her account registered a balance of £0.00.

Before long, her phone was cut off. Then her electricity.

I think of Morgan licking the sugar out of an empty packet, in a house gone dark. Think of her looking at the packet of rat poison and thinking, 'How much longer?' Wondering how long it was before she put her head to the wall for the first time wanting to see if plaster dust and breeze block could fill her belly.

'I don't understand it, really, not in these small places,' says Dunwoody. 'Why wouldn't she just walk down the hill and ask for food? Or call the police and report a fraud? Or anything.'

Buzz says, 'Yes, but loads of people die where you could ask the same thing. Last winter, how many thousand pensioners was it died from the cold? All they had to do was phone the gas company or speak to a neighbour, but instead they let themselves freeze. Every year, thousands of people.'

'That's true, but still. Why let yourself starve?'

There are a few answers to that, or none. We now know – from medical records and the documents I recovered from the cottage – that Morgan suffered a minor stroke some eight months back. She was assessed as having minor cognitive impairment, but perhaps those assessments were wrong. They sometimes are. She'd had mental-health problems too – depression, mostly – and those things might have returned. And her nearest neighbours weren't of her kind or class. And, with the death of coal-mining in these areas, none of these communities are what they used to be. And perhaps Morgan had some strange old-fashioned pride around begging. Or thought she'd sort things out with the bank. Or suffered some further stroke. Or had some petty feud with the people in the shop or the health centre. Or some combination of all these things and more.

We never finally know the truth, never learn the full map of any crime. Motivations and choices recede endlessly from view.

I don't say this though. Just read the paperwork as the others chat. Dunwoody looks at his empty beer glass and says, 'I'd swear I got the first round in.'

Buzz gets up to get more drinks. Breakell can't drink – he's driving – and I don't.

I hold up one of the documents. A letter from social services. 'She used to get fortnightly care visits. Someone cancelled them.'

'Who? Morgan?'

'Well, according to this, yes,' I say, 'but this letter is dated June of this year.'

Dunwoody shrugs. His face is pink and the beer has already risen to his eyes. He has a close-trimmed beard, which his mother probably thinks is strawberry-blond. To everyone else, it's ginger.

'Maybe Hayley Morgan wrote that letter, cancelling those visits, or maybe she didn't. Her account was emptied about four days after this letter was sent. Stayed empty, every day after that.'

Buzz comes back with the beers. Dunwoody takes his, but his eyes are on me.

I say, 'Hayley Morgan died because she was starving. And she was starving because she was robbed. If someone deliberately prevented care visits, in an effort to perpetuate their fraud, you could argue that that individual recklessly endangered Hayley Morgan's life. That's not payroll fraud. That's manslaughter.'

Dunwoody takes the letter from me, but the letter is not the point. You need three ingredients to make up a constructive manslaughter. First, an unlawful act. Second, an act likely to cause harm to the person affected. Third, death, though neither foreseen nor intended, results. As far as I can see it, we have a big *yes* on points one and three and a slightly more doubtful *yes* to point two. The case law is mostly built on the assumption that the harm-causing act is directly physical in nature. Punching someone in the face in one notable case, or pulling a replica gun on someone with a weak heart in another.

Stealing money and cancelling visits from social workers. Could those things add up to manslaughter? I think they could.

I think they *did*.

'I don't know,' says Dunwoody, 'I'm not sure.' But he hasn't touched his beer and his eyes have lost some of their pinkishness. There's anxiety there too, a rapid lateral movement of the pupils.

Which is good. If Hayley Morgan's death was no more than a nasty accident, Dunwoody has already investigated as rigorously as anyone would expect. If we're looking at a crime which stands only one rung down from murder, he's been sloppy. Slow to get to the scene. Insufficient in his demand for resources. Lazy in supervision.

He pulls out his phone. No signal.

'Sod it.'

He walks out into the car park. Buzz looks at me. This isn't his case. He's part amused by the scene he's just witnessed, part keen to have the last part explained.

'If I were him, I'd be calling my colleagues in Leicester. He should have been on their case from the start.'

Buzz rubs my back and I half close my eyes as I give myself over to the rub. Jon Breakell, feeling like a spare part probably, goes to have a pee.

'We should go on holiday,' Buzz says. 'You and me. Somewhere nice.'

'That would be nice.'

'Get some sun.'

I nod.

'You've got leave, have you?'

I stare at him. I almost never take leave. I do it only when I have to, and then never know what to do with it. That's changed a bit since I've been going out with Buzz. He books holidays, makes all the arrangements, tells me what to pay him for my share. I've no idea how many days' holiday I have owing. He knows that, I'm sure.

Buzz lets me hang a moment, then grins. 'You've got twenty-three days, including fifteen carried over from last year, and you need to use those or you'll lose 'em.'

'Oh.'

'I thought maybe Greece? Or Turkey? Somewhere still hot enough for beaches and swimming.'

I nod. 'That sounds . . .' I'm not sure what I'm meant to say next, so just nod some more, then tuck my head against his shoulder as Jon Breakell returns.

'I'll make the arrangements.'

A little wriggle of emotion escapes from somewhere behind my sternum. An elusive quicksilver flash that I can't identify and that's out of sight before I can pin it out for examination.

I say, 'Don't forget my course.'

I've got a training course coming up. A four-week residential thing in London. Buzz says, 'I won't. We'll go after that.'

His voice twists a bit as he speaks. He doesn't like me going on the course, but doesn't want to rehash that argument now.

Under the table, I knead his thigh.

Then the front door bangs open and Dunwoody enters. A blue twilight briefly framed behind him. Brown hills and white moths, papery in the lamplight.

'Leicestershire police have visited the address.' His voice is throaty. 'A family of eight. A Mr and Mrs Desai, his mother and five children. The husband is a hospital porter. Wife is a stay-at-home mum. Oldest child just turned fourteen. No computer present on the property. Two phones, both seized.'

He stops. His face is still in motion, though. He's feeling something, though I'm not sure what or how to describe it. The pressure of great things, perhaps. The responsibility and the fear.

I stretch my legs out. Pushing my toes out and down, feeling the burn in my calves and thighs. Feeling present. Happy.

'Payroll fraud,' I say. 'It's a beautiful thing.'

5

A beautiful thing, but strange.

Krishna Desai, the hospital porter, is not our T.M. Baron. Jon and I drove out to interview him under caution. He was helpful and friendly, though not all that comfortable speaking English. He disclaimed all knowledge of a T.M. Baron, said he didn't use a computer, but his children were taught about them at school. At the end of the interview, we asked him to fill out a short feedback form on a police website and he filled out his name slowly. He wasn't all that familiar with the keyboard and didn't know how to use a mouse. When it came to entering data other than his name, he looked at us, eyes asking what he was meant to do next.

The bank which gave T.M. Baron an account had a stored copy of the original ID and utility bill. Both things look authentic, but neither are. You can buy a top quality fake driving licence on the web for about forty pounds. A fake utility bill comes in at around thirty pounds, less if you shop around or buy in bulk.

Baron's account was interesting, though. He set up his account with an initial balance of a hundred pounds in late February 2010. A few weeks later, money started to flow into the account from Hayley Morgan and Adele Gibson, money whose origin we know to be fraudulent. Gibson – a woman with learning difficulties – managed her loss of income with no problems, because her careworker was more attentive, but

Gibson herself is not remotely plausible as a suspect.

As for the money, every month or so, all cash in the account was transferred to a bank in Spain. We don't yet know what happened at the Spanish end of things.

Sometime towards the end of June, however, arrangements changed. The accounts of Adele Gibson and Hayley Morgan started to be stripped completely. Cleaned out. It happened a bit earlier with Morgan than with Gibson, but between the end of June and the second week of July both those accounts were drained completely. Funds no longer went to Spain, but were taken out in cash from a variety of different cashpoints ranging from Reading to Cardiff and as far west as Exeter. The total sums extracted in that way amount to around £5,600.

We're trying to match CCTV footage against the dates and times of the cash withdrawals, but we've nothing useful so far. It seems like a long shot.

We've investigated the Cardiff store manager, the person best placed to commit the fraud, but he seems clean. His family holidayed at home this year, in an effort to save up for a kitchen extension. Not quite the behaviour of a successful fraudster. We'll continue to probe his finances – or Jon Breakell will – but the guy doesn't seem like our man. He's not even that bright.

We've looked at any business visitors to the store management team, but although there were a number – maintenance staff, haulage contractors – no one who rang alarm bells.

Social services has managed to find the letter sent by 'Hayley Morgan' cancelling her care visits. The paper is typed and printed on an ordinary household printer. The signature is not Hayley Morgan's, but the forgery was close enough that social services were hardly to blame for not noticing. Morgan did not, however, possess a computer or a printer or, we think, computer skills and that was something that her care worker should have noticed. Then again, her regular care worker was going off on maternity leave and her replacement was just learning the ropes. Yes, things should have been done better but, no, nothing happened that amounted to outright negligence.

And yet: a woman died because someone snipped her lifeline. Plaster dust under her gums, rat poison in her veins.

That's not quite how it's seen in the office, however. The manpower shortage in the Fraud Squad has been somewhat remedied by a couple of people returning from sickness and the secondment of an inspector from Swansea. We in Major Crime still aren't busy, except that an ugly motor accident – kids dropping stones off a motorway bridge, hitting a windscreen and triggering an eight-vehicle pile-up which killed two outright – has to be treated as a case of involuntary manslaughter, the culprits not yet identified with certainty.

And in the meantime, my little fraud inquiry, such as it was, has dwindled, the same way as Hayley Morgan's body seemed to shrink from the first moment I found her. Investigation hasn't ended, but it's being pursued in a way that means it won't ever be brought to a satisfactory close. The crime is being badged as a corporate fraud, now terminated, the culprit assumed to be living abroad.

After a tedious Monday briefing – the road accident, some boring burglaries, a dull stabbing, progress reports on some prosecution cases at least two of which I'm meant to be helping with – I pursue DCI Dennis Jackson to his office.

Jackson likes me but he doesn't allow that to get in the way of some good old-fashioned bollockings, which he delivers with panache and conviction when the occasion warrants.

'Good morning, Fiona. You've got that look.'

'A passion for Keeping South Wales Safe,' I say. 'That look?'

'You can get me a coffee, black, no sugar. I'll give you about five minutes before I have to do some actual work.'

I go to the kitchenette and get him his coffee. Make myself peppermint tea at the same time. Return to his office. A black leatherette sofa and a sideways view out towards Bute Park.

'Did the five minutes include making coffee? I don't think—'

'Fiona, let's just see how fast we can do this, shall we? You're going to tell me that the whoever-she-is Morgan death needs further investigation.'

'Hayley and yes.'

'You're going to call my attention to the fact that a crucial letter was forged and that the forgery contributed to Morgan's death.'

'I am.'

'You're going to add that the financial transactions we've been able to trace so far don't look like routine payroll fraud.'

'No, they don't.'

'And you'll use those things to talk up a case of constructive manslaughter.'

'It *is* manslaughter. An unlawful act leading to unintended death. That's manslaughter.'

'OK, then I'll look down at my list of current tasks and assignments and I'll find myself agreeing with DI Dunwoody's assessment that our limited resources could be better deployed elsewhere, particularly as our friends and colleagues in Fraud now have the manpower to take this on. If a manslaughter charge arises from their investigation, we'll do what's necessary to assist any prosecution.'

'Except that, as you keep telling me, I'm a cheap resource of doubtful reliability. If I spent more time on the Morgan case, I probably wouldn't even be missed.'

Cheap resource: the last time I had a proper telling-off from Jackson was when he discovered that I hadn't filled out any overtime sheets for five months. These things matter, apparently.

'*Very* doubtful,' mutters Jackson, his attention on his computer. He flicks through what's been done so far.

When you get to Jackson's level of seniority, you're not a field officer any more. You seldom get to visit crime scenes, interview suspects, force entry. The stink of these things reaches you only at second-hand, from the officers who were there and the reports they compile. But every senior copper was once a plod. They don't lose their sense of smell, they just get the scent from different sources.

Jackson reviews the case notes with swift precision. His fingers are heavy on the computer, but also rapid. Deft.

He lifts his eyes to me again. Dark eyes, shaggily browed.

'Look, you lot have covered most of the basics already. And for all we know there's a guy called T.M. Baron living on the Costa del Crime, in which case the Fraud boys will just get an EAW and have him picked up.'

EAW: a European Arrest Warrant. A delightfully simple procedure.

'The money won't stop in Spain and our perpetrator isn't called T.M. Baron.'

I can't prove that, of course, but most payroll fraud is visibly stupid. Inflated salaries, implausible bonuses, zero deductions, addresses and bank details that track straight through to someone with access to the corporate payroll system. This fraud was clean enough that, for sixteen months, it went untraced. Anyone with the sophistication and patience to set it up wouldn't be stupid enough to sit in a villa near Torremolinos, waiting to be arrested.

'Probably not.'

'And remember, we don't know how large this fraud really is.'

Jackson works his eyebrows at me, so I add, 'It was a very clean fraud, which implies some professionalism and organisation. But organised crime isn't interested in a couple of thousand pounds a month. They'd need far more than that to make it worth their while. My guess: if we really take a look at this, we'll find numerous other small frauds built on the same basic model and tracing through to the same ultimate destination.'

I don't say, because Jackson is smart enough to see it for himself, that the Morgan–Gibson fraud almost certainly involved a minimum of two people. There's the T.M. Baron character: whoever it was that collected the first sixteen months' worth of payments. Then there's the lower-level idiot who started emptying the Morgan–Gibson accounts. Who blew the whole racket up for a gain of just £5,600.

An end of summer wasp crawls against Jackson's office window, butting its head against an obstacle it doesn't understand and can't overcome. Jackson stares at the wasp with a face that has the emptiness of sculpture.

He looks back at his computer, hits some buttons.

'Your course starts soon, doesn't it?'

'Next week.'

Jackson ponders a little further. His version of pondering involves hitting the flat of his hand softly against the top of his desk and staring into the middle distance.

'Look, I take your point, but I think we need to leave this with Fraud for now. I'll talk to – who's that new guy over from Swansea?'

'Rhodri Stephens.'

'I'll talk to him. Tell him we take this seriously, that we think there's a manslaughter prosecution floating around here. We'll give them time to make a case of it, see where they get to.'

Because my face doesn't instantly assume the 'yes, O Mighty One' reverence that all senior officers think is their due, Jackson adds, 'Fiona, fraud is a job for the Fraud Squad.

It is not a job for Major Crime and it is not your job to tell me mine.'

'No, sir.'

'I think that's our five minutes. Thank you for the coffee.'

'You're welcome.'

'Good luck with the course.'

I nod and leave the room.

6

It's three weeks later, but feels more. I'm in a shit flat close to where the M1 disgorges into London, a long stone's throw from Brent Cross. I'm on the eighth floor of an eleven-storey building. One of the lifts is out of order and the curtains on my windows are made of unlined orange cotton. My kitchen contains a packet of sliced bread, some margarine, some peppermint tea bags and a tin of beans. I don't have a can opener.

It is midnight, and I have to be at work in Wembley by four. I'm not allowed my car here, and the journey time by public transport is an hour.

So far this week, I have averaged less than four hours sleep a night.

I put some margarine on a slice of bread and eat it, standing up, looking out of the window. There's music coming from the flat above me. Music and an argument.

I'd like to call Buzz. Not about anything, just to chat. Hear his voice, learn what's been going on at the office. Laugh a bit too much at one of his jokes, just for the pleasure of feeling his pleasure at my appreciation.

We've been going out for slightly more than a year. I would say it's been my longest ever relationship but in truth it's been my first ever relationship. First proper one. I remember when we first started dating I thought, *I realise I would like to be Dave Brydon's girlfriend. The sort who would remember his birthday, act appropriately in front of his parents and think to wear their most expensive knickers on St Valentine's Day.* And I've ticked those boxes, all of them. I haven't just remembered his birthday, but I got everything right at Christmas and have, mostly, remembered our important anniversaries. I don't get waves of love from his parents – him a manager at a national building products company, her the deputy head of a village school in the Forest of Dean – but my mishaps and misdemeanours have all been fairly minor, all explainable as *That's just Fi for you, I'm afraid.* I even got Valentine's Day right too. I couldn't quite believe that fully grown adults took all that commercial red-heart pap seriously, but I checked with my sister beforehand who told me yes, they really did. So I did it. Played the part. Wore a nice black dress with expensive undies, red and slutty, underneath. Let Buzz take me to dinner. Expressed surprise and delight when, inevitably, a dozen red roses were produced. Let myself be coaxed into drinking a whole glass and a half of champagne – a lot for me – and happily shared a chocolate pudding glazed with raspberry coulis in the shape of a heart. Then we went back to Buzz's place where we made red and slutty love, saying that we loved each other and meaning it.

I look at my phone. It's mine, not something issued by the training course. All my numbers pre-programmed. A couple of taps and I'm talking to a yawning Buzzman.

But I'm not allowed to phone him. Not him, not Mam or Dad, not Ant or Kay. No one at work. No one.

So I don't.

Just stand at the window, eat bread and margarine, listen to the argument above me. Traffic curls down the A406. I can't see the mouth of the M1, but somehow you feel its presence. Exhaust-fumed, grimy and congested. An ill-tempered beast, belching lorries. My hair feels greasy but I don't have a hairdryer here and I don't want to go to bed with wet hair.

I'm out of clean underwear, so I wash three pairs of knickers in the bathroom sink and hang them out on a radiator. They won't be dry in the morning.

I do my teeth, but without fervour. Look at my hair, which *is* greasy. Still don't wash it.

Bed.

My bed is made up of a second-hand mattress lying directly on the floor. Sheets clean enough and the duvet warm. I think if my eyes were like other people's, they'd be aching to close. I'd be half asleep already. But it doesn't work like that for me. I am tired, but that doesn't always mean I find it easy to sleep. So I just lie down and look at the light on the ceiling until sleep overtakes me. When it does, it's dreamless and dark.

The alarm clock rings at two forty. It's dark outside and the flat is cold.

Still wrapped in my duvet, I walk to the shower, get it hot, then step into it. Wash my hair. Wash everything else. Do you have to brush your teeth if you last brushed them less than three hours ago? Don't know, but I do anyway.

My knickers are still roughly as damp as they were when I hung them out last night. I choose the least wet.

Get dressed. My uniform consists of a pale grey polo shirt, a pale grey fleece top, black trousers, which I had to supply myself, and a mid-blue tabard which is in a unisex style and fit and consequently too big for me. I put it all on. The shirt, fleece and tabard all have the same corporate logo: YCS Cleaning and a meaningless geometrical logo in orange and blue.

Into the kitchen. Ponder the breakfast menu briefly. Opt for bread and margarine, but don't manage to eat much.

Then off to work. There's a direct bus which is theoretically faster, but it's unreliable and I've already had a warning for being late. So I walk to Cricklewood station, take a night bus in to Baker Street, take a second bus out to the Harrow Road and walk from there. It's a ridiculous way to make the journey

– an hour to travel about five miles – but it gets me there on time.

We gather in the dark, my colleagues and I. Six of us. Me, Amina, Ruqia, Diwata, Maria and someone whose name I'm not quite sure of. I think Milenka. Amina's huge smile cleaves the darkness. I smile back, though I doubt if my version cleaves quite the same.

Maria has cigarettes. I want one badly but I bummed a cigarette off her yesterday and in this world you need to give back. It's cold out and though I'm wrapped up, I still feel it.

At five to four, a black Honda Accord pulls up. Marcus Conway, our boss. He greets us, ticks our names off his list, then unlocks the main office door and leads us down to the service basement where the cleaning stuff is kept. A trolley each. Cleaning stuff. Large transparent waste sack. Spare liners for the office bins.

We're each allocated a different floor, because they don't like us talking to each other when we're working. When Conway gives us an instruction, we've been trained to answer, 'Yes, Mr Conway.' To start with, that all felt a little Victorian-mill-owner to me and I've never been the best little Victorian factory girl. But if it's good enough for Amina, it's good enough for me and when Conway tells me, 'Fiona, you'll take the fourth floor. All the computers need cleaning and the internal office windows. Have you got that?', I just mutter, 'Yes, Mr Conway.' And when he asks me to check I have the right cleaning kit for the screens and keyboards, I do check, just as he asks, then say it again.

And off I go, with my yellow trolley and a polyester tabard that reaches to my knees.

Oddly, it's the cleaning I find hardest about all this. Not that I have to work hard, I'm OK with that. But the actual process of cleaning itself. Wipe, dust, empty. Wipe, dust, empty. My brain can't stick with the routine. It keeps firing

31

off elsewhere. I honestly try my hardest, but my hardest is a bit ramshackle. Sometimes I do everything I'm meant to do. Other times, I realise I forgot to empty half the bins, or have left a waste bag in the middle of a corridor, or haven't cleaned the toilets. But I do my best.

We work at this office from four till just before six, then at another, larger, office from six to almost nine. In the City, I've heard that you can get as much as £7.20 per hour. Out here, though, we're strictly minimum wage, no sick pay, no long-term contracts, no holiday pay, no nothing.

At nine, we have to remove our tabards and empty out our pockets. That's Conway's way to show us that he's alive to the risk of us stealing. But he knows and we know that if we nicked anything, it would be cash and we would hide it in our underwear, so all the pocket-emptying is really no more than panto.

Today, unusually, I have free time between nine and five. Normally we have to meet for coursework. Lessons on surveillance methods. Case studies. Lots of legal stuff. We have to know the Regulation of Investigatory Powers Act pretty much backwards, but there's a lot of other law too. The Police and Criminal Evidence Act, of course. The Criminal Procedure and Investigations Act. European law and court rulings.

This is the National Undercover Training and Assessment course and it's the toughest course offered by the police service. Most people who apply are rejected. Even when you're accepted onto the course, 85 per cent of students fail.

I'm not even sure why I applied. A memo came round last year asking if anyone was interested and I said yes. No real reason. Curiosity, I suppose.

Buzz hates the idea of me working undercover. He doesn't like the danger. He doesn't like the loss of contact. It took me time to realise it, but he's hurt that I even applied for the course. As though it was some kind of snub to him.

I've mended things since then, I think. Told him that I have no intention of doing one of those marathon infiltrations. The things that last years and mess with your brain. I told him what might even be the truth: that I hate being told I can't do something, so I want to make sure that I've got the ability to do it if I want to. Which I won't.

As far as I'm concerned, that's logical. As far as Buzz goes – well, I don't know, but it'll be better once the course is over.

The course isn't mostly about law. We learn about managing a second identity, or 'legend' as it's called by the undercover specialists who teach us. I'm Fiona Grey now. Fiona isn't pretending to be a cleaner, she *is* a cleaner. We learn how to construct our pasts. Invent them. Get paperwork in the new names, get a history. Learn that history so it starts to become ours.

And we learn about danger. Infiltration is a tactic we only ever use against organised crime, or groups thought to be planning acts of violence or terror. Make a mistake on an infiltration and it's not going to be a 'Whoops, sorry, Sarge' moment. It's going to be a shot to the back of the head, bag in the river type moment.

We hear stories of undercover officers who have simply disappeared. Missing, presumed dead. Hear what happens when things go wrong.

The best sessions are briefings given by actual practitioners. Accounts of what it's actually like. The dangers, the situations you get into. When we started, most of the questions had to do with the drama of the chase. Making contact with the bad guys. Gaining their trust. Executing the bust. The armed raids and the car chases. By now, though, our interest has shifted. My fellow students ask about what it's like to be cut off from family. How you get through Christmas. What it's like to live in fear.

The answers get more truthful too. One guy – Steve, a London DS – said he was on a job that lasted twenty-two months. Unfortunately his marriage only lasted eighteen of them. One of my fellow students asked him whether he regretted his decision to take the assignment. He said, 'Every day, mate. Literally every day.'

Today, though, we have a break, our first on the course. My cleaning money has been very late in coming through to my bank account – my Fiona Grey account, that is – hence my rather basic eating and hygiene arrangements. I assume the money was held up by the course authorities. They can't replicate the fear of a real infiltration, but they can reproduce some of the stresses. Hence the isolation, the long hours, the lack of sleep, the constant little indignities.

They have all of us on two jobs, antisocial hours. I clean in the morning, waitress in the evening. The waitressing runs from six to eleven, or more like midnight on busy nights. It's not every night of the week, because our training often runs into the evenings, but it mops up what little free time I might have.

I sleep in between the waitressing and the cleaning. Make use of any spare half hours that come my way. Doze on trains.

When I try the bank again today, my money has come through and I withdraw fifty pounds. Spend most of it on a cheap hairdryer, a can opener and some ready-meals. Sit in a café and do my law revision.

It feels like luxury this: to have time and money. Those things and clean hair.

I take my time.

When I'm done, I go back to the flat. Collect dirty clothes to take to the launderette. I should take one of my law books, but I don't.

When I'm sitting, snoozing, waiting for the spin cycle to end, a guy parks himself next to me on the slatted wooden bench. I wake up, shift away. The guy is middle-aged, heavy, close-cropped hair. A Londoner.

'What's your name, love?'

'Fiona.'

He thumps his chest and says, 'Dez.'

I shrug.

'You're with YCS, right?'

I shrug again. I'm still wearing their damn fleece.

'Listen, sweetheart, I've got a little job that needs doing, all right? Won't get you into any trouble and it's worth a hundred quid, cash.'

The machine next to me stops spinning. I try the handle, but it's got one of those stupid safety releases which make you wait a minute before anything happens.

It's hard not to smile.

This course isn't mostly theoretical. It's not mostly about learning the law. Really, they shove you into a situation, deprive you of sleep, and see if you can cope. This man, 'Dez', is the next step. He'll ask me to do something illegal – steal something, plant something, I don't know what. I'll demur the right length of time, then say yes. The pressure will ratchet up. Less sleep, more phoney danger.

And they'll try to fool me. A police officer will 'recognise' me as a buddy of his from Hendon. Or someone will call me Griffiths, not Grey, my new name, and see how I respond.

I'll do just fine, I already know it. If I'd filled in my personality questionnaires honestly, they'd never have selected me for the course. Too vulnerable. History of mental disorder. Blah, blah.

Truth is, though, I'm pretty much ideal for this kind of work. The hardest thing about going undercover is the stress. The isolation, the fear, the risk of discovery. But my world is mostly like that anyway. I have problems with sleep. I'm used to isolation. It's my default state and I have to work hard to avoid it. As for the stuff that happens to people when they're alone and under stress – dissociation, loss of normal feelings – well, I've already won the gold ticket in that particular lottery. A little menial work in north-west London hardly registers.

When the safety thing clicks on the washing machine. I transfer my stuff into the dryer. Put in two quid. Set it going.

Dez tries again. A hundred quid to take a black notebook from a locked drawer in the Wembley office.

I say, 'I'll lose my job.'

When he tries again, I pull my stuff, still wet, from the dryer and walk out of the launderette.

7

The course ends. Twenty of us started. Twelve left before completion, in most cases, I think, because they went half nuts and called home, just to hear a friendly voice. That sort of thing is an instant fail.

Of the eight who stuck it through to the end, just three pass. I'm one of them.

I have a one-on-one session with the DCI overseeing the course on the final day. He riffles through feedback forms and test sheets. Weak sunlight comes in from the window behind him. I'm still in my Fiona Grey outfit, YCS fleece and all. I notice that the window needs cleaning. The ledge beneath it needs a good dust, and the keys on the computer keyboard are covered in little hillocks of finger oil and dirt. I could clean this room completely in eight minutes.

'This is good,' he says, waving at the paperwork. 'You probably don't need me to tell you that.'

'Thank you.'

'Did you enjoy it? Did you enjoy the experience?'

A hard question for me at the best of times. Other people seem to have a ready understanding of what they like and what they don't. I don't have that easy access. I know I like Buzz, the police service, the investigation of murder, and my family. I like hills and wild places and driving long distances when the sun is setting. Anything else – I don't really know.

I say, 'Yes, sir.'

'You know, most of the courses we run, that's the answer we want. People learn better if they're having a good time. With this one, that answer always slightly worries me. You *should* find this stuff difficult. It's all very well working undercover, but you need to come back into regular service too. The police force will need you back. So will your family, your loved ones. Are you married?'

'No.' His face wants more of an answer than that, so I add, 'I'm in a long-term relationship, though.'

The DCI jabs his chest with his index finger. 'Divorced. Two kids. They're only just starting to talk to me again. I'm fifty-four.'

I don't know what to say to that. I'm either Fiona Griffiths, a police officer. Or Fiona Grey, a cleaner. Neither of me is a marriage counsellor.

The wastebin needs emptying and the clear plastic rubbish sack hangs loose around the lip of the bin. We were taught to tie a knot in the plastic, so it sat tight.

'What I'm saying is, you need to prioritise your life. Your family life, your friends, your CID career. If an assignment comes up, and you want to do it, then do. But don't be attracted by the glamour. This isn't glamorous, it's hard. And mostly not worth it.'

'No, sir.'

The officers who do those marathon infiltrations – two years, three years – draw only their regular salary. No overtime, modest bonus. If they have a wife and kids, they're allowed to visit once a month, no more.

'Well.' He stands up. I'm not sure what the purpose of this interview was, or if the DCI thinks that purpose has been accomplished. I stand up too.

'Congratulations again. We've been very impressed.'

'Thank you, sir.'

I leave.

I could go home straight away. I've been given my car keys back, my bank cards, all the stuff that was taken from me at the start.

And I will go back, soon. Buzz is expecting me. But first things first. I drive into Ealing, an ugly estate near Drayton Green. Corrugated concrete walls and brown pebbledash. Rotary clothes dryers standing on balconies. A car without tyres.

I don't park too close – my car is very Fiona Griffiths, not at all Fiona Grey – and walk into the estate, checking the flat number I need from a little handwritten slip of paper.

Amina's handwriting. Her flat.

She was the one real friend I made at YCS. Neither her life nor mine allowed much leisure, but we liked each other. Hung out when we could.

I ring the bell, but knock as well. Glass door, single glazed.

Amina opens it. That huge smile when she sees me. Baby lying in a cot in the tiny hallway. A man in a purple shirt sits in the front room talking loudly on the phone. A language I don't recognise, but Somali I assume.

Amina brings me through to the kitchen. The man glances at me, but not for long. The kitchen is a mess. Amina has been barbecuing lamb kidneys using an oven rack laid directly over the gas hob. Everything is splattered with fat. A vegetable broth stands in a large saucepan to the side. Smells of cumin, cardamom, cloves. There is a motorbike standing where you'd expect there to be a table. Tools and rags, but not much sign of action.

I tell Amina I've lost my flat. That I'm leaving London.

She doesn't understand right away – her English isn't brilliant – but when she does, she looks upset.

'You can't go,' she says, waving a long black finger at me, then hugging me. As she steps back again, she adjusts her headscarf.

'I have to.'

Amina looks sad. She keeps readjusting her face to hide her sadness, but it keeps coming back.

'Can you give these back to Mr Conway? I haven't told him.'

I give Amina my YCS stuff in a plastic bag. Conway won't be surprised at my sudden disappearance. His workforce changes with every passing wind.

'Where are you going?'

'I'm not sure yet. Maybe Manchester.' I shrug.

Manchester: my Fiona Grey legend involves a long-term, but abusive, relationship with a guy in Manchester. The abusive part is good because it means I don't have to talk about it much. Also because it gives my legend a kind of messy unity. The kind of work I was doing in Wembley is essentially done only by immigrants. I was the only native Briton under Conway's command, the only one to speak English as a first language. Aside from Milenka, I was the only one with white skin. People like me only turn out to clean toilets at four in the morning if their lives have gone badly astray somewhere. Abuse, in the case of Fiona Grey. God knows what in the case of Fiona Griffiths.

The baby in the hall starts crying. The man in the purple shirt shouts through to us. Amina's eyes change and I say, 'I'll go.'

We hug again.

Amina gets the baby. I open the front door. Amina says, 'Wait,' goes through to the kitchen, and comes back with some brown cake wrapped in a piece of kitchen towel. 'Shushumow,' she says.

'Shushumow?'

She repeats the word, gives me that smile again, and closes the door.

Back at my car, I call Buzz.

40

'Hey, stranger.'

His voice is warm, full of love. I don't quite feel as I ought to in return. I feel clumsy and cut off from the person I was.

I act the part though. Act Fiona Griffiths, the one who's in love with a handsome policeman, and as I get into role, my feelings start to come back a bit. I don't quite feel like her exactly, but perhaps I might do with a little more practice.

We chat for a while, then hang up.

Plan for tonight is: drive home, get changed, fancy meal, lots of sex. The classic Buzz solution to any complex emotional situation, except that the first three parts of the formula are prone to change or cancellation without notice.

When I'm on the M4, I try nibbling one of the shushumow cakes, but they're way too sweet for me and I throw them out of the window when I'm crossing the Severn Bridge.

Croeso i Gymru.

Welcome to Wales.

8

We do, as it happens, implement the formula, just as planned. I go to my house, wash and change. Buzz has booked us a table at the restaurant where we had our first date. I don't know if there's meant to be some kind of significance in that but, if there is, I cooperate by wearing the outfit I wore then. Dark blue dress, silver and jet bead necklace, nice shoes.

I drive there. Make a hash of parking, which isn't like me, and get a bit lost in Pontcanna before finding my way to the right side of Cathedral Road, where I'm meant to be.

I realise I'm nervous. I don't know why.

I'm first to arrive. Sit all ladylike at the table, while a waiter brings me a menu, a glass tumbler holding breadsticks, and a glass of fizzy water. He lights a candle with a cigarette lighter.

I watch with professional interest. I wasn't a particularly good waitress, but I wasn't working in the candle-'n'-breadstick sort of place. Mine was a Tex-Mex joint that sold beer by the pitcher and had a big Friday night trade in after-work parties. I took orders, carried plates, fetched drinks, didn't mess anything up too much or too often, and occasionally remembered to smile. I did OK.

I sit there, waiting for Buzz, counting my breaths and trying to feel my feet.

A year and four months since I was last here.

Then all of a sudden, Buzz is here, in front of me. Disconcertingly strange and overwhelmingly familiar at the same time. He crushes me into a hug and smells completely of him.

'You look smashing, love,' he says, and I feel giddy.

We slowly settle, or I do. Buzz tells me about how he's been. I say little bits about the course, though I'm not meant to say too much. Something happens with food. I think I'm probably a bit wooden to start with, but Buzz knows not to take too much notice. I warm up.

And by the time we're eating our main course – steak for him, trout for me – Buzz says, 'OK. Holiday.'

He says it in a way that makes me realise this isn't just a welcome-back-Fi evening, it's something more than that, I'm not quite sure what.

I give him a big smile and say, 'Holiday! Tell me more.'

'OK, we wanted sunny, we wanted beaches, we wanted hot.'

I nod. 'Yes.' Another big smile, unloaded for free.

'Turkey, Greece, Morocco. All lovely, but they'd probably have been better last month than next month, so' – pause for dramatic effect – 'I'm thinking the Caribbean. Either Florida, Mexico, or one of the islands.'

I'm all ready and primed to give him the response he wants, but I'm not sure what that is. Delight, I assume, and I give out plenty of that, but I have a feeling I'm missing something. Buzz spreads brochures over the table. Coloured pictures, blue seas, white sands. Men in red shorts chasing balls. Lots of women, with legs much longer than mine, wearing bikinis and smiling like Moonies.

I say, 'Oh Buzz, this looks amazing.' Turn some pages, say it again, or some variant of the same thing.

I still think I'm missing something, but I'm not sure what. Buzz doesn't give any clues or, if he does, I can't read them.

'So,' he says, once the plates have been cleared and someone has asked us about puddings, and we've said no, just coffee, except that I'll have peppermint tea instead of coffee, and can we have the bill at the same time, please. 'So?'

'It looks amazing.'

'But which one?' He sorts out the brochures. Shows me the best Florida option, the best Yucatan one, the best island one, which is apparently a resort hotel in Saint Lucia.

He wants me to choose.

I interrogate his face, trying to figure out which one he likes. He sees me doing that and says, 'No, Fi. I want you to choose. Whichever one you like. Let's make it special.'

That last phrase, I've learned, is code for doesn't-matter-if-it's-expensive, but that is itself, I think, code for doesn't-matter-if-it's-expensive-but-let's-not-go-crazy-now.

The Saint Lucia place is the most expensive, the Yucatan place is the cheapest, so I put my hands down on Florida and say, 'I love this.'

He does that Buzz thing of looking into my eyes and saying, 'Are you sure now? It's what you want?'

I say yes, say it emphatically. And in saying it, it becomes true, or true enough. I'm lucky to have this man, who does these things for me. Who is this patient.

I say, 'Do you remember when we first came here? What a pain I was?'

'Not a pain, exactly . . .' Buzz's gallantry kicks automatically into gear, then hits the Hill of Truth and loses momentum fast. 'But not easy, no.'

'I was wearing this.' I touch the base of my neck at the join of my collarbones. My gesture includes both necklace and dress.

'I know. I remember.'

I've realised what it is I'm meant to say. The thing I was missing before.

'I missed you,' I said. 'Four weeks. It felt like a long time.'

Buzz's eyes melt and he says, 'Me too.'

When we get home, we do have sex. First once, fast and energetically, because we both need it. Then we chat a bit, and Buzz makes tea and brings it back to bed, and then we have sex again, but slowly and properly, and I no longer feel weird at all, or no more than always.

And when he's done, and his eyes are drooping, and I think I've done everything that a supergreat and perfect girlfriend is meant to do on evenings like these, I sit across his thighs, bouncing gently up and down.

'You haven't told me what happened to the Hayley Morgan thing.'

'Bloody hell, Fi. Really? Nothing's happened with the Hayley Morgan thing.'

I consider that response, but think it deserves another bounce. '*Something* must have happened.'

'Fraud Squad stuff, isn't it? They've interviewed everyone at the superstore, checked if anyone is driving a Jag when they ought to be driving a Fiesta, that sort of thing.'

'What about SOCA?'

SOCA: the Serious and Organised Crime Agency, which handles major league fraud, among other things.

'SOCA? It's not big enough for them. You know that.'

I give an annoyed grunt, which coincides with another bounce, which hurts Buzz enough that he lifts me off him, making a noise in the back of his throat which tells me I need to behave.

'Sorry, love.'

'Do you *ever* sleep?'

'When I was at YCS, my work day started at four a.m. I had to set the alarm for two forty.'

'What's YCS?'

He doesn't want an answer to that question, though. He wants to be allowed to get some rest without me annoying

45

him. I turn the lights off and give him a kiss. 'Sleep well, old man. I missed you.'

'I missed you too.'

It feels like the truth, both ways round.

I think about wearing a bikini on white Floridian sands. Buzz in red shorts chasing a ball, like a golden retriever after a stick.

I do love Buzz. Love him the best way I am able, which might not be a very good best. And I wonder, not for the first time, if he is simply mistaken about me. If he would not be happier with someone else.

His snores deflect the question. I snuggle down beside him and go to sleep.

9

The office, Monday morning. The normality seems strange. I feel like I've been away a million years. Most people have hardly noticed I've been gone.

Bev Rowlands, says, '*Fi!* How was your course?'

'It was fine. Quite fun, actually.'

'God, I'd never do anything like that,' says Bev, then starts telling me about an outdoor training course she did once where she had to climb up some rope netting strung between two pine trees.

I don't quite understand the point of the story, but say 'gosh' anyway.

As we're chatting, DCI Jackson walks past and says, 'Well done, Fiona,' but doesn't stop.

The morning briefing is full of busy nothings. Huw Bowen's manslaughter case, the one I initially wanted, has turned dull. No new murders. No proper assaults, no good ones. A presentation from some traffic officers about various pre-Christmas campaigns they're running. A talk about cost-cutting and the correct use of community support officers.

When I use the Ladies, I notice that the mirror has streak marks and the soap dispenser nozzles are gummed up. I use paper towels to remove the streak marks and do a basic job on the soap nozzles too.

I'm tasked to process paperwork on a couple of cases that are coming to court. Someone assigns me to help on a team that is developing advice on how to avoid thefts from vehicles. The first of our meetings takes an hour and forty minutes and the gist of our advice will be, 'Lock your car and hide your valuables.' Or, to simplify further, 'Don't be a bloody idiot.'

I suggest that as a slogan and everyone looks at me.

I read all the statements accumulated by the Fraud Squad inquiry. They've done just as Buzz said. Interviewed everyone local. Checked for unexpected inflows of money. Checked anyone with access to the store's management suite on the day when the offending payroll entries were made. Verified with Swindon that those entries were in fact made locally. And that's it. The inquiry hasn't been closed, exactly, but it's been effectively killed all the same. The T.M. Baron money went from the UK to Spain to Belize and we haven't yet been able to track it beyond that point.

One morning, on the way into work, I buy one of those big chocolate cookies, still warm from the oven and chewy in the middle. Make a big cup of black coffee, no sugar. Take these gifts to DCI Jackson's office. Tell him what I want. Say, 'Pretty please.'

'You don't give up, do you?'

He's not bothered by my request as such, but he's wary of offending his counterparts in Fraud.

'There *is* a dead body here,' I say. 'This is our case too.'

'Yes.'

'And I don't need much time. If I can't sort things quickly, I'll leave it.'

He asks what I specifically want to do. I tell him.

'OK. I'll speak to Fraud. But here's the deal. I'll get Owen to give you proper instructions. You complete those instructions as written. You complete them within a day. And normal rules apply, Fiona, OK?'

Normal rules: that's Jackson-speak for me not doing anything to piss him off.

'Yes, sir.'

I stand and offer my very best salute. Saluting senior officers is pretty much unheard of these days. Police officers are required to salute at Remembrance Day services and in the presence of a hearse or the sovereign, but those things don't come along every day and it's possible that my mark of respect is lacking a certain technical precision.

'Fiona, we're done. You look like a gay man waving.'

I leave the room. As well as the coffee and cookie, I brought a file full of the Morgan paperwork, in case Jackson wanted to inspect it. He didn't, but the door has a heavy self-closing mechanism and I find it hard to open with my one free hand. In the end, I have to put the folder down, use both hands on the door, then pick up the folder when I have it open.

Jackson stares at me. His eyes are impassive, but his lips move. The only words that come out are, 'One day. Normal rules.'

10

Swindon. Roundabouts and distribution centres. Big white industrial sheds surrounded by dwarf willows and artificial lakes. Wire fencing.

I park in a 250-bay car park. Sign myself in, in a high, glass-fronted lobby. Get a plastic badge and am told to go to the third floor. Three people waiting for the lift: two men and a woman, all in dark grey suits. The woman is saying something about warehousing issues in Poland, but falls silent when the lift comes. We travel up in silence.

On the third floor, there's another reception desk. I'm feeling a bit spacey – I often do in these places – so I have to blink a few times before finding the name I need.

'Kevin. Kevin Tildesley,' I say, when I'm done.

The woman behind the desk says something. I sit down. There are magazines on a low table – *Furniture World*, *Furniture Today* – but I resist their lure.

Every ten seconds or so something electronic bleeps. I look at my hands and try to remember who I am.

Then Tildesley arrives and I feel immediately less weird. He takes me through to a small conference room with a view out over the dwarf willows and the phoney lake. Tildesley feels more cheerful this time, less stressed. I guess he's feeling more secure about his job. That the mess won't end up being blamed on him.

I explain why I'm here. Tell the truth. About T.M. Baron,

and the money that went to Spain, and the money that was withdrawn in cash. Tell him about Hayley Morgan and how she died.

'Christ,' he says. 'Jesus.'

No one really knows what it's like to die from a combination of rat poison and starvation, but it isn't good. The poison in question was a second generation anti-coagulant. The stuff works by thinning the blood so much that the body's capillaries become dangerously permeable. Blood starts to leak into joints and muscles, so that victims literally bleed to death, though the bleeding is all internal. Scientific studies of haemophiliac pain suggest that the effect is moderately to severely painful. And not particularly fast.

'We've done what we can to chase up the ultimate recipients of the cash, but the money has long gone offshore. Outside the EU, even. So we need to work on the front end. When the scam was set up. How it was set up. How it was kept going.'

'OK. Yes. OK. As you can imagine, there's been an inquiry here.' Tildesley raises his eyebrows in an imagine-the-drama kind of way. 'Some of our historical procedures were, quite frankly, lax, and of course on the audit side . . .'

We get into the nuts and bolts. Tildesley isn't that great at explaining things, but he does understand his subject.

Historically – that is, in the Days Before Kevin – payroll was administered both locally and nationally. So the system was constructed and audited at national level, but it made use of inputs generated locally. 'So if, let's say, the manager of the Bridgend store needed to hire some extra staff for Christmas, he'd have made a request in the regular way. We'd approve that sort of thing instantaneously, normally. Then he'd have entered the names and payment details at store level, and the data would have flowed through to our national payment system.'

'OK. I get that. But assuming that the boss of the Cardiff

store wasn't fiddling the system himself – and we don't think that he was – how come he didn't instantly notice the fraud? It's a big store, but there aren't *that* many employees.'

Tildesley is shaking his head. Now that he's not worried about keeping his job, he likes the excitement. Feels like the Swindon-accountant version of a trawler captain caught in a Newfoundland storm. Water waist-high on the foredeck and foam seething on a lee shore.

'Yes, but that was the clever thing. We assess performance store-by-store and region-by-region. Now obviously lots of our costs are completely local. What a store uses in terms of power, for example, or their staffing bill. But you've got other costs that are regional, and others that are national. So all our buying activity is national, but a lot of our marketing and promotion might be regional. The way we work that out is we allocate a set proportion of regional costs to each store in the area. Same thing with our national costs. That way, we get a fair view of the profitability of each store.'

I nod. 'OK . . .'

'And our two individuals – Morgan and Gibson – were given a *regional* coding, not a local one, not a national one. So the store manager saw the names, and assumed they had nothing directly to do with him. The national payroll team saw that these two names were inputted via the Cardiff store, and assumed it was some regional activity being led out of Cardiff. Both ends of the operation thought the other one was in control.'

Tildesley thrusts papers over the table at me to show the deliciousness of the scam. I don't completely understand, but don't think I need to.

'But someone, somewhere, once sat down at a computer and created these false profiles, correct?'

'Correct.'

'And that computer was physically located in Cardiff, in Swindon or somewhere else?'

'Cardiff.'

'You're sure?'

'Certain.' Tildesley starts telling me why. Something to do with the input coding.

'And presumably any member of the Cardiff store could have got access to those computers? I mean, shop-floor staff probably weren't meant to play around with the payroll system, but they'd have had physical access to the space.'

'Yes. But we always talk about three levels of access. Physical, network, finance. Physical access: OK, you have rules and procedures, but you know those things are going to be breached. Shop-floor workers take their lunch break. Chat with a secretary. Look at the internet from an office PC.

'Level two access – access to the firm's intranet and systems – that's password-protected. Passwords change every month and they're unique to every user. We have a complete log of who signs in when and for how long.'

Sure enough, Tildesley pushes a folder at me: a printout of computer log-ons, sorted by date, running back two years.

'Level three access – getting to move money around – that's the biggie.' Tildesley starts to explain it all. It's complex in detail, but simple in essence. The Swindon head office regards its individual stores with distaste, the way Marie Antoinette thought of her stablehands. Swindon makes the decisions. The stores get to stack shelves and operate cash tills. Any financial decisions above a thousand pounds require authorisation from head office. Not even the Cardiff store manager has standing authority to spend the firm's cash.

I ask Kevin if the store keeps visitor sign-in books for people who come to the store on business. He tells me that those things are computerised now. He makes a call. A girl with a milky face and a navy dress brings a pile of printouts, still warm from the printer.

I ask Kevin if he has a record of any external consultants who had access to the store over the last two and half years. The answer is no, not exactly, but he can find records of any payments made to consultants in the South Wales region, plus the dates of those payments, plus the invoices. I ask for copies of the lot.

And by the time we're done, I have been here two hours and have a stack of printouts four inches high. Kevin and the girl with the milky face see me to the lifts, my very own guard of honour.

I say to the girl, 'I like your dress.'

I don't particularly. I have no feelings on the subject. But I know women say these things to each other, so I try saying it now and again. The disciplines of Planet Normal.

The girl starts telling me about her dress, while I express interest with just a tint of excitement. The lift comes and I leave.

On the way back to Cardiff, I stop at the Leigh Delamere service station for fuel and lunch. Brie and rocket sandwich. A plastic salad thing, which I buy from some sense of duty. Fruit smoothie. But mostly, I just sit there with my printouts and my laptop. Researching.

Call Kevin. Can he tell me which specific computer the data was entered on?

He can't, but he'll speak to the IT people.

I try eating my salad with the plastic fork provided. It bounces off the baby tomatoes, has difficulty with the cucumber, but handles the sweetcorn as easy as *la*.

I call our forensic computer team in Cardiff, the ones who deal with computer frauds and kiddie-porn. Anything really complex is handled by the Hi Tech Crime Unit at SOCA, but our guys are fine with the basics. I ask a few questions, get a few answers.

Find a way of cornering my tomatoes against the plastic wall of the salad bowl and successfully impale them, every last one of them.

Get a call back from Kevin, who has an IT guy with him, another Kevin. Kevin Two starts speaking a language I don't really understand, even though nearly all of the words seem to be English. Then he gives me what I want: the serial number of the computer from which the fraud was committed.

Phone Dunwoody. I need his permission to do what I want to do next. He squirms. Doesn't like the responsibility of decision, but knows Jackson has authorised my researches so he doesn't have much option. Says OK.

I phone our computer people back and ask them to send someone to the store. Say I'll be there in an hour.

I'm there in an hour and ten. Our guy is already there: Mark Lampley, jeans and a T-shirt, worn under a jacket. He's drinking tea, not working. I'm about to be pissed off at him, except he pre-empts me. Taps the desktop, says, 'Trojan horse. Computer is totally compromised.'

I make my IT face at him and he explains further.

'A Trojan horse is any kind of application which allows a remote user to control a computer. Basically, once the program's installed it just sits in the background. If someone wants to control it from outside, they can.'

'How much knowledge do you need to create something like this?'

'Well, I doubt if the software's original. This looks like a basic Slavebot app to me.'

'But you need to be an IT specialist, yes?'

'Ideally, yes.'

One of Kevin's invoices showed that Red Dragon Systems, a computer consultancy based down in the Bay, had done work for the store over an eight week period last spring, a period ending about eleven weeks before the payroll fraud began. The Fraud Squad investigation had focused on the period immediately around the fraudulent payroll request itself, so they hadn't even noticed Red Dragon's involvement.

The store sign-in data indicates that the firm had three consultants working on the project: Saj Kureishi, Andrew Peters, Colin Cooper.

I look at Mark. He looks at me. Puts his mug down with a bang.

'Let's go and arrest some criminals,' he says.

11

We arrest no one.

We do go down to Red Dragon Systems. Myself, Lampley, someone from the Fraud Squad, plus a couple of uniforms for good measure. Peters and Cooper are both there, scared at finding themselves surrounded by cops and marched off to Cathays under caution.

But not Kureishi. He went missing in about late June. Hasn't been in to work. Not responding to messages left at his home address, on his mobile or on his IM accounts.

We start to do the basics, of course. Interview Peters and Cooper. Seize computers from Red Dragon, including the machine that belonged to Kureishi. Start to check personal bank accounts.

We don't get far. When we start to enter Kureishi's details on the PNC database, a basic cross-check flags up a case of possible interest. Two weeks ago, Devon and Cornwall police were called to a small rural property which was rented out in the summer months. The owner, there to do a bit of end-of-season DIY, found, along with the wasp nests and the leaf-filled gutter, the body of an Asian man. The corpse was duct-taped to a chair, his hands hacked off. There were no other signs of violence, meaning that the man was left to bleed to death.

I've seen the crime scene photos. The man's brown face has gone a kind of ash grey. His eyes are open and his mouth pulled back in an expression of mild astonishment. It's as though he saw something, while dying, which caused him a mild, detached, almost philosophical amusement. A last wry chuckle at a fading world.

I know not to read too much into these expressions. They arise not as the result of emotion, but of physiognomy, the body hardening, then softening, into its final shape. But, either way, I like the pictures. Have them printed in full colour. Pin them up around my desk.

The pool of blood on the man's knees, thighs and floor has turned a deep rust brown, like the shadows in a forest of autumn beech.

We check the corpse's DNA against samples collected from Kureishi's home and workplace. Also drive Peters and Cooper down to Exeter to confirm the ID. It's him. What's more, Kureishi's work computer contains copies of the Trojan horse software installed at the superstore. The other Red Dragon computers are clean.

The forged 'Hayley Morgan' letter received by Social Services matches the paper, envelope, printer and toner ink used by Red Dragon.

Our fraud officers check, very discreetly, some other corporate addresses where Kureishi did consultancy work. They check five computers at which he was known to have worked. All five are infected with the same Trojan horse. Three of those computers are able to access the payroll systems of the companies in which they are located.

These things arouse a flurry of activity. A meeting is held jointly between the Devon and Cornwall Major Crime Unit, the Serious Fraud Office, SOCA and ourselves. We are represented by DI Mick Adams of our Fraud unit, Dennis Jackson and myself.

I've never been in one of these things before: big beasts loping around a carcass, figuring out their dominance hierarchy. I'm only here as a little courtesy from Jackson, who recognises my role in connecting Kureishi to the fraud.

The man from the SFO, a pinched, black-suited man, is the first to fold his hand.

'The *size* of the fraud is perhaps large enough,' he says. 'We're not really *equipped* to handle frauds of less than a million or so, but this *may* pass muster on that account. On the other hand, we have to *ask*, is this case likely to be of *widespread* public concern? Does it call for our *specialist* knowledge? I have to say, I think we might *prefer* to leave the matter in your, no doubt capable, hands.'

The no doubt capable hands round the table look at the SFO guy in much the same way as they'd study a Bangkok ladyboy in full regalia. Appalled disbelief.

Jackson, taking charge, says, 'OK.'

'Our main concern, really, is with the smooth functioning of *financial markets.*'

The SFO guy looks set to go on, explaining why the case is beneath him, but Jackson just says again, 'OK. Thank you for coming,' and gestures at the door.

The SFO guy halts, looks bemused, then gathers up his papers and leaves.

No one says anything, but no one needs to. If the atmosphere in the room could be distilled down to a single word, that word would begin with a 'w' and rhyme with banker.

That leaves us, our West country cousins, and SOCA. The Devon and Cornwall force are represented by a DCI, Jackson's counterpart, and her gopher. The DCI, Mary Widdicombe, says, 'This isn't our fraud, but it is our murder. We also recognise that the murder, almost certainly, arose as a consequence of the fraud. We don't care how you,' she makes a gesture that includes the rest of us, 'investigate the fraud. We just need to know that your inquiry will have the investigation and prosecution of this murder as a central objective. And we will need to have one of our officers seconded to the core investigation team.'

Widdicombe – dark brown hair worn long, blue eyes, but a strong jaw, strong demeanour – holds her gaze steady as she says the last bit, but we all know that her last remarks are aimed at SOCA.

The senior SOCA representative here is a man called Adrian Brattenbury. He seems perfectly sensible, but the agency has strong linkages with the security services and is viewed as more than a little suspect by many police officers. SOCA likes to talk about its ability to 'disrupt organised crime' and prides itself on its intelligence-led investigative approach. Which is all good. Organised crime needs to be disrupted and a stupidity-led approach is unlikely to pay dividends. On the other hand, good intelligence tends to become all about the preservation of sources, while any competent police investigation has to end with doors being kicked down and bad guys being led away in handcuffs. For simple coppers, like Jackson, Widdicombe and myself, it's hard to see how organised crime is being disrupted if we don't see the heads of major crime organisations being successfully prosecuted in a British courtroom.

But still. Widdicombe hasn't exactly folded her hand, but she's taking a pace back from the carcass. That leaves Brattenbury and Jackson still facing off.

'I'm with Mary,' says Jackson. 'Fraud on this scale – not to mention potentially complicated IT issues – that's not something we particularly want to handle. But we need a prosecution out of this. A Cardiff resident was murdered. The frauds took place here. We need to know that the perpetrators will be brought to justice and in a timely manner.'

Brattenbury has dark curly hair, a bright pink shirt, charcoal pinstripe suit and an air of intelligence, which I like. He says, 'Yes, of course. Look, our objectives are the same as yours. We want to put criminals behind bars.'

'We'd need staff on the team. Seconded to you, but reporting to me.'

'Yes. Yes, we do usually work with local staff. We need to. Our regional offices are very lean. Obviously, on a live case, we have to be very careful about who knows what, we're very rigorous about protecting our officers, but—'

'No.' Jackson isn't loud, but he doesn't have to be. 'No. That phrase, that attitude. It's a *no*. Mary's got a murder. I've got a fraud at least, maybe a manslaughter as well. If you boys and girls at SOCA want a piece of this, it's on our terms. And those terms do not include cutting me or Mary out of the loop. We're not negotiating here. And by the way, Mary and I are detective chief inspectors. We know something about protecting our bloody officers and we're not about to take lessons from you.'

He looks at Widdicombe, who nods once, briefly.

They both look at Brattenbury, who clears his throat and says, 'I'm sure we can sort something out.'

Jackson says, 'We *are* sorting something out. If you need to make a call, the office next door is free.'

Brattenbury heads off with his phone. To me, Jackson says, 'Fiona, get us some drinks, would you?'

I take orders and go off to fetch coffees. I'm aware that I'm representing the South Wales force and am proud that my coffee-making skills have been called upon. I seek to excel.

By the time I return, all is sweetness and light.

Jackson, Adams, Widdicombe, Brattenbury and Widdicombe's gopher are standing by the conference room window getting a guided tour of central Cardiff from Jackson's stabbing index finger. I'm not welcome on his tour bus. 'OK, Fiona, thank you,' meaning that my services are no longer required.

I leave.

And that's it. I hear nothing further. As I understand things, Mick Adams from our Fraud Squad is seconded to the SOCA inquiry. Presumably someone of similar rank from Devon and Cornwall. Presumably Jackson and Widdicombe get what they need. But nothing filters down to me.

I'm only partly sorry. Whatever else this case may be, it's going to involve a lot of complex computer analysis, a lot of painstaking financial audits. That kind of work is tailor-made for SOCA – they inherited the whole of what used to be the National Hi-tech Crime Unit and they have forensic financial skills second only to those of the SFO. And none of that appeals to me. Much as I relish Kureishi's exsanguinated corpse, much as I like the odour of organised crime that floats over the entire investigation, I'm not interested in computers or financial accounts. I like the objects of the inquiry, but not its probable methods. I go back to my busy little detective constable life, being given orders by people I don't always respect, executing those orders, writing up a completed action report and repeating the process. We have no interesting murders in stock at the moment, but we have our normal helping of assault, rape and violent stupidity. It's a thin diet, but I get by.

The one real highlight: I point out an anomaly in the case so far to Dennis Jackson. The superstore fraud involved two unwitting accomplices: Adele Gibson and Hayley Morgan. They were excellent choices for the fraud in one way, because they were real people, with real addresses. The audit software used to detect payroll frauds would never have flashed an alert faced with these names.

Yet, I don't think the names were chosen by accident. Hayley Morgan was an isolated stroke victim with some cognitive impairments. Adele Gibson is learning impaired and relies on a social worker for help with basic household finance and the like. People like that don't always have the tools needed to challenge strange behaviour in their finances – and until the last few months, they hadn't actually been made any worse off by the scam. They were carefully chosen targets. Chosen by someone in a position to pick.

I nudge Jackson. He nudges the Fraud Squad. They

discover that Sajid Kureishi's sister-in-law, Razia Riaz, worked as a receptionist at Cardiff Social Care Services in Grangetown. Discover that she had interfered with the flow of correspondence in order to keep care workers in the dark.

She's arrested and charged with fraud. Under interrogation, she admitted that she had, a year and a half back, obtained the signatures needed from Adele Gibson and Hayley Morgan to gain access to their bank accounts. I wasn't present at the arrest or the interrogation, but Gethin Stephens, the new Fraud Squad DI, told me that she was a nasty piece of work, venomous and vindictive, and with no apparent remorse for the consequences of her actions.

The CPS are considering a manslaughter charge and I hope they go ahead.

And that's the story as we now have it. Kureishi found a way to penetrate corporate computers. His sister-in-law found a way to generate appropriate payroll dummies for the fraud. The pair of them obtained some false identity documents and set up a bank account which they used to channel their money. The first of them is dead, the second awaiting prosecution. We don't know quite why Kureishi went on the run and probably never will, but he must have got scared that his partners in organised crime were getting tired of him. He stole what he could. Ran when he could. And got killed anyway.

That's all I really know. I do my regular work and try to remember that I have a life.

When Buzz asks if I have a swimsuit, I say I have no swimsuits but two bikinis. He asks if my passport is valid. I say that I've checked and it is.

And strange to say, I find I'm excited by the prospect of holiday. I've never felt that before. I've normally avoided holiday completely or approached it with a kind of anxiety. But this feels different. And when Buzz says, 'Are you looking forward to it?', I say, 'I am, I really am.' When he laughs at me, I laugh too.

12

Wednesday 9 November. Two weeks and two days before Buzz and I fly out to Miami. I get a call from Jackson.

'Do you have a minute?' he says. He speaks with an unusual gentleness, the way he might if I actually had a choice.

I go up. His office: a large, black leatherette sofa, a couple of art prints on the wall, one of those pointless office plants – a stringy palmate thing, that sits in a ceramic pot full of what looks like ceramic gravel.

On the sofa, Brattenbury, wearing a dark jacket over a plum-coloured V-neck. He looks cooler than coppers are meant to look. Makes Jackson look older and tireder than he really is.

I sit down.

'Fiona, you remember Adrian Brattenbury. He's the Senior Investigating Officer on Operation Tinker.'

'*Tinker?*'

Brattenbury says, 'The computer allocates names. We don't pick 'em.'

'Adrian, if you want to give Fiona a quick overview.'

There's a smoked glass coffee table in front of the sofa. Papers on it, including some six by ten photo sheets, but turned so I can't see them.

Brattenbury nods, but first looks straight at me and says, 'Nice to meet you properly. I understand Dennis here has a lot of faith in you.'

I don't know what to say to that, so I just sit. When

Brattenbury figures out that I'm not going to say anything, he continues, 'Tinker. It's turning into a biggie. Thanks to your work in identifying Kureishi, we've been able to trace nine different frauds, eight of those payroll-related. One of them an expense-based thing: the same, but different. Total *monthly* amount stolen is in excess of a quarter of a million pounds. At the current rate, about three point eight million a year.'

Perhaps I look surprised, because he adds, 'We haven't closed anything down. Not yet. If we do, our chances of securing convictions on the perpetrators fall to about zero. These are big companies for the most part and most of them have an existing policy of cooperating with police investigation. Those that don't – well, they're on board for now. How long that goes on for, I don't know. But for the time being, we're OK.'

He waits to see if I want to say something, but I still don't, so he continues, 'It looks like the basic mechanics of the fraud were initially set up by Kureishi. He installed software that gave external access to payroll. We're confident he was not the ultimate beneficiary of the fraud. We simply can't find enough money or signs of heavy spending. And the set-up looks remarkably professional. The fraud involves over a hundred and fifty dummy UK bank accounts. The money siphons via Spain, Portugal or Jersey to Belize. The Belize bank account is fronted by nominees and owned by a shell company in the British Virgin Islands. That shell company in turn is owned by a foundation in Panama. We've got the best investigators we have trying to crack that little nut open, but frankly our chances are very low. And even if we peel things back to Panama, they'll quite likely just pull the money back through a whole lot of anonymous shell companies, through difficult or corrupt jurisdictions, and we'll get nowhere at all.'

It occurs to me that Jersey and the British Virgin Islands are both under the jurisdiction of the British government, and that the Queen is head of state in Belize. It also occurs to me that making these places world centres for shell companies, nominee accounts, loosely controlled money and zero corporate taxation is not necessarily consistent with what our government is there to do.

I don't say this, though. Just sit there and try to look intelligent.

Brattenbury continues. 'Our assumption is that even if Kureishi originated the fraud, he lost control of it to criminals with far more extensive resources and experience. Kureishi got greedy or had some falling-out with his employers. They handled that the way these guys tend to do. Our primary investigative goal is therefore to find the ultimate controllers of this fraud and to bring them to justice. Charges of fraud and murder.'

I nod. I still don't know why I'm here, except that I think I do.

I keep looking at the six by tens.

I am feeling something. A cold distance that comes between me and my body, a band of December fog. I normally like to pursue these feelings, to see if I can understand and name them, but the time and place for that exercise is not now. Not now and not here.

'Your furniture superstore,' says Brattenbury. 'That was the smallest fraud, the earliest, and the least sophisticated. I think you'd call it a proof of concept test. They've been building from there. The current frauds, the larger ones, are built on a much larger scale and need more . . . more care and attention.'

I nod. Keep looking at the pictures. Keep feeling that December fog.

'With the bigger companies, backdoor access to a single computer terminal doesn't give the fraudsters what they need. They need someone onsite as well. Basically, they use that initial opening to design the fraud. To figure out the company's systems, how to get around the safeguards. Then, when they've figured out a scam that will work, they recruit a mole within the company. The mole executes the plan and monitors it.'

I say, or try to say, 'A payroll clerk, someone like that,' but no words seem to come out, so I clear my throat and try again.

'Yes, exactly,' he says when he understands me. 'Exactly.'

He goes on talking. The current plan is to terminate most of the frauds in what Brattenbury calls a 'natural' way. Basically, he intends to nudge the companies' internal auditors to make the checks that will expose the fraud, seemingly as part of the company's regular audit process.

'We do, however, want to leave two or three of the bigger scams running. We don't want the perpetrators to feel they've been found out. Luckily, the two biggest scams affect insurance companies, both of whom pay out tens of millions of pounds annually as a result of organised crime, so they're particularly keen to be helpful. They've given us as much systems access as we need. We can see literally every single keystroke, every mouseclick on the relevant computers.'

I nod. I'm not particularly good with computers, but I know these things aren't particularly difficult. You can get remote monitoring software for twenty or thirty pounds online. If the corporate's IT staff are being helpful, you can probably achieve the same effect by tweaking a few settings on some admin panel.

I also know, though, that you don't break organised crime syndicates by computer monitoring alone.

'We have identified the local moles. That's not hard, as you know. But we don't want the moles, we want the people controlling them. And the people profiting from them. And we've got nowhere. Nowhere at all. We haven't closed with the enemy because, the truth is, we've no idea *who* the enemy is.'

I nod. I don't seem to have a working voicebox, so I stop trying to use it.

'Infiltration,' says Brattenbury. 'We want to plant an operative in their camp. Make some identifications. Get some surveillance going.'

Nod.

Stare down at the six by tens.

Brattenbury has, I'm sure, noticed the direction of my gaze before now, but this is the first time he responds directly. He flips the photos over one by one, leaving just a singleton still face down on the table.

The photos are of people. Mugshots and full length profiles. One of them is of me. I'm wearing something from Next. Pale blue blouse, cardigan, grey skirt, dark court shoes. Bland, safe, officey.

There are four other photos, all of men. Men in their thirties or younger forties. Short hair. Muscular, or at least tough-looking. Narrow eyes, strong jaws. The men are all wearing jeans. Dark shirts or T-shirts. Casual jackets, one leather, one denim, the two others not far removed from the same denim-leather school of couture. Four men with a whiff of the macho.

I recognise three of the men: my colleagues. One I don't, but I assume he's a copper too, just one I haven't met. The three men I recognise have all worked undercover.

I know where this is going.

'I understand you've just completed your undercover course.'

'Yes.'

'Did very well. An unusually strong performance, I'm told.'

I shrug. 'It was a training thing, not a real thing.' That's not wonderful English, but at least my voice seems to be working again.

'That's perfectly true. There's a huge difference and yet the training is designed for real life. By people who have lived that life.'

Nod.

'Fiona, we need a payroll clerk. Someone who *looks* like a payroll clerk. Someone who could do the job of a payroll clerk. We need an outstanding investigator and someone with nerve. Preferably also someone local. We could bring in someone from Birmingham, say, but then they look like someone being brought in for a reason. They'll be the first person our targets will suspect.'

Nod.

There's a glance between Jackson and Brattenbury. Jackson reaches out and flips the last photo. It's of Kureishi. His corpse. Not a shot I've seen before. This one is full frontal. It takes a moment to notice that he has stumps in place of hands. There's blood all over his legs. From this angle, the look on his face isn't one of astonishment, but of anguish. Either that, or I'm just viewing it differently.

'Fiona.' This is Jackson talking. 'I want you to know that you do not have to accept this assignment. I want you to know that we regard it as exceptionally dangerous. If you are exposed, the likelihood is that you end up like this.' He taps the photo of Kureishi. 'If you say no, that will not be held against you in any way at all. Not when it comes to promotion. Not when it comes to allocating work. Not in any way at all. Do you understand?'

Nod.

'I need you to say yes or no.'

'Yes. I understand.'

My voice is gravel moving on sandpaper. Cinders blowing in an empty grate.

Another look passes between the two men.

Brattenbury says, 'I'd like to offer you the job. Your task would be to infiltrate the organisation and help us destroy it. You will continue to be employed here, by the South Wales CID. You'll be seconded, on a temporary basis, to us at SOCA. I'll be your case officer, but you'll also have a reporting line direct to Dennis here. You'll be able to reach either of us at any point.

'We'll work with your Fiona Grey legend. We'll have you under our protection the entire time. We'll surveille your flat and your workplace. We'll have armed response officers ready should the situation ever call for it. But I don't want to pretend these things are perfect. They never are. As Dennis says, this is a dangerous game. It's OK to say no.'

'Yes.' Because neither of the men react, I say it again, more clearly this time. 'I mean, yes, I'll take the job.'

Brattenbury doesn't move. It's as though he doesn't want to move in case he breaks some meniscus that is only just holding its tension.

Jackson is the opposite. He does a tiny double-take, as though checking he heard me right, then moves in quickly, forcefully, to say, 'Fiona, you're not to make this decision on the fly. You need to think about it. Your chap, now. Sergeant Brydon. You'll need to talk to him. You can't talk about this to your family or friends or other loved ones, but you need to think about them.'

'Yes.'

'This could be a long assignment.' Jackson has some of my course paperwork in front of him. Paperwork in which I stated that I only wanted short duration assignments. 'You have to think about the consequences. Not just for you, but for those around you.'

'Yes.' I don't say anything for a while and nor does anyone else. Then: 'I've got a holiday coming up. In Florida.'

Brattenbury nods. 'We don't have to get in the way of that. It might be a good idea, actually.' Gives me a half smile. 'Perhaps go easy on the tan.'

'I don't know anything about payroll.'

Brattenbury smiles again. 'The company we want to place you in is an outfit called Western Vale. An insurance company. They use a system called Total Payroll Solutions. TPS. It's standard software, easy to use. As luck would have it, this office uses identical software. So do half the offices in this city. If you're up for this, we'll start training you tomorrow. We'll need to do some work on your legend. Get you familiar with the duties of a payroll clerk. Start the infiltration as soon as you get back from holiday.'

His face asks, *Anything else?*

I nod. I can't see that there's much else to say.

I stand up. Or rather: two of me stand up. Fiona Griffiths, a policewoman, and Fiona Grey, a cleaner. Fiona Griffiths is comfortable enough in this environment: in a room with two senior officers and neither of them yelling at her. Fiona Grey feels out of place. As a cleaner, I was used to exiting a building before the employees turned up. I don't know what to do under this scrutiny. Just look at the floor and wait to be dismissed.

Brattenbury says, 'I'll see you tomorrow. We'll get started then.'

Jackson says, 'Think about it, Fiona. Think about it and talk it over.'

He wants to hold my gaze, but he can't find it. Whoever hoovered the room didn't push the cleaning head properly under the sofa, so there's a shadow line of dust visible beneath the seat. The miniature palm tree in its ceramic pot is dropping brown leaf curls on the carpet.

Fiona Grey says, 'Yes, sir,' and leaves the room.

13

Florida. Blue seas, white sands. Men in red shorts. Women – women, including me – in itsy-bitsy bikinis, walking hand in hand with their men, down these implausible, glittering coasts.

We live in an hotel block painted the colour of ice cream. Have the use of a pool where the sunbeds match the umbrellas and a bamboo- and rush-covered bar opens at eleven in the morning. I paint my toenails while Buzz does lengths. He reads a book about the war in Iraq. I have a paperback novel and a book of philosophy by Colin McGinn. I don't read either. Mostly just leaf through women's magazines left by other holiday-makers.

Nothing feels real.

Buzz was not happy with me. Not happy at all. We had the only proper argument we've ever really had. He couldn't understand why I would take the Tinker assignment. Felt hurt. Maybe even frightened for me. I'm not sure. I was very slow to decode his feelings. Could only feel his anger. Felt his anger and responded stupidly.

'You had Bosnia,' I said. 'Risking your life to defend the citizens of some other country. I'm a police officer. I've got a duty to *our* citizens.'

'There are other ways to do your duty, Fi.'

'Oh, because girls should stay clear of the rough stuff? Leave that to the lads, eh? Maybe they could put me in Family

Liaison. I could look pretty and hand out the paper tissues.'

I was stupid. Said stupid, hurtful things.

We argued, badly, and didn't make up before we went to sleep.

It was my fault. As we reviewed things the following day, I realised that for Buzz these things are simple. If you're single, you can do what you like. Male or female, no distinctions. Any degree of danger acceptable.

But he doesn't see my situation, or his, that way. In his eyes, we've given up our freedom for the relationship. There are escapes we can no longer take, dangers we may no longer face. Buzz, I realise, sees his life with a straightforwardness I am unable to match. Realise too that the commitment he makes to me is as total and uncomplicated as the one he expects from me in return.

When I finally understand these things, I apologise, sincerely, for my behaviour the night before. I don't cry, because tears don't come easily to me, but I feel a kind of pricking in my eyes. Feel something liquid, or molten, loose inside me.

I say, 'Buzz, I would like to do this, because I've accepted the assignment and because I want to do something like this, at least once, so I know what it's like. But if you say I can't do it, I won't. I'll say no to Brattenbury. Say no to Jackson. And if I *do* do it, then I'll never do anything like it again. Nothing so long-term. Nothing where the dangers are so obvious.'

Buzz holds my face between his hands. His eyes are as big as a labrador's. He's so serious, I want to laugh.

'That's real, Fi, is it?'

'Yes. It's a promise.'

He's moved. Emotions move in his face like the wind over Cardiff Bay. Compared with me, he's so easily explained. I am constantly learning from his simplicity.

'Well, then. OK.'

'OK?'

'I think you should do it. I think you should be bloody careful. I hope you'll see sense and choose to back out. But if you want to do it, you should do it.'

His big eyes get bigger. We have make-up sex of the sort that we should have had the night before.

And then – well, I think everything is all right. We don't argue again. Start to make plans. Once I've slipped into being Fiona Grey full-time, I won't be allowed to see Buzz more than once a month. Shouldn't ever speak to him outside that time. But Buzz says, and I agree, that some rules are made to be broken. We figure out safe ways to communicate if need be.

I start to work with Brattenbury. Spend days in our payroll department, learning my way round the system that powers the accounts. Learn about employment contracts and induction packs, payroll files and attendance trackers. Learn to generate P60s and P45s. Memorise HMRC rules on NI rates, statutory payments, and a host of other things. I work hard. I'm not particularly great with numbers, but the rest of it I find easy. I'm overqualified for this work.

Evenings, and any other time I have spare, I work with Brattenbury. My legend takes shape. Fiona Grey grows a past, a present. Get a set of documents that are all fake, but the lie they tell starts to become so complete, it feels more like truth.

Brattenbury comes round to my house with a female colleague. The two of them look at my wardrobe and tell me what Fiona Grey can and can't take with her. Most of my clothes are off limits. Not because I've got so much classy stuff, but because Fiona Grey, poor lass, can't afford even average stuff.

Brattenbury gives me £160 and tells me to go to Primark. The female colleague comes with me, shepherding me through the store, editing my choices. I put everything that's washable through at least five wash cycles, using a high-bleach detergent.

I buy shoes, second-hand, from eBay. Pay £1.99 for one pair, £2.50 for some second-hand black boots. Wonder who is selling shoes for these prices.

Brattenbury doesn't want me to get a haircut. Tells me to cut it by myself, in front of a mirror, if I want it shorter.

I don't mind his bossiness. I like his attention to detail.

He tells me that Fiona Grey has had a rough time in Manchester. She was physically abused. Had some run-ins with the police. Wants to emigrate.

It's a good story. Undercover operating procedure demands that every legend should offer a 'bribe' and a 'bully'. For most people, the 'bribe' will simply be an offer of cash. If an officer is infiltrating a jewel-robbery team, his jewel-robbing colleagues will assume that any newcomer will be working for cash, just as they are. But these things are never constructed in a one-size-fits-all way. An officer infiltrating a group of neo-fascists will need to be 'motivated' by ideology. For Fiona Grey, the mistreated little payroll clerk, a simple appeal to avarice would never be entirely persuasive. Give her the chance to leave the country, though, and she might be induced into anything.

'And the "bully" part?'

Brattenbury raises his eyebrows. 'You're wanted by the Greater Manchester Police. That'll be a real thing, by the way. We'll create a crime report for a stabbing incident and set up an alert on the PNC names database. If you come into contact with the regular police, you'll be brought up to Manchester for questioning.'

'It's just I was thinking, maybe something lower tech could work too. As a supplementary item.'

'Such as?'

'Well, sir, when I was a student, I became reasonably

75

proficient in growing cannabis. Obviously, I never inhaled and—'

Brattenbury just laughs. 'OK. Good. A little home horticulture. Why not?'

'And if possible, sir—'

'If possible, you'd like me to keep your supervising officer in the dark about this particular element of your legend? That's fine. It wouldn't be the first time.'

Undercover officers are permitted to break the law as long as any breaches are reasonably necessary for the purpose in hand. If you want to infiltrate that gang of neo-fascists, for example, they'll probably need to see you smash a window, throw a punch, pull a blade, or attack a policeman. Those things are necessary, but they give case officers the heebie-jeebies: do too little and you may expose the officer as a plant. Do too much, and you'll be in front of a disciplinary inquiry for exceeding your brief. By those standards, a few puffs of weed hardly signify.

I also meet Roy Williams, a brother officer in CID, and one of the few beside me to have passed the undercover training course.

Roy is an ex-rugby player, with a broken nose, some partially visible tattoos, and hair that's cut with those electric clippers, leaving the kind of fuzz you measure in sixteenths of an inch. When he wears T-shirts, his biceps bulge like bratwurst tied with string.

He doesn't exactly look like your classic payroll type, but he does look splendidly like an undercover policeman.

Brattenbury explains, 'They know that we've found Kureishi. They'll guess we've uncovered those frauds, at least some of them. What they won't know is whether we believe Kureishi to have been the main perpetrator or whether we suspect wider organised crime involvement. Either way though, they'll expect us to poke around. So Roy here will do the poking. We're going to train him up, Fiona, same as you. Infiltrate him. Do everything right, just as if he were the main thrust of our investigation. In effect, we'll show the bad guys that we're looking around. I imagine they'll stay well clear from any involvement. In due course, we'll stand Roy down and the bad guys will think we've folded our investigation. Think of him as a red herring, if you like.'

If he's a red herring, Roy is certainly a well-muscled one. Also one who has acute difficulty with even the basics of payroll. We end up working together, side by side in the police's own payroll department. Roy isn't that bad with numbers, not really, but he has a kind of allergy to them. Both the numbers and the paperwork. The endless computer screens. We get the same training, but it's always me that helps out Roy. Helping him actually makes me learn faster and more confidently. I'm good at this, I realise. I'll make it as a payroll clerk.

Perhaps that realisation, or the job itself, or the awareness of what will follow makes me increasingly adopt the colours of my new habitat. I wear neat little dresses from Next. Court shoes and pencil skirts. Give myself a dab or two of perfume in the morning, the first time I've done that, I think, since joining the police.

As I blend in, Roy seems to blend out. He starts the day in suit and tie – the compulsory wear of male payroll clerking – but he quickly sheds the jacket, then the tie is loosened and by lunchtime his sleeves are rolled up, his gold signet ring is tapping anxiously against his teeth, and his eyes hold the agonised look of a man who knows that a P11(D) has to be inspected for accuracy but who is long past caring what the hell a P11(D) is meant to signify.

We take lunch together most days. Roy talks about cases he's worked on and asks me about my past. I don't answer him, not really, and tell him he's doing fine. We get together socially too. Me and Buzz, Roy and his wife Katie. Except that's the wrong pairing really, the wrong way of expressing it. Roy is so entirely blokey that he ends up talking sport and policing with Buzz. I end up talking girl-stuff with Katie. She's ten years younger than Roy, and visibly adoring of him. Katie was in charge of supper, but told Roy to look after things while she put their two-year-old daughter to bed. Roy forgot and I forgot to remind him, so I chat with Katie over a piece of chicken that is halfway to becoming coal. We talk about her daughter and her desire for more children. She asks about me and Buzz. She is sweet and wide-eyed and easily awed and charming.

The next day I tell Roy he's lucky, and I mean it.

I don't think anyone could say the same to Buzz, or not in quite the same way, at any rate.

And through all this, Brattenbury doesn't tell me much about Tinker. Says I'll be more natural if I know fairly little. That's OK with me. Brattenbury has the air of a man who knows what he's doing.

Before coming out to Florida, I also did what I could to make things right with my family. Saw my parents, my two sisters. Told them I was going to be on secondment to a Human Trafficking Unit, based in London but starting with a six-month capacity-building mission to the Balkans. Dad was protective, almost jealous. He was like this when I went off to Cambridge too. Mam said she'll miss me, but she'll be fine. My sisters weren't that fussed.

And here I am in Florida, as the year starts to tilt into Christmas, my toenails painted and my itsy-bitsy bikinis unnaturally bright under this almost tropical sun.

Buzz and I have a nice time. I don't swim much. Wear sun cream with a protection factor of fifty. Also broadbrimmed hats and, when I'm not under the shade of a sun umbrella, I'm quick to cover myself in long skirts, loose cotton tops.

My pale skin doesn't change colour much. Buzz goes a

classic Welsh pink, then tilts over into a proper golden tan. He laughs at my milky limbs.

Buzz swims. We both read, or pretend do. Go on long walks down those improbable beaches. Make a couple of excursions to supposed local attractions that don't, in fact, seem very attractive.

We make love in a hotel room, darkened by a venetian blind and a ceiling fan revolving slowly above our heads.

On the penultimate evening of our stay, Buzz insists on our having a full romantic experience.

French cuisine. View over the sea. Candles and big menus. In the lobby, lobsters idle in a lurid aquarium, unaware that their only remaining life-task is to seduce a diner into ordering their execution. No wonder they turn red when they're cooked. That's when they realise how stupid they've been.

And after the wine is poured, and the candles lit, and the waiters sent away, Buzz gets out a tiny box. A jewellery box. He passes it over the table.

Makes a short speech. Schmaltzy down to the last cliché, but so earnestly delivered that my heart can't help but be moved. He ends down on one knee, saying, 'Fi, will you marry me?'

I say, 'Yes.'

The diamond is a solitaire and Buzz has chosen a ring that fits perfectly.

Nothing feels real.

14

It's five days before Christmas and my last night in Cardiff, or my last as Fiona Griffiths.

We've had – my mam, dad, two sisters and me – an early Christmas. The full works. Turkey, roast potatoes, bread sauce, stuffing, bacon rolls, Brussels, carrots, gravy, redcurrant jelly. All that, plus present-giving by the tree, carols on the sound system, crackers and paper hats, and all those endless waves of further food: Christmas pudding, trifle, fruit, nuts, chocolate, mince pies. Assault troops storming an already exhausted digestive system.

I surrender before finishing my first helping of turkey.

Dad's giving most of us electronics this year. An iPad for me. An upgraded smartphone for Kay. The same but different for Ant. Mam – who never learned how to programme her video recorder, who only ever taped programmes by waiting, live, for them to start, then holding the control at arm's length and stabbing at its buttons with a look approaching terror on her face – Mam gets a day out to a fancy spa and a machine which describes itself as a 6 in 1 Ultrasonic Liposuction Vacuum Cavitation Multipolar All-Bio Natureworld Slimming Device. Mam looks baffled and thrilled in about equal measure. Kay, envious, asks if she can use it.

Dad tries to get us all to watch *The Sound of Music* in the living room, but Kay and Ant want to go and play with their toys, and Mam wants to start washing up and 'get a few things ready for supper'.

Dad looks at me and says, 'Come on then, Fi, love.'

We go through to his studio, a place semi-detached from the main house and a place that is entirely Dad's. His mess, his toys, his energy.

He shows me some of his newest acquisitions. His latest thing is 1920s-themed American diners. He has an autographed photo of Al Capone. Some stamped tin sheets which will form the ceiling of his next bar. Some Tiffany-style light fittings.

Dad doesn't have taste, exactly. He acquires the hideous and the beautiful with the same awed reverence. What he does have, however, is a collector's appetite. That satelessness. So he doesn't stop buying stuff just because he has enough. He buys because the stuff is there, available. Dad still seems like a five-year-old in a sweet shop: amazed wonder that the world has so many good things in it. His bars and clubs succeed, I think, because they give to the customer that sense of the prolific. A gift of abundance.

Dad is slow to settle.

'Lord, your mother does feed us,' he complains, pouring glasses of fizzy water for us both.

'Thanks for my iPad,' I say. 'And the money.'

Dad had put £2,500 in cash in an envelope with my card.

'Oh, you're welcome, love. You'll need it in Sarajevo.'

Sarajevo: where I've told my family I'll be for Christmas. Working with Balkan law enforcement agencies. Only Dad doesn't say the word like that. He puts inverted commas round it. A smile nibbling at the foundations.

I shrug. Not confirming, not denying.

'See, if I had a cynical mind, I'd say that maybe you're not quite telling the whole truth about things. I mean, I'm sure you have a good reason, love, I'm not having a go. Just –

well, they have phones in that part of the world these days. And flights home. And a little part of me says that if you were spending six months helping Albanian ladies, or whatever, you'd still be calling home and seeing us for weekends now and again.'

I smile. 'But if I weren't going to Sarajevo, I probably couldn't tell you where I *was* going.'

'No, that's true.'

'Dad.' I sit forward. We're on facing leather chesterfields. There's a coal-effect gas fire flickering on our left. Picture windows, black against the night, behind Dad. 'Your clubs and your bars, they're legitimate businesses, I know that. Maybe there are little fiddles in there – I don't know, tax things, employment things, whatever – but they're basically straight. What I don't know, what I don't *really* know, is whether any of your former business interests are still active.'

'No. I've given up on all that.'

Dad's answer doesn't come immediately. And it comes out as a rumble, low in the throat. It's as though he hadn't used his voice for years. Was trying it out again, like a frock coat being shaken out. A chimney pipe swept free of soot.

'And I don't know, don't *really* know, if any of your friends are still playing the old tables, dancing to the old tunes.'

Dad's head goes back at that. Beyond the gaze of the shaded lamplight. The gas fire paints his features in dim shades of flame and copper.

'Lord, love, I have so many friends . . .'

'Of course.' Dad knows everyone and everyone he knows is a friend. 'I didn't mean that. I meant the people you were closest to. Uncle Em, people like that.'

'We're old men now. And those were young men's games.'

If this were a police interview, I'd want something more specific than that, but I'm not an interrogator and this isn't a suspect.

I can still hear, from across the little patio that separates this studio from the main house, the faint lilt of Christmas carols. They are a thousand miles away, audible only intermittently, like those undependable freaks of shortwave radio.

'Dad, I'm going to ask you a question. If you answer it with a "yes", I'll drop my current assignment. I won't give a reason. I won't have to give one. I'll just go about my ordinary business, the way I did before. I won't impede any current police investigations, but I won't assist them either.'

Dad nods, inviting the question. I think his lips move – a 'Lord, Fi, love,' most likely, or something along those lines – but no actual sound emerges. I wait just a second or two longer, trying to read this silence. Trying, vainly, to read the shadows in his face.

Then, 'Do you, or do people close to you, have anything to do with a man called Sajid "Saj" Kureishi? Or the death of a woman called Hayley Morgan? Or with a fraud that has affected a number of local companies?' I name them all, the companies which have lost money.

Dad assembles his features in the shadowlands, then brings his face forward into the light.

'That's three questions. At least.'

'And that's not an answer to any of them.'

Again that throat rumble. Frock coats and chimney pipes.

'No, love. I've nothing to do with any of that. Like I told you, I'm straighter than straight these days.'

That wasn't, in fact, what Dad said. He told me that he was no longer involved in his old games – primarily the purchase and resale of stolen cars – but avoided any statement about his current operations.

But still. I asked my question, got my answer.

I say, 'I'm not going to Sarajevo. I'm going to be working undercover. It'll be a longish assignment. I don't really know how long.'

'It'll be hard for your mother.'

'Yes.'

'And dangerous, I suppose. How did Hayley Morgan die?'

'She was starving. Ended up eating rat poison. Saj Kureishi was taped to a chair and had his hands hacked off. He bled to death.'

'Bloody hell, love! You don't give yourself an easy life, do you?'

I half smile at that. You could say the same of my pa. Lads from the old Tiger Bay, where Dad came from, were meant to work on the docks, indulge in petty crime or, if they were smart and ambitious, get a place at a grammar school and work their way into a white-collar job in the port authority or local government. He chose none of those options.

'I might need help along the way. If I do, Mam mustn't know. Buzz mustn't know. It would be just me and you.'

Dad nods, relaxes. This is an easy one for him. If I ask for help, he'll give it. He always has done, always will.

'Of course, love. Whatever you need.'

It's the first answer he's given me which I believe completely.

15

Four thirty p.m. on Christmas Eve.

I have a black bag with my stuff in it. Eighteen pounds in cash. I avoided sleeping much last night, so I look pretty rough. I haven't washed my hair for four days and I usually need to wash it daily.

I have the name of a homeless hostel that's not too far away. Make my way there. The streets heave with the last thrashing of a city centre Christmas. Men getting tanked up in the pub before going home to face their families. Everything green and red and gold. Everything that can be made to twinkle twinkling like fury.

The hostel is full.

I don't know what to do. It's the one Brattenbury told me to go to. I think maybe he knew it would be full. The man at the reception desk tells me to sit down and gives me a cup of tea. I drink it slowly as he phones around. Finds a place that has space. He gives me a map and explains carefully, twice, how to get there. I say thanks. He asks me if I've eaten. I shrug and say, 'sort of'. He asks if I've got any money, and I say, 'I'm fine.'

Finish my tea. Walk over to the other hostel. A big white building. Those boxy modern windows that look efficient, but somehow inhuman, as if belonging to a posh sort of jail. There's a little patch of lawn in front, pitted with black because of the season. The back and side of the hostel

85

are protected by fiercely spiked steel-grey railings.

I find the entrance. Two men outside. Raggedy-bearded. Sharing a roll-up cigarette.

'All right?' one of the men says.

I duck the question and go inside. The man who asked the question holds the door for me, as I find it hard to manage with my bag.

There's another reception desk here. Also rows of leaflets, noticeboards, chirpily phrased ads for therapy groups and back-to-work initiatives.

I say, 'I'm Fiona. I think someone called about me.'

The woman on duty – plump, black T-shirt worn under a patterned Christmas cardigan, and a face that is both tough and loving – says, 'Fiona, yes. Fiona Grey, right?'

'Yes.'

She tells me her name: Abs, short for Abigail. She gives me forms to fill in. I can't fill them all out. Partly because I don't want that level of intrusion into my notional past. Mostly because Fiona Grey wouldn't want to.

I fill in the main bits and wave my pen over the remaining blank areas. 'I'm not going to stay long,' I say.

'Do you have a place to go to?'

'Not yet.'

'Friends or family?'

I shrug.

'Have you got anything lined up with the council? Put in an application form for housing?'

I tell her no, but say they have to house me because I'm from the area.

She grimaces, tells me it doesn't work quite like that. Asks me what money I have. I say 'twenty quid' and show her what I have.

'OK, we're going to have to do this properly, but maybe not on Christmas Eve, eh, Fiona *fach*? Do you have towels?'

I shake my head.

She books me in for three days. Charges me £1.00 for the towels, refundable if I return them clean. Twenty pence for a sachet of shampoo.

She takes me up to a room. Two bunkbeds, two other women already sharing. Everything very clean. Lockers on the landing where I can keep my cash and papers.

'No smoking anywhere in the building. You need to read and sign our policy on aggression, drugs and alcohol. We operate a no-tolerance policy and we do mean no tolerance. Showers down the hall there. Breakfast at eight. Christmas lunch at twelve. It's 50p for breakfast, £1.50 for the lunch, but you won't want to miss that.'

I say thanks. Drop my bag.

The other two women are called Sophie and Mared. I say who I am, but we don't talk much. They're both alcoholic, I think. There's something brightly unstable about them anyway.

I take a shower. Wash my hair. Put on clothes from my bag. Dark jeans. Black boots. T-shirt, dark jumper and jacket. Wash my old underwear and T-shirt in the sink, take them back to my room to hang out.

Mared says, 'There's a laundry room, you know.'

I say, 'oh,' but hang my clothes out just the same.

I quite like the hostel. Christmas lunch – everything overcooked, but big portions, warm and lots of gravy – is crowded, smelly and companionable. I sit next to a man who spends the entire time telling me about his past as a butcher. He doesn't ask a single question about me, or not really. I eat everything, then fall asleep in the TV room.

On Boxing Day, Abs sits me down and goes through my history. I say I was in a relationship in Manchester. Say that it didn't work out.

'Was there physical violence? Did he hit you?'

I shrug.

'Did you report it to the police?'

I shake my head.

'Do you have children? Are there any children involved?'

Shake.

'OK. Are you sure?'

I nod. 'I don't have kids.'

She goes through other things. My connection with Cardiff. My existing family. My job history. Any skills I have.

I say, 'I've always worked.'

'OK, good. That's good.'

Abs digs it all out of me. I'm a cleaner now. Used to do clerical work. Filing, admin. Payroll. 'I've got qualifications.'

Abs wants to know more. I tell her I got all my payroll certificates.

'Do you still have them?'

'No.'

Abs wants me to make a Reintegration Plan with her. I don't do it that day, or the next. But before New Year's Eve is breaking out in the city centre like a small war, I have a draft Plan. Its gist: get a job, get accommodation, get a life. Don't live with someone who hits me. Abs says, 'You can do this, you know. Anyone can end up here as a one-off thing. That's just bad luck. The trick is not to end up here again.' I say thank you, and she hugs me.

16

I get a job. Cleaning again. Minimum wage. Start at five, work through to two o'clock. Offices and other commercial property.

I like it, like everything about it. I like the early starts. I like the routine and the pressure. I become quite good at it, definitely one of the better cleaners. I'm still a bit forgetful, especially in the big open plan offices, but I enjoy doing the floors and I'm ace on bathrooms and toilets. I like the sparkle from a properly cleaned mirror and the gleam from a row of clean white ceramic loos. I also like the invisibility. The way no one notices you when you clean around them. People might slightly lower their voices when they speak to each other in my presence, but not much. I've become like one of those minor modern inconveniences: a swipe-card entry system or a telephone menu. Something that irritates briefly and is then ignored. My best friend is a Filipina, Juvy Barretto. She has six teeth and bad English, but we smile a lot. She helps me with the big offices, telling me what to do when I get confused. I help her with the bathrooms, where she doesn't move as fast as I do.

So I mop, I clean, I dust, I hoover. I'm seldom late. I never complain. I don't pick stupid fights with anyone. I'm issued with a new tabard – smart, polyester, navy blue – and I take good care of it. Wash it. Iron it. Keep it nice.

I make sandwiches at the hostel and eat them for lunch.

Abs has got me a single room to myself – tiny, but I don't mind that.

And she's got big plans for me, Abs has. She wants me to get my own place. I'm not on any kind of priority housing list because I'm single, no kids, no health issues and no recent connection with the area. On the other hand, I'm earning good money now. After deductions, I'm making £189 a week. I have to pay £28 to the hostel – quite a lot, but I'm in work – and then meals and transport costs another £55. I try to avoid expensive stuff, meat especially, and walk as much as I can, but there are limits.

In any case, I'm making money and I start looking for properties to rent. Find a place on the A470 North Road, just by the intersection with Western Avenue. It's a studio flat. All-in-one bedroom, living room, kitchenette. Shared bathroom down the hall. The bed is a single with a lumpy mattress. The living room part of the set-up consists of a giant brown velour armchair, a Formica table and two folding metal chairs. The kitchenette comprises a tiny sink, a two-ring hob and a microwave. There's a big brown wardrobe of the sort that grandmothers used to keep in order to give small children nightmares. It smells of mothballs and something else, I'm not sure what. I'm on the second floor and my window looks out onto no fewer than nine lanes of traffic. The A470 itself, plus slip roads leading on and off the main ramp. There are always lights, always noise, always traffic.

I like almost everything about it. I like the roads outside, their neon brightness. I like the way there isn't too much of anything: one room, one bed, one armchair, one table, one sink. I like the smallness, especially. If I sit in my giant velour armchair, I can touch the bed with my right arm and, almost, the little kitchen range with my left. It's harder for me to get lost, physically or metaphorically.

Because the only address I can give is a homeless shelter –

I'm not even DSS – my potential landlord wants two and a half months' deposit from me upfront. That's a lot more than I can afford, but Abs helps me take out a loan from a social housing fund. The loan doesn't just cover the deposit, but also things like bedding. When I get the money and sign my rental agreement, she's genuinely thrilled for me. I'm thrilled for myself, actually. Proud. She tells me about a Freecycle place which helps people starting out or, like me, restarting. I get as much as I can for free. A nice man drives the stuff over to my place in his lunch break. I try to give him two pounds, but he tells me not to worry. He calls me 'love'.

Abs makes me promise to come in for weekly counselling and 'life planning sessions'. She wants to get me out of the minimum wage cleaning racket and into the sunny uplands of payroll clerking. She's checked with the Institute of Payroll Professionals and found that they have a log of my payroll certificates: a log which shows the extent of SOCA's always confident reach. Abs gives me reprints of my past glories.

'We run a mentoring service as part of our reintegration work,' she says. 'We've got a mentor who's heard about your case and who's really keen to work with you, Adrian Boothby.'

Boothby: what Adrian Brattenbury has chosen to call himself for these purposes.

I promise to come in for mentoring. Say I'm keen to get back into payroll.

When I meet Brattenbury for the first time since before Florida, it's the end of January and a grey rain beats against the window of the little room that the hostel sets aside for these things.

Brattenbury is tanned and fit-looking. Skiing, at a guess. He's wearing a dark blue shirt, open-necked. By police standards, Adrian Brattenbury is a very dapper chap.

He says, 'How was your Christmas?'

'Good actually. I've been enjoying myself.'

He assumes I'm being ironic and makes the necessary ironic smile in return, but I'm being sincere.

'Time to get you in play,' he says. He outlines his plans. I'm happy with his suggestions. He seems both intelligent and trustworthy, and he'll need to be both. He doesn't give me much detail on the workplace I'm going to. 'Fiona Grey wouldn't have any background, so you shouldn't either.' Logic I agree with.

On Tinker, he tells me what they have: not much. 'We haven't been able to track the money. All those Panama foundations and BVI shell companies – they're totally opaque. As far as the individual frauds are concerned, we know the local moles. We think we've identified their handler.' He flips a photo at me. A thirty-something man. Short dark hair, starting to thin. The photo was taken on a street somewhere and shows him in a grey wool coat and navy scarf. The photo tells me nothing. The man could be an accountant or a murderer. Or both. 'We think this is the guy, but until we get up close and personal, we won't know.'

I look at the photo. If I'm the tethered goat, is this to be my lion?

Brattenbury wants the keys to my room. I've only got one set, but I give them to him. He says he'll leave them back here at the hostel later.

'We'll wire up your room. Audio and video. You won't find anything even if you search for it. We'll do the same for your workplace when we get you in there. We're also going to embed devices in your personal items. Bag, coats, buttons, that sort of thing. The devices themselves are tiny, it's battery power that limits us, so please choose chunky over sleek. These things will be found if searched for by an expert, but they'll elude any ordinary search. We get our kit from the same outfit that handles the intelligence services, so it's as good as it gets.'

He slides a phone over to me. Cheap, non-contract. With

receipt showing a cash payment. 'Phone. They would need an electronics lab to detect the alterations we've made to this. Keep it with you whenever you can, so we can track your physical presence at all times. And keep it charged. The phone will pull down more battery power than you might expect.'

He gives me data too. Code words for use in emergency. Words that will get an armed response unit to me as fast as possible. But we both know that I may or may not be able to deploy those words. If my phone has been removed, and if I'm not at home or at work, I'll be out of contact. I doubt if Saj Kureishi had code words or an armed response team at his disposal, but if he did, they wouldn't have been of much use to him, strapped to a chair in an empty house in the empty country just south of Barnstaple.

I think of Kureishi's face. The expression that looks astonished from one point of view, anguished from another. Wonder if these things ever mean anything.

'You OK?' says Brattenbury, winding up.

'Yes, sir.'

A smile twitches at his mouth. 'You don't really need to "sir" me, not here.'

'No.' I'm not exactly known as a maximum deference type, so I'm not sure why I've started sirring now. 'I think it's Fiona Grey. I think she says "sir".'

Brattenbury looks quizzically amused. 'Well, whatever you want.'

'Thank you, sir.'

And I sit there noticing dust marks while Brattenbury talks at me and a grey rain washes the window outside.

17

Payroll. As Brattenbury promised, there's a job up for grabs with Western Vale, an insurance company. The Cardiff office manages back-office functions for the entire national network, which is one of the six biggest domestic insurers in the UK, so it's a big department. The job is an entry-level thing, paying twelve thousand pounds per annum for a probationary six months. Fourteen grand thereafter. By Fiona Grey standards, it's definitely a step up in the world.

I have to interview for the post. Win it fair and square. There are written tests and an interview. I don't have anything officey in my wardrobe, so go to Matalan the day before and buy a new grey skirt, shoes and jacket. I'm about to add a blouse, when a woman says to me, 'You're small, dear. Have you tried the children's section? There's no VAT.' So I do, and discover that I can get a two-pack of polycotton blouses for £7, which strikes me as exceptionally good value. I think of getting three packs, except that it would seem presumptuous, so I don't.

The written tests go fine. I have a double first from Cambridge in philosophy – the Fiona Griffiths me does, anyway – and I breeze through tests on Filing, Writing a Business Letter, and Numeracy.

The interview goes fine too, I think. The charity which runs the hostel has a business outreach programme – that's how they secured Brattenbury/Boothby as my mentor, or how they think they did – and the human resources person interviewing me treats me delicately, as though I'm half fragile ornament, half unexploded bomb. I try to act like neither. I worry that my jacket looks too cheap.

When she asks for references, I give Mr Conway's name at YCS and the name of my boss, Euan Tanner, at my current cleaning job. 'I haven't said anything to them yet,' I say.

'Don't worry. We'll only ask if we're offering you the job.' The human resources person – blond bob, professionally friendly eyes – squeezes out a smile at me, all lipsticked up and minty-fresh. I do my best to reciprocate, but suspect I fall short on professionalism, lipstick and all-round mintiness.

When she asks me if I have any questions, I say, 'No, I don't. I really want to do this. I'm a very hard worker.'

I get the job.

Start on 20 February. I'm sorry to give up my cleaning work – indeed, I try to find out whether it will be possible to do a five to eight-thirty shift, prior to the start of my working day in payroll. It's possible in principle, but the transport links don't work out, so reluctantly I give the position up completely. Ask to be considered for the early shift, if they get work in my area.

Say goodbye to Juvy. We hug.

Use my life savings to buy more office wear from Matalan. The store offers exceptional value. I don't know why I haven't used it more in the past.

And make a new life in payroll. In at nine, out at five. Eat lunch in the office canteen. Timidly get to know my colleagues, who have gleaned little glimpses of my dark history. Homelessness. Cleaning work. Rumours about a violent relationship somewhere up north. There are eight people in our little team. Six women, two men. Neither of the men look much like Roy Williams. Plenty of the women look like me. Or like smarter, more together versions of me, at any rate.

I'd like to meet up with Roy, learn how he's getting on, but my role prohibits any such thing. And his infiltration is running a few weeks behind mine. His payroll purgatory lies ahead.

Meantime, I process pay. Deal with leavers and joiners. Overtime and bonuses. Issue forms, chase HMRC, respond to queries, tabulate numbers. I get to know the Total Payroll Solutions software in painfully intimate detail.

I don't enjoy this job, not really. Quite often it gets to five p.m., and I can't think where the day's gone. I have to keep checking the clock to have any sense of time. When we leave the building, it's getting dark and always cold. If it's not raining I walk home – it takes forty minutes – to save the bus fare. The walk takes me straight past the police headquarters, my beloved Cathays, but I stay on the wrong side of the North Road. Don't let myself even peer in at the windows, even though there's a tiny chance that I might glimpse a brief view of Buzz, framed against the light of some conference room window.

I've seen him twice since Florida. I had one day with him in January, a day which we treated the way a long-term prisoner in a US state penitentiary might treat his once-annual conjugal visit. My February visit was slightly less fevered, but still steamy.

Because I'm not yet 'in play' as Brattenbury puts it, I'm allowed to see Buzz in his own flat. From now on, though, it'll all be off-site locations which SOCA will arrange. When I see Buzz, he gives me the engagement ring and I wear it with joy. Take it off, sadly, when I leave.

We say lots of nice things to each other, of course. Keep those Floridian promises alive and warm in these Welsh winter damps. But I realise that I treasure that diamond glitter not least because it's an emblem of all I thought I'd never have. To have recovered from my illness enough that a sane man could want to marry me. To have recovered enough that I could even think to marry. *Mirabile dictu.*

I can't stop looking at the ring when I'm wearing it. Buzz sees me looking and is fit to burst with pride and love.

Fiona Grey, meanwhile, little by little improves her life. She puts money aside for her housing loan. Buys a plate, a bowl, a mug, a saucepan. She doesn't buy cutlery, because she's stolen plenty from the canteen at work. She buys a tiny second-hand TV, but no licence.

We also buy a second-hand laptop. We can't access the internet at home – Fiona Grey fails every credit check, so no one will give her a contract – but we can sometimes get to the library before it closes. There we look at our emigration options. New Zealand and Australia look difficult. Canada looks hopeful. The United States looks possible, but expensive. We download some forms, make enquiries. Set up a Post Office savings account as Fiona Grey.

But it's not all personal improvement. There's a seedy-looking café in the studenty bit of Cathays which does vegan and organic food. I buy two cannabis plants from the hippy who serves coffee there. We celebrate our deal by smoking a joint out by the dustbins at the back. It's my first smoke since I arrived back in Cardiff.

Brattenbury, I see weekly. He reviews everything I do in meticulous detail. When I tell him I put my name down for an early morning cleaning shift, he pounces on it. 'Why? Why do that? Why add the pressure?'

'Cover, sir. It's what Fiona Grey would do.'

'You can shape who she is. You don't have to give yourself one and a half jobs, on top of the one you do for us.'

I shrug. 'That's what any SIO would say to any undercover officer. So no undercover officer would take the cleaning job.

So it's a perfect job to take, if I get the chance.'

Brattenbury disapproves, but since I don't actually have an offer of cleaning work, he lets it go.

Jackson, too, I see on and off. He has appointed himself my chief welfare officer. He's like a possessive dad who can't quite let his daughter live her own life at university. He asks me if I'm eating enough. If it's OK with Buzz and with my family.

I laugh at him and don't call him sir.

With Brattenbury, things are more practical. He tells me stuff, drills me in stuff. The use of recording devices. The way the plan is shaping up.

'Audio and video surveillance are in place. Ditto network access. We don't know if Tinker have installed recording equipment, but we have to assume they do. You should assume your PC is compromised as well.'

'Yes, sir.'

'And meantime, we've "infiltrated" Roy Williams into Fielding Insurance.' Brattenbury's fingers walk inverted commas through the empty air. 'I think he'll do perfectly.'

'He's a natural payroll type,' I murmur. 'Duck to water.'

'Yes.' Brattenbury laughs. 'I've seldom seen an officer less happy in his role. But we've done a proper job with him, actually. Wired him up. Surveilled his flat and his workplace. The whole works. We want it to appear as though we're taking the kind of countermeasures that the Tinker gang would expect us to take. We don't want to look suspiciously sloppy.'

'No, sir.'

He scrutinises me. 'You've got your computer?'

'Yes, sir. And I've been getting online when I can.'

'Good. And your savings account?'

'Done.'

'Your horticultural projects?'

'Thriving.'

'Good.' He explores my face with his eyes. I don't know

what he finds there. Fiona Grey tends to look away from authority, so my eyes stay close to the floor. My hands are in my lap. I don't think that's how I sit normally, but I can't remember how I was before. This is me now.

'We'll make our move soon. Are you ready? Or ready enough?'

'Yes, sir.'

'OK. Stay safe.'

18

Stay safe. I've been in my post four weeks and two days, when uniformed officers enter our offices and arrest one of my co-workers, the department's deputy manager, Ellen Keith.

The charge is fraud. Keith has, apparently, been using her managerial privileges to falsify her own payroll. Excessive overtime. Unsubstantiated expense claims. Insufficient deductions for tax. A classic example of the successful crook getting too greedy and overreaching themselves.

At my next meeting with Brattenbury, he tells me they were lucky. 'She wasn't just stealing on behalf of Tinker. She started stealing on behalf of herself. Doing it quite incompetently too. So it was a nice, easy arrest. We didn't have to disturb the Tinker operation. From the gang's point of view, they've just watched us take down a rogue part of their operation. In some ways, they'll be relieved to have lost her.'

'Won't Tinker be worried that she might spill the beans?'

'Maybe, but I severely doubt she has any beans to spill. If you were Tinker, you'd tell her as little as possible and use false names and neutral meeting points.'

He shrugs. Nothing is risk free. Not in his world, not in mine. Brattenbury has lost some of his tan, but that look of health continues to illuminate the office. I wonder how I come across. Not like that, I think.

When he resumes he says, 'From Western Vale alone, they are currently stealing £73,000 a month, via twenty-nine different fraudulent payroll accounts. They aren't going to risk losing that.'

'No, sir.'

'They'll be looking to replace Keith. They'll make their checks – we expect them to be thorough – then come after their chosen replacement.'

'Yes, sir.'

Brattenbury, I think, is expecting me to a bit more gung-ho. A bit more let's-get-these-bastards, guv, but that's not quite my style, or not Fiona Grey's anyway. He seems dissatisfied by my lack of response and keep prodding away at it restlessly. I say 'yes, sir' when I need to and otherwise don't say much.

After half an hour, I say, 'Is that all you needed, sir?' and he says, 'Yes.'

At work, meanwhile, we talk about Keith's fall from grace in shocked whispers. She'd been a bright, vivacious, even raucous presence, with carmine nails and suits in orange, red and bottle green. Those things are now being reinterpreted as signs of peeping criminality. We get visits and lectures from compliance officers, from audit, from the executive suite.

Me, I just do what I do. Live frugally. Save what I can. Wear my rubbish clothes from Matalan. Work hard.

I do decide to cut my hair and trim it myself in my little sink. It's not a very good job, maybe, but good enough. The hair got a bit shorter, which is what I was aiming at.

And one evening when I drop in at the hostel for a warm meal and a bit of social life, Abs looks up from some paperwork and says, 'Oh, Fi, there was a man here yesterday, asking after you. A friend of yours.'

'Oh?'

'A Vic somebody?'

I shrug. I don't know a Vic. Abs says, 'We don't give out personal information. He doesn't have your address or anything like that.'

I say good, and give her a pound for an evening meal.

And then one night, about two weeks after Keith's departure, I come home from a visit to the library to find my door unlocked and a man sitting in my giant velour armchair. Mid-thirties, give or take. Thinning on top. Clean shaven. Grey suit, pale blue shirt. The man from Brattenbury's photo.

I stand in my doorway, staring.

I probably look frightened. Maybe I am frightened. I'm not sure.

He says, 'Sorry, come in. I mean, this is your room, isn't it?'

I half close the door. Drop my bag. Sit on the bed.

'Nice place.'

I don't say anything to that. It *isn't* a nice place. There's nothing nice about it. I just happen to like it.

'I'm Vic. Victor. But everyone calls me Vic.'

'How did you get in?'

'I picked the lock.' He shows me his lock picks. I have a set just like it, but not here. 'I'm not here to hurt you. Sorry, I should have said that straight out.'

'You a friend of Rick's?'

'Rick? I don't know a Rick. No. Nothing to do with me.'

Rick: the name of my abusive, if theoretical, ex-boyfriend.

'You from Manchester?'

'No, love. You don't know me. I've got nothing to do with any of whatever that is. I'm here because I want to help out. Honestly. Look, shall I put the kettle on? *Is* there a kettle?'

There's only a saucepan and one mug, but I let him make me peppermint tea. There's nothing for him to drink out of and no tea or coffee, so he has to make do. He puts my mug down on the little bedside table. I'm still sitting on the bed, coat still on.

'I didn't know you were a gardener, Fiona,' he says, gesturing towards the cupboard.

I keep my cannabis plants in the cupboard, with a low-

102

power heat lamp to keep them happy. I don't say anything. Not about the fact that he's looked in the cupboard, nor about the fact he knows my name.

I take the tea. I want to pull my knees up towards my chin, but I'm wearing a skirt and can't do that easily, not with him here.

'You work at Western Vale, right? New job.'

I don't say anything.

'Look, there's something you could do for me. I'd pay you.'

I shake my head.

'Easily done. Five minutes, literally. I'd pay a grand. Cash.'

My head is still shaking. 'No. I'd like you to leave, please. I don't want . . .' Fiona Grey isn't very assertive and I can't look at this man. I look at the side of the armchair and talk to the floor.

'Thing is, if I happened to call Western Vale and say I think they ought to get you to do a drugs test, you might not have a job afterwards. Then what? Back to the cleaning? Back home to Manchester? I don't think you'd make it to Canada or Australia or wherever you wanted to go next.'

I do draw my knees up now. Wrap my arms around my calves. I think I rock. It feels something like that. If I say anything, I probably say, 'Please.'

Vic, I think, studies me for a while. I'm not sure. I'm not looking.

Then I hear him stand up and he says, 'Look, this is all a bit fast for you, isn't it? Tell you what, just think it over. Don't do anything stupid. I won't do anything. And maybe we'll go out tomorrow for a drink, somewhere nice, and we'll just talk it over.'

I don't say anything. Just hug my legs.

'If I come round tomorrow, maybe. Shall we say six?'

Fiona finds it hard to say much, but she does manage to get

103

out the words, 'Don't come here.' She doesn't get them out very loudly, though, and Vic says, 'What?' before realising. Then he says, 'OK, let's meet somewhere. You choose. What sort of place? A wine bar maybe? A pub?'

I'm not a very good conversationalist, so I let these questions go.

Vic gives me space to answer, then says, 'OK, how about The Grape and The Grain, half past six. Do you know where that is?'

I do. It's a wannabe upmarket wine bar, a ten- or fifteen-minute walk into town from here. I nod, just enough for Vic to see the nod.

'Half past six tomorrow then,' he says.

That's not really a confirmation of an arrangement, not on his lips. It's more like a reiteration of a threat. Be there, or . . .

But I nod.

I'll be there.

Vic stands at the door and checks the room. I feel his gaze on me, on my bed, my chair, my few possessions. It's as though he's taking an inventory and I'm his Item One.

When he goes, I lock the door after him. Then sit on the bed again. Back against the wall, knees under my chin, arms round my legs. The full teenage angst pose, with a little bit of rocking thrown in, I think.

I'm not faking it, or not really.

Yes, I'm aware that Henderson is probably bugging my room. Watching my next moves. But Fiona Grey isn't pretending to be a cleaner. She is a cleaner. A cleaner with aspirations for a higher, brighter, easier life that's all of a sudden looking lower, dirtier and harder than she'd ever wanted.

I stay hugging my legs until I get cold. Then wrap the duvet round me and hug some more. Then, much later, roll a joint, a big one, and smoke out of the window. When I look at my watch, it's one in the morning and I haven't eaten anything since lunch. But I'm not hungry. I do my teeth in the sink. Strip down to my underwear. Go to bed.

I lie there, two people at once. Fiona Grey is thinking about tomorrow. She *is* scared, I can feel it. Her hopeless past about to swallow her once-hopeful future.

Fiona Griffiths is a more elusive quantity. She ought to be happy with the way things are going, but if she is, I can't feel it.

Was Vic there when Kureishi was killed? Was he the man who wielded the hatchet? Maybe. It hardly matters. Certainly not morally, but not legally speaking either. The doctrine of common purpose means you don't have to wield the hatchet to count as a murderer.

Fiona Griffiths lies in bed, staring up at her dark ceiling, listening to the traffic. Different tunes. Cars leaving the slip road make one kind of sound, as they brake for the lights. But that's the descant to the main road's bass. The sound I like the best is the foot-to-the-floor sound of vehicles as they climb the A470 flyover. Metal angels ascending to a tarmac heaven.

This Fiona wonders what she's got herself into. Whether she'll ever get herself out. She wonders if Brattenbury has been watching all this. If Henderson is.

She's hoping yes.

19

The Grape and The Grain. Ten to seven.

It's a miserable day. Not freezing, but cold. Not raining steadily, but heavy intermittent downpours. A blustery wind blows in from the Atlantic, foul-tempered and hostile. I'm wearing office clothes, a mac, scarf and woolly hat. The mac isn't warm enough or properly waterproof even. I got it second-hand because the good coats cost £40, even in Matalan.

I was here early. Six twenty. Have been walking up and down since then looking in at the warmly lit windows and feeling out of place. One of my boots has a hole in the sole and my foot is sodden.

But in the end, I go in.

It's a smart bar, nicely done. Dark wooden floor. Scrubbed wooden bar. Lots of heavy fittings: oak casks, brass nautical lamps, a huge glass bowl filled with wine corks and dried hops.

I stand, dripping, in the entrance area as men in suits and women in tailored outfits talk, laugh, fiddle with their phones. A waiter with a stubbly beard and a blue neckerchief approaches. He's wearing a smile but I have this vision of him simply clearing me away, the way you might if you came into your kitchen and found a dead pigeon or a stray drowned mouse making a mess of your scrubbed limestone floors.

I stand there, dripping, waiting to be tidied. Wet cotton mops and metal buckets.

But I'm not tidied. Vic emerges from behind a raw oak pillar. My face must change somehow, because the waiter swings round, sees Vic. Some look is exchanged, and the waiter waves me over to where Vic has a table waiting.

'You made it,' he says.

He clucks around me, a fussy uncle. He wants me to remove my coat, but I keep it on. Take off my hat, but keep it close.

He wants me to choose a drink. Pushes a long wine list at me, tells me to order anything. I ask for water. He tells me again to order *anything*, meaning that water doesn't count, so I say orange juice, a small one.

He orders another glass of red wine for him, a bowl of olives, toasted ciabatta slices and olive oil, a selection of antipasti, and my orange juice.

I sit there with my bag on my lap. The bag is wired for sound. So is my coat.

'Filthy day, isn't it? I don't mind it cold, but this is vile.'

I don't say anything. Maybe shrug. Look sideways.

'Listen, love, you're frightened, aren't you? And that's my fault. I think I frightened you yesterday. Let's just get to know each other a bit maybe.'

'How do you know my name?'

'OK, full disclosure, we took a look at your laptop when you were out. Checked your room. We like to know a little about the people we work with. That's how I know you're thinking of emigrating down under. Get some sunshine, eh? Not like this.'

'Canada.'

'Canada, is it?'

'Or America. I don't know. Wherever.'

Vic pauses to see if my little conversational spurt will run anywhere. It doesn't, so he puts his shoulder to the wheel once again.

'What is it? Need a break? Or just start again somewhere,

107

completely fresh. I've always thought about doing that. Just going somewhere else, starting with a clean slate, see what happens. Bit of an adventure.'

Since I don't respond to that, he says, 'But it's tough, isn't it? If you're married to an Aussie, or whatever, then it's hi, Sheila, come in, g'day. If not, then it's do you have the skills, do you have the money? Fact is, if you've got the cash, then anything can happen. If not . . .' He shrugs.

My mouth moves but doesn't actually say anything, so Vic puts his shoulder to the wheel once again.

'You've got your payroll skills. Those are good qualifications, aren't they? The sort of thing that might help get you a visa. But, you know, is payroll here the same as payroll there? I don't know how far those qualifications stretch. You don't have anything like nursing, do you? That's a good one. Or school teacher. Everyone needs teachers.'

There's a pause.

I do my share of pausing, but this moment belongs to Vic. He's using it the way we use silences in interrogation. Dropping uncomfortable facts on the table and allowing them to swell in the emptiness.

I don't say anything.

A waiter comes with drinks and food and we wait as the table is spread with good things. When he leaves, Vic drops a letter on the table.

The letterhead belongs to a British law firm, headquartered in London. The letter starts, *Dear Mr Henderson, Thank you for your enquiry about a subject, Miss Fiona Grey, who is seeking to emigrate to an English-speaking country in the southern hemisphere, preferably Australia or New Zealand. We understand that Miss Grey (a) speaks fluent English, (b) has no criminal record, (c) holds NVQ-type certifications in payroll, (d) has no family overseas . . .*

Vic flips me straight to the last paragraph. *We feel confident*

of being able to progress this matter and look forward to receiving
further instructions from you.

'Money,' says Vic. 'It's all about money. Getting some dick-for-brains lawyer to package you up so you look like God's gift to Oz, or wherever the hell you want to go.' He waves the letter in the air, before folding it back into his pocket. 'Let's say twelve K for the lawyers, plus maybe ten or twenty in your bank account so you can prove financial solidity. Allow a bit more for any bullshit qualifications you might need to acquire. Thirty or forty grand and you can live in Oz. Not on some temporary visa thing, but for life. Become a citizen. Or Canada. Or New Zealand. These guys' – tapping his pocket – 'they'll sort you out.'

Vic watches my face. Looks pleased with the result.

Says, 'Not so scary now, am I?'

He grins.

If Brattenbury looks like an unusually dapper policeman, then Vic looks like an unusually dapper gang member. He's wearing a nicely fitted jacket in brown tweed herringbone. Lining in damson silk. A black woollen rollneck that might even be cashmere. I have to remind myself that these neatly manicured hands might yet be the ones that swung the hatchet. Part of me wants to ask. Wants to say, 'What is it like, to sit in bars like this, to wear clothes like this, and to know that you and your friends cut a man's hands off and let him bleed to death as you watched and he screamed?'

But I don't.

Don't say that, or anything else. But when he says, 'Here, why don't we get that wet coat off,' I do put my hand to my throat and undo the first couple of buttons. Reach for an olive. And, for the first time, catch Vic's eyes and don't look away.

20

Saturday is my favourite day of the week. A day for play, work and self-improvement. I spend most of my day at the hostel, which isn't only a place for people like me to get shelter for the night. It runs a drop-in centre too. Group therapy. Skills workshops.

I fit right in. Fiona Griffiths's various injuries and vulnerabilities are somewhat different to those of Fiona Grey, but both of us feel comfortable with this beat-up, muddled, slightly crazy level of society. We can be ourselves. We disappoint no one's expectations. If we let a little craziness show, that's OK. People don't notice or, if they do, don't care.

I've joined a regular Saturday morning session on domestic violence. Fiona Grey doesn't contribute much, but when she does, people listen and understand. She and I both listen to other people's tragedies and are stunned at the ordinary braveries we hear. The braveries and stupidities. The two things, hand in hand. We feel moved to be there. I sign up for a counselling course which takes place one weekend a month in Birmingham. If I attend all four weekends, I get a diploma.

Later in the afternoon, Fiona and I also attend classes on Cooking For Yourself. The class is brilliantly practical. It's not one of those things that's all about potato ricers and how to get a glass-like finish on your crème brûlée. We're told things like where to buy the cheapest saucepans and how to cook a nutritious meal for less than £1.50. I've learned heaps of stuff I never knew.

There's also an Anger and Anxiety Management course which looks good. Also one on Life Skills which sounds enticingly ambitious. I sign up for the first one, leave the second for later.

Mostly, though, I like the hostel for its social side. There's a games room where I've been learning to play table football. My best friend is an ex-addict, ex-soldier, ex-husband, called Gary. He was the raggedy-bearded man who held the door open for me my first night here and is one of the senior members of Cardiff's *Big Issue* fraternity. He and I share roll-up tobacco and life stories, but Gary's not really a table football type and my regular partner is a woman called, impressively, Clementina who speaks a kind of gypsy-English I don't completely understand. But she is a constant cackle of laughter and has a whip-like action in front of goal which compensates for my deficiencies in defence. We smoke, play table football, and drink lots of tea. I haven't smoked or drunk as much tea as this since the last time I was in a mental hospital.

All this and I meet my 'mentor' Adrian Brattenbury, who goes by a different name here, of course.

We meet, in late morning, up in a tiny room on the top floor, one set aside for various different types of counselling. It boasts two small armchairs and three inspirational prints: of a waterfall, the sun setting behind clouds, and an autumn forest.

I sit where I can see the window, not the prints.

Brattenbury waits until he has my attention, then his eyes move to a small wicker hamper on the table. He whips it open with a *ta-daa*.

It's rich-person food. A half bottle of champagne. Bagels with salmon and cream cheese. Orange juice, freshly squeezed.

A flask of coffee. A heated dish with sausages, mushrooms and egg. Real china, metal cutlery. A champagne glass hunkered down in its own satin-lined compartment.

He reaches for the champagne, but his words are strictly business. 'Audio, absolutely crystal. Bag and coat. Courtroom quality. Easily enough there for a conviction. Wham, bam, and thank you, ma'am.'

He tries to whip off the cork to coincide with the *ma'am*, but his timing falls narrowly astray. He's good with the bottle, though. One of these people who holds the thing by its bottom, knows how far to fill the glass without spillage, an easy twist to prevent drips at the end.

'Bucks fizz or as it is?' he asks, waving the orange juice.

'I don't really drink. Sorry, sir.'

'You don't drink? That's a you thing, or a Fiona Grey thing?'

I shrug. I don't understand the question. 'I'll just have orange juice, if that's OK.'

He pours orange juice. 'And coffee?'

'I mostly avoid caffeine. Sorry.'

'Well.' Brattenbury looks uncertain how to react. Like a parent whose six-year-old has just rejected a Christmas present. His face flickers through various different options, before it settles for Brightly Optimistic. 'Never mind. Just help yourself to whatever you do want.' The hand gesture which accompanies the invitation doesn't look brightly optimistic to me. A hint of thunderclouds.

I start to eat the sausages.

At the library, I have to check in my bag and coat. Brattenbury has installed one of his guys as a cloakroom attendant and, by the time I'm in line to collect my stuff at closing time, the audio data has been collected and the memory cleared. If I want to leave a message, I simply speak into one of my devices before checking it in.

I receive instructions at the same time. Brattenbury has his messages printed on the inside of food wrappers, Twix and KitKat mostly, then rewraps them around the original chocolate. A cute touch that. I can't let Vic and his buddies find me in possession of any messages, but nor do I want to have to burn, shred, eat or otherwise destroy ordinary slips of paper. If I was seen doing that it would be almost as dangerous as being found with the original. So I just open up my chocolate, read the message while I'm eating, then chuck the waste into any street bin. Occasionally I get messages via Western Vale's internal mail, but not mostly.

'Well, if you're not going to . . .'

Brattenbury helps himself to champagne, which seems to restore his mood. He's in his Saturday attire. Dark jeans, suede shoes, suede jacket, pale blue shirt. It's a look which vaguely suggests the casual without, I think, actually being anything of the sort. But that's OK. I prefer my spymasters to be sticklers for detail. He has the pinkish, self-righteous glow of a man who has already visited the gym.

I finish my first sausage. I want Brattenbury to tell me what they've found out about Vic, but I don't ask. Start on some egg.

'Vic Henderson. Not his real name, of course. Apartment down on the Bay. We've installed surveillance. Non-intrusive. Got permission to listen in to his landline. We weren't able to do that before because we didn't have sufficient grounds for a warrant. Thanks to you, we do now.'

I wait for him to tell me more. He waits for me to ask him a question.

I help myself to mushrooms.

I'm a slow eater.

He says, 'We don't yet have useful data, but it's only been two days. He's careful.'

113

I put my fork down. 'Vic must have reported back on me. Must have done.'

'He uses a disposable mobile phone. We're trying to intercept it, but he's been careful so far.'

There are lots of ways to be careful. You can take the battery out of the phone, rendering it invisible except when you make or receive a call. You can change phones frequently. You can make sure your calls are encrypted. Or you can use your phone only in places, like the centre of Cardiff, where no interesting location data is imparted. It's pretty much impossible to intercept a call on a phone whose number and location you don't know.

'His movements?'

'He's careful. Full of tricks.' Brattenbury doesn't elaborate, but it's not that hard to shake off a tail. Hopping on and off public transport, reversing course, entering public buildings. The tricks used in any spy movie are still reliable ways to evade pursuit. And, of course, Brattenbury's surveillance guys have to be acutely careful not to be identified, or 'burned', because any slip on their part could easily compromise me. 'But we're patient,' he says. 'These guys always lose patience before we do. The key thing is getting access and you've given us that. We think Henderson is probably a handler, nothing more. We suspect that the gang probably has a finance expert. Probably also a computer guy, unless that's the same person. Maybe also an overall boss, if that's how they organise themselves. So perhaps three to four people in total, and you've given us one of them.'

I go on doing damage to the meal in front of me. But slowly. I've eaten one and a half small sausages, a spoonful of egg, some mushrooms.

I don't know about Henderson losing patience. This scam has been running for eighteen months, has already netted

114

millions and caused at least two deaths. Henderson, it seems to me, is not a slapdash type.

'When Henderson checked out your room, he did a basic search for surveillance equipment. He'd have found anything with a transmitter, but we didn't give him that pleasure. He didn't find the devices we have in place. He did install a basic audio and video device here.' He shows me stills taken from his own video feed. The photos show Henderson unscrewing the face plate from a power socket and replacing it with one taken from his pocket. 'It takes a power feed from your own mains electrical supply so it'll be on 24/7. It *does* transmit data, so they can pick it up remotely. You need to assume you're always on show.'

The socket faces my velour armchair.

'Do you know how much of the room it captures? Do I have *any* privacy?'

'That's a fair question. I don't know the answer. I'll find out and let you know.'

I don't much like the idea of getting dressed and undressed in front of Henderson's watchful eye. He doesn't seem pervy, but you don't need to be a perv to get kicks from such things. And who knows who is actually watching this feed? Who, and how many?

'Thank you.'

I'm done on the hot food and push the plate back. Peer into the hamper.

'Listen, Fiona, we've had a big review meeting. Dennis Jackson was there and . . . some senior people from the agency.'

I reach for the bagel and cream cheese.

It's strange, in a way, the amount of one-size-only food that exists. I'm a bit under fifty kilos and just a couple of inches over five feet. I buy my clothes in petite ranges, and choose a size to fit my not-very-bulky frame. My dear Buzz, who is not that far off being twice my weight, buys his clothes from places that suit his much larger figure. In the field of clothing, the logic of size compels universal obedience, as it ought to. But when it comes to food, people give me the same size bagel that they'd give to Buzz. They don't figure out that my bagel-needs aren't going to be equivalent to his.

I start saying this to Brattenbury. I say, 'They don't do bagels in small, do they? They ought to.'

'I think we need to start talking about exfiltration. We need to take it slow.'

I stop chewing. Stop talking.

'I'm talking months, not weeks.'

I swallow.

'I know it's hard. I know the pressures, believe me. But we've got our breakthrough and we need to protect it.'

I say, '*Ex*filtration?'

'It's a stupid word, I know that.'

I clear my mouth, push my food away. Say, 'You must be fucking joking.' Then, remembering etiquette, correct myself. 'I mean, you must be fucking joking, *sir*.'

'You're questioning my decision?'

'No. I mean, it's not a question.'

Brattenbury flushes like a girl when he's angry. He has lovely rosy cheeks that bring the best out of his dark curls and blue eyes. It's his best look, I think.

'Do I understand you to be disagreeing with the need to get you out? Or the pace with which I'm intending to do it?'

'I'm not quitting. I've only just started.'

'You've given us Henderson. He'll give us everyone else. Fiona, this isn't the first time we've done this kind of thing.'

'Oh, really? Let me see what exactly we have so far. We have one man with a false name. We don't have any of his contacts or connections. We have confirmation that these people are exceptionally cautious in their communications and movements. We have one person, *one*, where we can plausibly secure a conviction, and even then only for fraud. We have nothing else. Fuck all. And you want me to quit?'

We glare at each other.

Glare until the moment passes. Morphs into something that's the same, but a bit different.

Brattenbury says, 'I'm guessing this is a Fiona Griffiths thing, is it? More you, less Fiona Grey?'

'Don't tell me that Jackson didn't warn you. He warns everyone else.'

'He might have communicated something along those lines.'

'I haven't started *investigating* anything yet. I haven't had the chance till now.'

'You don't have a chance now. You won't get it. If you start to poke around, ask questions, whatever, you're going to find yourself in the same place as Saj Kureishi. We're not prepared to take that risk.'

'It's not *your* risk. It's mine.'

'Constable, you report to me. To me and to DCI Jackson. And we're not asking about your preferences. We're giving orders. You are still a police officer.'

We do the glaring thing again for a bit, then one of us, maybe him, starts smiling and we can't quite remember what we're arguing about.

'We'll talk about this next week, shall we?' he says. 'For now, steady as she goes.'

'Yes, sir.'

'These are dangerous men. Competent and ruthless.'

'Yes, sir.'

'Do you need . . .? On the social side of things. Are you getting enough support? Is there more we could be doing for you?'

'No, sir.' I want to tell Brattenbury about all the good

things the hostel has to offer, but feel he might be alarmed by my enthusiasm.

He stares at me.

I sit there, hands in my lap, wondering what he sees. I wonder what I would see, if I were him. I don't have those questions when I'm with Abs, or Gary, or Clementina. I was going to add, 'or Buzz', but realise that I have those questions with him most of all.

As if reading my thoughts, Brattenbury says, 'You're engaged now, I understand.'

'Yes, sir.'

'Take care with that. Those things are precious.'

'Yes.'

'OK. Good. And I'll talk to Dennis Jackson about your desire to . . . to deepen the infiltration. It'll be his call as much as mine.'

'Yes, sir. Thank you.'

'Anything else?'

'No, sir, except . . .'

He raises his eyebrows, inviting more.

I hesitate. Am I really going to say this?

I find that I am.

'There's a private investigation of my own, which I'm interested in pursuing. It won't conflict with Tinker. I just wondered whether SOCA might have any data that goes beyond what I can find from regular police sources.'

Brattenbury's face is illuminated with surprise. A fairground, garlanded with coloured lights.

'And the object of this inquiry . . .?'

'Thomas Griffiths. My father.'

'There are *police* files on your *father*?'

I shrug. Invite Brattenbury to look at his laptop.

He does so. I can't see the screen, so don't know if he's

118

looking at SOCA material or our own files, but our own files are extensive enough.

Brattenbury's surprise grows visibly as he investigates. 'Three prosecutions? Four?'

'Five, actually. There's one in nineteen eighty-two you might have missed. The full package is two armed robberies, then one each of possession of a firearm, kidnap and arson. He was never really an arsonist though. Not his *métier*.'

Brattenbury continues to study the screen in front of him, but I already know the story. My dad was Cardiff's crime boss for a decade or so in the eighties and early nineties. Before that, he was working his way up. After that, he started to move sideways into more legitimate lines of work. He was suspected of countless crimes. Prosecuted for five. Convicted of none. Cardiff's most innocent man: at one time his favourite joke.

'You want to nail your father?'

'No. I would never do that. It's just there are certain questions I have about my own past. Questions that are, I'm sure, tied up with my father's career. My investigation is about that. About the past, not the present. It's about me really, not him.'

Brattenbury, I bet, would love the full story, but I'm not about to share it. The bare facts, however, are these. One sunny day in June 1986, my mother and father found me in the back of Dad's open-top Jag as they came out of chapel. I was aged about two. I had a camera round my neck, with just one photo on the film: a photo of me, in the back of the car. I was clean and tidy. No signs of abuse. But I didn't speak. No one came to claim me. My parents, who had been trying for children, adopted me as soon as they could. Looked after me, cared for me, loved me. Loved me as fully and as well as, I hope, I love them now.

But those missing two years of life: I know nothing of them. Wouldn't care particularly, except that when I was a teenager,

119

apparently out of nowhere, I became mentally ill. As ill as it is possible to be. Depressed. Dissociated. Depersonalised. It got so that I couldn't feel anything. No emotion. No physical sensation. For two years, or thereabouts, I went around convinced I was dead.

Cotard's Syndrome: mine, an unfortunately classic manifestation.

For various reasons, I've become sure that my Cotard's Syndrome in my teenage years traces back, somehow, to those missing two years of life. The missing me, the dead me: one and the same. Yet to focus back on the past is to be not quite precise. I'm *still* not normal. Still struggle to achieve those things that other people find straightforward. The ghost of my Cotard's still haunts my ordinary life.

These days, I'm largely OK with my own craziness. I accept it, the way the lame accept their limp, the deaf their world of silence. But my version of normal never feels very stable. It always feels as though it could tip back into that place of deathliness and I've never thought I could survive another sojourn in that place. My long-term survival requires me to find a reliable balance. A resting point.

And I think the truth would help me. The truth about my puzzling origin. It's for that reason that I care.

'Does Dennis know about this?'

'He knows about my father, of course. Every copper of that generation knew about my dad. About *my* desire to find out more – no. That's not something I would share with my colleagues.'

Brattenbury pushes back from his laptop.

'SOCA wasn't in existence, of course . . .'

'I know.'

SOCA is a relatively recent beast. It replaced the National Crime Squad, which in turn replaced the old regional Crime Squads. But the data of those old organisations lives on. And there's always the question of whether my father is as clean as he now claims to be.

'I'll take a look.'

'Thank you.'

'I can't promise that I'll find anything or that I'll be able to tell you if I do . . .'

'I understand.'

'Anything else, Constable?' His tone is one of amusement.

'Yes, actually. The one other name I'm interested in is that of Gareth Glyn. It's probably nothing, but . . .'

I give Brattenbury a quick outline of what I know. In nineteen ninety-two, a mid-ranking executive at a big construction firm came to the police alleging extensive corruption in the award of municipal contracts and in various city planning decisions. Though he never named my father, my father's empire was, at that time, extensive enough that he'd have been the prime suspect for any such allegation. An investigation was made, but with no outcome. Glyn lost his job. Worked as a consultant for a while, then retired with ill health. In 2002, he walked out on his wife and was never heard of again.

A plain enough story, except that when I tracked down Delia Glyn, the abandoned wife, she told me that Gareth Glyn had been killed as a way to silence him.

Delia Glyn was on a number of psychiatric medications when she told me this. She was visibly somewhat crazed. And she was, in every way, very far from being a credible witness. But my inquiry won't end up in court and some of the people she named – in her rambling, repetitive, obsessive way – as being involved in the theoretical murder are people whom I know Dad to have known or worked with.

'That's not much of a connection,' comments Brattenbury, even as he notes down the major details.

'No. But it's like that with my dad. The people who know stuff won't tell it. And if I start asking around too obviously, he'll know that I'm looking and then the shutters really will come down.'

Brattenbury stares at his computer a little more. He is now, I'm pretty sure, looking at a SOCA profile, not a police one. 'Impressive. An impressive career.' He looks at me, with curiosity. 'Like father, like daughter, eh?'

I don't know quite what to say to that. Dad *isn't* my biological father. He was a criminal and I'm in law enforcement. Yet we are more similar than almost anyone else I know.

Brattenbury sees I'm not going to answer him, so he tells me to take care and starts to pack up. I go down to the games room, find Gary, and we spend some time smoking outside and chatting. He was in some fierce firefights in Afghanistan, came home a different person. Bad dreams. Occasional heavy drinking. Anger. He lost his wife to another man. Has been homeless ever since.

No lives are easy. I tell him that and he laughs till he coughs.

At four in the afternoon, I leave. Buy some groceries, so I can practise my new-found cooking skills. But also go to a hardware store, where I buy a security chain for my door. It costs £9.99, which feels like a lot, but the screwdriver only costs 95p, which seems good value. I ask at the checkout if I need anything else to fix the chain to my door. The girl – my age, friendly – isn't sure and directs me to someone called Ted, who asks if I have a drill. I say no. He says, do I have a bradawl. I say I don't know what that is. He gets me one – basically, a sharp pointy thing – and charges an extra £1.99, which seems unfair if a screwdriver is only 95p.

On my way home – walking, because I feel I spent too much in the hardware shop – I get a text from the cleaning company. Their central Cardiff unit needs a new cleaner to start on Monday. Am I interested? I text back saying, yes. Remind them I can only do the first shift, the pre-breakfast one.

When I get home, tired, I try to fit the security chain. The bradawl doesn't seem to work at all, or at least I'm not strong enough to make it do its thing. Upstairs from me, there's a man called Jason, a bus driver, post-divorce. He's got an actual flat. Bedroom, bathroom, living room/kitchen. An aristocrat of the low-rent world, but a nice guy for all that. I knock on his door and ask for help.

He's happy to oblige. He gets the chain fixing onto the softwood door frame with ease, but the door itself is plywood and even Jason can't force the stupid bradawl into the wood far enough to make room for the screw. He asks if I have a drill and I say no. He asks if I have a hammer. I say, I've got a saucepan.

Jason whacks the bradawl with my saucepan and – after a lot of whacking, a lot of noise and some inventive swearing – the track part of the mechanism goes up. The screws are only about three quarters of an inch long and quite slim, so I'm not at all sure that the chain will resist serious attack, but maybe that doesn't matter.

When he's done, I cook us a celebratory meal in my now wobbly saucepan. A one-pot meal of squash, tomatoes and lentils. It doesn't taste quite the same as when we made it at the hostel but, after Jason goes to get some salt from his flat, it tastes OK.

We watch TV and eat. Me in the armchair, Jason on the floor beside. When he goes back to his room, I go with him and ask if I can send a text from his phone. Text Brattenbury, saying, AM UP EARLY MONDAY. WATCH ME. F. Delete the text once I've sent it.

Jason says, 'We should do this again sometime. It's easy to get lonely in here.' I agree, warmly, on both counts.

It's been a wonderful day.

21

On Monday, my phone vibrates a silent alarm at 3.55 a.m., but I'm already awake.

I leave the room dark and slip out to the bathroom. Have a shower and get dressed in the bathroom. When I come back, it's 4.08 and I flip the lights on. My giant velour armchair squats like a hibernating bear. In the narrow space between armchair, wardrobe and kitchen area, I creep around putting on coat, hat and scarf. There's not much food kicking around, but I eat something anyway. I'm out and onto the street by 4.13.

It's a cold day. Directly overhead the sky is clear, but the streets are wet and a mass of inky cloud rides at anchor over the Bristol Channel.

I walk south. Lamplight softens the blackness, but the pavements are poorly lit and I'm well wrapped.

There's not much traffic. Whatever is there moves at the edge of the speed limit, or just a little more. I'm not particularly good with car makes and models, but I put any obvious commercial vehicles to one side – vans, milk floats, lorries – and pay attention to the rest. Try to keep a log of them using three letters from their licence plate. Silver Volvo HGM. Burgundy Corolla SSW. Repeat each identification in my head before dropping it from attention and turning to the next vehicle to pass.

The city is quiet. Just my walking feet and these passing

cars. A burr of engines, a splash of tyres. From somewhere beyond the Mynachdy Road, you can sense the river and the darkness of Bute Park. A deeper silence, owl-haunted.

When cars approach, I turn my head as though shielding my eyes from the headlamps. I walk fast, but I walk fast anyway. At some point, I'm not sure when, it starts to rain again. A gentle drizzle.

By the time I'm approaching the bridge over the railway line, I think maybe I've got this wrong. Perhaps they're less careful than Brattenbury thought. Or somehow know about my cleaning job.

As it turns out: neither.

A silver Audi TT drives north, on the far side of the road. I catch its number plate as it passes. Silver Audi RBO. There's a hesitation in its movement, as though its driver touched the brakes briefly on seeing me.

I do nothing. Just walk on.

At this point, the road has a raised central reservation and cars can't simply do a U-turn. I don't look round, but I do hear the car speed up, then brake hard. I'm guessing it's making a turn by the Texaco garage. Sure enough, the same car, driving slowly now, passes again. Silver Audi RBO.

I keep on walking.

The car drives ahead and out of sight. It can't do anything else, not really. Vic's boys won't have the resources to arrange a multi-vehicle surveillance given no notice at all, long before dawn on a Monday morning. And in any case, those things are hard to manage at a time when there's virtually no traffic, virtually no pedestrians.

I cross the bridge and go on walking.

The Audi is parked up ahead on Blackweir Terrace, lights off. I walk straight past it. Want to glance into the windows, but don't.

Walk on until I'm out of sight of the car, then stop. Prop my bag on a low wall and root around for tobacco and cigarette papers. Roll a ciggy, then walk on, smoking.

My cigarette ploy wasted a minute, maybe more, so the Audi gets its timings a little wrong. Passes me again before it really wants to. It goes past the left turn onto Colum Road, so I take the turn and start walking south towards the university buildings. I'm moving faster now, almost running.

A few moments later, I hear a car enter the road behind me.

I bolt into Colum Drive, a dead-end, as it happens, but unless you know this area you might not know that. Press myself against the doorway of the first building I come to.

The Audi follows me into the cul-de-sac, then realises its mistake, but also realises it's too late to make amends. It stops abruptly, tyres losing traction briefly on the wet road. When the car stops, it feels very still indeed. A composition in black, silver and glass.

I step out from the doorway and approach. Tap on the car window. After a brief hesitation, the glass descends.

There's a woman at the wheel. Forties, maybe. Blonde. Shoulder-length hair held back in a grip. Blue woollen coat worn over a dark jumper.

I kick the door. Hard. I'm wearing boots and kick hard enough to dent the panel.

'Who the *fuck* are you? What the *fuck* are you doing?'

'I've been . . . look, sorry, I've lost someone. I thought you might be her.'

'You've *lost* someone?' I kick the door again. 'Who *are* you?'

'I'm . . . um . . . Alison.'

I almost feel sorry for 'Alison'. I don't know what her role in the whole set-up is, but I'm pretty sure that motorised surveillance isn't her particular sphere of excellence. I guess she was assigned to this chase just because she happened to be closest.

'Alison? And who have you lost, Alison?'

'Look, it was a mistake, OK?'

'Who have you lost? You said you'd lost someone.'

Alison hesitates and, to help her make up her mind, I kick her car again. Not the door this time, but the rear panel. It wasn't a particularly good kick, but every dent is another four hundred quid on a car like this.

She loses her patience. 'Can you *stop* doing that?' Her voice is shrill. She gets out to look at the damage and, I guess, keep me from doing any more.

'Yes, if you stop *fucking* stalking me.'

Kick.

While we're having our version of a catfight, a man walks past. Jeans and waxed jacket. Something carried under his arm.

'You ladies all right?'

A car rides down Colum Road behind us, illuminating our faces. We stare briefly into the glare.

'Yeah, we're all right,' I say sulkily.

The man goes. The car goes.

Alison looks at her Audi with disbelief. 'Jesus,' she says. 'Jesus.'

'Just leave me alone, OK?' I look at my watch. 'You're making me late.'

'Late for what? I can give you a lift if you like.' Alison sees a way to rescue something from this shambles. 'To make up,' she says. 'I didn't mean to scare you.'

Our stand-off prolongs itself for another moment. Her peace-making and my suspicion grapple in this rain-softened darkness.

I throw my cigarette into a puddle. Sulkily tell Alison she can drop me at the top of Fitzalan Place.

Get cautiously into her car, which smells of leather and new carpet. I sit in my wet coat and keep my bag on my lap. I don't put my seatbelt on and a red warning light disapproves of my recklessness. Something pings.

Alison drives smoothly. Puts her indicator on, even where the junctions are completely clear. The wipers silently clear the rain. Her face is slightly illuminated in red.

'You're up early,' she says, trying again.

I don't answer.

We pass through the silent university buildings, the grey stones of the National Museum. My beloved Cathays, the police HQ, is just a couple of blocks away. I'd love to catch even a glimpse of it, but don't let myself stare.

When she drops me, I say, 'Look, sorry about your car, yeah? It's just that stuff freaks me out.'

On the other side of the road, there's a knot of people in dark coats. The orange stab of a cigarette.

'Meeting someone?' says Alison.

She really, really isn't very good at this.

'Yes,' I say, 'I'm meeting friends.'

I cross the road. Eight women. Nine including me. It's four fifty-five and my cleaning day is about to start. Over the road, the Audi sits there, hazard lights blinking, as Alison phones through the results of her morning adventures.

Who are you, Alison? I wonder. I'm fairly sure I'm about to find out.

22

A long working day.

From five to eight thirty, office cleaning. Acres of open cubicles under fluorescent tube lighting. A million yards of nylon carpet. A thousand dustbins. A hundred bathrooms, ceramics gleaming, floor tiles astonishing in their whiteness.

I do my stuff. Don't get praised or rebuked. My main cleaning partner is a woman, Lowri, who seems sour. She does all the hoovering. I do the bins and most of the dusting. She wipes her nose and tells me about her allergies.

At half-eight, I use the Ladies to change into something a bit more formal for the office: skirt and jacket in place of trousers and a fleece. Get peppermint tea and a pastry from a coffee shop. Am at my desk in Western Vale by just before nine.

Do my payroll work, which I go on finding hard to love. It's as though we live in some bureaucrats' heaven, where people, names, dates of birth flow over our desk and through our hands in a stream that has no start and no end. HMRC floats over our every transaction like the remote but threatening God of some failing Amazonian tribe.

We pay homage and buy hot drinks from a vending machine at 20p a cup.

Yesterday, I did the thing that Henderson paid me a grand to do. Nothing illegal. Not at this stage. He simply wanted me to change the assignment list that our department head,

Krissy Philips, keeps on a spreadsheet in her office. There's no particular magic about that list. Mostly it's just a way of making sure that work is divided evenly between Philips's worker bees. When everyone else went to lunch, I just waited around, pretending I had a personal call to make. Then just walked into Philips's office, pulled up the spreadsheet, and switched forty-eight names from other people to me. Switched the same number of my names back to them, so no one's total workload was either greater or less. The whole thing took seven minutes. One person, not from our department, entered while I was working, then went away again when he saw the place empty.

The switch of names means that the twenty-nine false payroll accounts now come under my jurisdiction. I haven't yet falsified anything. All I've done so far is ensure that no one else in the department will locate the fraud and expose it.

When I'd done what Henderson asked, I called him on his mobile and told him. He told me to meet him that evening at The Grape and The Grain, gave me a thousand pounds in cash, told me I'd done well. Said there might be more jobs down the road.

He offered me a drink. I said no and he didn't press. He didn't say anything more about the immigration lawyer and I didn't ask. Just walked out into the night, holding my bag tight against my side.

The next morning, I paid the money into my Post Office savings account. Any spare money I have left over at the end of the week goes in the same place. When I take my laptop to the library in the evenings, I check out immigration lawyers. And it's true: immigration law is basically a matter of cash. Pay the right guy enough and he'll find a way to sneak you through the system. It's good to know. I start making lists.

One puzzle: Henderson asked me to switch forty-eight names, but Brattenbury is only aware of a fraud affecting twenty-nine. When we met on Saturday, Brattenbury promised to check his figures but neither he nor I have an easy explanation of the discrepancy.

At eleven this morning, the internal mail comes round. There's an envelope for me – from Brattenbury, though nothing says so. Inside, a single sheet. A map of my studio apartment. Dotted lines mark out the expected field of vision of Henderson's surveillance. It's good news, on the whole. He can see the entire living area of the apartment, but not much of the bed and the area where I usually get changed is also out of sight. I realise that if I move the wardrobe by just a few inches, I'll shield the bed completely.

I put the sheet aside with some other documents. Forty minutes later, take the whole stack to the shredder and destroy the lot.

At lunchtime, I 'forget' my mobile and use a colleague's phone to text Buzz. OK TO DELIVER GOODS. FXXX. Delete the text from the Sent folder. Return the phone.

Work hard. But by four o'clock, I'm yawning. I've been up for twelve hours and working for nearly eleven. I drink peppermint tea and look at spreadsheets.

Leave at five. Buy some groceries and a sandwich. Buy a coat hook for the back of the door.

Walk home through Bute Park. Walk aimlessly. Watch the river from the bridge. Move between the formal beds and the long wooded walks. I can't see anyone following me, and I come into Bute Park often enough that my movements won't look suspicious.

I eat my sandwich next to some bushes by the river. Throw bits of bread to some waterbirds – two coots and some sort of wagtail – but they treat my offerings with contempt. Next to me, in the dark of the bushes, an envelope gleams white. I reach for it and put it in my bag. Throw the rest of my sandwich away and the wagtail, alarmed, flies off downriver.

That evening, I go to Jason's flat and offer to make supper for us. He says, OK and do we need anything? I say no, but show him the coat hook and where I want it.

As he starts to wrestle with my bradawl, I start to cook.

Start to cook, but also float over to his computer, which is switched on. Open up his web browser. Click Options on the browser menu, then select Security. The Security tab should really be called an Insecurity tab because, among other flim-flam, it asks if I want to see Saved Passwords. I do. Get a list of sites – only about a quarter of them porno – with stored usernames. I click the button that offers to Show Passwords. It says, 'Are you sure?' which doesn't strike me as the world's most testing security interrogation. I select 'Yes' and a complete list appears on screen.

OLIVIA06.

The name of his daughter and the year of her birth. A single password controlling a million different accounts. *Thank you, Olivia. Thank you, Jason.* The simple perils of fatherly love.

I close everything and go back to the stove.

That night before I go to bed, I throw open my window and make myself a joint, a big one, fat with hash.

Smoke it, slowly, with a cup of peppermint tea and a box of chocolates – a little extra gift from Buzz – on the arm of the chair.

Normally at this stage in a murder investigation, I'm very well acquainted with the victims. Have their faces pinned up by my desk. At home, even. The faces of the dead, photographed at the scene of their death. Postcards sent from their world to ours.

I find it strange, disorienting, not having those images available to me. It seems almost irreverent to go chasing off after murderers without the victims at the cold dead centre of the chase. A wedding without a bride. A feast without wine.

I've also felt uncomfortable being so far removed from

Brattenbury's inquiry. From one perspective, of course, I'm the steel point on the tip of SOCA's javelin. The thing that forces entry, opens the flesh, does the damage. But I'm also a copper and a Cambridge graduate. The policewoman in me wants to see the inquiry's records. To see the data remorselessly collecting. Lists of names, dates, phone calls, bank transfers. Witness statements and officers' reports. The Cambridge graduate in me likes the same thing. Puts her trust in paperwork, the primary sources for any inquiry.

It's not even that Brattenbury *can't* keep me abreast of these things in the limited time we have available, it's that he doesn't want to. The undercover operating manual says that the more fully I live in role, the less likely I am to commit an error. So Brattenbury tells me the minimum, tries to restrict every investigative impulse I have.

He's a good investigator, but careful. And I don't do well with careful.

I eat a chocolate, finish my joint, finish my tea, get ready for bed.

I'm conscious of Henderson's camera now, but not paranoid. If I pass it in my underwear, I don't care too much. I'm beginning to feel like I've got weapons of my own.

When Jason fixed the coat hook on my door, the extra protrusion meant it kept banging up against the wardrobe. So we shifted the wardrobe sideways. Only a few inches, but enough.

In the envelope Buzz left for me was the iPad my dad gave me for Christmas, also the cash, and also the name of a street in Llandaff, just across the river from here.

In bed, under the duvet, hidden from Henderson's gaze, I turn the iPad on, wait for it to scout out the local wireless networks. It finds a few – it would do in here – and I poke around until I find Jason's. The system asks me for a password and I offer it Jason's tender homage to his daughter. OLIVIA06.

133

The tablet thinks about that, then admits me, unaccusingly, to the world of the digital. Working under the duvet, I start to explore the world I've been missing.

A world of investigation and the faces of the dead.

23

Pontcanna. One of those posh streets that run down along-side Cathedral Road. I'm sitting on a doorstep, or Fiona Grey is. Same old coat, same old bag. Plane trees not yet in leaf, but you can feel them getting ready. A hidden murmur.

It's eleven fifteen in the morning.

I've been here two hours.

In the house behind me lives 'Alison'. Real name: Anna Quintrell. Occupation: dodgy accountant. Having internet access via my iPad means that I can, finally, get to see the data being assembled by Brattenbury's team. When I had my run-in with Quintrell, Brattenbury's guys were there to document it. The man in a waxed jacket who asked us if we were all right was one of his men. So was the driver who fixed us in his headlights, a simple way to ensure that his partner's video was properly lit.

The Audi was registered to Anna Quintrell, address here in Pontcanna. A basic PNC check revealed that Quintrell was cited in a major false accounting case three years back. She escaped conviction because of errors made by the CPS during prosecution, but she was kicked out of the Association of Chartered Accountants and must have had difficulty earning an honest crust since that point.

According to the Tinker case notes, Quintrell's house will soon be, and perhaps already is, under surveillance. I imagine they won't enter the house itself – that would be too crude for Brattenbury – but they'll find a way to enter one of the houses to either side. Perhaps both. Before Christmas, when I was still getting briefed, one of the SOCA technical guys told me they can do the whole job – enter the house, place the bug, make good, withdraw – in ten to fifteen minutes. They don't even need to enter the suspect's property, which means the chance of detection is close to zero.

But Fiona Grey can't rely on police data for her info. When I was at work, I called the various different Audi garages in Cardiff, saying that I'd brought an Audi TT in for repairs to the bodywork. The first two garages blanked me. The receptionist at the third said, 'Ah yes, Anna Quintrell, isn't it?' I said yes and complained that I hadn't yet had an estimate through. The receptionist apologised and said she was sure one had been sent. I asked them to confirm where they were sending it and the woman gave me the address whose doorstep I'm sitting on now.

Deception is so easy, I wonder why it isn't more common.

Time moves on.

Plane trees print abstract shapes on the pavement. Kids pass, with mothers in tow. A delivery man brings a parcel to the house across the street.

I think Quintrell is at home. She didn't answer the door when I arrived, but I'm pretty sure I've heard movements from within. There are net curtains on the windows.

According to the Tinker case notes, the mole at Fielding Insurance has been arrested, meaning that Roy Williams is about to 'go live'.

I think about Hayley Morgan. I've looked at all the scene-of-crime photos now, about a million times. There's something beautifully quiet in the lighting. The gentle light of a Vermeer painting. Filtered by glass, falling on slate flags, finding the sheen in cooking pots and old plaster. All that, and Hayley Morgan's little corpse. Restrained and peaceful, like a scatter of apples on a linen cloth.

I haven't really got to know her. I'd like to visit her again.

At twelve thirty, a police car glides up the road and stops. A couple of uniforms step out and approach me. I don't recognise them, nor they me.

'Are you all right?'

'Yes.'

'Been here a while, haven't you?'

'I'm waiting for someone.'

They ask my name and who I'm waiting for and what my business is. I answer 'Fiona Jones' to the first question: Fiona Grey is a wanted woman. The other questions I don't have to answer, so I don't. The officers try to get me to go away and come back later. Demand to see ID. I do have my Fiona Grey ID on me, as it happens, but I don't have to hand it over, so I don't. I'm not committing any offence by being here so there's nothing anyone can do to shift me. They hassle me a bit more, then retreat to their patrol car and sit there another minute or two, lights flashing. When the car leaves, the street feels very empty. In the house diagonally opposite me, a woman comes to the front door, stares at me for thirty seconds, then disappears again.

I like this street. I think maybe plane trees are my favourite sort.

When one of the mums returns from wherever she's been, minus the kids this time, I smile at her but she looks away.

At two fifteen, a black BMW noses down the road and parks. Vic Henderson gets out, straightens his jacket, blips his car locked. He starts walking towards me, but before he does, there's just a brief moment where he settles his expression. His face is now smoothed into a friendly, civilised, let's-all-be-reasonable look, but I don't think that's what it was saying when I first noticed it. He was twenty yards away from me, perhaps more, and the moment was fleeting, but I think there was something fierce in that face. Something brutal.

An easy violence.

I try to keep everything out of my expression. No hope, no surprise, no fear, no expectation.

The little path up to the front step is paved in two-inch tiles, black and white. A black-painted iron gate. Henderson has his hand on the latch before he speaks.

'Fiona.'

I shrug, or half shrug. I don't even know if the movement is visible through my coat.

'You've been here a while, eh?'

Shrug.

'OK. Let's go in.'

'She's not there.'

'I think you might be wrong about that.'

Henderson rings on the doorbell, then steps to the window and raps on it, putting his face to the glass so whoever's inside can see him if they choose to.

A moment later, the door unlocks. Anna Quintrell – 'Alison' – opens it. She stares down at me. She's wearing a red skirt and dark top. Make-up, hair glossily perfect. When I saw her before, she didn't look like this, but I imagine she'd been pulled out of bed at very short notice. She looked good, given that.

Quintrell says, 'Come in.' Henderson stands between me and the road. I have a sudden sense of being herded.

I stand, awkwardly nervous, until Quintrell steps back. The hallway opens up. I hesitate a moment longer, then step inside.

They lead me through to the kitchen. A surprisingly large modern extension. Big windows looking out onto one of those Japanese-style modern gardens. Slatted decking, potted ferns, concealed lighting.

No one asks me to sit, so I stand there, in my coat, holding my bag against my belly.

Henderson and Quintrell exchange glances. Then it's Henderson, not Quintrell, who asks, 'Do you want anything to drink?'

I do one of my invisible shrugs, then clear my throat. Say, 'I'll have a glass of water, please.'

Quintrell gets me a glass. I sit down at the kitchen table. Some blond wood, Nordic thing. The sort that looks almost identical to an IKEA table but costs five times more.

Henderson tells Quintrell to make him coffee, then says, 'Fiona, we're not very happy with you. Not happy at all.'

I say nothing.

'Now Anna and I have colleagues. And we've been talking about you. A long and difficult discussion, if I'm honest.'

I say nothing. Quintrell stands by her Italian coffee maker and does whatever you have to do to make those things work.

'There are two schools of thought,' Henderson continues. 'School one says you're more trouble than you're worth. We make a call to your bosses, tell them to give you a drug test, have you removed from Western Vale. Perhaps we also give your name to the police, just to see if they're interested.'

I don't know what my face shows at that. What I do know is that Fiona Grey feels frightened. Actual fear that tightens up the belly, sends its cold fingers into the capillaries and nerve endings.

That's a good reaction, of course. Fiona Grey is a 'person wanted in connection with' a stabbing in Manchester. If the police who arrived earlier had taken my ID, the system would have flagged me up and they'd have taken me into custody, awaiting further instructions from their colleagues in Greater Manchester.

But more interesting to me is the way I feel Fiona Grey's emotions more easily than my own. I've been frightened before, of course, and fear is one of the feelings that, I think, I identify more reliably than some others. But still. Fiona

Grey feels fear and – *boom!* – it's there throughout her body. She feels it with an immediacy and naturalness that I seldom manage on my own account.

I don't know what my face shows, but it shows something. I can tell that Henderson is pleased.

'Of course, if you have nothing to hide, the police won't be interested, will they?'

I still don't say anything, so he continues.

'The second school of thought says we give you another chance. A chance to show us that you can do what we need you to do. Without causing problems. Without doing twelve hundred pounds' worth of damage to Anna's car here. And without causing a scene at her home address. Getting the police called out.'

He stares at me. A vivisectionist pondering where to make the next incision.

Quintrell comes to the table with two of those tiny white espresso cups. I grip my water. I haven't yet touched it.

Stare at Henderson.

'And I'd love to tell you that we've come to a decision. But we haven't. We really haven't.'

'What you did to my car was totally uncalled for.' Quintrell has a taut asperity in her voice. A wintriness. 'It was vandalism, pure and simple.'

'The question is,' says Henderson, 'what you can do to put things right. Whether you *want* to put things right.'

This is bullying. There's not even a would-you-like-a-drink pretence about it now. Henderson has an unconcealed aggression that seems natural to him. Quintrell isn't physically threatening in the same way, but there's something cruel in the room now. Blood in the water and a skirmish of sharks.

I say, sulkily, 'She followed me. I didn't know she had anything to do with you.'

'I don't care. Do you understand that? I don't care.'

Henderson forces me to look at him. 'My colleagues and I have a lot at stake here. You can help us or you can get in the way. If you get in the way, we will discard you. Do you understand?'

I nod.

'So,' Henderson says. 'We need an answer. Are you going to help us?'

When I learned French at school – and I was never very good at languages – I remember a lesson on how to ask questions. You could create a question by sticking *Est-ce que* onto the start of a sentence. Or you could invert the subject and the verb. Or, simplest of all, you could just end your sentence with the phrase *n'est-ce pas*, but – and this was the bit that stuck with me – you could only do that if you were expecting the answer *yes*.

At the time, that struck me as a weirdly pointless piece of grammar. Why ask a question to which you already knew the answer? But the more I've studied interrogation, the more I realise that the French have got it right. More than half the time, we ask questions whose answers we think we know. Often enough, you ask the question *because* you know the answer and because you want to force the other person to acknowledge that fact.

This is one of those times.

A question expecting the answer 'yes'.

I stare down at my hands. Don't catch Henderson's eye. I mumble, 'I don't know what you want. I don't know anything about you.'

I can't see anything except my hands white around my water glass. A spread of expensive Scandinavian table. But I somehow feel an exchange of glances over my head. I don't know what those glances say, but Henderson rips into an old-fashioned police-style grilling, each question coming at me fast, hard and low.

I don't change position. Speak my answers into my glass or just move my head.

'You took a job cleaning. Why?'

'Earn some money.'

'Did you tell Western Vale?'

Head-shake.

'Are you planning to keep both jobs?'

Nod.

'But you didn't tell me. Why not?'

Shrug.

'I said why not?'

'I didn't know I was meant to.'

'Well you know now, don't you? If you work for us, we need to know what you're up to. At all times. Do you understand?'

Nod. 'Yes.'

'You go to the homeless hostel still, even though you're no longer homeless. Why?'

'People. There are courses and stuff. And just to hang out.'

He probes away at that. I let him find out about Boothby. I realise that Brattenbury will now kill those weekly 'mentoring' visits. Too much of a security risk. I can't say I'm sorry, but I realise I've half-deliberately severed another link with my previous life. Another connection to Planet Normal.

Henderson gets a who's who of my friends at the hostel, then moves on to other things.

'Why were you worried by Anna's car? Why did you react the way you did?'

'She was stalking me.' I say that a bit angrily. Or defiantly. But I don't shift my gaze from the glass in front of me.

'So you did twelve hundred pounds' worth of damage?'

'She wouldn't say who she was. She freaked me out.'

Henderson allows that answer to stand for a moment or two before he resumes.

'You found out her name and address. Why?'

'I was freaked out. I said.'

'How did you obtain the information?'

'I rang the garage.'

'How did you know which garage?'

'I rang all of them.'

Another short pause. Henderson, I assume, knows what I've just said to be true. If he can hear my phone calls from work and see what I do on the computer, then he has pretty full insight into my affairs.

'And you came here why?'

'I didn't want to be scared. I thought if I came . . .'

'You thought if you came, what?'

'I'd find out what was going on. I thought . . . You don't know how scary it is. It was four in the morning and she was being weird.'

There's a pause. A change of tempo. Into the silence, I say, 'Is it all right if I smoke? Sorry. I can go outside.'

Again, that unseen exchange of glances over my head. Quintrell says, 'You can go into the garden if you like. Don't leave your cigarette butt lying around.'

'Thank you.'

I get up. Meekly. Head for the garden but can't manage the sliding door. Have to wait for Quintrell, tsking, to rescue me. I say thank you again.

Outside, amongst the glazed earthenware and ornamental bamboos, I roll a cigarette and start smoking it. I have a bit of weed with me but, though I'm tempted, don't add that to the mix. Inside, in the kitchen, Henderson and Quintrell are locked in serious conversation. Henderson makes a phone call, keeps darting glances out at me.

I smoke one cigarette fast and needily, then a second one more slowly.

I quite like this garden. It's paved in some kind of stone, edged in brick, and has a stone bench shaded by next door's

143

magnolia. The day isn't sunny, but it's trying. It's halfway there.

I wonder what Kureishi's house was like. The house he had before he went on the run. Before he ended up in an end-of-season let in Devon, taped to a chair and his life's blood spurting from his wrists. I usually get to see those things. It's odd working undercover and being so remote from the corpses.

When I've finished my second cigarette, I gather up the two butts and the matches into a Rizla paper and stand outside the kitchen door waiting to be readmitted.

Henderson finishes his phone call, none too hurried, then signals to Quintrell that she can let me back in.

I throw the cigarette bits away, then sit back at the table. I keep my eyes forty-five degrees below the horizontal and say to Quintrell, 'I'm sorry about your car.'

Henderson likes that. 'Good. OK. Good. That's a better attitude. Now, Anna, remind me exactly how much the car cost to fix.'

'Nine eighty, plus VAT. Eleven seventy-six, all told.'

'OK. Fiona, we gave you a thousand pounds last week for doing five minutes' work. I think you need to give that to Anna. I'm sure she'll be happy to overlook the rest, won't you, Anna?'

'Yes. A thousand would be fine.'

'Fiona?'

I nod. Sulkily: 'OK.'

'Good. That's settled. Now look, Fiona, we've decided we would like to try to work with you again. One more chance. If you behave yourself, there'll be a lot more money to come. More money and we'll help with your emigration. Our promise to you is that, if you do well over the next year, we'll make it possible for you to leave the country to wherever it is you want to go. We'll pay for the lawyer. If we need to provide proof of any training qualifications, we'll arrange for that too.'

He goes on. Tells me, and my two recording devices, exactly what he wants. Looking after what he calls my 'portfolio' of payroll assignments. He tells me, in plain English, that some of the people receiving salaries are fictional.

'That doesn't need to affect you,' he says. 'We need you to keep their tax records up to date, enter their overtime payments, all the stuff you would normally do. Can you manage that?'

I nod.

'It's stealing. You realise that? There's no point in doing this if you're going to lose your nerve.'

'I'll be OK,' I mumble.

He stares at me. His gaze is a laser-sight roving over my face and forehead. A red dot tracking the contours.

'You may find that some of the names *aren't* fictional,' he says. 'About thirty names are fictional. The rest are real. But we need you to treat them much the same way. If any questions arise about those names, if anyone challenges you, or if you notice any unusual activity, you tell me at once.'

'OK.'

'And I mean at once, do you understand?'

'Yes.'

'And I need you to stay in communication with us, me or Anna, all the time. One of us will meet you every week and we'll check over your portfolio. If your employment arrangements vary, or if you want to take a holiday, or if you have a day off sick, or you want to leave Cardiff, you tell us *before* you do anything. Is that clear?'

'Yes.'

'You can contact us by simply sending an email to yourself from your computer at work. We will be able to see that email. Don't put anything secret in that email. Just say, for example,

"I need a sick day" or "please can we talk" and we'll do the rest. Do you understand?'

'Yes.'

'And from time to time, we will keep an eye on you. That might be Anna, or it might be me, or it might be someone else.'

'I don't want to be followed.'

'As long as you work for us, we want to be sure that you *are* working for us and no one else.'

'I still don't think you should stalk me. It's creepy.'

Henderson says, with emphasis, 'I don't care *what* you think. If we want to keep an eye on you, we will. If you notice us – and you probably won't – you will not overreact the way you did on Monday. Is that clear?'

Shrug. Mumble. 'Yes.'

'You need to mean that. I should warn you, we can be quite tough with colleagues who don't do as they've promised.'

I shrug.

'And I do mean tough. You wouldn't like it.'

I don't react to that much. The way Henderson says what he says makes me think he either is the man who killed Kureishi or a very intimate conspirator. Either way, a murderer in my books.

'That also means that as far as you are concerned, you've never met me, never met Anna. Do you understand?'

I give him something that's halfway between a shrug or a nod.

He studies me a moment longer, then unpins his gaze. 'Good. Excellent.' His signal for a change of mood. Enough bullying. Now for phoney-niceness. Except I don't respond the way I'm meant to.

I stay stubbornly silent for a moment or two. Then, 'You haven't told me what I'm getting.'

'We're going to pay you properly. And, if you perform well,

we'll arrange for your emigration. I've said that.'

'I need to know how much.'

Henderson tries to divert me, but Fiona Grey isn't to be diverted. She hangs tough. Henderson offers a grand a month plus an immigration visa to an English-speaking country in twelve months' time. Fiona Grey holds out for three grand a month, plus the visa. We end up settling at a thousand a month for the first four months. Then two for the next four. Then two point five grand a month for the next four.

I insist on writing it down. Ask for the name of the lawyer. Ask for details of when I'll get my visa, what's involved, what Henderson means when he says he'll provide proof of my training qualifications.

He answers with increasing terseness, but his answers indicate that he's done his research, that he knows what he's talking about. To the last question, he says simply, 'If we need to fabricate something, we will.'

'Fabricate? You mean, make something up?'

'Yes. Provide false documents, that sort of thing.'

When I have the main points written down – on the back of an envelope that Quintrell has fished from her bin – I get Henderson to initial them.

I can feel I'm angering him, but the anger is good. A police spy would have made all this easier. A police spy wouldn't have sat for five hours on a suspect's doorstep. Fiona Grey may be difficult to manage, but she's beginning to earn these people's trust.

And when we're done, when Fiona has her 'contract' tucked into her bag, she asks, 'Where's the nearest Post Office, please?'

Quintrell says that there's one at the top of Pontcanna Street.

Fiona says, 'I'll get your money.'

And we all troop out together. A warm afternoon. The

plane trees are still marking shadows on the pavement. I get the money and hand it over. Henderson and Quintrell walk away together, talking animatedly.

As for me, this is my first day of approximate holiday since Florida: although I turned up at my cleaning shift as normal at 4.00 am, I told Western Vale that I wasn't coming in that day. I celebrate my freedom by buying a sandwich and a bottle of orange juice. Take them to Llandaff Fields and eat by the weir, where the black water breaks into a temporary, troubled white.

Life is good, I think. But when I bring Buzz to mind – try to remember what he looks like, what he feels like – I retrieve nothing but shadows.

I try thinking about our engagement. Our theoretical wedding. Me in a white dress, a veil, a froth of petticoats. Buzz, dark-suited, next to me, speaking his responses with that broad-chested male confidence. Shapes beyond us in the dimness: friends, family, those people you have to invite.

The whole idea seems inconceivably distant. Like something half recalled from childhood. Disney misremembered.

I do what I always do to centre myself. Breathing exercises. Try to feel my body. And allow my mind to seek sanctuary in the places it finds most restful. Hayley Morgan's tiny body, Kureishi's anguished surprise. Those things help a bit, but not as much as usual. I think, *It's not surprising. I'm Fiona Grey now. Fiona Griffiths is hardly even here sometimes. There are whole days when I barely remember that I'm her.* A strange death this, to be alive in theory and present so little in the ways that matter.

A strange death this, for me who has been so strangely dead before.

I eat my sandwich and black water streams endlessly to the sea.

24

May. Wet and cold. The year began with warnings of drought, but already flooding has affected thousands of homes. Power lines have been down. Rivers gurgle through living rooms. In Somerset, a pub landlord shows a TV reporter the dead fish he found floating behind his bar.

I don't mind the weather. It suits me, suits Fiona Grey. The two of us settle further into our odd life, making our home here.

I buy more boots from a charity shop, hoping these ones are more waterproof.

I've expanded my repertoire of one-pot cooking until I'm almost competent. Jason and I take turns to cook for each other. He's better than I am, but we enjoy the company.

Meantime, my Saturdays at the hostel go on being beautiful things, all the better because Brattenbury does indeed cancel his weekly visits as a security precaution. I use the extra time to start my Anger and Anxiety Management course, which is surprisingly useful. Our tutor gives us a handout with Ten Things to Remember printed out on bright yellow paper and I stick it up on my fridge. I look at it most nights.

Clementina and I are knocked out of the table football tournament in the first round, because she had been out drinking the night before and couldn't focus very well. I was useless, as always, but it was nice being part of a team.

And I am now for the first time, guilty of criminal fraud.

I start to manage my portfolio as Henderson and Quintrell instruct me. Sometimes I'm told to go to Quintrell's house and I sit there in her kitchen, at her fancy Scandinavian table, showing her copies of payslips and HMRC input forms. She gives me a glass of water, but never offers me anything else to eat or drink. She doesn't use my name ever. Never says please or thank you. Just checks my work. Says, 'OK,' if it's all right and, 'No, this is wrong,' or 'You've made an error,' if there's something she wants me to change.

If the phone rings or there's something she needs to do on the computer, I just sit and wait till she's finished or ask to go out in the garden and have a smoke. Because she doesn't like me leaving ash in her garden, I carry plastic bags in my coat pocket and make sure that I put any ash, matches and cigarette butts in there when I'm finished.

Other times I meet Henderson. He's nicer to me. We had our first 'portfolio review' meeting at The Grape and The Grain, and he kept trying to get me something to eat and drink. I had another orange juice and ate some of his olives. At the end of that session, he said, 'I don't think you like it here, do you?'

I said, 'It's OK.'

He said, 'We could do it somewhere else if you liked. We could do it at your place?'

I said OK, but he wasn't to let himself in. He had to come when I was there. So far, he's come, good as gold, at the appointed time and waited outside for me to let him in. I quite like him, is the truth of it. I often like the bad guys.

Brattenbury I've seen just the once. It was five in the morning. I entered one of my corporate washrooms, ready to clean it, and found him sitting on the row of basins. He gave me a bollocking for my stunt with Anna Quintrell, but his performance wasn't up to Dennis Jackson's standards, not remotely. Too English and too polite, somehow. All

Oxbridgey cricket whites, where Jackson is a mud-splattered rugby red.

I said, 'Yes sir,' when I needed to, and kept glancing sideways to inspect the state of the bathroom.

When Brattenbury was finished, we shared a moment's silence.

I said, 'You've been surveilling Henderson, of course . . .'

'Yes. And got nothing. We can't push it too hard, because we can't let him identify us. He burns off any vehicle-based pursuit. So we followed him with a chopper. He pulled into a filling station, one of the sort with a big overhead canopy. Left in a different vehicle. Same thing with his phone. He uses disposable phones and encrypted lines. It's rare, that level of care. Unusual.'

'That's bad luck, that is.'

'Yes.'

'I mean, a careful criminal and a reckless undercover officer. What are the chances?'

He laughs at that and the mood changes.

I say, 'Look, you won't want to know this, but I've got an iPad.'

'*What?*'

I tell him. That I've got an iPad. That it's fully secured with a sixteen digit alphanumeric password. That I get network access via a neighbour.

'You *asked* a *neighbour* for his password?' Brattenbury is incredulous.

So am I. '*No.* I stole it. I'll work better if I'm kept in the loop.'

I can see Brattenbury wondering whether to fire off another lecture at me, but it's too early in the morning for all of that. He asks where I keep the tablet – behind the radiator in the shared bathroom is the answer – and tells me he'll sort out a better hiding place.

I say, 'They found Quintrell by looking around for a not-too-scrupulous accountant. A simple Google search, quite likely. When Kureishi went walkabout, they'd have needed an IT guy in a hurry. They might have found one the same way.'

Brattenbury considers that. The ANPR systems – Automatic Number Plate Recognition – are nationwide and hold data for years. In principle, if Henderson and Quintrell drove to recruit a none-too-clean IT guy, a combination of careful computer searches and ANPR tracking could provide a big clue as to who they took on board.

'Good thought. We'll look into it.'

He eases himself off the basin unit with a grimace. He's wearing suede shoes, chinos, a pale blue herringbone shirt and a dark jacket. No tie. I start to unload cleaning bottles from my trolley, ready to start on the mirrors.

He says, 'You're nuts, taking this cleaning job. Any time you want to quit . . .'

I shake my head. 'You're wrong, actually. I'm just nuts, full stop.'

'I've got a present for you, by the way. I wasn't sure how to deliver it, but you seem to have solved that problem.'

A present? I stare at Brattenbury, suddenly hungry.

He nods. 'Mr Griffiths and Mr Glyn. There's a lot of material. On your dad mostly, but . . . I'll beam it over to you.'

His words have an odd effect on me. Palms wettening. Pulse increasing. I recognise the tickle of fear, but there's something else here as well.

I say, 'You know when you're excited? That's quite like being scared, isn't it? I mean, it's like they're next-door feelings, almost the same thing.'

Brattenbury stares at me, as though I've said something strange. He doesn't say anything, but his face tells me yes. He looks at me a moment longer then drops his eyes. Picks up a bottle of glass cleaner, as though studying the ingredients.

'Take care, Fiona. These cases do get to people. Even when they think they're immune.'

I say whatever it is I think I'm meant to say. Then watch him leave. Brown brogues and ironed chinos. A mirror person walking in a mirror world. I pick up my cloths and start to clean.

25

Mr Griffiths and Mr Glyn.

My father and a man who once came to the police with a story about city council corruption. A story that was investigated and for which no firm evidence was ever found. A man who – years later – vanished without trace. His wife, a slightly crazed woman with depressive and obsessive tendencies aplenty, alleges, again without evidence, that he was murdered. By whom, she doesn't know.

Not much to work with, but it's all I've got.

And that night, working under the covers of my bed, I use my iPad to explore the trove sent to me by Brattenbury. Police files, old databases, paper records scanned into the digital age. Ancient caves, explored by lamplight.

SOCA inherited the files that were originally compiled by the old Regional Crime Squads. Those squads have a faintly dated feel to them now. They somehow recall the era of bubble perms, flared jeans, loose fists and misogyny. But in their day, those RCSs were as good as they got. Well-resourced, well-trained, and they broke some huge cases.

Much of that old data has already been available to me via normal police routes, but not all of it. And given that my father was a target of intense police investigation and surveillance for the best part of fifteen years, the two pools of data – the police set and the RCS one – are enormous. Simply comparing one collection against the other is a monumental task.

It's also one that I find hard to perform given the limitations I'm working under. I can't take physical notes, because I can't take the risk of Henderson finding them. I *can* take digital notes, but I can't type fast on an iPad, especially not when lying clam-like between my lumpy mattress and my second-hand polyester duvet – nor can I even sit up to work, because I can't allow Henderson or his team to see any hint of light from my screen.

By the end of that first week exploring Brattenbury's gift, I realise I need more breathing room, literal and figurative. I can't do much Monday to Friday, because of my work commitments. I can't do much on Saturday, because Saturdays are my day for the hostel, for my Anxiety and Anger Management course, for table football, for laundry, for smoking ciggies with Gary and, in general, for my entire social life outside cleaning, payroll and my once-monthly conjugal visit with Buzz.

So that leaves Sunday. The one day of the week where I've never had a settled routine, where I've deliberately kept my movements a little random, unpredictable. Mostly, I've spent those Sundays walking. Bute Park sometimes. Along the Taff. Sometimes just frequented coffee shops in the city centre, or window-shopped, or smoked the occasional bit of weed with the hippy guy in the veggie café. Other times, I've roamed further afield. Gone down to the seashore. Fed the gulls. Been as far out as Penarth, where I've watched the brown waves beat against a brown shoreline as container ships ride the horizon.

On some of these trips, I know I've been followed. Down at Hamadryad Park once, I saw Henderson's own BMW, both when I entered and then two hours later as I was walking back up towards the hostel. On another occasion – the weekend before Henderson made contact – I saw a blue Astra once too often for it to be coincidence. The driver – male, thirty-something, army crew cut – looked just about right for one of Henderson's cronies.

I didn't react. Didn't do my Quintrell number on it. Just told Brattenbury via an audio message delivered through the library cloakroom. Gave him the number plate, let him trace it from there.

But since those early inspections, I think Henderson has either dropped the direct surveillance, or cut it back hard. So, while I remain watchful, I think I have more freedom than I had.

I use it.

That Sunday, I have a lie-in, which means getting up at seven or even seven-thirty. Make breakfast and eat it at my Formica table. Read a bit. Sit at the window and stare out. Then take myself out for a wander. The kind of wander that looks utterly convincing, yet almost impossible to monitor with discretion. So I stop in front of shop windows. Enter pedestrianised areas, linger, then leave. Stop at a café, have a cup of tea, watch the road from the window, leave abruptly.

I do all that and, by half past ten, I'm confident no one is following me. I enter the park by Blackweir Woods, cross the river, and walk rapidly up into Llandaff. No one could follow me by car, because the parks and river crossing are pedestrian-only. There are few people about and none who I see more than once.

In Llandaff, I go to the street address which Buzz gave me in the package with the iPad. There, as promised, stands my very sleek, very white Alfa Romeo Guilietta. I grope inside the rear wheel arch. Find a small magnet, which holds my car key. Within minutes I'm scooting out of Cardiff, unseen and unpursued.

I want to make the most of it, this freedom. I want to touch the pedal to the metal and see if it's really true that the car can do 135 miles per hour.

I bet it can, but I play safe. Miss Grey and DC Griffiths both have reasons to keep a low profile, so we skim along the motorway doing not a whisper over eighty – or *almost* not a whisper – and enjoy the sound of the exhaust and the trees racing away behind us.

We play for a while, then turn serious. Buy a mobile broadband dongle from an electronics store and zoom up to Blaengwynfi, to Hayley Morgan's little cottage.

We break in. It's easily done: the police files noted a broken lock on the rear door. The door was secured by a combination lock and the case records have given me the combination.

The house is empty and cold. Nothing much has changed. The window I broke has been reglazed. In the middle of the living room floor, there are some evidence boxes containing items removed from the property and now returned. The boxes make the place look more empty, not less.

Morgan died intestate and with no surviving relatives. The house is therefore being swallowed by the Crown.

Bona vacantia: ownerless goods. A medieval doctrine permitting seizure.

I set up in the kitchen. The little stone-flagged kitchen, where Morgan's corpse feels present even now. So present, indeed, that I keep turning to check if it's there. Plug in my dongle. I've taken care to ensure that my broadband service provider is one that gets signal up here. The speed isn't brilliant, but it's OK.

Start work.

When I'm thirsty, I drink water from the tap, skirting the place where Hayley once lay. I don't eat, though, not inside the house. Not with Hayley's toothmarks still etched into the plaster. Coal ash and plaster dust.

That first day, I work for six hours. Don't accomplish anything of shattering usefulness, but you don't always know what's useful at the time you do it.

The following Sunday, I work for eight hours. Bring tulips too. Flowers for Hayley. My little gift.

The Sunday after that, I glimpse Henderson's BMW as I'm walking down the North Road, then a little later the blue Astra. That's good. Very good. If they want to know what Fiona Grey is up to, I'm happy to show them. She does a lot of window shopping. Wedding dress shops, in particular, hold her gaze, but she's got catholic tastes. She also loves the displays in upmarket patisseries, studies menus, loves looking at the kind of shoes no office cleaner could ever afford. She never buys much, though. Cheap sandwiches in see-through packets or a burger sold from a van. A cup of tea, sipped dry over forty-five minutes, bought in a city centre coffee shop that makes the Sunday newspapers available for free. At twelve thirty, a fit of extravagance takes her to a half-price movie matinee. A black and white weepie. Barbara Stanwyck sacrificing everything for a daughter who, in my opinion, could use a good slap. After that, we drift around a little more. Spend half an hour in Waterstones. Buy a self-help book which Fiona Grey chooses but which, it suddenly occurs to me as we count our money together at the till, will be of great interest to me too. Then we sit in the park, wishing we had food for the birds. When we see a man throw a sandwich in the bin, we leave it a respectable length of time, then fish it out and use that.

It's gone six before I'm back at my bedsit. I've not seen Henderson again since the morning, but I think I did see Astra-man in the Hayes and, in any case, I'm guessing Henderson had more than himself and one other guy on the job. If they did a half-reasonable job of tracking me, they'll have chalked me up as the world's least suspicious recruit. A lonely young woman whose life is as empty as she says it is.

Brattenbury has traced the Astra, of course. The car was bought for cash eight months ago. It's registered to a false name and address, but he used ANPR data to track the car's approximate home location, then sent plainclothes officers borrowed from the South Wales force to locate it exactly. Then had the road watched, until the man was identified: Allan Wiley, living in a small terraced house in the west of Cardiff. We don't believe Wiley is his real name, but Brattenbury now has another home to bug, another landline to tap.

No useful data yet, but these things take time. And another blank space in our knowledge of Tinker has been filled.

After that Sunday, I don't experience any further physical surveillance. I stay vigilant, but use my liberty to spend more time up at Hayley's cottage. Long, beautiful hours of work. Long, beautiful days, with light summer rains greening the air and sheep bleating a stone's toss from the window.

Each time I visit, I bring fresh flowers.

Hayley and I get along well. She likes me, I think, for all the red-faced barbarity of we living folk. Our grossness. For my part, I find Hayley's spirit well-suited to this little house. This *bona vacantia*. We enjoy ourselves.

And a fortnight after my Barbara Stanwyck Sunday, I'm going through Brattenbury's files again, when I realise I've missed something. Brattenbury's original email contained a link to a Gareth Glyn document in the National Crime Squad archives. I'd missed the link, because it hadn't occurred to me that Glyn could have been of interest to the NCS – the successor agency to those Regional Crime Squads and the immediate predecessor of SOCA itself. I was thinking of him only as a route to my father.

Mistake.

I click on the link and get five lines of text on the SOCA intranet.

Those five lines tell me that one of the intelligence services – identity redacted, but almost certainly MI5 – came to the NCS in late 2001 asking for any data they might hold on

Gareth Glyn. The NCS held none and said so. End of.

Five lines that glow like a beacon in my darkness.

A beacon, a clue, a line of inquiry.

The timescales are these. Gareth Glyn made his accusations of impropriety in the planning process in the mid-eighties. I was born – I guess – in early- to mid-1984. My whereabouts for the next two or two-and-a-half years are a complete mystery to me. Then, on a sunny June day in 1986, I turned up in the back of an open-top Jaguar outside Chapel. The Jaguar belonging to the man who became my father.

Skip forward fifteen years. Gareth Glyn, in the meantime, has lost his job, has worked as a freelance consultant with ordinary, unspectacular success. He's living with his batty, depressive wife, who might not have been quite as batty or as depressive back then. So far, so nothing. Then, in late 2001, a national intelligence agency asks the country's senior criminal investigation agency for data on this nothing-man. A few months later, he vanishes, leaving his wife alleging murder. Her (paranoid, non-credible) list of the guilty did *not* include my father but *did* include plenty of people he knew or had dealings with or was highly likely to have known.

As a lead, if this were a police inquiry, it would be so faint as to be almost useless.

But this isn't a police inquiry. It's my inquiry. And every more ordinary lead – every allegation against him, every suspicion held by my past colleagues – has been researched diligently and found barren. That's the negative reason for my interest. What else have I got?

But there are more positive ones too. First, the timing is good. The Gareth Glyn affair – the original allegation, investigation and his departure from his job – the timing of all that correlates perfectly with my own strange arrival into life.

Then too, the obliqueness is good. In a funny way, I was never going to get into my father's past by treading the same routes that my police colleagues had already beaten into mud. My father's defences against legal attack have proved impeccable time and again. The only way around those defences is, I'm sure, to bypass them completely. To come into his affairs at an angle so obscure, so apparently irrelevant, that it might not have occurred to him to protect against investigation. Gareth Glyn ticks that box, and then some. His wife never once mentioned my father. Nor did Glyn. It was only DCI Yorath, now retired, who made the connection, saying, in essence, that if anyone had been skimming money from construction contracts, it would have been my dad.

And finally, whatever it was that deposited me in the back of my father's car, it had to *matter*. Girls don't simply appear out of thin air for run-of-the-mill reasons. Delia Glyn's allegations of murder might simply be the wanderings of an unhappy woman's mind, but a specific interest from MI5 – an interest only just pre-dating his disappearance – make it clear that *something* was going on. Something significant, something big.

Big enough, perhaps, to cause a little girl to appear out of thin air.

For the first time in a long time, I feel that shiver of investigative excitement. That sense of heat, a glimpse of light.

That day, I brought Hayley a bunch of pink and white stocks. Thick clusters of flowers and perfume, spicy and rich. But they don't quite feel enough. I walk outside. Scavenge the hedgerows and come back with a bunch of wildflowers. Nothing really good, but plenty of cow parsley and some branches of wild cherry blossom. Hayley has no vases, but she has jugs and mugs aplenty and I bestow my flowers round the room, till it looks like a wedding festival.

That night, I drive back – park in Llandaff, careful about who sees me – but can't return home straight away. I need company, the company of the living, so go down to the hostel

161

and spend the whole evening there. Watching telly. Listening to Clementina's impenetrable anecdotes. Smoking with Gary's *Big Issue* mates, but not him, because he's on the piss and is banned from the hostel until he sobers.

It's a lovely evening, capping off another wonderful day. Fiona Grey is a happy creature. I'm lucky to have her.

26

Early June.

Summer in the city, except that the city seems trapped in a gloomy cycle of brisk winds and scudding, intermittent rain. At the weekend, the Queen celebrated her Jubilee with a small armada of boats crowding the Thames. But the river was grey and furious, the wind unceasing, the rain constant. I didn't watch most of the coverage – I was down at the hostel, engaged in laundry chores and table football – but found something impressive about the sheer wetness of the whole episode. That people endured it. That they chose to.

And through all of this my life continues to progress. In the early mornings, I clean. During the day, I do my payroll clerking and manage Henderson's fraud. See either Quintrell or Henderson at least once a week. Sometimes more.

When Henderson's on duty, he comes to my flat. The last couple of times, he's been businesslike and brisk, but he seems different this time. More open. More widely curious.

As I get on my eccentrically bottomed saucepan on to heat water for tea, he inspects my studio in detail. The yellow sheet on the fridge. My meagre kitchen utensils. The interior of my wardrobe: its few clothes and not-very-healthy cannabis plants.

He says, 'You could get somewhere better now, couldn't you? You've got two jobs, plus what we pay you.'

'I'm saving up.'

'For emigration?'

I nod.

'You hate it here that much?'

I glance out of the window. At the nine-lane road. The rain. Spray-paint graffiti on a garden wall. At the metallic insects and their unreachable heaven.

He laughs and says, 'You're probably right. You're probably right.'

His curiosity also extends to my laptop.

'You don't get internet in here? You don't want it?'

I shrug and look fiercely down.

I don't know if Henderson ever had a police training, or similar, but I wouldn't be surprised. Most interrogators rush things. Fill the silence. Henderson is happy to scrutinise. To let these little micro-expressions talk to him.

He studies me a while, then pushes again. 'You can get deals for nothing these days. Fifteen quid a month, something like that.'

I start speaking, choke a bit, clear my throat and try a second time. 'It's on contract.'

'On contract?' Henderson is puzzled for a moment, then figures it out. 'It's your credit rating, is it?'

'They want past addresses. I haven't always had all this.' I wave a hand at my newly come by opulence. The Sun King showing off a newly landscaped deer park.

'Look, if you want—'

I shake my head. 'I go to the library. It's fine.'

Again, Henderson inspects me. I don't meet his eye. I seldom do. Just let him hold me under his gaze until he's done.

It's a curious feeling to be appraised like this. If I had to bet, I'd say that Henderson was in the room when Kureishi was killed and, quite likely, the one swinging the chopper. That edge of brutality never feels far distant. Like rocks lying underwater with nothing showing but a curl of white foam and too much seething silence. Yet I don't dislike spending time with him. He's kinder to me than Quintrell is. Something more human, even in his cruelty.

As if reading my thoughts, he produces a small gift from his bag. 'Here. For you.'

A small chocolate cake in a box, tied with a pink ribbon.

I realise the cake comes from one of the posh patisseries whose windows so attracted Fiona Grey on one of her Sunday wanderings. Henderson is creepy enough to follow her, nice enough to buy her cake.

I can't do the maths on that, but say thank you anyway.

'OK, shall we take a look at what you've been up to?'

I get out my papers. Forms, photocopies, lists. Place them in front of him on the little Formica table. Say, 'Do you want tea?'

Henderson looks uncertain. A man trying to work out whether it would be more polite to say yes or no. He chooses yes.

The water in my funny saucepan is boiling now, so I get out my only mug and a bowl. Make peppermint tea in the bowl for me, tea in the mug for him. Cut two slices of cake and put them on a plate.

'I don't have milk, sorry, but if you want, I can . . .'

'No, that's fine. As long as it's hot and wet, eh?'

He sits at the Formica table and pores over my documents.

I sit on the arm of my armchair and watch the rain, the cars, the first glow from sodium street lights. Nibble cake.

Henderson isn't picky the way Quintrell is. I don't know what he checks, to be honest. I don't think he has the accountancy skills to know what's right and what isn't. The few times he's tried to question things in my work, he's revealed a pretty slim understanding of the underlying mechanics.

But it's nice, these sessions. For the first time, I feel properly attuned to the corpses that brought me here. Hayley Morgan: a troubled woman, who ate rat poison and plaster sooner than walk down the hill to ask for help. Saj Kureishi: a thief who fell out with his bosses and sold his life for £5,600. Their presences are with me now.

And my iPad has made me feel less isolated. Brattenbury's boys have built a very secure nest for the machine, in the bathroom boxwork. When I'm not using my internet connection to research my father and Gareth Glyn, I spend my time trawling the Tinker data too.

It's impressive. Brattenbury has, I'd estimate, a team equivalent to about thirty full-time officers. Some of those are borrowed from my own department at Cathays. Others are head-office analysts. Computer technicians in south London. Communications experts in Cheltenham. SOCA's own surveillance specialists.

Armed officers too. Until I saw the case files properly, I hadn't realised the effort that goes into protecting me. Every time I've met Henderson or Quintrell, Brattenbury has had a minimum of two armed officers within sixty seconds of me. There are, right now, two armed officers in a van waiting on Laytonia Road. Three further uniformed officers, two of them armed, in a patrol car no more than half a mile distant.

And yet – what have we accomplished? Almost nothing. We have nothing to justify a murder charge. We could certainly nail both Henderson and Quintrell for fraud, but this case demands charges far bigger than merely that. The Astraman, Allan Wiley, we can't attach to any crime, though we're certain he's part of the group. Indeed, Henderson talks a lot about 'his colleagues' and implies the existence of a substantial organisation behind him, yet we can't even glimpse it, let alone destroy it.

Brattenbury did follow up on my suggestion about trying to track a Kureishi replacement. They looked for times and dates when Henderson and Quintrell seemed to be in the same place. There were numerous matches in Cardiff – just what you'd expect from two mobile people living together in the same, mid-sized city – but almost none elsewhere. There was a time they were both in Central London – CCTV shows their cars making use of the same car park – but it proved impossible to link that visit to any dodgy IT consultant living locally. On another occasion, they both made use of the same hotel just outside Heathrow airport. They were day visitors only, neither of them spending a night there, but both made use of the car park for a full eight hours.

Aside from those frustratingly suggestive encounters, there was a possible rendezvous in Swansea, but the overlap time might have been no more than twenty or thirty minutes, suggesting that the 'meeting' was no more than coincidence. Another possible rendezvous in Chepstow, but on a race day, which could suggest either coincidence or a social encounter.

Brattenbury has done what I'd have wanted to do in his place. Try to find IT consultants of doubtful honesty and link them to any of these places. No joy.

He's also obtained guest data for the relevant dates from the airport hotel, but the names don't correlate with anything useful, either on our own national databases or on those available via Interpol. In any case, the hotel only registers actual guests. Those who make use of the hotel's ample conference and business facilities aren't separately registered. Brattenbury also checked on those booking conference suites. Henderson's name doesn't show up, but most of the bookings are made in company names, many of which are untraceable.

Efforts to track Tinker's money have also failed. Run into the golden sands of the Virgin Islands. Lost in the bougainvillea-scented shades of Panama and Belize.

Surveillance of Henderson has still thrown up nothing of value. He travels to London frequently. Goes abroad – Paris,

Geneva, Barcelona – fairly often, but for short trips. SOCA's surveillance guys seem to think that he doesn't normally care if he's followed. On occasions when he does, he is scrupulous about losing any tail before going wherever it is he goes.

On one occasion, just one, we have something which *might* be suggestive. It was on a day when Brattenbury's guys were certain that he was deliberately avoiding surveillance. Drove south-west, then abruptly turned back towards Cardiff, dived off to the coast, then twisted and turned in Penarth and Grangetown until he'd burned off any tails. And yet ninety minutes after we'd lost him, he showed up again ordering lunch at a bistro in the Cardiff city centre.

The sighting was completely random – one of Brattenbury's men was getting an end-of-shift hamburger and just happened to make the identification – but the implications are interesting. Henderson had last been seen in the Cardiff Bay area. Assuming he'd spent thirty minutes doing whatever it was he was doing that day, he couldn't have travelled more than twenty or thirty minutes from Cardiff to do it.

That's enough time, just about, to get as far as Newport, not enough to get to Swansea. Love Newport though I do, it's hardly a world centre of sophisticated criminal activity, which suggests that whatever Henderson was up to was taking place in Cardiff . . . except that he might simply have changed his mind, had a call cancelling any meeting, or any other of a thousand things. To some extent, Brattenbury's guys have been able to track Henderson's movements prior to the bistro by reviewing CCTV footage, but the trail died in one of the little side roads off the Hayes. Another dead end.

The plain fact is that Brattenbury has discovered almost nothing of value, and shabby little Fiona Grey remains the only ace in his denuded deck.

So I sit there, on the arm of my slumbering, velour bear, sipping my tea and feeling the rain. I have a murderer and two corpses for company. The steel tip of a javelin that is travelling nowhere.

Henderson sits at my Formica table and studies my documents.

And then – it all changes. I sense it from the way Henderson looks up at me from the table. His face has a gravity in it. A weight.

'This is good, Fiona. It's all good.'

I don't say anything to that. Not even a 'thank you'. Henderson doesn't expect one. We both know this is an introduction to something else.

'Even Anna thinks so. I know she doesn't always show it.'

I don't answer.

The thing that Henderson isn't saying is now the biggest thing in the room. Bigger than my armchair. Bigger than either of us.

'And you're happy with us, are you? You've got no complaints?'

I'm not here any more. This is Fiona Grey's world, not mine, and it's she who sits in her grey skirt and white child's polycotton blouse, staring out at Henderson. She's scared, I feel it. I think she's right to be.

I don't say anything and Henderson continues softly.

'Because you've done well, we want to ramp it up. We want to slightly increase the work you do for us and the money too.'

My mouth moves and after a bit words come out. 'What work?'

'It'll be easy enough. Nothing difficult. Like I say, we're pleased with you.'

I have my hands crossed over my stomach. Henderson nice is more frightening than Henderson nasty.

'You have nineteen names in your portfolio where everything is just ordinary, yes? Where you don't yet do anything?'

Don't answer. Just stare.

The light in the room is starting to fade. Shadows crawl out to join the twilight. Car headlights pass like alien moons.

'It's simple enough. We just want you to keep an eye on things. If a monthly payslip comes past your desk and registers a change from what you'd expect, we want you to make a note of the irregularity and simply make the correction you normally would. Basically, all I'm saying is that these payslips might start to look a bit funny from time to time and we just want you to keep an eye on them for us. Not just payslips, but P60s, overtime forms, submissions to HMRC, anything like that. Is that clear?'

I nod. It's *very* clear and if Brattenbury is listening to all this, I bet he's nodding too. SOCA has some fancy computer experts and if they're listening in, I bet they're nodding most of all.

'For the first few weeks, you'll be seeing a bit more of me and Anna. Probably best we meet at her house. Maybe Tuesdays and Thursdays. Is that OK?'

Nod.

'Good.' The thing that Henderson isn't saying is still here. A creature of these emerging shadows. He says, 'You haven't asked about your pay. I said I'd increase it.'

I say nothing.

He says, 'We'll double it. Is that fair? From right now.'

Through cracked lips: 'What about my lawyer?'

He doesn't hear me at first, but when he does, he says, 'As soon as you start this new work, we'll take you to London and you can get started with the lawyer. We'll push things forward as quick as we can.'

My mouth opens and closes in a thank-you-ish sort of way.

'But look. There's one more thing. This operation involves a lot of trust and you haven't been with us long. We *like* you, but I wouldn't say we *know* you.'

That sounds like a formula Henderson had thought of before entering the room. He reaches for his bag. Produces a laptop. Fires up.

'Come and sit here, please, Fiona.'

He indicates the folding metal chair he's been sitting at. I sit as he instructs.

'I'm sorry about this. It's going to be a bit unpleasant, but it makes a point.'

He navigates to a video site. Calls up a clip that's got a private listing. The clip is eight minutes long. The first three minutes show a cat fooling around in a garden. The garden looks more American than British. I assume the video's just nicked from YouTube. A blind.

But Henderson doesn't bother with the cat. Drags the cursor through to the start of the fourth minute, where the screen changes.

The picture is familiar and unfamiliar. It's of Sajid Kureishi. Alive. Bound to his chair. Hands still attached to his arms. He's talking, fast, terrified, almost incoherent.

Henderson, looking at my face, jumps to mute the sound, and Kureishi's voice disappears.

But not his anguish. Not his astonishment.

The video is shot in close up, so nothing much is visible in the picture except Kureishi's face, chest and arms.

Then the murder.

A few slashes with a billhook. The sort of thing used to lay hedges and slay brambles. I can't see whoever is wielding the tool, but I do notice that Henderson isn't looking at the screen. I don't know what that means except perhaps that he's more likely a murderer-for-business than a murderer-for-pleasure.

First one hand goes, then the other. Blood jets fast and horribly initially, then slows down to a flow, a trickle, a drip. Kureishi's blood, Kureishi's life.

I can't look. Or sort of do, because Henderson checks to see I have my eyes on the screen, but sort of don't too.

I discover something about myself. Me and Fiona Grey, the both of us. We hate what we've just seen. Hate and loathe it. Hate and loathe everything about everyone with any part in that video's creation. It's not the presence of death that bothers me. I enjoy the company of the dead. But murder is different and murderers are different.

I vow to myself, again, that I will see Henderson jailed for this. Him and all his brood.

Henderson murmurs, 'This was a man who let us down. And we don't permit that. If you do what we ask, you'll be fine. We'll help you leave the country. Make sure you have cash in your pocket. Some qualifications. Everything you need. If not – well, you know what happens.'

I'm in shock. Me personally, I guess, but Fiona Grey is for sure, and she's in control here. She clasps her belly, hugs and rocks.

Even before the video has ended, before Kureishi's life has finally dripped away, Henderson has closed the video software, deleted the file, folded the laptop.

He puts the laptop in his bag. Shifts his cup of tea – half drunk – to the sink.

He moves like an undertaker, treading softly in the silence.

I think he wants a reaction from me. Or wants to find my eye so he can say something. Fiona gives him neither option. When he pauses by the sink, she says, quietly, 'Please leave my room. Please just go.'

He hesitates another second. Glances towards his own video-transmitter down by the skirting board. Then leaves.

The door closes with the gentleness of death.

I don't know how long I sit there. An hour maybe, perhaps two. The violence still echoes round the room. Kureishi's shrieks dangle from the light fittings, ricochet from the walls. Blood drips from the tap.

I've been present at scenes of violence before. Not as a bystander, either, but as a participant. Yet nothing has affected me like this video. It's not just Fiona Grey who is shocked. I am too. We hug each other and rock.

I've wondered sometimes why I came into policing. I know I like solving puzzles. I know I like the dead. Like the comfort of rules and hierarchies, however bad I am at following their strictures. But now, I think, I've found the real answer. The core of it. I like *this* because I hate *that*. Have to solve crimes because I can't abide the violence that generates them.

Whenever I close my eyes, I see the descending billhook. Those knotted brown wrists. The way it took more than one stroke to sever them.

And then Fiona, my companion Fiona, shifts from her seat. Starts shoving clothes into her only bag. She has more possessions now than will fit into that bag, so she has to be selective. This skirt, yes. That jumper, no. She takes her saucepan, mug, a couple of plastic bags of dried leaves and flowers from her cannabis plants. The yellow page of Anger and Anxiety advice from the fridge door.

The yellow page has ten tips, good ones. Developed by people who know what people like Fiona and I need. But they missed some crucial points. *Tip Eleven*: Do not allow murderers into your home. *Tip Twelve*: Do not watch footage of a recent murder. *Tip Thirteen*: Do not live undercover. Do not separate yourself from the people who love you. Do not reject the good advice of the man who wants to be your husband.

Tip Fourteen: Escape while you can.

Fiona puts on a cardigan, a coat, picks up her bag and leaves the apartment.

It's still raining. It's a forty-five minute walk to the bus station, but forty-five minutes it is.

Fiona walks steadily. On Wellington Street, a man stops her and asks for directions. She gives them. Feels something slip into her pocket. Ten minutes after the man has gone, she checks her pocket. Finds a mobile phone.

Beyond the railway line, but before the din and chaos of the bus station itself, she uses the phone to call Brattenbury. His personal mobile. He answers at the first ring.

'Fiona, are you OK?'

'Yes.'

He tells me that there are armed police who have me in direct view. That it's my call if I want to 'come in' as he puts it.

'I'd quite like to nail this fucker, sir. And all his fucker friends.'

That doesn't quite sound like my voice, but it's close enough.

'Yes. I would too. What's your plan?'

There are a couple of options. Basically: go walkabout and come back again. Or just go walkabout.

I argue for the latter. 'At the moment they trust me about eighty or ninety per cent. We've got to get them to a straight one hundred. We can't leave them in any doubt.'

He agrees. Since the mole has been arrested at Fielding Insurance, we believe that I'm the only payroll insider that Tinker still has. They need me. And we need them to trust me.

'Do you know where you want to go?'

I do. It has to be somewhere I can be traced. I say what I'm proposing.

'Ah yes. And you had an employment reference from them, didn't you?'

'Two, actually. One for my cleaning job, one for payroll.

And I left my laptop in my room. That'll have my application letter on it.'

'Perfect. Go for it.'

I say, 'Those nineteen names. I think we know what they're up to now.'

'You think? I'm not sure. But we'll see. Good luck, Fiona. Take care, stay safe.'

I walk into the bus station. Buy some fast food. Eat some of it. Put the phone into the paper bag with the remains of my meal and throw the whole lot away.

There's a bus leaving for London in five minutes. I buy a ticket, sit at the back.

We pull out of the city on sodden roads. Midnight tarmac spins endlessly from our departing tyres. Black water plunging to the sea.

27

That first night in London, I spend in Victoria Bus Station. Buying hot drinks in all-night cafés when I get too cold. Otherwise trying to snatch little fragments of sleep on seats designed to deter the homeless.

A man stinking of piss and alcohol tries to make a pass at me. There are two Transport Police officers close by. They watch, but don't intervene. I don't summon them.

I miss Gary from the hostel. His raggedy beard and tobacco-stained laugh.

When I sleep, I see Kureishi. His face as the first blow falls. Just that moment, again and again. I shake myself from sleep as soon I can scramble out of its pit.

At seven, I go into the Ladies and try to sort myself out in the mirror. Fiona Grey looks exhausted and shocked. We do something with her hair. Put some blusher on, some eye make-up. She doesn't look good, but she doesn't look scary either. She did before.

I find it easier to deal with her appearance than my own.

I buy a bacon roll and a cup of tea. Make them last.

Then take the tube across town to Ealing. Walk to Amina's house.

She's not there. No sign of Man in Purple Shirt. No sign of the baby.

I sit outside and wait. It's not raining today and it's warmer here than Cardiff.

Smoke one cigarette that's only tobacco. Smoke another that's mostly weed.

Amina turns up at half past two. She doesn't see me straight away, but when she does, her face breaks into that huge, genuine, lovely smile of hers.

'Fiona, my friend!' she says and hugs me.

She takes me into her house. Leaves me there while she fetches her baby from a neighbour. The motorbike is still sitting in the kitchen. Ditto the spatters of fat. The smell of lamb kidney and cumin seeds. There aren't any rags or tools by the motorbike though. Few hints of a man in the house.

Amina confirms as much when she returns. 'It is just me and Asad now.' Asad, the baby.

I say I've got nowhere to stay.

She says, 'You are my friend. You stay with me.'

And I do.

We spend that first day smoking, playing with the baby and cooking. I ask her about the man who was here before, and she just says, 'He is away.' I don't know if *away* means 'in a different place but returning' or if it means 'gone for ever'. I don't pry.

At the end of the day, I give Amina fifty pounds. 'For rent,' I say. She tells me I don't have to, but keeps the money.

I call Mr Conway at YCS and ask him if he has any work available. I say, 'I don't mind if I have to work some extra hours to start with.' Meaning: it's OK if I work four hours and he pays me for two. YCS isn't particularly exploitative, but they all cut corners where they can. Conway takes my phone number and says he'll see.

There are only two bedrooms in the flat – no beds, just mattresses on the floor – and Asad has a room all to himself. I'm happy to sleep in the living room, but Amina is perplexed and, I think, upset by my assumption. It's clear she's used to sleeping many to a bed and so when it comes to the evening, we just go upstairs together. My short, milky limbs lying next to her long, ebony ones. 'We are sisters now,' Amina announces and turns out the light.

I still see Kureishi when I close my eyes, but it's better now that I'm not alone. I sleep badly, but it's not awful.

The first morning, Amina goes out to work leaving Asad – 'his name means lion' – with a neighbour. I tidy the house and try to bring order to the kitchen.

That afternoon, Conway does call. Asks me in for work the next day. I don't know if Brattenbury found a way to nudge that forward or if Conway really is that short of almost-reliable cleaners. I'm guessing a bit of both.

And, pretty soon, Amina and I find our rhythm.

We leave the house at just after three. Work from four to nine, cleaning offices for YCS. Then Amina leaves for a job at a local hotel which keeps her busy until early afternoon. I go straight back to the flat and retrieve the lion, Asad, from the neighbour. Then I keep him clean and entertained. Do what I can to clean in the kitchen. Get the house a bit tidier. All this, until Amina returns.

She usually criticises my cooking, which I can understand, but is also strangely dismissive of my efforts to clean, although the place is already a million times cleaner than it was. I've already filled five black sacks with rubbish and have got through three packets of kitchen cleaning cloths and two bottles of cleaning fluid, all of which I bought with my own money. But Amina's sourness doesn't tip over into anything serious and before too long we're friends again. Spend the afternoons watching TV, which Amina doesn't understand very well, and singing Asad songs in Arabic and Somali which I don't understand at all. Amina and I go to bed at eight. We don't cuddle or touch particularly, but if we happen to wake up skin to skin, that doesn't bother either of us. It's a nice way to pass the night.

At the weekend, there's some kind of gathering of the family or clan and Amina and I work like slaves cooking and tidying and getting things ready. The people who come are almost all men or older boys. I mostly stay in the kitchen and help with the dishes. When it's obvious that Amina needs help to clear the living room, I ask her if I ought to wear a headscarf. She says no, but there is something dark in her face, so I go upstairs and borrow one of her scarves anyway. No alcohol is served, but the men all chew khat and have teeth ranging from dark-yellow to almost-black.

And that's my life.

Amina says we are sisters, but when she returns home from work, and I greet her at the door, with a clean baby in my arms, a tidy kitchen, a hoovered floor, the laundry drying upstairs, and something bubbling on the stove, I feel like something more than that. A wife. A helpmeet. Once, and it was only once, I spilled something in the kitchen – meat, quite an expensive item in our budgets – and Amina, quick as a flash, slapped me across the face and cursed me in Somali. I apologised quickly and after a minute or two, Amina relented and started smiling again. 'But you are a very clumsy woman. Your mother did not teach you.'

Teach you: Amina's limbs are longer and more beautiful than mine, but they bear scars which, she told me, came from her mother beating her with wire. I'm not sure, on the whole, that I'd like to be a Somali wife, sister or daughter. Not permanently, anyway.

On the fifth day, I have a long phone call with Brattenbury, from a payphone in Drayton Park. I say, 'That Heathrow hotel. We've got CCTV of incoming guests?'

Brattenbury has to double-check, but says yes. He reminds me that day-users of the hotel don't need to register.

'But there were some Indian faces there, as I remember?'

Amina doesn't have an internet connection and my iPad is still in Cardiff. But I'm pretty sure there were.

'I think so.'

'We know when Henderson and Quintrell arrived and left the hotel that day. Can you check those times against flights to and from Bangalore?'

'Bangalore? Why Bangalore?'

I tell him.

He checks on his computer as I hold the line. 'Well, bloody hell.'

He tells me that a flight came in from Bangalore that morning. The time would have been enough for someone to have come through immigration, showered in the business lounge, and come on to the hotel. The flight time back tallied reasonably well with Quintrell and Henderson's departure too.

I say, 'I think we need to check the passenger manifest. Also, can we get number plates for every car in the hotel car park that day?'

'Yes. We'll get onto that immediately.'

On the seventh day, I speak to Brattenbury again. He says, 'That Heathrow hotel.'

'Yes?'

'OK, whoever books a conference room has to sign for a key. We got a handwriting specialist to check those signatures. No "Vic Henderson" on the list of course, but we've got one signature that tallies pretty well with samples of his handwriting we've taken from his house.'

'OK, good.'

'That particular conference room was originally booked for an hour after the Bangalore flight was due to land. As you say, Bangalore is basically India's answer to Silicon Valley. It's heaving with IT types. So your guess looked spot on.'

'Yes?'

'Wait, it gets better. Quintrell and Henderson *didn't* arrive then, though. Hotel CCTV pictures has them arriving at the hotel *three* hours after the flight was due to come in. So your guess looked bad, except that . . .'

'Don't tell me—'

'Yep. The flight was delayed. Some refuelling problem in Bangalore. Two hours late arriving. Henderson and Quintrell just shifted their arrival time accordingly. Oh, and the meeting broke up just in time for the flight back home.'

'Bingo!'

'Yes, quite. And we can compare passenger manifests for the journey there and back. Both flights were fully booked but only sixteen passengers came for the day only. So our guy is one of those.'

'Guy or *guys*. These boys don't do things by halves.'

'No. Look, I think we need to bring you in for a day. You should meet Susan Knowles, who's leading the IT part of all this. You'll like her.'

I say yes, that's a good idea.

Later that day, I give Amina another fifty pounds of rent money. Forty pounds for food. She takes the cash and doesn't tell me I don't need to give it.

On the tenth day, I take a train into central London. Follow a route prescribed for me by Brattenbury. I'm walking up the Earl's Court Road when a grey Mondeo draws up alongside me. Two men inside, windows wound down.

'All right, love, we're on your team,' says one. 'No one on you.'

The other says, 'Adrian's got a hotel room round the corner. Nice place too.'

He's right. It's one of those boutiquey hotels you see in the magazines. Designery and secluded. Ornate Victorian brickwork crowded with window-boxes, each one a fury of nasturtiums and scarlet marigolds.

Inside, Brattenbury takes me up to a suite. A small but lovely sitting room and, behind, an invisible bedroom. There's a woman there: sleek, late thirties, red-headed, intelligent. She introduces herself as Susan Knowles. She's from the part of SOCA that used to be the Hi-Tech Crime Unit, though she's nobody's idea of a geek.

She shakes my hand and says, 'Adrian's wondergirl. Nice to meet you at last.'

Adrian's wondergirl doesn't quite know how to answer that so, as he fusses with glasses and bottled water in the corner, I make meaningless small talk instead. She studies me carefully, as though I'm an unusual specimen, an object of gossip.

I let her scrutinise away. A butterfly preening under the lepidopterist's lens.

As Brattenbury rejoins us, we turn straight to business. The first item for discussion is my portfolio of names. The twenty-nine where we know a fraud is currently active. The nineteen further names, where the individuals concerned are, in fact, regular employees of Western Vale, doing their regular work at a regular salary.

Brattenbury says, 'Do you have any ideas about what those nineteen names might be all about?'

I tell them what I think's going on.

Knowles says, 'Yes, we think the same.' She trails off and in the silence we feel the shadow of a larger crime, concealed within one that is already large enough, one that has already taken two lives.

'It's no wonder they killed Kureishi,' I said. 'When you think what they're playing for.'

'And it would explain why they're quite so security-conscious,' says Brattenbury.

'Flying in IT consultants from Bangalore. That's a completely new one in my experience,' adds Knowles.

There's a tiny silence in which we all try to ignore the fact that, if the stakes are as high as we think they are, the life of one little payroll clerk won't figure much.

Instead, we do what all coppers do in a case that's not making sufficient progress. We turn to detail. Knowles wants to know exactly what's happening, payroll-wise, with those nineteen names. Anything odd as regards tax, or overtime, or any of the other matters that cross my desk.

I give, from memory, a very full description of what I've been doing.

At one point Knowles is worried that I'm inventing stuff to please her, and she says, 'This is a lot of detail, Fiona. Are you sure you remember all this correctly?'

I say, 'I can't be certain, no, but I knew this would be important so I invented mnemonics to help me remember. Plus I used a spreadsheet to keep notes of what was happening as I went along, then closed the spreadsheet without saving it.' I look at Brattenbury and say, 'I assume . . .?'

He nods. He's got a pad in front of him which, I now realise, he's been consulting while I was speaking with Susan. 'We reconstructed the spreadsheet from the log of your key strokes. Your spreadsheet didn't cover everything you've just been discussing, but where I can check your memory against what you wrote in the spreadsheet . . .' His gaze turns to Susan. 'She's better than ninety per cent accurate. Maybe even ninety-five.'

Susan gives me a smile, big, warm and genuine. One that starts in the eyes and stays there after the lips have finished their thing. There's also, I note, a darted look between her and Brattenbury. His look, I think, says, *See what I mean?*

And from that point on – I don't know. I've never encountered anything like it. The pair of them start treating me like an adult. The way, I imagine, senior officers routinely deal with one another. Brattenbury and Knowles share information, suggest possible lines of inquiry, ask for my opinion. At one point, I complain that my police-coding restricts my ability to see some of SOCA's Tinker files. Knowles just nods and, off a look from Brattenbury, says, 'I'll get that fixed.'

And, I think, I become a better officer. Less obstreperous. Easier to work with. I even – is this possible? – become almost tentative in my opinions and suggestions. Collegiate.

I feel both junior and special. Junior, because I am. By rank, age and experience. But also those intangibles. They're both Londoners. Cardiff is, to them, not a capital city, but a provincial one, Western Vale, not a huge company. This fraud, just another case.

That, plus all those other little things. Those indicators of sophistication that people like these let fall like beads. Knowles wears ankle-skimming jeans in a sort of greeny yellow. Lavender cardigan worn over a pale grey T-shirt. The outfit is impeccably casual. Weekend wear. Not-trying-too-hard wear. And yet. The jeans are flatteringly skinny without being remotely tarty. The outfit is casual, but accessorised with a watch and bracelet, both of which look glossily expensive. The jeans themselves – what colour are they even? I call them greeny yellow because I don't have the vocabulary to be more precise. I guess Knowles herself would call them lime yellow, or greengage, or dusky citrus, or some other term which she'd produce without self-consciousness. When Brattenbury asks us if we want tea or coffee, she says, 'Oh, I'd love an Americano. No, actually, you know what, I'll have a caffè mocha, semi-skimmed, no cream,' and all that – the initial order, the reversal, the precision of the final request – comes without that flicker of *ooh, look at me* which almost any Welsh woman would feel the need to insert. Any Welsh woman, including me, and when Knowles says 'caffè mocha', she says it in a way which indicates both that she is reasonably comfortable in Italian and that she doesn't need to show off about it.

I say, 'Can I just have a peppermint tea, please?' and Knowles smiles at me, nicely, as if I've done something charming.

At the same time, I have something that they don't. I'm still the tip on the end of their javelin. Still their only lead of consequence.

And, too, I'm aware of their respect. Has Knowles ever done anything like this? Has Brattenbury? I don't know, but I doubt it. This hotel, the designery suite and the riot of windowboxes, is their way of saying, *We know this is hard. You're doing well. Hang in there.*

At one point, I say, 'Are we sure they'll come and get me? It's been eleven days.'

Brattenbury says, 'They *have to* come and get you. You're the only payroll clerk they've got. We keep dangling Roy Williams in front of their noses and they're not interested. And as for earning their trust, you've done everything a police spy wouldn't have done. Operationally speaking, I think things have gone pretty much perfectly.'

I laugh: I think Brattenbury has just forgiven my catfight with Quintrell.

Susan says, 'I saw pictures of what you did to her Audi. They've gone viral in the office.'

We talk about the Tinker team. When we started the project we assumed a shortish list of personnel. Our first hypothesised team composition ran as follows:

??? – Boss
Vic Henderson – Security & operations
Saj Kureishi – IT guy
??? – possible additional gang members

Already, that list has been expanded. Our list now looks like this:

??? – Boss

Vic Henderson, Allan Wiley [plus others???] – Security &
   operations
Anna Quintrell – accounting
Bangalore consultant[s] – IT
??? – possible additional gang members

I say, 'All that funny money in the Caribbean. Those Panamanian foundations and all the rest of it. You need to know what you're doing to set that stuff up. I can't see Quintrell knowing enough to do that. Or Henderson.'

'True,' says Brattenbury. 'But you can just buy that kind of expertise in. London's a world centre for that kind of knowhow.'

'Right. But if you're holding a big get-to-know-you meeting with your new IT guys, wouldn't you want *everyone* there? I mean, all the systems will have to coordinate. Getting the money offshore. Hiding it when it's there.'

Brattenbury and Susan share a look. He says, 'Yes, worth a look.'

She flips open a laptop, calling up a SOCA screen with a list of all the vehicles parked in the hotel car park on the relevant day. The vehicles and their owners. Brattenbury, meanwhile, is dragging a bunch of files from a black document case.

SOCA's data systems look a little different from ours, but the principle is the same. The hotel car park saw a total of 127 cars present for all or part of the meeting time. SOCA's analysts have already pulled together names, addresses, vehicle types, entry and exit times, home phone data, usually mobile data too. Often job descriptions. Links to Facebook and other online pages. They've even used Google Street View to collect photos of the car owners' homes and another website to collect guesstimated market prices.

I say, 'The guy we're looking for has got a nice car and an expensive house.'

Susan filters the data to include only properties worth

186

£750,000 or more.

'That's not a lot for London,' she cautions.

Thirty-two names are left.

'Let's try a million.'

Twenty-four names.

Susan tries a few other filters – car values, length of stay, any phone use to or from the South Wales area – but they don't seem to shed much light. We go back to the twenty-four.

'We don't have to do this now,' Brattenbury says.

I stare at him. Like I have something better to do.

He shrugs. From one of his folders, he pulls out a bunch of stapled sheets, one bunch for each of the 127 cars parked. He starts picking out the twenty-four individuals we're now concerned with. As he's doing that, Susan kicks off her shoes and does a series of stretches. Yoga probably.

Someone's ordered sandwiches from room service, and a big tray of them arrive.

We eat sandwiches and play hunt-the-villain.

We've got lots of accountants, bankers, lawyers, management consultants, that sort of thing. But given that this is a business hotel outside Heathrow, we'd have expected nothing less. Brattenbury finds a lawyer, cautioned for cocaine use while at university, speciality in European tax law, big house in Chelsea, recent phone use to and from South Wales.

'Sounds good,' says Susan.

'Mmm,' I say, and reach for more food.

'Try these. They're goat's cheese and roasted pepper.'

'Thing is,' I say, 'phone use to South Wales looks too blatant, doesn't it? If we know anything about these boys, it's that they're a hundred per cent on anything to do with security. Outside an emergency, it would be all disposable phones, bought for cash.'

'It's his sister,' says Susan, looking at her laptop. 'I've got

187

her Facebook page up. She runs a small stud farm outside . . . wherever that is.'

'Mynyddislwyn,' I say, helping her with the place name. 'Outside Pontllanfraith.'

There's nothing in my pile of stuff which interests me. I reach for Susan's discards. Start to work through them. Reach the sixth name down.

James Wyatt. A London accountant. Working for a firm just outside the big four. Background in audit, but now a 'consultant', whatever that means. Nothing particularly interesting in that, except that an article in *Accountancy World* magazine, dating four years back, happens to link him to a company called Bay Properties. Which is majority owned by a man named David Marr-Phillips. A man who lives in Cardiff and whose integrity and lawful conduct I do not completely trust.

Is this the slimmest of all slim leads? Or nothing at all?

Mr Wyatt drives a Porsche Boxter. Value: about forty-five thousand pounds. Lives off the Old Brompton Road in London. Two-bedroom flats in the road go for more than one point five million, and it's not quite clear from the data we have whether Wyatt has a flat or a house.

'What do accountants earn?' I ask. 'Used to be, um, a senior audit manager,' and I name the firm.

'We can check,' says Brattenbury. He calls his office. Gives instructions to a colleague.

Susan is online, checking a salary guide published by a London recruitment consultancy. 'A hundred K,' she says. 'That's an upper limit, unless the guy is very experienced.'

'He's thirty-four,' I say, checking. 'Lives near here. Is that a flat or a house?'

Brattenbury makes another call. To the grey-Mondeo men from earlier, I'm guessing. He tells them to attempt a 'delivery' to the address, scope out whether Wyatt has the whole property or just one floor.

I study Wyatt's call log. Plenty of international calls there – not too surprising, given the kind of names we're looking at – including a good few to the United States. Only, I think I'm right in saying that the US shares its '1' country code prefix not just with Canada, but the Caribbean too.

'Susan,' I say, 'can you check area code 345 for me?'

She does.

The Cayman Islands.

'Area code 284?'

'British Virgin Islands.'

About the same time, Brattenbury gets a couple of texts in.

Looking over my shoulder at the call logs, he says, 'At his last place of work, the guy earned about £125,000, including bonuses. That house he's living in, he's got all of it. Value about two and a half, three million.'

There's a pause, then someone says, 'Gotcha.'

I think the someone was me.

'Yes, gotcha,' murmurs Brattenbury. He calls the office. He wants surveillance on Wyatt's house, but will need an interception warrant. We don't actually have any evidence of Wyatt's involvement in crime, but the circumstantial evidence we have is powerfully suggestive and the crimes here are big ones. I don't think Brattenbury will have much difficulty in obtaining what he needs.

Our putative list of gang members grows another name:

James Wyatt (?) – offshore finance specialist

If I could, I'd work all night on this. I'd turn the lights down, eat at strange hours, make a nest of pillows and cushions on the floor, access every database I could think of, trace every lead no matter how minor. Once, on a different case, we made a breakthrough because I found, on the suspect's partner's niece's Facebook page, a photo of a school concert with one face partially out of frame. I used a combination of Photoshop and online facial analysis software to determine that the out-of-frame face was highly consistent with that of our suspect. I then visited the Facebook page of every other parent and schoolchild present that night until I found a photo that was unmistakably of our guy, placing him in Cardiff when he'd claimed to be in Porthcawl. The case wasn't even a big deal. A handling stolen goods charge with a probable six-month sentence. I didn't even tell the DI leading the investigation how I'd found the photo, because I wasn't really assigned to the inquiry and I prefer to hide how obsessive I actually am.

But, much as I'd love to stay and work through the night, my cover demands that I go back to Amina's.

Out on the street, with Brattenbury and Susan both saying goodbye to me on the steps of the hotel, I feel weird. Like I'm suspended in the gap between two lives, unsure which is mine. I feel colourless and weightless. An air bubble waiting to dress itself in somebody else's clothes.

I say, 'I am Fiona Grey. A cleaner.'

The man who looks like Adrian Brattenbury says, 'Yes, and you are also Fiona Griffiths, a very capable police officer.'

The woman who has hair like something out of Titian and whose long green legs are like a daffodil unfolding, gives me a hug.

I don't know what to say, so I blink instead.

Brattenbury says something. Maybe, 'Stay safe.' That's what he normally says.

I can't feel my body at all and I look down to check that my legs are still there.

They are, but they don't look right.

The man who looks like Brattenbury says more things. The woman too. I don't know what she says exactly, but she smiles nicely.

I do something, or say something, or at any rate, I find myself walking away up the street. As soon as I think it safe to do so, I stare down at my legs, and maybe hit them with my hand, to see if I can feel anything. I don't succeed or not really, except that I think the Fiona Grey person starts to thicken and the other one, the one who is a policewoman, starts to dissipate.

When I reach the corner, I look back and see Brattenbury and the other one deep in conversation on the steps of the hotel, flicking glances up the road as I disappear.

28

Back at Amina's place, I find my balance again, or sort of.

I clean. We play with Asad. I fret about whether Tinker will come and find me or not.

One afternoon, the thirteenth day, I walk down to the railway station. Drayton, the area where Amina lives, is not lovely, but at its best it has a quiet suburban charm. Almost villagey. Ice cream vans and privet hedges. Quiet roads and dads who wash their cars at the weekend.

There's a phone box there, an old-fashioned thing. I use it to call Buzz, a breach of procedure.

Buzz answers. Says, 'Babe, are you OK?'

I say yes, as I always do, then, 'Buzz, when we can – I mean, as soon as it's safe – can we do something weddingy together? Maybe look at dresses or, I don't know, venues?'

'I'm not meant to see your dress before the big day.'

'I know, but can we anyway?'

He says yes. He always does.

I say, 'And Buzzman, can you do me a favour?' I ask him to print a good colour photo of Henderson off from police records and leave it for Gary at the hostel. 'Say it's from me. And that I'll be in touch.'

'Who's Gary?'

'A homeless guy. Bit of an alkie. A *Big Issue* seller.'

'You want me to hand over data from a top secret police

inquiry to an alcoholic homeless man, with probable mental-health issues?'

'He was an NCO in the Royal Welch Fusiliers. Expertise in signals. Combat experience. And he's a buddy. He'd walk through fire for me.'

'I know, Fi, but when he's pissed, if he starts talking in a pub . . .'

'Gary? In a pub? Paying two pound fifty a pint? You have to be joking. When Gary gets pissed he buys two litre bottles of Diamond White for three quid and change, and drinks on a park bench until he's too drunk to see.'

'If you're sure . . .'

'I'm sure.'

'And naturally you'll have consulted your senior investigating officer about this strategy.'

I laugh at that. I tried raising the matter once. Brattenbury heard me out, but said, snobbily, 'He's not an appropriate person,' as though we were discussing a new member for the Athenaeum.

'That's not the same thing at all,' I object. 'My senior investigating officer isn't allowed to sleep with me.'

The conversation changes tack at that point, Buzz's thoughts turning to just how little he's been able to exercise his fiancé-privileges in recent months.

We talk rubbish for a few minutes, then hang up.

A butterfly settles on the phone box in front of me. The air smells of sunshine on plastic. I lift the handset again so I can hear the dial tone, which sounds like Buzz's bass rumble.

I'm scared that I'm losing myself. I feel spacey and unsure.

It's a relief when, the very next day – day fourteen, a Wednesday – Amina and I complete our early morning shift for YCS, and walk out onto the street to find a black BMW purring on the kerb.

Henderson is inside it. Gestures me over.

Amina sees the gesture. I've told her nothing about where I've been or what I've been doing since I last saw her, but men in black cars have a significance that crosses any boundary of language or culture. She looks at me and at Henderson. Her face has that fierce, impassive African quality, unbroken by any smile.

She says, 'You need to get Asad,' then stalks off, without a glance back.

I don't go over to Henderson. Sit on the granite steps of the office I've just cleaned and start to roll a cigarette.

Henderson parks, illegally, and comes over.

'May I?' he says, wanting to sit beside me.

I don't say yes and I don't say no, so he sits anyway.

'Look, Fiona, we screwed up. I'm sorry. I shouldn't have done what I did. It was horrible. It scared you. I'm sorry.'

I don't say anything, but I've got my cigarette rolled now and I light up.

I wish it was a big fat spliff with handfuls of sweet Griffithsian weed in it, but there are times when the thin brown taste of tobacco just has to do instead.

'If I'm being honest, I have to say I didn't like doing that. You and me, I think we had trust anyway. Some of my colleagues, they haven't met you, they felt we had to do more. And they were wrong. They pushed too hard. *I* did. *I* pushed too hard. I want to say sorry.'

I shrug. It's an apology which has nothing to do with repentance. No sorry-we-murdered-that-guy. No sorry-to-have-threatened-you. Not even an *I, Vic Henderson, apologise for being a total arsehole*, because his 'apology' took care to make clear that he had been forced into doing something he'd argued against. And, I note, nowhere did Henderson suggest that the threat of murder he levelled at me that night has been lifted, not even one iota. The threat is still there, still alive. His only apology is for the manner of presentation.

194

Fuck you, I think. *Fuck you and I'll see you in jail.*

What I say is nothing at all.

A parking warden comes down the road towards Henderson's BMW. We both see the warden. Henderson says, 'Look, are you OK coming with me, just while I move the car?'

I go on smoking. *Fuck you. Fuck your car.*

'OK, shit. Look – no, it doesn't matter.'

We watch as the warden photographs the BMW. Starts to make out a ticket. I finish my ciggy.

'I've got something for you.' He has a document wallet with him. Hands it over.

There are qualifications inside. A couple for nursing. One for primary education. Another for something to do with speech therapy. They all look pukka, all made out in the name of Fiona Grey.

'I don't really know what you want. But it's got to be something that would make you count as a skilled migrant for immigration purposes. If you want to choose something else, we'll sort it out.'

'I can't be a nurse. You can't put me in charge of patients when I don't know anything about nursing.'

'This stuff just gets you your visa. You can work as anything you like.'

'Even so. It's not right.'

'OK, then be something else. If you need references, we'll fix those too.'

'You keep talking about this lawyer, but I've never met him. How do I even know he's real?'

'He's real, all right. We can go right there if you like.'

Henderson is hopeful. He waves at his now-beticketed car.

'I don't want *your* lawyer. I want one that I choose.'

Henderson does a little double-take, then says, 'OK.'

'You pay the bills, but he's my lawyer.'

'OK.'

'And you've got to get me my old job back. And my flat.'

'It's still there. Both. The job and the flat.'

'I was on probation. It was a six-month probationary thing.'

'You've been sick. We arranged for a doctor to send in a sick note. Your workmates sent you a card.'

'Really?'

I'm moved by this. Pulled by different emotions. Impressed at Henderson's organisation. The care taken to keep me in play. Also touched that my workmates bothered to send me a card. I've never even bonded with them, not really. I still prefer cleaning to payroll.

Henderson says, 'Are we good? Are you ready to come back to Cardiff?'

'I've got to get Asad.'

He doesn't know who Asad is, but he opens the car door and I get in.

29

Arriving back: a whirl of activity.

That night, I resuscitate my cannabis plants, which have resented my absence but don't look as though they'll die to punish me. Jason cooks me a cabbage and bacon hotpot and I build a spliff that uses four Rizla papers and is loaded with so much grass that it threatens to burst at the seams.

I dream again of Kureishi – bad dreams, violent and too vivid – but the dope softens those edges. I can see myself smoking a lot if the dreams keep coming.

At Western Vale, lots to catch up on. My 'portfolio' was in reasonably good shape before I left, so although my colleagues had to cover for me in my absence, they didn't find any horrendous giveaways that their junior payroll clerk might be stealing tens of thousands of pounds a month. I tell everyone I was sick. Gastroenteritis. People say, Yes, it's been going around. People always say that, I realise, no matter how true or untrue it is.

At work that day, I make a list of immigration lawyers.

Henderson wants a major 'portfolio review' on Saturday at Quintrell's house. I say no. He puts pressure on me, but I say I have to go to the hostel. Say I can do Sunday instead. He agrees, reluctantly. We arrange to meet at ten in the morning.

At the hostel, I find that Clementina has deserted me for a table-football partner who can actually play. She tells me a long story, almost none of which I understand. I try to find Gary, but he's nowhere around.

I catch up on my Anger and Anxiety Management course. Our tutor is a breathlessly optimistic woman, Melinda, who wears ethnic jewellery and lots of bangles. I go on learning a lot. Melinda says, 'Sometimes you might not notice your feelings directly, but you can often notice the results. For example, if you have problems sleeping, you might be anxious about something. Or if you find yourself getting obsessive, that could easily be because of some inner anxiety.'

She lists a few other things and ask us if any of them are familiar to us. A few people put up their hands. I don't, then realise that I tick every one of those symptoms.

Sleep: on weeknights, I seldom get more than four or five hours' sleep. At weekends, I try to lie in, but seldom manage more than five hours' real sleep.

Obsession: no need to ask what Buzz would say about that. Or DCI Jackson. Even Brattenbury. I think of my untaken holidays. My endless uncharged-for overtime.

Losing touch with friends and family. Working undercover is basically a way to guarantee extreme social isolation. I was warned about this repeatedly and ignored every warning.

Melinda is on something else now, but I raise my hand anyway.

'Yes, Fiona, did you have a question?'

'No. Just I think I have those things. The signs of anxiety.'

'OK, which ones?' She starts to go through her list again.

'All of them,' I say. 'All of them.'

We do Signs of Anger too. One of the signs is Unpredictable Outbursts (including Acts of Violence). I don't raise my hand on this one, but my record on Acts of Violence is not something I'd care to share with my bosses. Melinda says, 'Sometimes you might actually end up hurting someone.' I don't tell her that I've killed one person outright, another person sort-of, and have inflicted reasonably serious injuries on a further five. That sort of thing can get you thrown off even the best courses.

At the end of the session, I ask Melinda for any handouts from the week before. I'm going to put them all up on my fridge.

When I leave the hostel, I wander outside looking for Gary. If he's getting drunk, he'll be on a park bench somewhere with his mates. If he's sober, he'll be selling the *Big Issue*, trying to make the most of the last Saturday shoppers.

He's sober.

Selling the magazine outside Cardiff Castle. He puts his mags down and we share a ciggy. I ask if he's going to drink tonight. He says no. 'Liver's fucking killing me,' an assessment which is no doubt medically accurate. I ask him if he can get over to Pontcanna tomorrow morning.

'What time?'

I tell him.

'What for?'

I tell him. Not the truth, but close enough. A version which basically just says, Henderson is a fucker and I want to know more about him. Say that he drives a black BMW and supply the registration number.

Gary's happy enough with that. I don't know if he believes me, but it doesn't really matter if he does. The hostel is full of people with mental-health issues. We have delusions, pick quarrels, get angry over nothing. If Gary thinks I'm a wacko, he's welcome.

On Sunday, I go to Quintrell's house. Gary is there, nursing a shopping trolley full of trash and a plastic bottle of cider. I wink at him. He's enjoying his surveillance role too much to wink back but Gary, even when drunk, isn't a trolley-pusher, so I know he's on the case.

Henderson arrives shortly after me. I don't know if Gary's

clocked him, but I'll find out later. Quintrell gets me my normal glass of water and doesn't offer to take my coat, but Fiona Grey and I are more assertive now. We give Quintrell our coat to hang and ask for herbal tea. Quintrell fumes, but a look from Henderson makes her do as we ask.

Fuck you too, I think, as she brings my tea over. *And fuck you too*.

We go over the portfolio: Henderson, Quintrell and Team Fiona.

There's a pushiness now which wasn't here before. A good sign. The SOCA surveillance boys now have a good audio feed from Quintrell's house, so I assume Brattenbury will be listening in.

I hope he enjoys it.

With the Kureishi-vintage frauds down to just one that's still operative, the Tinker gang have got to get the most from me that they can. And we think we now know what they're up to.

It's still speculative, of course, but our best guess is this. Kureishi, to begin with, was working for himself, almost experimentally perhaps. His job made it easy for him to gain control of corporate computers. He set up the first little frauds in a kind of boutique way, with his sister-in-law as his co-conspirator.

As his ambitions progressed, he came into contact, we don't know how, with Henderson's gang. Perhaps he needed help with arranging the movement of money overseas. Or perhaps some of the IT stuff was beyond him. Or perhaps he needed Quintrell's expertise. Or something else. In any case, the Tinker crew took Kureishi's work and professionalised it. Expanded the scale. Eliminated those little giveaways which first alerted Swindon Kevin to the fraud.

We don't know what caused the breakdown in relations between Kureishi and the rest. Perhaps Kureishi got greedy. Or felt muscled out of his own enterprise. In any event, at some point he pushed things too far, realised his life was in danger, and went on the run, stealing money from Gibson and Morgan to fund his few months of liberty.

A small-time crook who learned what it was like to play in the bigger leagues.

For a long time, my SOCA colleagues assumed – as did I – that the purpose of the fraud was simply the money skimmed through my work and through that of my fellow moles.

We now think we were wrong. The clue, all along, were those nineteen dummy names in my portfolio. The clue, also, was that meeting in Heathrow, the plane from Bangalore. Clues which hint that the actual 'profits' from the various frauds so far have been just a way to fund an investment in a much larger IT project. One managed from the UK, but executed – or mostly executed – by professional IT technicians in Bangalore.

What's more, if we're right that James Wyatt is part of the gang, it's becoming increasingly clear that Tinker is bigger than we had ever envisaged. Bigger, and better organised. Indeed, it's alarming that we still have no real product from our watching and listening. Henderson, we know, is clearly a pro, but we all doubt that either Quintrell or Wyatt have any real training in evading surveillance, yet we've never traced a call to a number that looks of real interest, nor overhead any conversation of substance.

I also come to see that I'm more important to this group than I – or perhaps even they – had ever realised.

Quintrell is going through my work. Picks up an email I sent to HMRC.

'No, look, this is wrong.' She is scolding. Testy. It's not just her manner, it's that she genuinely doesn't like me. Doesn't like me in her house. Doesn't like my new assertiveness, resents the support I seem to be getting from Henderson. 'You've got the coding wrong—'

'I haven't.'

'You have. You've put—'

'I *haven't*.'

We get into a dispute. There's a narrow technical way in which Quintrell is right. The thing she wants me to do is theoretically correct, but because the tax coding in question is an unusual one, I would need to get a manager to sign off on it.

I explain this and say, 'Of course, if you want me to get my boss involved . . .'

'No.' Henderson's interjection is firm. 'You're right, Fiona. You did the right thing.' He glares at Quintrell.

Thirty minutes later, something similar arises. Quintrell is again right in theory, but she doesn't know the way that payroll departments actually operate and she doesn't know the TPS software in the same excruciating detail that I do. Her way of approaching something would increase the risk of detection. My way would reduce it.

Quintrell and I get into one of our fights. This doesn't end with my kicking her kitchen in – more's the pity – but it does end with Henderson breaking us up.

'Look, Fiona, this is really helpful. There are things in what you've said, which . . . we're going to have to think about.'

He drums his fingers briefly, plays with his phone. 'Look, would you mind stepping outside a moment? Maybe have a cigarette?'

Quintrell escorts me to the garden door. I roll a cigarette, topped up with weed, and smoke it under the magnolia. Put ash anywhere I want. Ditto the match. Ditto, when I'm finished, the butt.

And fuck you too.

When I left the kitchen, Quintrell and Henderson had an

intense exchange for a few minutes, then Henderson called a halt and made a call. I hoped that he'd stay in the kitchen, for the sake of Brattenbury's audio recording, but he soon moves out onto the street. We haven't been able to intercept his mobile calls because he protects his line well, encrypting his calls and replacing his handset at regular intervals.

Quintrell moves around in the kitchen. When she darts a look out at me, it's full of malice.

I wonder how she'll enjoy prison. I hope she goes to one of those dark Victorian places. Long corridors, overhead lights, and brick cells higher than they are wide. The sort of prison that looks like a workhouse and sounds like a sermon.

When Henderson comes back, his face is carefully upbeat.

'OK, fantastic. I think we had a really good session there. Really useful.'

He sounds like an organised crime version of Melinda. I imagine him wearing bangles and an African scarf knotted in his hair.

Because of the weed I've just smoked, I giggle a bit and ask for biscuits.

As Quintrell fetches them, Henderson says he wants me to 'meet the team. We really want to bring you into the centre of this project, so to speak.' He makes it sound like I've won some Employee of the Month contest. I think I'm meant to coo with happiness.

I don't coo.

'We've got to find dates that work. There are a lot of people to coordinate.'

I say, 'You keep telling me what *you* want. You haven't asked me what *I* want.'

Henderson – no bangles, no headscarf – swallows down his impatience.

'OK. What you do *you* want?'

I get out my list of lawyers: a shortlist of six.

'I want to choose a lawyer. I want you to pay his fees. I want a date for my visa.'

'OK, Fiona, I know. And I've already said—'

'You've *said* all sorts of things. But you haven't *done* anything.'

Sit there. Eating biscuits. Feeling giggly.

Henderson has one hand in a fist. Is using the other to knead it. It's an odd gesture. Like the fist wants to hit me and the other hand is trying to calm it.

'All right,' he says. 'That's fair. I'll make calls and get something in place.'

'*I'll* make the calls,' I say. 'You pay the bills. When I've chosen my lawyer, I'll ask him to bill me in advance. When you've paid, I don't mind helping.'

Henderson's face is fire and smoke. There's a blackness in his face which wasn't there even when he was showing me his Kureishi video.

But I win.

'OK,' he says. 'OK. But let's get a move on.'

I finish my biscuit, and agree.

30

I see my four of my list of six lawyers. Henderson is my chauffeur for the day. Driving me from fancy London office to fancy London office. He waits downstairs, tightly angry in his BMW. Illegally parked, on the lookout for wardens.

I'm upstairs, getting the nicey-nicey treatment from men who bill their time at £350 an hour. The first guy seems genuinely warm, but not in a hurry. I rule him out immediately. The second guy treats me like the most unimportant part of his day. Number three: I don't know, because he doesn't turn up and leaves me in the hands of a junior associate, who is male but probably shaves about as often as I do.

Number four – George Noble – seems vaguely lecherous. Fat lips, fat cheeks, fleshy hands. A gold signet ring. One of those colourful ties which deeply conventional people wear if they're eager to seem rebellious. But his acquisitive, desirous nature appeals to me.

I say, 'How soon can I get out of here?'

'Which country?'

'Whichever's fastest. It needs to be English-speaking, that's all.'

'Is budget an issue?'

'No.'

He likes that response. He smiles and a thread of saliva hangs from the inside of his upper lip. My résumé – fake as it is – hardly suggests I'm in a position to be reckless about budget, but Henderson has clearly promised enough that Noble isn't worried about payment. I don't know what Noble believes about me, but I doubt if he's too finicky about his ethics.

'New Zealand is fastest.'

'Then New Zealand it is.'

'Your sponsor, Mr Henderson, tells me you have quite a varied skillset.'

'It's a question of what we emphasise. I don't want them to think I'm a flake.'

'You're a qualified speech therapist?'

'Yes.'

'And have worked in a registered practice for three years or more? They will check.'

'Yes.'

'Then we'll go with that. Do you have any New Zealand connections?'

I shrug. 'I'm Welsh. I like sheep.'

That smile again. Then, 'Your English is obviously fluent. Any other languages?'

'Welsh.'

Noble raises his eyebrows, as though no reasonable government department would count that as a language.

I say, 'The impudence of the government is appalling. *Mae haerllygrwydd y llywodraeth yn ddychrynllyd.* It's proof of linguistic competence. Important in my line of work.'

'OK, fair enough. Any criminal convictions?'

'No.'

'They will check.'

'They can check all they want.' And they can: a 'person wanted in connection with . . .' won't show on any search that Immigration New Zealand has access to.

Noble asks a few other questions, but I should be an easy case. I'll be a skilled migrant, the sort that New Zealand wants to encourage. He says, 'Most delays are caused by poorly completed application forms. After that, it's down to how quickly the authorities are able to confirm employment details and the like. Our form will have no errors in it. The rest . . .' He shrugs. 'A matter of weeks.'

When I get downstairs, Henderson is still at the wheel. A takeaway coffee in one hand. Phone pressed to his ear with the other.

Gary *did* get a good view of Henderson the other day in Pontcanna. He hasn't seen Henderson around town, but says he's on the case. He enjoys the challenge, I think. I've told him to patrol the town centre. I've asked Gary to start with that little side street off the Hayes where we lost track of him once, then work outwards from there. A long job, infinitely tedious, but selling the *Big Issue* is the best cover you can get. And it's not like Gary has anything more pressing to do.

Meantime, I wait by the passenger door until Henderson completes his call and allows me back.

'Next one,' he says grimly, putting the car into gear.

'We can go home. I'm going to work with Mr Noble.'

We encounter congestion and delays as far as Heathrow, then the motorway opens up. When we pass Slough and Windsor, we are travelling at eighty-seven miles per hour. When we pass Maidenhead, the needle touches a hundred and the BMW is as quiet as a church in winter.

As we cross into Wales, Henderson clears his throat and says, 'We're going to need you for a few days. At the end of next week. We'll have a team of people together and I'll need you to work with us the way you've been working with myself and Anna. You've been very helpful so far.'

I shrug. Low cloud rolls over the hills ahead of us. A grey Atlantic fretting at a stony coast. This is Wales as the Saxons first saw it. The Romans before them, the Celts before them. Low cloud and sombre hills.

'That video. I'm sorry you saw it.'

'It's not about seeing it. It's that you did it.'

'It wasn't necessarily me.' Henderson glances over, changing the subject. 'I've got a present for you. On the back seat.'

I look behind me. Retrieve an Amazon box. It's full of books. *A Career in Speech and Language Therapy. Basic Medical Science for Speech and Language Therapy Students. Children's Speech Disorders.* A few others too.

'In case you did actually want to work as a speech therapist. I don't know. But in case you did.'

Henderson is less articulate than usual. A faint embarrassment sketches his cheekbones.

'Thank you,' I say. 'Thank you.'

31

It's a week after the lawyer trip. Two weeks since that Sunday in Quintrell's kitchen. I'm in Quintrell's house again, but upstairs. Her bedroom.

There's a black bin liner on the bed. Some casual sports clothes. Tracksuit bottoms. Training shoes. Socks. T-shirt. A fleece. Underwear. An eye-mask and something in black cotton.

I say, 'You're serious?'

Henderson says, 'It's a precaution. Your safety as much as ours.'

I shrug, as though I don't care. As though this sort of thing is completely routine. A monthly fire drill, a matter of corporate compliance. Truth is, though, Fiona Grey feels this moment. I do too, I think. The creep of fear. The realisation that I am about to step out of my world and into another. A world where the rewards are measured in Amazon gifts, the punishments meted out with billhooks.

Henderson gives a few brief instructions to Quintrell, then leaves the room. I can hear him pacing the corridor beyond. Thick cream carpet and Redouté rose prints in gold frames on the wall.

I keep my clothes on, sit on the bed. I say to Quintrell, 'This is a lovely house.'

'Thank you.'

I see three versions of myself in her dressing table mirror. But

209

all the versions look undersized and somehow monochrome. A payroll clerk in shabby clothes. Quintrell stands beside me, skinny jeans and a lambswool jumper in bottle green. Low-heeled brown boots. Gold earrings and bracelets. She has more clothes in a small travel suitcase at the foot of the bed. I've brought a couple of my speech therapy books, because Henderson told me I might have time on my hands. Nothing else. He didn't even want me to bring a toothbrush.

I pick up the things laid out for me and point at the en-suite bathroom. 'Can I go in there? I'll leave the door open.'

'Sorry. I need to watch.'

So I strip. Not just down to my underwear, but completely. Stand there under the light as Quintrell examines me. Nothing taped to my skin. No little bits of electronics, nothing.

I have some scarring on my buttocks and left side, the result of a skin graft operation I had eighteen months back. Quintrell runs her hands down the white lines on the edge of my rib cage, as though testing the tissue. I think she's curious how I got the scars, but she doesn't ask.

'OK,' she says, pulling back. She doesn't like this any more than I do. Doesn't like it, isn't good at it.

She takes my clothes though. Extracts my phone from my jacket pocket. Leaves that out on the dressing table. Then, with a nod, signals that I can change into the other stuff. It doesn't fit brilliantly – I have to tuck the waistband over on itself to stop the trouser bottoms slopping under my heels – but it's OK. I put on the T-shirt and just hold the fleece. The shoes are a size too big, but still comfortable.

Quintrell throws open the door and Henderson re-enters.

He has an RF scanner on him and something else. A handheld metal detector, I think. He sweeps me all over. Asks me to sit on the bed and examines my scalp, like a mother checking for nits. Checks my mouth, ears, nostrils.

'Good.'

He takes the battery out of my phone, then sweeps carefully for any residual transmissions. Checks the books too, though he only gave those to me a few days back.

Thank God, Brattenbury determined that it was unsafe for me to take any type of recording, transmitting or tracking device to this meeting, so I'm here completely clean. Brattenbury said, 'Go to the meeting as Fiona Grey. Inhabit her as fully as you can. *Be* her. Don't worry about collecting evidence, making recordings, identifying faces, nothing like that. Just play your part and when we make our move, get down on the fucking floor and don't move a fucking inch.'

It was the first time I've ever heard Brattenbury properly swear.

'Yes, sir,' I said and meant it. Not just the assent, but the obedience to command.

Make our move: that's Brattenbury-speak for a raid conducted by the SCO19 firearms command. Glass and bullets everywhere. Men in black, with Kevlar body armour and automatic weapons. Shattered wood and shouting.

You bet I'll be a good little detective constable. I'll lie down on the fucking floor and not move a fucking inch. Me and Fiona Grey, the two of us together.

Henderson puts my possessions, except for the books, in a bin liner, which he leaves in the corridor outside. Tells me I'll probably want to put the fleece on. I do. He picks up the eye-mask and the black cotton thing, and we all go downstairs.

To Henderson's car. The rear windows are shaded by those perforated black sun screens people put up to reduce glare. They effectively hide anything in the back of the car.

Quintrell and I sit in the rear seats, the invisible ones. Henderson fiddles around outside, checking for tracking devices. I say to Quintrell, 'Did you have to do all this too? When you started?'

She says, 'Everyone gets checked. It's for all our security.'

That's not quite an answer, but all I'm going to get. When Henderson is satisfied that his car is clean, he opens my door and passes me the eye-mask. I put it on and my world goes dark.

'Head forward.'

I lean forward and feel the black cotton hood come down over my head. It's secured with a knot in the pullcord at the back. My breath feels suddenly hot and clammy. The walls of the world are close at hand.

I hope to God Brattenbury knows what he's doing.

Get down on the fucking floor and don't move a fucking inch.

32

I don't know how long I'm in that car. I can't check my watch, because my head is hooded and because my watch is in a dustbin liner in Quintrell's bedroom.

But after perhaps fifteen minutes of city traffic, Henderson says, 'We're going to leave this car and enter a second vehicle. I'm going to open your door. I'm going to escort you to that other vehicle. You will get inside and wait until we move off again. Is that clear?'

I say, 'Yes.'

My door opens and I get out, Henderson's hand on my upper arm. There's a brief rush of city air: sooty and warm. There's a buzz of traffic noise, but the buzz has a hard quality to it, a compactness, which makes me think we're in a narrow alley, or something like it. Something tucked away, out of sight. We walk a few paces and Henderson guides my hand to the roof of the car and an open door. I get inside. He says, 'Please lie,' and I do. I feel him on the rear seats beside me, also lying. The car moves off again. Quintrell, presumably, at the wheel.

It's a sweet move.

A black BMW with a male driver enters a little side street. Some completely different vehicle exits with a woman at the wheel. No passengers visible. It's not the kind of move which defeats all opposition, but you either need a stroke of luck – a fortuitous sightline, a tiny slip by those executing

213

the manoeuvre – or highly intrusive surveillance. Brattenbury can't risk the latter, and is unlikely to benefit from the former. As it happens, I know that Brattenbury won't bother with more than cursory surveillance. Nothing out of the normal, that's the watchword now.

After a bit, I can feel Henderson raise his head. He'll be checking for any tail. He gives Quintrell brief, clipped instructions – 'Go left here. Stop. Move off. You see that side road coming up after the lights? Make a sudden turn into the road, and drive fast for a hundred yards.' I feel the car swaying to his command.

After a while, he's satisfied. 'We're clear,' he announces. 'You can pull over.'

The car stops. Quintrell gets out and sits next to me in the back. I hear her fixing screens to the windows. Don't want the little hooded girl attracting the wrong kind of attention.

Henderson is about to take the wheel, but first he tells me, 'I'm going to give you something to listen to. What do you like listening to?'

'Anything.'

'OK. Stereophonics maybe? We'll start with that. Lean forwards, please.'

I lean forward. Quintrell arranges a headband on me that contains speakers over the ears. The music comes out way too loud at first. I complain and Quintrell adjusts the settings a bit, puts the thing on shuffle.

It's still loud, though. I can hear almost nothing else. I lose touch with the movement of the car too, whether it's fast or slow, jerky or not. In my altered world, I can only feel my breath fingering the folds of black cotton, the pressure of the eye-mask, the clamour of some indie rockers from the Valleys.

I think, *For all I know, Henderson knows who I am.*

I think, *For all I know, he is taking me away to kill me.*

I can't connect with those thoughts, though. Not really.

Can't connect with anything much. Not Brattenbury. Not Buzz. Not my real mission here. So I let my thoughts go wherever they feel most comfortable and that turns out to be a Fiona Grey place, not a me place. I think of my time with Amina. Her saying, 'We are sisters now,' as she turned out the light. Think of my lecherous lawyer, George Noble, and the visa he will secure.

Speech therapy? I've looked at those books which Henderson brought me and I like them. If I wanted, at the end of this, I could make a new life for myself in New Zealand, teaching disabled kids to practise saying *la-la-la* and *ta-ta-ta*. That idea doesn't feel ridiculous. Part of me wants it. Part of me is already there. A small, clean office in a small, clean town. Green hills on the horizon and rugby burbling from the radio.

La-la-la.

Ta-ta-ta.

And again, please. *La-la-la. Ta-ta-ta.* One more time.

I don't try to read direction from the movements of the car. For one thing, I can't. For another thing, I already know where I'm going, or assume I do.

As soon as Henderson started talking about bringing me 'into the centre of this project', I told Brattenbury. He checked flights in and out of Bangalore. Checked bookings for hotel and conference centres within a thirty-minute perimeter of Heathrow.

Easy pickings. Henderson had booked another conference suite in another Heathrow hotel, taking it for five days, and had called to check such things as availability of sufficient power points and the existence of a secure data connection. He'd also booked hotel rooms for himself plus four at a second hotel a few minutes' drive away.

Brattenbury is working now to have the hotel rooms and conference suite wired for sound and images. He's planted SOCA operatives acting as maids and waiters. He's got the hotel managements to agree to share their booking data with him. If they hadn't agreed, he'd have secured a warrant.

I wonder if Brattenbury has told those managements what the firearms boys of SCO19 might do to their daintily manicured conference suites. I'm guessing not.

Brattenbury told me: 'As far as you can, Fiona, just relax. We've done this before. We're not expecting armed resistance. And in any case, we will move in with overwhelming force.'

I said, 'Yes, sir.'

'They may seek to intimidate or threaten you. They may wish to remind you of Sajid Kureishi and what happens to those who cross them. But you have nothing to fear. They need your expertise. This is the endgame now.'

'Yes, sir.'

'Remember that these people are highly security conscious, so please don't be concerned if they take precautions.'

'No, sir.'

Precautions. Being stripped. An intimate skin, hair and cavity search. A change of clothes. Eye-mask. Hood. A switch of cars. Rock music. *Please don't be concerned.*

I'm not concerned.

Not concerned, that is, until after some hours have, I guess, passed. Enough hours, easily, to get us to Heathrow. We left Pontcanna at half past two, so it must be after six now, perhaps well after.

Then the going changes abruptly. A couple of steep ascents. Hard bends in the road. A left turn onto a rough surface. Too rough for tarmac, no matter how potholed. A country track. Unmetalled. At one point Henderson misjudges something and the car bottom scrapes on something hard. In a gap between tracks, I hear Henderson swear softly. Quintrell starts to say something, but Kelly Jones from the Stereophonics starts to tell me, yet again, about laying back, head on the grass, and I can't hear anything more.

The car stops.

Doors bang open and closed. Henderson removes the headphones from me and says, 'We're here. Are you OK?'

'Do I have to listen to any more Stereophonics?'

'No.'

'Then I'm OK.'

The noise and the sightlessness has disoriented me. I can feel my voice is clumsy. Not my own.

Henderson tells me that he's going to lead me inside. It's not just my voice which is clumsy. It's my movements too. I clamber out OK, but have pins and needles in my thigh and ask to lean against the car, waiting for feeling to return.

As we stand there, a fox yelps somewhere in the silence. A bird breaks cover from a tree. I hear its heavy flapping overhead. There is no engine noise, no jets.

Either Heathrow has decided to close its flightpaths down for the day or we aren't within a hundred miles of the place and Adrian Brattenbury has no idea where I am.

Please don't be concerned.

Then, when I'm ready, Henderson takes me by an arm and leads me over to a door. We go inside and down a few steps. Henderson asks me to sit and I lower myself gingerly on what turns out to be a soft surface, a sofa or bed.

'Lean forward, please.'

I lower my head. The movement bares the nape of my neck. Vertebrae forming landing lights for the executioner's axe, the murderer's billhook.

No axe, no billhook.

Henderson fiddles with the pullcord, catches my hair, apologises, undoes the knot. Removes hood and eye-mask.

There's way too much light around me and I immediately close my eyes. Henderson rubs the top of my back. 'OK, take your time. I know these things are disorienting, believe me. Just say if you want anything to eat or drink.'

217

I do take my time and slowly make sense of my surroundings.

I'm in a small white-painted room, no phone, no windows. There's a bed, on which I'm now sitting, a bedside table, a lamp, a chest of drawers, a small sink. There's a glass vase containing daffodils by the bed. I touch them: they're real, not fake. The bed has clean linen, a set of folded towels, a bathrobe. On the chest of drawers, there is a packet of clean underwear, a couple of T-shirts, socks. Also a toothbrush, toothpaste, two bars of that tiny paper-wrapped hotel soap, and some pale green shampoo in a clear plastic bottle.

I stand up, move around, recover my senses. The T-shirts are in XS, my size. I open the shampoo and sniff. It smells of apple.

'Apple,' I say.

Henderson watches me reorder myself. Says, 'This is your room. Anna will be staying just next to you.' He taps the wall. 'The accommodation here is fairly basic, but if there's anything you want or need, please ask and we will try to provide it. Toilet and shower room here.' He leads me upstairs. 'Exercise room. More bedrooms through there. Common room here.'

The 'common room' is painted white, beige carpet. Chairs and sofas. A TV screen. Some books and magazines. A little kitchenette with tea and coffee things, a little sink. Bottles of water. A wicker basket that contains small plastic packets of biscuits. There are more flowers here. More daffs. No windows.

At the head of the little flight of steps, commanding the front door, there's a man in an old flannel shirt and a leather jacket. He is reading the *Sun*. He is developing a slight paunch, but is otherwise muscled and tough-looking. On a little table beside him, he has a cup of tea, some lo-cal sweeteners, two chocolate digestives, and a pistol.

I don't know much about guns, but I think this is a Glock, a standard police weapon.

I don't know much about lo-cal sweeteners, but I do know they're less effective when taken with chocolate digestives.

'This is Geoff,' says Henderson. 'He's here to look after us.'

Geoff waves a hand. Quintrell – who's changed into a knee-length black dress – exits her room, trots upstairs, and goes through a big wooden door, which leads I don't know where.

Something clicks. Back at her house, when I was getting ready to strip, I was struck by her clothes. Jeans and a jumper. Not the sort of thing that a woman like Quintrell would have worn to a big business meeting in a Heathrow hotel. She's attached to her own self-image as a professional woman. She'd have worn a skirt or a dress. Heels. A trouser suit at the very minimum. Quintrell's initial outfit tells me that we're in proper countryside. Not some golf-club-'n'-country-club version of the countryside either, but the real thing. A place with farm animals, ditches, bad tracks and muck.

We will move in with overwhelming force, Brattenbury promised me, but he probably didn't know how easy a promise it would be to keep. How much force do you need to overwhelm an empty conference room? How many men needed to arrest a room full of absences?

Please don't be concerned.

'Am I in prison?' I ask, which isn't a very eloquent way to phrase the question, but is the way it comes out.

'The meeting rooms are through here,' says Henderson. 'Your presence there will be required off and on over the next few days. Meals will be served either there or in the common room. You'll find that the windows are all shuttered. I request that you do not make any attempt to look out of them. Also that you do not go outside. Is that clear?'

'You mean "yes". That's the answer to my question.'

'The answer to your question is "no". You will be here for a few days, then we will return you to Cardiff. While you are here, we ask you to respect a few rules. That's all.'

He asks if I want anything. I say I want to shower, then eat. He tells me that Geoff will sort me out. He's impatient to get away. I can hear voices and footfall from the door that Quintrell went through. The occasional burst of noisy laughter. Henderson has not been unkind particularly, but my claims on his patience are expiring fast.

I let him go.

I ask Geoff about food. He produces a menu. Scrambled egg. Ditto, with bacon, sausage and tomato. A range of sandwiches. Soup of the day.

'Soup of the *day*?' I say. 'What *is* this place?'

'Soup today was parsnip. Didn't taste of much, I don't think. They do a good sandwich though. They do chips too, if you want them.'

I ask for a sandwich, some salad, no chips. He calls someone with my order. An intercom thing, not an external line. There are no external lines here that I've seen. No mobile phones either. 'Give it twenty minutes,' he advises. 'They've got their hands full at the moment.'

I get a towel from my bed and go to the shower room.

After a few hours with my head in that hood, my breath hanging wet and foggy around my cheeks, I feel clammy and unclean. I spend ten minutes under the shower. A blast of warm water and soap. Wash my hair and dry it with one of those built-in dryers that hotels have.

Stare at myself in the mirror.

Fiona Grey, looking vaguely sporty in her pale grey trackies and white T-shirt. Hair longer than I'm used to. A face that means nothing to me, or nothing I can read anyway.

We look at each other through the glass for a while, then grow bored.

I go off to find Geoff.

Ask if he has a ciggy. He says no, and the common room is

no smoking. But he says can get me some ciggies and there's a small room where I can smoke.

Ask if there's any chance of getting some weed. He laughs and says, 'Doubt it.'

I say, 'What time is it?'

He checks his watch – not disguising the dial – and says coming up to nine o'clock. That's more than six hours after we left Quintrell's house. Enough time to have gone pretty much anywhere in England or Wales. Time enough to reach southern Scotland.

Geoff says, 'It's weird, isn't it, not knowing the time. Gets you disoriented.'

He also says, dropping his voice, 'And just so you know, I'm Special Branch. Here to keep an eye on you. Any problems, I'm on it.'

I don't say much to that. My sandwich comes. There's a knock at the door, Geoff enters a passcode to open it, deals with whoever's at the door. The food arrives on a tray that someone's nicked from McDonald's. It's a 'club' sandwich, which turns out to mean chicken, bacon and some bits of salad.

I eat. Drink some water. Read about speech therapy.

Then Geoff goes off for a pee, taking his Glock with him when he goes. I lope out of the common room, through the doors that Quintrell and Henderson both used.

Emerge into a large, converted barn. Stone walls, partially exposed. Huge timber beams. A fancy wooden atrium, double doors beyond, shading the noise of a dozen or more voices. I open the door. A sudden loudening of the conversation. Some Indian faces. White ones. A couple of waitresses, dressed in black, holding trays, but also standing close to each other. Village girls, I guess. Not pros. Close to each other, because they're not used to this kind of thing and are buddying up for mutual support.

221

No one really notices my entry, except the waitresses. One of them offers me a drink, the other a tray of canapés. I ignore the canapés, take a glass of red wine.

Quintrell is close to me, but is standing with her back to me, talking to an Indian guy in a suit. Henderson is the far side of the room, side on to me. I don't really notice the room itself. Just have an impression of it. One impressive stone wall. A big fireplace with a log fire crackling away. Copper wall lamps, expensive-looking. A couple of big timber pillars, supporting a gallery. Raw oak. Everything fancy.

I push through the people to Henderson. I don't think he sees me, as such, just sees movement in his peripheral vision, turns to check it. He's wearing a dark suit, white shirt, silk tie.

'Fiona,' he says, or starts to say.

Might have said more, except that by this time I've thrown my red wine in his face. My glass too.

Leaped at him.

Kicking. Hitting. Scratching. Biting.

This isn't fighting the way my friend Lev taught me. There's no science in this, no carefully gauged aggression. This is strictly playground stuff. Fiona Grey keeps her nails fairly long, and I feel them drag down Henderson's cheek. Feel her fist knot in his thinning hair.

I'm shouting too. She is, or I am. I don't know. We're not always so separate. A stream of swearwords mostly. Nothing very inventive. 'You stupid fucking buggering shit-wanker.' That sort of thing.

Henderson doesn't resist much. That is: he protects himself from my assault but doesn't seek to harm me back. Any billhook action is strictly off limits. But this fight is eighteen-to-one, and I'm the one.

My left arm is yanked from behind. Yanked and twisted. My right arm is also seized. A forearm closes over my throat and darkness instantly starts to overtake me.

I'm aware that my legs are thrashing. Kicking out at anything I can reach. But my shoes are soft and can't do much damage. In any case, my legs too are pinioned. Geoff materialises beside me. Passes his pistol to Henderson, who holds it loosely. Geoff cuffs my wrists behind my back. Someone forces me down into a chair. The person who was choking me removes their hold and light starts to return to my world.

A world of confusion.

Henderson is dabbing his cheeks with a paper napkin. Has wine everywhere. But there's blood on him as well as wine, and I realise that a fair bit of the blood is mine. I think I cut myself on the wine glass somehow. In any case, I've got a gash on my knees and a graze all down my forearm. My joints scream from their various pummellings.

The confusion isn't merely physical. There's a ripple of social confusion too. It's not every cocktail party which is enlivened by unexpected assault, and at first people aren't sure how to react. I'm fairly sure that while I was being choked someone swiped me hard across the face. A backhand slap that seemed to loosen the teeth in my mouth. But I can also see that my actions have provoked amusement. Henderson is too suave to be your classic bruiser, but he knows how to handle himself and he was never at great physical risk from a girl who takes her T-shirts in size XS. A couple of the Indians are laughing openly at me and speaking to each other in some language other than English. There's a circle of faces, checking that Henderson is OK, rebuking me in different accents, and laughing.

One of the waitresses tiptoes into the circle. Starts mopping up wine and broken glass with kitchen towel and a plastic dustpan. She doesn't catch my eye. When her efforts to clean up start flicking round my feet, someone drags my chair backwards and me with it.

I say, sulkily, through a swelling lip, 'We're all fucked. You

223

know that? That guy there' – I'm nodding at Geoff – 'he's a pig. Special Branch. You think you're all so clever with the strip searches and bollocks, and you let a fucking copper right into your stupid fucking meeting.'

There's more. I say more. But I don't really know what. Fiona Grey doesn't cry any more than I do, but she's distraught. As far as she sees the world, everything's just turned to shit. Instead of speech therapy, New Zealand, and a pocketful of cash, she's looking at a prison sentence, investigation by the Manchester police, and no chance of ever emigrating.

As I speak, more to myself than anyone else, hair falling in front of my face, I become aware of Henderson's voice saying, 'Fiona. Fiona.'

I don't respond, or not properly. Just kick out, catch his shin, swear some more.

So he slaps me. Hard.

Hard enough I'm half thrown from my chair. I might even fall, except that someone has my handcuffed wrists in their grip and their hold steadies me.

This time I feel blood in my mouth and there's enough force in the blow that I don't want another.

I just mumble, 'Fuck off,' and try to turn away.

But Henderson's not for turning. Staying clear of my legs, he tells me that Geoff is not Special Branch. That he's assigned to tell all newcomers the same thing. That it's a test of loyalty. That I should have calmly reported the comment to him, Henderson, at the next opportunity. That instead, I have caused an unnecessary drama and, he manages to indicate, a good bit of damage to a decent suit.

He says these things with a quiet, emphatic force. As though telling me these things were a slightly less flavoursome version of hitting me.

'Do you understand what I'm telling you? Geoff, will

you please tell Fiona that you are not a policeman working undercover.'

Geoff does as he's asked, and other people weigh in too. The consensus in the room is that I overreacted wildly. That I somehow owe an apology to them all for interrupting their precious party. For damaging something as beautiful and valuable as Vic Henderson's Italian grey suit.

At the same time, as it becomes clearer that I am not a threat, that no one has been hurt, that this whole thing has been the most temporary of tempests, I become the very best form of party entertainment: a thing of merriment. A person that everyone can ridicule without breaching etiquette. One of the Indian guys is re-enacting my assault, with explosions of laughter from those around him. Quintrell's face is a study of dislike and contempt.

And then – it's all over. Geoff releases me from my handcuffs. A waitress brings kitchen towel for me to wipe at. Henderson and I shake hands. Someone gives me a glass of white wine, which I neither drink nor use as a weapon.

One of the waitresses offers me a canapé.

I say, 'Is there any blood on my face?'

She says, 'A bit,' and helps me wipe it off. I say I made a bit of a fool of myself. She tells me not to worry, no harm done. I ask her for a packet of cigarettes and she'll say she'll see what she can do.

Her accent is Welsh, for sure, but not Cardiff, and not North Wales. The accent of the Valleys is a bit different from the accents you hear further into Wales, Powys and Ceredigion, and I think her accent isn't Valleys, but I wouldn't swear to it. We don't talk for all that long.

I try standing up, but feel wobbly, so sit back down.

I'm in sports shoes, T-shirt and trackie bottoms. The men here – and it's mostly men – are, apart from Geoff, all in suits and ties. Quintrell is in black dress and clicky heels. Also she doesn't have blood, wine and glass all over her clothes.

Henderson goes off to change. When he returns, he introduces me to a man who calls himself Ramesh.

'Ram is leading the software side of things,' Henderson says. 'He's going to need your operational knowledge to make sure we get a really robust system. Garbage in, garbage out, right, Ram?'

Ramesh shakes my hand and laughs at me some more. I think the laughter is meant to be jovial and inclusive, but it doesn't feel that way.

Then the waitress comes with cigarettes and matches. I say thanks, smile at Ramesh and leave. The waitress points out the smoking room for me, but then enters a code on the keypad next to the main door, releases the lock and leaves. I slip out after her, in the wake of the closing door. I don't want to sit indoors in some shuttered room and Fiona Grey doesn't either. It's been a rough day for us both.

So we just sit outside on the steps to the barn. The sun has set, but a summer twilight still hovers in the trees. There's a big farmhouse to the right, with some windows lit up, but the view from the barn is mostly of a cobbled courtyard, some old agricultural buildings, and trees. Oak. Ash. A punky fringe of hawthorn. Over in the distance somewhere, I can just see the top lamp of a telecoms tower, a red beacon in the night.

The steps to the barn are a reddish sandstone, flaking at the edges. I play with the stone and break off a flake. Pocket it. Get stone dust under my nails.

I smoke.

Fiona Griffiths never used to smoke much. Weed often, tobacco almost never. Fiona Grey is a bit different. Less weed, more tobacco. I wonder vaguely if I'll ever kick her habit.

The party behind me begins to break up. People start exiting the barn.

I guess the barn itself only accommodates lower-level staff.

The more important, or more trusted, members of the team are in the farmhouse itself. Quintrell, for all her airs, is strictly servant class, like me.

I also wonder about the party I just witnessed.

When I entered the room, I didn't look around much. Just sought out Henderson and attacked him. But I had an impression of numbers. Numbers, and the mix between white faces and brown. At a rough guess, and excluding the waitresses, I reckon there were about twenty people, with around two white faces for every brown one. By the time the Fiona-'n'-Vic show was over, however, I'd say the room was significantly emptier, with about equal numbers of British and Indian faces. I've also something of a suspicion that Henderson's attention was only partly on me, through all that fight scene. I think he was also looking elsewhere, checking that the people who had to vacate the room because of my intrusive presence were indeed vacating.

I've got a feeling that Allan, the Astra-man, was present in the room. It would make sense.

I smoke another cigarette.

I can hear the churring of a nightjar. The distant movement of farm machinery.

Henderson materialises behind me. I'm disobeying his instructions and I think he's hesitating about how to react.

Gently, is the answer.

He sits beside me and I offer him a cigarette. He lights it from the glowing tip of mine.

'Bit of a show back there,' he comments.

'Sorry.'

'Well, I'm sorry too. Sorry for hitting you. I didn't need to do that.'

I shrug. 'I hit you.'

'Well, sorry anyway.'

'I've had worse,' I say, and Fiona Grey has. Much worse.

We smoke a while, without conversation.

Beyond the telecoms tower, and to the right, a low moon appears between loose cloud.

'What's the time?' I ask.

'Quarter to eleven. Bedtime, almost. We start early.'

'Vic?'

'Yes?'

'I want to go home. Sorry. I don't think I fit here. I can't do what you want me to do.'

Vic looks at me in the moonlight.

Reaches out and draws me to him. An arm round my shoulder, pressing me against his warmth. He kisses me softly on the top of my head.

'You're fine, Fiona. What you did in there—'

'It's not just that. It's everything. I should have said when you first came. When I left Manchester, I wanted to change my life. I wanted to be different.'

He kisses me again. A kiss that could easily be paternal. Or ex-boyfriendy. A kiss which is intimate but also respectful of boundaries. Yet I think he's angling for more. I think if I turned my face up to his, turned my lips up to his, I could drink from that well as deep as I liked.

I'm tempted. Not just Fiona Grey, but me too. I feel a good old-fashioned desire tugging at me in this soft summer night. My once-a-month conjugal visits with Buzz feel as distant as fairy tales. I lean into Henderson, my head against his shoulder. Enjoying his presence, but keeping the barriers up.

No well-drinking for me tonight.

He's been holding his cigarette away from me during this, now takes one last drag and stubs it out. He's not really a smoker, I don't think. He's smoked barely half the cigarette and when he stubs it, he has an odd action, one which breaks the cigarette where the tobacco meets the filter. In the hostel,

228

someone would pick up the unsmoked tobacco for a roll-up. I can feel myself wanting to do the same.

'Fiona, I don't think you realise how much we depend on you. We've had other people doing what you do, but you're the only one who really gets it. The other day with Anna, when you had those disagreements with her, you were always right. We need that woman. We need you.'

'Sorry, Vic. But I've made up my mind. I do want to go home. I won't tell anyone about anything. I don't want to cause trouble.'

We argue a bit. He says he can't let me go home. That there's no one to take me. I say I can't face meeting all the people who were laughing at me this evening. Say I hate my clothes. That they make me feel like riff-raff amongst all those suits. The laughing stock.

'They weren't laughing *at* you . . .' he starts.

'They were. You know they were.'

'Look, they haven't met you yet. They don't know how good you are.'

'They'll still laugh. *Look* at me.'

'We can get you clothes.'

'You already did. You got me horrible polycotton tracksuit trousers that don't fit.'

Vic sighs. 'Look, give me a list of stuff you want. I'll get one of the girls to get it for you.'

He means one of the waitresses.

I don't give way too soon, and it takes another cigarette and another kiss on the dome of my head before he shifts from the step. When he does, he crosses the moonlit yard to the farmhouse. Comes back five minutes later with the waitress. Pen and paper.

I shoo Henderson away and go through stuff I want with the waitress. I know I'm not allowed to ask her what town we're near, and know Henderson will check, so I just say,

229

'There's a Gap in town is there?' and the girl, Nia, hesitates a moment, then says, Yes, she should think so.

We make a list. I want a dress, some tights, some smart shoes. Trousers. Skirt. Two or three different tops. I give my sizes. The dress, I say, has to be in petite. That the full size ones never fit me. I say I need something for smart, something for more relaxed.

Nia is helpful actually. Sounds like she used to work as a shop assistant. When we have a list, we OK it with Henderson. It'll be three or four hundred quid, I would guess, but separate a girl from her wardrobe and you pay the price. He accepts my request with one of those patient male sighs.

Nia goes.

Henderson says, 'Feel ready for tomorrow?'

'No.'

'You'll be fine. You'll be great, actually.'

'If anyone is horrible to me while I'm here, I'll walk out.'

Henderson gives me a look which I decode as meaning, 'If you walk out of here, I will kill you.' Perhaps there's also a whiff of, 'And I'd regret that, because I enjoyed our moment on the step.'

I say, 'Where are we anyway?'

He waves his hand at the night. 'Somewhere in the universe. Does it matter?'

'Not really.' I put my hands on his shoulder, in that intimate/not-intimate ex-girlfriend way, and give him a light kiss on his cheek. There's a long rip on his left hand cheek, ending with a flap of skin and some thickly clotted tissue, dark as ox-blood. My handiwork. 'Thank you for being nice to me.'

He rubs my arm and says goodnight.

I turn to go in. Henderson isn't about to follow. He's with the big boys in the farmhouse.

'Don't come out here again, please. We need you to stay in the barn. This evening was a one-off.'

I nod.

My submissive nod. My obedient one.

That's the thing about we battered women. Our 'stop' never really means 'stop'. The average victim of domestic violence suffers thirty assaults before she reports anything and that number is only a guess. It could easily be much more. Henderson's technique – hit then kiss – is the abuser's way to maintain control. And Fiona Grey is under control again. She's going to see out her time here, good as gold.

33

I sleep for ever, or it seems that way. Kureishi comes to me in my dreams, his darkened screaming, but there's something muffled about his presence this time. As though he's been muted. As though there's glass between him and me. That doesn't feel like a comfortable fact, though. It feels sinister, like when music plays softly in a horror film and the pretty teenager decides to explore the empty house. I can't find Hayley, though I do try.

When I wake up, I patter upstairs in my bathrobe. Geoff is around. A couple of Indians are watching a cricket match on TV.

I ask Geoff to sort me out some breakfast – eggs, orange juice, herbal tea – and ask him what time it is. After nine is the answer, which means I've slept almost ten hours. Fiona Griffiths never sleeps that long. Fiona Grey seldom does either.

Shower.

Eat.

Talk rubbish with Geoff, who seems nice, apart from the Glock, the handcuffs and the whole organised-crime thing.

I put on underwear and a clean T-shirt, but apart from that I don't get dressed, just stick to the bathrobe. My tracksuit trousers *are* horrible. Wrong size, torn, stained. And just horrible.

My neck feels sore from the blows I took last night. Also my arms ache down their whole length. It's not safe handcuffing people behind their backs. Certainly not if you're hitting them at the same time and yanking at their wrists. I stretch a bit, but not much. I'm not convinced it really helps.

Go back to my room and read speech therapy stuff.

Phonation is the term given to the vibration of the vocal folds. Sounds that involve the vibration of the vocal folds are said to be voiced. If there is no vocal fold vibration, the sounds are said to be unvoiced, or voiceless.

I sit there feeling my vocal cords vibrate when I say *ga-ga-ga* and *da-da-da*. Feel them not vibrate when I say *ka-ka-ka* and *ta-ta-ta*. The voiced and the voiceless.

I sit there, doing the exercises, concentrating on my sound production, when the door opens.

Henderson is there, holding two big bags from Gap.

'How's it going?' he asks, meaning the speech therapy.

'I like it. It'll suit me.'

'Good.'

I don't really know how Henderson sees the endgame. Does he plan to kill me, drop me in a river somewhere, wipe away a possible loose end? Or is the visa thing for real? Will he let me go?

Mostly, I think the latter. Murder sounds tidy, but it usually isn't. The crime brings massively resourced police investigations like nothing else. I think I'll get a lecture about the importance of keeping my mouth shut, but apart from that I'll be allowed to go.

Probably.

Henderson puts the bags on the bed. 'Clothes.'

I take a look. There's a grey dress, a nice tweed skirt, some jeans, a belt, a couple of smart shirts, two pairs of shoes, tights, some other bits. It's good. Better than Fiona Grey's own wardrobe. Probably better than mine, if I'm honest.

The sizes look right, but I won't know until I try stuff on.

'Thank you.'

'And look. I got you a present. This is from me.'

Henderson produces, with a flourish, a brown leather attaché case. There's a yellow legal notepad inside, a couple of pens, and a sharp pencil.

I'm speechless. It's one of the nicest presents anyone's ever given me.

'Is it OK?' he asks.

I nod. 'It's really nice.'

'Anna says you can use her make-up if you need any.' Then quickly adds, 'Not that you do. You look great.'

There's not a chance that Quintrell volunteered the use of her cosmetics, which means Henderson bullied her into it. Keeping me pliable is part of his job, certainly, but he's not merely a thug. The best criminals never are. They always have a little something extra. A touch of class.

'Thank you.'

I look at him. His right hand has grazed knuckles and there's a bruise over his right eye which I didn't put there.

'Your eye,' I say. 'That wasn't me.'

'No. It wasn't. I've had a long night.' His face twitches. 'I've not gone to bed yet.'

There's something open-ended in the way he says that. A memory of yesterday evening. Those kisses in the twilight.

I think that if I stood up now and approached, if I put my arms to him, touched his neck, we would be making love within the minute. I feel those tugs of lust eddying round the room, kicking up like dust devils.

My lust as much as his.

His mouth is slightly open.

I say, 'Vic, I don't think we should.'

'No.'

'I'd like to.'

'Same here.'

234

'Thanks for all this. Especially this.' I indicate the attaché case. 'It's really thoughtful.'

'You're welcome.'

He come close, lifts me, and kisses me. Kisses hard. Without consent. One of those kisses that reaches down to my feet.

I'm gasping when he pulls away, and not with outrage.

He says, 'Remember. You're good the way you are. Just be yourself and love yourself.'

The unexpectedness of the remark catches me off-guard momentarily. Then I realise what he's talking about. It's a slogan from the list I'd taped to my fridge door. Henderson must have remembered it from the last time he was in my room. The time he showed me the Kureishi murder video.

I say, 'They're good classes those. If you want me to sign you up . . .'

He grins.

Reaches for the attaché case and pulls out a sheet of A4 from an inside compartment I hadn't explored.

'Your agenda for the weekend,' he says.

It's a list of meetings, with times, attendees, draft topics. The heading on the list is strand two: product design. The attendees are marked by initials. I'm there as FG. Quintrell is there as AQ. There are other initials too, ones I don't recognise. There is no attendee marked as VH.

'Strand two? What are the other strands?'

Henderson considers before answering. The man is a walking, talking security screen. It would be the same whether he was making love to me or chopping my hands off. A coolly considered appraisal of risks and rewards.

The appraisal, in this case, comes up positive, and he says, 'Strand one is security. That's my specialist subject. Strand three is distribution. How we roll out the system when we have it. Strand four is finance. How the money moves around.'

'I never knew organised crime was so well organised.'

'It's that or jail, and I've promised myself never to end up in jail.' He checks his watch. 'Your first meeting is at twelve. I won't be there, but I'll see you around.'

'You took my watch. My only clock is Geoff and he's a bit too highly armed for my taste.'

Henderson shakes out the Gap bags over the bed. A watch falls out. Brown leather strap. Gold face. Not obviously tacky. He sets it to the correct time and tosses it to me.

'Your watch, ma'am.'

I put it on.

It's odd this. I'm still half naked. In T-shirt and bathrobe, yes, but that's still more naked than most things. Those eddies of lust have abated but still swirl around the room, snatching at ankles, trembling on the back of the neck.

I say, 'Vic?'

'Yes?'

'Sit down. You're a mess.'

He does.

I run warm water in the sink, wet a corner of the towel, wipe the cut on his knuckles, dab at the bruise over his eye. He's got a small mark on his jacket, blood from the look of it, and I kneel down, work at the mark until it's mostly gone. He's the sort of man who would have a monobrow if he didn't work at it, and I pluck away a couple of stray hairs.

'There,' I tell him, as I resettle his jacket and stand back.

'Thank you.' The possibility of another kiss blooms in the air between us, then vanishes. He says, 'Please follow the rules, by the way. Going outside yesterday, that needs to be an exception.'

'Yes, sir.' Then, standing back, by the daffodils, I murmur, 'You're a good kisser, Vic.'

'You too, Fi.' He uses the intimate version of my name instinctively. So naturally it takes me a moment to realise.

'Maybe sometime before you head off to Kiwi-land, we could go away somewhere and forget about being sensible.'

I nod. What I say is, 'Maybe one day I'll fall for a good guy. It would make life easier.'

Henderson goes for the door, half opens it, says, 'Nah. Good guys are boring.' Leaves.

I get dressed. Grey dress with black velvet at the neck and on the sleeves. Little brown belt. Dark tights and clicky heels. Attaché case.

I do go next door to Quintrell's room. She's there, and lets me use her make-up without even being too grumpy about it. I'm not great with make-up, but there's a cut over my lip which looks better for some concealer. Quintrell even helps me apply it.

I say, 'I don't want to fight you, Anna.'

'I know.'

'Can we maybe start again? As if nothing had ever happened.'

'OK. Yes. OK.'

She's not very communicative, but there's a little rush of emotion in her face. I can't read it. She probably finds all this difficult too. Henderson is core Tinker. Quintrell is no more than a hired hand. A temporary asset, like me.

I think we ought to hug or something like that. Seal the deal. But Quintrell remains pulled back and withdrawn. So I just say, 'Brilliant, thank you.'

She smiles. It's not a natural one, but effort counts for something too. She still doesn't like me but at least we can be temporary allies.

Back in my room, I take the flake of rock I took from the step yesterday and crumble it up. Little red particles of grit. Meaningless to me, but eloquent enough under a microscope. I scatter the grit through my clothes. A pinch goes into the crack between the wall of my shoe and the insole. A smear gets rubbed into the hem of a blue shirt, the seam of my dress. I distribute the stuff around till it's all gone. Effectively invisible.

Then I start to work on the towel that I used on Henderson's blood marks. Some of the blood is his, but maybe not all of it. I take a bloodied thread from the towel and drop it into the inside seam of the pocket on my white shirt. A bit of lint, no more. Take the eyebrow hairs I plucked and put them into a jeans pocket. Although Henderson's eye was bruised, the skin wasn't broken, yet there was something – I think blood – matting the eyebrows.

Then wash the towel. Hang it out. Tidy my tiny room.

I like these small spaces. They swaddle me. I find them soothing.

I don't think about Quintrell much. She's a fraudster and a fool, but she's not a murderer and she's not the progenitor of this scheme. We have enough evidence on her to convict her for all that she's done.

Henderson, though, he's a different matter. I think about him and me, about the kiss we had and the dust devils we sought to ignore. Most of all, I think about what I said to him. *Maybe one day I'll fall for a good guy.* That was a good Fiona Grey-ish thing to say. That poor lass has had few enough good men in her forlorn little life and the bad guys keep barging their way in.

But me? I'm engaged to a handsome police sergeant, who loves me and is patient with me. Who has a perfect service record, in the police and in the army. Who is stable, calm and kind. Who is honourable by instinct and by belief. Who is tall and strong and (if you happen to like freckles) is sandily handsome. I *have* fallen for a good guy, haven't I? Fallen hard and fallen well.

But I don't know if it was just Fiona Grey making that comment about good guys or if it was me too. And if it was me too, what sense can I make of it? I've always been attracted to Buzz. Always thought, *God, I'm lucky that this man feels this way about me.* Thought, *The love of Buzz and my family are the best things in my life, bar nothing. They're the reasons I make it through the day.*

I suspect I'm probably just experiencing what most undercover officers go through, sooner or later on assignment. The madness of isolation. A desire for intimate contact, because intimacy feels like an adequate substitute for truth. If I did have sex with Henderson, I wouldn't even quite count it as infidelity. It would be just one of those things. An operational exigency.

At five to twelve, there's a tap at my door. Quintrell is there: smart green dress, black jacket, dark tights, heels. She says, 'Ready?' and we walk upstairs together.

34

Those meetings! Like nothing else I've ever encountered. Perhaps it's always like this in the private sector. The suits. The agendas. The two types of bottled water and the thermoses of hot drinks.

There are eight of us in total. Ramesh has three colleagues with him, but he is clearly the most senior. All four speak good English. I know nothing about IT, but clearly these guys do. Clear too that they have further programmers back in Bangalore. We're seeing the gleam of helmets, not the entire battle force.

Then there are two British guys. One, a Londoner, who calls himself Terry. Late thirties, early forties. Short hair, black shirt, a suit which probably cost a lot of money, and a gold watch which is almost certainly some expensive branded thing. Then we are also, occasionally, graced with the presence of James Wyatt. He calls himself Phil but I recognise him from the surveillance photos on our system. He tells us that he is mostly on the finance side. That he's just here to chip in, if he can help. That he doesn't understand all the 'techie stuff'.

He pretends to be modest, but really his intention is to emphasise that he's in *finance*, a holy land altogether higher and finer than the swamplands of IT. What he would think of Fiona Grey's habitat of payroll clerking and homeless shelters, I can't even imagine. He wears a striped blue shirt with an all-white collar. He has a handkerchief that matches his tie. I think, *Fuck you too, Jimmy boy.* Think how well that tie-and-hanky combo will go down in a Category A all-male clink. *And fuck you too.*

Ramesh and gang are the programmers-in-chief. Terry is there to manage and direct. 'Specify, program, beta-launch, full launch. And test, test, test, test.' Terry's phrase. As far as I can tell we're mid beta-launch. Those nineteen payroll accounts which I've been monitoring are the dummy run. Something much bigger lies beyond them.

Quintrell and I hear endless talk about field selection, dummy classes, remote users, filter value resets, UI objects, array correlations, and pagination widgets. People say things to each other like, 'but if the MySQL data is firewalled, we might have to dehash the passwords.' There's are occasionally little linguistic misunderstandings between the Indian and British sides of the room, but Ramesh – or Ram, as everyone calls him – normally grasps these things first, then explains whatever it is rapidly to his colleagues in whatever language it is they speak. Not Hindi, I think. I don't think Hindi goes that far south, so maybe Tamil or Kannada or some language I've never heard of.

Quintrell doesn't understand the IT talk any more than I do. We just let it wash by us, picnickers on the riverbank. But often enough, Terry or Ram will request clarification of something. How does HMRC handle maternity leave, if notification of that leave is delayed for some reason? If insufficient tax has been paid, is the amount owing recouped as a one-off thing or via the next year's tax coding? And precisely when are PAYE coding notices sent out and who specifically receives them?

Quintrell has her answer. I have mine. But we work together. She'll say something like, 'Well, the technically correct answer here would be . . .' And I say things like, 'Anna's absolutely right of course, but I suppose that in practice . . .'

We sit side by side, support each other's answers, and pour

water for each other. Although my first appearance arouses a prickle of remembered laughter, that soon dissipates under the pressure of work and, perhaps, my more businesslike appearance. Before long, Ram accepts me as part of the team, every bit as important as Quintrell herself. He calls us 'our lady experts' and, twice, 'our beautiful lady experts'. That sounds creepy, but he means it courteously, and neither Quintrell nor I are in the mood to be all feminist about these things, so we just do our best to be beautiful and expert all at once, and Quintrell at least does a good job on both fronts. She has lovely hair and good skin.

From time to time, Henderson enters the room, and just lounges around on one of the chairs at the side. If it's not him, it's usually Geoff. And if it's neither of those two, then it is indeed the man calling himself Allan Wiley. All three men are clearly part of the security group, but it seems to me that Henderson is the boss of this little unit.

I wonder if there are more of them than just these three. I'm thinking yes.

During our meetings, it's rare that Henderson or either of the others interjects, but when they do, it's always with a reminder about avoiding attention. At one point, a particular conversation led to one of the Indian guys saying, 'Yes, but ninety-nine point something of data returns are going to look fine. We'll get one or two weird results, that's all.' Henderson, who was in the room at the time, barked, 'That's exactly what we can't have. No weird results ever. That's the kind of thing that generates a call back to the software vendors, which we absolutely have to avoid.'

That line – 'no weird results ever' – becomes our slogan. A good slogan too. An important one. Because our aim, which I now understand properly for the first time, is breathtakingly audacious.

The family of software packages we're working with – Total

Payroll Solutions, or TPS – is the most widely used payroll system in the UK and, by far, the one most used by large corporations. Terry tells us that, in rough terms, the wages and salaries paid via TPS amount to about £170 billion. 'At least that,' he says. 'At least.'

That money has to be split up amongst millions of different employees, has to be apportioned out in tax and national insurance and everything else. Money that gets paid out, on time, in the correct amounts, all across the country. It's money that families depend on. The lifeblood of the economy, no less.

Henderson and his merry men aim to subvert that happy system. They aim to distribute a version of the software that almost exactly replicates the real thing, but which introduces what Terry and Ram are calling a 'skim'. If a company uses the software Ram and his guys are producing, they will see a tax bill that is very slightly too high. HMRC will see one that is very slightly too low. The payment system built into the software will skim the difference. The amount of the skim hasn't yet been finally settled, but it looks likely to be as little as one half of one tenth of one per cent of total payroll.

A skim that tiny might sound too small to be worth bothering with, but apply that to nigh on two hundred billion and you're talking almost a hundred million pounds. That's a hundred million *per annum*, a cool two million a week.

How long would it take a company to notice that it was being diddled? I'm not sure. I'm not an auditor and don't have that kind of experience. But I do know that my team at Western Vale would never spot it. We look for obvious mistakes not tiny little rounding errors. My old superstore buddy, Sir Kevin the Bold of Swindon, said the same thing. It took his firm eighteen months to notice a major error and Kevin was neither idle nor incompetent.

Nor do I think the taxman would notice the missing

money. To a weirdly huge degree, the British system operates on trust. If a company's numbers *look* like they're in order, HMRC seldom carries out any major investigation. And if they do investigate, they're looking for major fraud or gross incompetence. HMRC just doesn't have the resources to tease out a half of a tenth of a one per cent error in the data. It doesn't have the time, the staff or even the desire. Yet when you think about it, the crime being contemplated is breathtaking. So audacious, yet so simple in design and concept that you simply have to stand back and applaud its creators.

Applaud, then arrest them.

The system will also have what Terry calls a 'Fuck It button'. Basically, if it looks like the scam is busted, there'll be a feature which will allow a remote user to ramp the skim up to a full hundred per cent of all salary and taxes due. There's no way that either HMRC or any company would fail to notice that kind of rip-off. Any half-alert corporate would just rip the plug out of their central server and suspend all payments until the problem was identified and solved. But even if you had just a day or two in between hitting the Fuck It button and getting closed down completely, the amount of money you could steal in that time could easily be in eight digits. Maybe nine.

The hundred million pound heist.

I'm looking at the *Mona Lisa* of theft. The *Hamlet*. The Beethoven's Ninth.

I remember our original planning meeting at Cathays. The one with Jackson, Brattenbury, the DCI from Devon and Cornwall, and the little twerp from the SFO. The SFO guy said, 'We're not really *equipped* to handle frauds of less than a million or so.' He said, 'We have to *ask*, is this case likely to be of *widespread* public concern?'

Stupid fucker.

Stupid arrogant SFO fucker.

I think Kureishi was lucky to last as long as he did. I think *I've* been lucky, for that matter. With stakes like this, lives look cheap. This fraud, if it comes to fruition, will be by far the largest ever executed in Britain. Probably the world.

Our beautiful lady experts.

Please don't be concerned.

The little mystery of my portfolio of names – the twenty-nine fake names, the nineteen real ones – is also solved. The twenty-nine fake names were simply a way to generate enough money to cover this group's operating expenses. Not just the money I helped steal, but the money stolen by the various other payroll moles. All that was simply a way to raise the working capital. A temporary, regrettable expedient.

The nineteen other names were, however, the more important ones. Although in those cases there were real employees, drawing real salaries and paying real taxes, their payslips and so on were being generated not by the *real* version of the TPS software, but by Tinker's rip-off version. I needed to monitor the results so that any errors in the software could be immediately checked and corrected.

I'm finally seeing the full scale of the crime whose gathering shadow I've been living in for so long. Finally understanding who and what we're up against. I also realise that if my colleagues and I ever allow Henderson and friends to hit their Fuck It button, we'll be guilty of permitting the greatest crime on earth to take place under our noses. We have to let things run far enough that we can round up the perpetrators, but not so far that they can launch their attack. Like watching terrorists. The same delicate clockwork of risk.

The work is intense, and the schedule relentless. We work from twelve to two, break for sandwiches. Then two-thirty to five. Break for tea and biscuits. Then five-thirty to eight. The group had been running for three hours before Quintrell and I joined it.

Because our group is the largest one, we get the biggest and nicest room: the same one in which I caused a scene yesterday. When I'm bored by the talk of dummy classes and UI objects, I gaze around. That raw oak, stone wall, copper lamp thing is nice. Quietly expensive. Tasteful.

But there are other groups running elsewhere. There's one upstairs, because people come and go in the gallery above our heads. Sometimes stand there talking quietly and casting glances down at us. That's the 'distribution' group, I think. At times, one or two of Ram's boys go to join the distribution people upstairs, because product design and distribution need to be carefully coordinated.

I don't see anything of the finance and security meetings. I think they take place in the farmhouse. I'm pretty sure that my earlier suspicion is correct: that only the those in the innermost circle are allowed into the farmhouse.

And who is in the inner group? The million dollar question.

The annoying thing is that I probably saw them. I think they were here, in this room, yesterday: the handful of white faces who left the room when I burst in. The people whose absence was important enough that Henderson was checking that they were vacating even when I was ripping chunks out of his hair and ripping grooves down the side of his face.

I wonder if Henderson was worried that I might recognise them from somewhere. Or if it was just his instinct for perfect security at all times.

Could be the latter. Could be the former.

The only way to find out is to break into the farmhouse, but I seriously doubt my ability to do that and exit alive.

If I had Lev here, and enough weapons, we might chance it, but I don't have Lev, I don't have a weapon and I've no idea about the layout of the farm and farmhouse.

I notice that Geoff or Allan are always lingering at the top of the stairs, in easy view of the barn door, which is always locked and is released only by a six-digit code entered in a keypad to the side. Both men are always armed. Both trim enough too. Short-haired, alert, plenty of muscle. Military types, by the look of them, and comfortable with those handguns. The shutters over the big barn windows are bolted and padlocked.

I can forget about trying to get out of the farmhouse alive. Truth is, I probably wouldn't be able to get out of the barn.

The first day seems long, but we find a rhythm.

Quintrell and I are essential in terms of determining exactly what the software system needs to deliver, but we add nothing of value to the business of figuring out how to make it do so. Increasingly, therefore, after that long first day, we end up spending time in our bedrooms or in the common room, available to be called on as required. Neither of us watch TV all that much. We ask Geoff if he can get books or magazines for us. He can't, but Henderson comes over from the farmhouse with a stack of board games, and Quintrell and I find ourselves playing an endless game of Monopoly. Whenever one of us has too much money, we give it back to the bank or to the other. Whenever the board is getting too built up, we have a property clearance session, and tear down houses and hotels, foreclose on railways and utilities, strip the board back to something like its original nakedness.

I go to jail six times on my first day. After that I lose count.

Other people – Terry, Wyatt, Geoff, Henderson, and not Ram, but each of his colleagues – end up joining us as guests from time to time. I'm the boot. Quintrell is the racing car. Quintrell is moderately competitive. The Indians are all keen to amass huge fortunes, Terry too. Wyatt is too snobby to play for long. Geoff is too busy nursing his Glock to pay much attention and ends up giving money away and playing badly. Allan takes the game seriously. He's sporting one of those close-trimmed beards that circles his mouth only, and he rubs his chin as he worries whether it would be prudent to invest in a third house on Regent Street.

I try quite hard, I really do, but somehow always mismanage things and am always teetering on the edge of bankruptcy. Terry, who does well, gives me those orange and pink £100 and £500 notes to tide me over. He enjoys the munificence.

When I get bored, I pace around, up and down, side to side.

My arms get better, but my neck still aches.

And when I'm not being a beautiful lady expert, or playing Monopoly, or pacing around, or eating sandwiches or soup with the others in the main room upstairs, I lie on the bed in my room, reading my speech therapy books. When Henderson asks me how I'm getting on, I make him put his fingers on his larynx and tell him about phonation. I say 'bilabial plosive', and it almost sounds as if I know what I'm talking about.

After lunch on day five, a Sunday, Ram calls our group together and goes through a one hundred and twenty point checklist of items. I realise, to my surprise, that we've covered them all. There are still further matters – issues of technical design, nothing to do with Quintrell or myself – to be covered, but they don't need an accountant or a payroll clerk. Terry, discussing the matter with Ram, says to Henderson, 'No, Vic, we don't need them any more. I think we're done.'

Henderson looks at us, smiles, says, 'Time to go home.'

I put my stuff in a plastic bin liner that Geoff finds for me. Quintrell emerges from her room, neat as ever, towing her small suitcase, airport-style, behind her.

We go upstairs. Say goodbye to people. To Ram and his cohorts, to Terry and Wyatt. To Allan and Geoff. To those people from the 'distribution team' that we've got to know a bit in the course of our stay.

Henderson says, 'OK, Fiona, please.' A sentence which doesn't mean anything at all, except that he holds out eye-mask and hood, and in the moment when I see them in his hands, I experience a terror as clean and pure as any feeling I've ever known. I don't know if I say anything. I know I reach out my hand: this lady expert is going to cooperate with her gaoler and her seducer until her final breath. But my body has a reaction that simply bypasses my mind. Bypasses any sense of control, or will, or any number of secret identities.

I take the eye-mask, but I am trembling too much to pull it over my eyes.

We don't need them any more. I think we're done.

That could mean, 'Thank you for a fine job of work, now enjoy a well-earned rest.' Or it could mean, 'Kill the bitches.' Terry's eyes didn't flicker as he said what he said, but Henderson's eyes probably didn't flicker as he hacked Kureishi's hands off.

I tremble so much that it takes Henderson's fierce grip to keep me from falling.

He says, with that terrifying, controlled patience of his, 'We're taking you home. Nothing is going to happen to you. It's a routine security precaution.'

He puts the eye-mask on. His hands are gentle, but the compulsion is total.

'Head forward, please.'

I lean forward. I can feel my hair sliding either side of my neck. Baring it.

Will it be bullet or billhook? The strangler's rope or the hangman's noose?

I am still trembling.

The hood slides over my head. I keep my head bent as the cord is tied. Henderson keeps the cord fairly loose, but I can still feel its pressure on my throat as he pulls it tight.

The eye-mask alone is enough to block all light, but it's not secure. The hood doesn't block as much light, but prevents me from tampering with the eye-mask.

'There. You can put your head up.'

I straighten.

I am a beautiful lady expert in a black executioner's hood. My breaths are billows that completely fill this little space. Each time I inhale, folds of black cotton press like moth wings on my mouth.

I hear Henderson pick up my bin liner of stuff. He takes me and it to the car. My legs feel so weak, I feel at risk of falling and Henderson's hand is a crutch as much as a guide.

As he slots me into my seat, I murmur, 'Sorry, Vic.'

He says, 'That's OK. You're doing fine.'

I nod.

I don't disbelieve him, but my body has its own logic. I am still trembling.

Henderson puts my seat belt on. Reaching across me to clip me in. I can feel the weight of his body as he leans across me. I lean my hood forward until I can feel the fabric crumple against the crook of his neck. The hump of his shoulder under my lips.

'You're not making this easier,' he says mildly, as he tries to buckle me in.

I lean in to him fully. Rest against him. Somewhere beside us in the car, there is a swirl of dust and an eddy of oven-hot air.

He allows this to continue a moment or two, then pushes me back against my seat. Buckles me in.

'What music do you want?'

'Please, Vic, no headphones. Please.'

After a moment, 'OK.'

He goes to get Quintrell. She stumbles as she gets in beside me. Henderson talks her through it.

I hadn't realised it on the way here, but she's blindfolded too. Not hooded necessarily – she might be trusted enough by now not to remove an eye-mask – but she has no more idea of where we are than I have. I'm guessing Ram and the others are in the same position. Perhaps it's only the members of the elite 'security strand' who are privileged with this knowledge.

Henderson closes the door on Quintrell. My door is still open. He comes round to close it, but as he does so, I slip the catch on my seat belt. 'Whoops.'

Henderson reaches in to do me up again, then changes his mind. Takes my head in his hands and kisses me hard, through the cotton, on my lips. I kiss back. Hard. Pull his head against mine, my nails against his scalp. He has one hand on my left breast, the other on my neck.

The cotton round my mouth is soaking wet. My kisses from the inside meeting his from the outside.

Quintrell says, 'We're OK, are we?'

Henderson, pulling away, says, 'Yes.' He's panting slightly. I'm panting hard.

He strokes my breast, leans down to kiss it, bites gently, then buckles me in again.

I'm ridiculously aroused. Still frightened too. But it's hard to tell. I think there's a point at which the two feelings merge. It's the sort of thing I'd normally ask someone, but I can tell that wouldn't be clever. Instead, I touch the wet cloth against my upper lip and let my breathing slowly calm.

We drive off.

Henderson puts the radio on fairly loud for the first twenty minutes. Listening hard in the gaps and silences, I can't hear anything unusual. I guess the music and headphones on the way here were simply a tool to disorient me even further. Perhaps also guard against any conversational indiscretions between Quintrell and Henderson. After twenty minutes, Henderson asks if we want more music or silence. Quintrell and I both opt for silence.

I'm constantly impressed by the depth of security

precautions these guys take. Nothing is too much trouble. No risk too small to eliminate.

I wonder at my behaviour with Henderson.

I *am* attracted to him. Violently so. I wasn't the first time I met him, but these things can creep up on you. They do on me, anyway.

Sexual attraction isn't love, of course. Henderson is a murderer and a thief, who belongs in jail. But it's disconcerting to find myself almost uncontrollably in lust with this man, when I find it hard even to imagine my feelings for Buzz.

My darling Buzz seems of a different world. In this one, he's as real as a painted soldier. A toy.

And even as I press the cloth of my hood against my lip, breathe this cottony air still humid with those kisses, I realise that I have to see Buzz soon. Spend a weekend with him. Find those feelings I used to have. Not just those sweet high notes of love and respect, but the deep slow bass of the bedroom.

Brattenbury will worry about the operational implications, but I don't want to be like the DCI who oversaw my undercover training course. Fifty-four and trying to rebuild the ruins of a family. If Brattenbury wants his raggedy wondergirl to go on working for him, he'll have to compromise.

Meantime, as the car rolls on towards wherever Henderson is taking us, I try to think of myself in a wedding dress. Imagine the different bits of the ceremony. Myself, at the back of the church. Head in a cloud of white veil, a frill of bridesmaids behind. Stone columns and an altar window. The organ. Buzz willing me towards him. A press of gazes.

I try to imagine this. Try to make it real.

I pick threads from the car seat with my fingernail. Slip my shoe off and rub my stockinged foot into the tiny nylon curls of the floor carpet.

The car travels on, either to Cardiff or to death.

35

Cardiff, not death.

We switch cars in the car park as before. Henderson drives a little further, then releases me from my hood and mask. He drives Quintrell home, collects my bag of clothes. I stare out at the passing streets, almost overwhelmed by their ordinary beauty. Tidy gardens and Sunday strollers. A man repainting his window frames. The fluttering shade of plane trees.

I love all of it. The city boozers. The dead hotels. The shops selling cheap holidays or sugary doughnuts. I love it all.

When Henderson stops outside my building, he says, 'I could come up.' His voice is rough.

'You've got to get back, haven't you?'

'Yes.'

I'm torn between a stupid lust and a model of how I ought to behave. A model whose origin and purpose I cannot for the moment remember.

For a moment, we stand on the street. Facing each other, wanting each other, but frozen with indecision.

I realise that, for Henderson, this is partly a security issue. He isn't meant to take any action which might jeopardise his judgement. Sex with me would be an unnecessary risk.

I say, 'Before I go to New Zealand, will you take me away somewhere? Just you and me.'

'Yes.'

'No threats. No masks. No guns. No bollocks.'

'Yes.'

I pick up my two bin liners of clothes: the one from the barn and the one from Quintrell's house. Those and my fancy new attaché case. 'Have a good trip back.'

He kisses his fore- and index fingers. Touches them against my mouth. 'See you soon, Fi.'

He gets into his BMW and glides off. It's five o'clock on Wednesday afternoon. I've got a full day of work tomorrow.

First though, I go into town. To the hostel. They've got laundry rooms in the basement, and I prefer using them to the launderette.

I clean the stuff that needs cleaning, but make a package of the stuff I want forensically examined. Write a note for 'Adrian Boothby'. Leave the package and the note with Abs. Call Brattenbury on his mobile, but I go through to voicemail and leave a message. Get some food.

Gary is around. We go outside for a fag, and he says, 'I found your psycho guy,' meaning Henderson. He tells me that the guy uses an alternative health centre in the city centre, not far from where the CCTV lost him off the Hayes.

'It was definitely him,' says Gary. 'Do you want me to hurt him? I can if you want.'

'No, thanks. I just wanted to know how to find him.'

We smoke two ciggies, talk rubbish, share a joint.

Home.

In these city streets, Buzz is already starting to seem more real. Henderson is not unreal exactly, but more distant. There's a bridal shop near my room, a place of ivory silk and slim mannequins. Beaded bodices and white hands clasped over artificial flowers. I stare in through the windows, a fish seeking entry to the aquarium.

Before going to bed, I retrieve my iPad, log in to Tinker.

There's only one bit of news really, but it's a biggie.

Roy Williams, the undercover officer whose role was only

ever to act as a red herring, whose role was only ever to improve my cover and protection, has been abducted.

Had his briefing with Brattenbury as normal on Saturday. Raised nothing unusual. Used none of his emergency codes. Went home, cooked something and ate, then left the flat again, probably for the pub. He never turned up. Responds to none of his numbers. His car is parked in its normal place. No body has been found. A typed note, posted to his flat, read simply, PLEASE SUSPEND ANY CURRENT INVESTIGATIONS. IF YOU DO SO, MR 'PRYCE' WILL BE RETURNED UNHARMED BY CHRISTMAS.

Pryce: the name Roy used for his legend.

We have no clue as to what exact action provoked the abduction. The gradual closing down of Kureishi's frauds? Some bit of operational inattention by Roy himself? A crude piece of surveillance by Brattenbury's men which revealed too much of SOCA's interest in all this? Or Tinker's relentless concern for security taking one more logical step?

We don't know and won't know, but it puts us in a vastly difficult situation. Up till now, if we'd wanted to close down Tinker, we could simply have done so. Arrested all known participants. Alerted the company behind the real TPS software. Alerted every major payroll department in the land. We might not have secured all the arrests we wanted – nor all the *intelligence*, in SOCA's inevitable phrase – but by God we could smash the ring.

We can't do that now. Not in the same way. Any move we make now will be made with the acute awareness that Roy's life hangs in the balance.

Roy's life, and maybe mine – but it's Roy that I think about. He's thirty-seven years old and, like me, never wanted a long-duration undercover role. I can't imagine what Katie must be feeling. That's a literal truth in my case – I'm not good at those most ordinary human feelings – but I know it won't be good. Her distress must be beyond measure. And their daughter too. What do you say to a two-year-old? When *is* Daddy coming home?

Please don't be concerned.

These thoughts don't help, so I turn to something that might: Gary's news about Henderson. The alternative health place offers acupuncture, osteopathy, homeopathy, reiki, psychotherapy, and a variety of beauty treatments. Does Henderson have a joint problem? Maybe. Do men with a deep involvement in organised crime go in for acupuncture or reiki or psychotherapy? I doubt it, but what do I know? Was Henderson evading surveillance that day in order to protect his visit to that health centre? Or was it just one of those things? A cancelled meeting, and a massage and a meal out instead?

I send an email to Brattenbury, who'll want to get the place under surveillance. I'd like to do more, but time is short and other things come first.

Stop work at midnight, hoping for sleep, but nothing much comes to me except Kureishi's violent haunting. That, and Hayley Morgan's frail sadness.

36

The next steps follow rapidly. Follow as I assume they must.

My Thursday morning cleaning shift goes fine. Everything as normal. Lowri hoovers and complains about her allergies. I do the bins and the bathrooms, and every time I clean a mirror, I see Katie Williams. China-blue eyes and disbelief.

At eight thirty, I get changed. Croissant for breakfast. Get to Western Vale just after nine.

I've been away a bit recently – a two week 'illness' when I was in London with Amina and a few days 'holiday' just now – so I've a lot to catch up with. Emails and letters. Queries and forms.

I try to focus, but find it hard. I'm kissing Henderson through black cotton. Seeing Katie Williams in the mirror. Watching Kureishi's anguished face as his hands tumble from his arms.

At nine thirty, I research ways to destroy a computer's hard drive. There's a free program, DBAN, which promises to wipe a hard drive beyond the possibility of recovery. I download the software. Resume work.

At eleven o'clock, I get a cup of peppermint tea. The kitchenette has a view out over the junction where Adam Street meets the A4234. There is a police car below. Parked. Lights lazily flashing. It's joined by a second. Officers talking on the radio.

I go to my desk, change my black office shoes for the

training shoes I wear when I'm cleaning. Go back to the window. The cars are still there. One officer leaning on his vehicle. No one else.

I get my coat from the rack. Take anything personal from my desk and put it in my bag. Start the DBAN disk. Get it so that I just have to hit enter to start wiping my hard drive. Go over to Zara Jones in accounts, who doesn't particularly like me but whose desk has a good view of the lift lobby.

An elevator stops. Six uniformed police emerge. A crackle of radios, viewed through glass.

I say to Zara, 'Someone's got visitors.' Leave her and go to my desk.

Take my coat and bag. Start the procedure that wipes the hard drive. Then take the back stairs that lead down to the ground floor.

As I go down, I can see the black and white of a police officer's arm coming up. Radio noise.

I come off the stairs at the second floor. Claims Processing. Linger there until I can see officers ascend beyond me. Then back onto the stairs and quickly down. Into the lobby.

I fumble my security pass, then get it to work. The glass turnstile opens, and I make for the street. A security guard shouts 'Hey.'

I run.

Burst through the doors. Onto Adam Street. Head for Bute Terrace. I think if I get to the pedestrianised Hayes, I stand a chance of evading pursuit.

Sirens yowl behind me. I turn up Mary Ann Street, but a car comes screaming into it from higher up. I bet the lads are loving it. City centre chases are always the best.

I skip sideways into the Park Inn Hotel. A modern thing, like an ocean liner erupting from a tower block.

Inside, a huge white atrium. Modern bar. Mirrors. Red carpet on white tiles. A few people around: businessmen drinking coffee, reception staff. I try to look like them: a busy person, not a fugitive.

Head for the lifts. Hit the button.

But I'm too late. I was seen entering and a couple of coppers burst into the lobby. They see me and yell, 'Police! Stop!'

I slam the lift button in frustration at its slowness. Run for the stairs. There's a potted palm behind me and I tip it over as I pass. Hear one of the officers swear as he tangles with it.

I think I've made the stairs, but I'm wrong. One of my pursuers catches up. Slams into me, like a rugby back defending his try line. The wall and floor take it in turns to hit me with chunks of tile and plasterwork.

I say, 'Fuck off, fuck *off*!' Kick out. Bite something. A thumb, I think.

A pair of huge hands puts my wrists into handcuffs. The rigid sort, which I don't like. I kick again, but the ratchet bars tighten till the cuffs are secure even on my little wrists.

There are four policemen around me now. One is reading me my rights. Another is sucking his thumb. They're all wary of my legs.

They walk me out to the waiting squad car.

One of the coppers says, 'Now if you calm down, we'll take the restraints off.'

I say, 'Fuck off, I haven't done anything.'

He says, 'Well then, we'll go and talk about it. And if you haven't done anything, then—'

I elbow him in the side and try to grab the pouch that has keys to the cuffs.

I don't get anywhere, but the officers exchange glances and bundle me into the car, cuffs and all. In England and Wales, arrest is primarily a symbolic act. Wherever possible, 'arrest' is made simply by a police officer placing a hand on the suspect's shoulder, taking emblematic control of that person's freedom. If physical control – handcuffs, for example – is required, then it's applied to the minimum degree possible and for the shortest possible time. Chokeholds and the like are strictly forbidden. The use of cuffs on women and minors is regarded as inappropriate in almost all situations.

As ever, I like to be the exception.

When we get to the custody suite – down on Cardiff Bay, modern facility, all very fancy – they offer again to take the cuffs off. They make it sound as if they want to do me a favour, but the truth is that any half-awake custody sergeant would demand an explanation if he saw four bulky male officers escort a young woman inside, wearing restraints. I act badly enough, however, that the restraints stay on.

As I'm being booked in, I see Quintrell being processed too. No cuffs for her. She's in a blue and white summer dress, with matching shoes. She catches my eye, but we keep our faces closed. I can feel a bruise rising on my forehead where the floor hit me.

Custody processing isn't quick. Because I received some injuries in the arrest process, those things need to be evaluated by a medical professional. The arresting officers have to make a statement of their arrest and restraint techniques. I'm evaluated for my likelihood of self-harm and my shoelaces, belt, bra and tights are removed as a precaution. The female custody officer who removes these things tells me I can have them back if my risk-assessment changes. She offers me a hygiene pack, which I take. Because records show that Fiona Grey has been in custody before, in Manchester, it takes some time to access both national and local intelligence systems.

The lighting in the examination room is fierce and I have a swelling headache. I ask for, and receive, aspirin.

I have a brief interview with the duty solicitor. She seems like a nice woman – Barbara, mumsy, keen to help. I tell her to fuck off.

Then sit without speaking for ten minutes.

Then we're done.

At two fifteen, I'm taken to an interview room, a big one. Painted in those awful green-grey and cream colours that would make most people confess to anything, just for a change of decor.

DCI Jackson is there. And Mervyn Rogers, a good friend of mine from Major Crime. Also Brattenbury and Susan Knowles. And a forensics guy, Ryan, who I've had some dealings with in the past.

Jackson pumps my hand. Was quite close to giving me a hug, I think. Brattenbury too. Susan Knowles kisses me and says, '*Fiona!*' There is cake on the table – chocolate – and a plate of lasagne.

'Tuck in,' Jackson says. 'You must be starving.'

I'm not starving. I had something to eat six hours ago and I never eat much for lunch. But I know why they chose lasagne: Buzz once asked me what my favourite food was, because he wanted to cook something special. I've no idea what my favourite food is, so I said lasagne, because I thought I had to say something. So Buzz always cooks lasagne when he wants to be extra nice and Jackson would have asked Buzz what I'd most want, and Buzz would have said lasagne and chocolate cake, which I do certainly like.

I eat a bit.

Brattenbury says, 'You know about Roy?'

'Yes.'

'I'm sorry about not giving you more notice of this' – he means my arrest – 'but we had to get you out. We couldn't risk losing two officers.'

'I know,' I say, avoiding the question of whether I agree or not.

'Taking Quintrell at the same time: it's the perfect cover.'

I nod.

'The story is that we kept an eye on the Western Vale

261

payroll system after the arrest of Ellen Keith. We realised that the fraud was being perpetuated. Identified you as the perpetrator. Followed you to Quintrell's house. Uncovered her past. Figured out that you and she were in collusion. Secured audio surveillance on her house. Heard everything. Ba-ba-boom.'

'Have you arrested Henderson?'

'No. We're going to play dumb. We've got his voice on the tapes, of course, but we're going to treat him just as "Unidentified Male". When we interrogate Quintrell, we'll make it seem like getting an identification on him will be a major purpose of our inquiries. But we'd rather have him loose, so we can go on watching him. We only brought Quintrell in so we could get you out.'

'I understand.'

If Brattenbury was expecting me to be more gushing about my rescue, he manages his disappointment with nothing more than a micro-pause. He moves on to thank me for the package I left for him at the hostel. Ryan, the forensics guy, tells me that the blood on Henderson's clothing and eyebrow has been identified as belonging to Roy Williams. I'd guessed as much, but it's good to have it confirmed.

'How's Katie?' I ask.

Jackson says, 'Not good. Not at all good.'

'I could see her later, maybe. If that would help.'

'Yes, it might. Let's see.'

We talk business. Brattenbury's team realised fairly quickly that the entire Heathrow conference thing was just a blind. SCO19 were stood down, but by that point they had no idea where I was, where Quintrell was, where anyone was.

'We were very frightened for you,' says Brattenbury simply. 'Especially after Roy.'

'I don't think they've killed Roy. He's no use to them dead.'

'I agree, but still . . .'

He doesn't need to finish that sentence. Williams's life is in acute danger. We all know it. We sit for a moment in a ticking silence.

But silence doesn't help. Working does. I tell them all about the barn, the farmhouse, the computer project. I tell them about Ram and Terry and Phil and Geoff. Tell them about the Fuck It button. The button that would allow them to steal one hundred per cent of all payroll payments coming from all companies using the system.

The biggest theft in the world.

Jackson is visibly shocked, but also impressed. We all are. You can't be a police officer and not admire criminality at its most talented and audacious. These things are a privilege to witness.

I sketch out what I see now of Tinker's organisation. The full list is way longer than we'd ever imagined. And our gathering belief that we had identified most of the gang participants is proving to be way off target. Scarily far off. As we have it now, the organisation chart looks like this, with question marks denoting those people where we don't have final identities, addresses, or surveillance.

Security and operations: Henderson, Allan, Geoff
Product design: Quintrell, Terry, Ramesh + 3 colleagues
Distribution: ??? Three participants, maybe four
Finance: Wyatt, plus ??? three others
The owner / boss: ???

It's true I have some idea of numbers and faces in the distribution and finance strands, but it's desperately hard to recall a face well enough to derive an accurate image of it, particularly if there's a gap of a day or more, particularly if, as in my case, that day has not exactly been calm and without incident. And even if I were able to recall the faces, what then? Wyatt wouldn't have shown up in any search of police records. Identity searches like that only really work where a local force is trawling through a list of known troublemakers. They don't work when you're looking for some guy whose face Fiona Griffiths thinks she roughly remembers.

I think our organisation chart isn't complete.

'There were times when Henderson, Allan and Geoff were all together in the barn. But that would mean there was no one looking out for the farmhouse itself. No one protecting the big boss guy, assuming that the boss guy was present in the farmhouse the entire time. I don't think that's plausible. And the night that Roy Williams was abducted, Geoff and Allan were in the barn, at least some of the time. I just don't believe that Henderson picked Roy up by himself. It's not credible.'

Brattenbury agrees with my logic. 'One more security guy? Two?'

His pen hesitates over the whiteboard.

'I'm guessing, but I'd say two, minimum.'

Our organisation chart changes again, so that the first line reads:

Security and operations: Henderson, Allan, Geoff, plus ??? two other unknowns

Jackson grimaces, then changes the subject. 'Talk to me about location,' he says.

I give him what I have.

Nia's accent. South, Mid or West Wales, not Cardiff. Probably not Valleys.

The stone flake from the step. Ryan tells us that it's an example of Old Red Sandstone. There are instances of the stone as far distant as the Moray Firth, even Shetland, but the main deposit in the UK is in South Wales and the Welsh Marches. 'Pembrokeshire, Carmarthenshire, Powys,

264

Monmouthshire. That's basically the main area. There are outcrops in Herefordshire and Gloucestershire. Also Somerset and Devon. There are further tests we can do to specify location, but we don't have a lot of material to deal with.' He grimaces, but I don't apologise. Henderson searched my clothes, not intensively, but with attention before packing them in the bin liner. If I'd taken more stone, it would have been detected.

My clothes. I made a scene about what I had to wear because I wanted to make sure Henderson bought a long list of stuff. I gave Brattenbury details in my note last night: the grey dress, the brown belt, the shoes, the shirts, the jeans, the watch. Everything. 'I had my clothes no later than ten thirty in the morning. Everything was Gap branded. So there's a store somewhere which sold that list of clothes to a shopper, almost certainly paying cash, somewhere between opening time and ten a.m. or thereabouts. If we can get time and place for the transaction, we've got some coordinates to work with.'

The telecoms tower: it was neither very close by nor thirty miles distant. When the moon came out, there was an angle of, I guess, about ten degrees, between moon and tower. Henderson told me that the time was quarter to eleven, a time that was consistent with the level of darkness outside. Estimating the direction of the telecom tower from the angle of the moon should give us a bearing with which to work.

The car: the fibres I took from the second car – not Henderson's BMW but the one I only entered blindfolded – should with a little luck be sufficient to identify a make and perhaps even a model. I check with Henderson, 'You have video coverage of location where Henderson switched cars?' He nods, so I say, 'We check video for cars leaving the area at that time and driven by a lone female. Check any possibles against the fibre samples, and we should know which car I was carried in. There's a good chance that we'll get ANPR data on its movements.'

And finally, of course, the barn itself. When I paced up and down, I made careful measurements of both the main barn itself and the side buildings which housed our bedrooms and the common room. I give the measurements as accurately as I can. Draw it out. 'The renovation is fairly recent and expensive. Assuming they applied for planning permission, the application should be traceable. And if not – well, we can always go back over aerial images.'

Jackson and the others scribble furiously all through this. Jackson tells me that they're already asking Gap head office for store by store sales data. I ask how many stores they have in South Wales.

'Outside Cardiff? Not many. Ebbw Vale. Bridgend.'

I say, 'Try Ebbw. I think we were in the mountains. No lights. Minimal traffic. No planes. Nightjars. At least one or two steep ascents. I also think the telecoms tower was on elevated ground. There were trees between me and it, but its topmost lamp rose clear of the leaves. If we were in the mountains, it wouldn't make sense for someone to drive to Cardiff or Bridgend.'

'Good. We'll call Ebbw direct.'

There's a bit more discussion. Ryan is a bit negative on the fibres I collected from the car. He says you have two or three big carpet manufacturers who supply all the big car companies. We spiral off into technicalities.

I say, 'Look, I think we should have a little police brutality, if you don't mind.'

Jackson and Brattenbury exchange a look. Susan Knowles covers her mouth.

Jackson starts to talk, but I interrupt.

'Look, you're going to put me in a cell with Anna Quintrell, yes?'

'Yes.'

'So let me look the part, the way she imagines it, anyway. She's already seen me in handcuffs. We may as well add some colour. We want her to unload.'

'You've already taken a knock or two from when they brought you in.'

'Yes, but . . .' I shrug. I saw myself in the mirror when I was getting my medical inspection. A knock or two. No big deal.

Brattenbury says, 'Look, Fiona, I appreciate your—'

Jackson says, 'Actually, Adrian, I agree with Fiona here. Mervyn, this is your field of expertise, I believe.'

Rogers grins at me and says, 'I thought I'd never get the chance.' He leaves the room.

I eat some lasagne, which is now cold.

Brattenbury says, 'Fiona, this is remarkable work. You—'

Jackson interrupts him. 'Don't flatter her. She'll cock everything up. Or start shooting people.'

Rogers comes back into the room with a wooden hockey stick. I view it with some alarm. I do vaguely remember that one of Buzz's hockey team-mates works in the custody suite, but when I suggested police brutality, I wasn't thinking of this exactly. And Rogers looks like a man who knows how to use a hockey stick. Except maybe when it comes to hitting hockey balls.

'Don't worry,' he says cheerfully. 'This looks worse than it is. Here, take these.' He gives me some aspirin. 'Reduces pain, increases bruising.'

I've already had as many aspirin as I'm meant to take, but I crunch up what he gives me and swallow the dust with some cold tea.

'Give it twenty minutes,' Rogers advises.

Jackson nods. Says, 'This farmhouse, wherever it is. You think Roy Williams is there?'

'Yes.'

'Any actual evidence?'

'No. But they've taken acute care to protect the place. Roy Williams will be a prize asset for them. Why give yourself two locations to worry about when you could focus on a single site?'

A bit of chat about that too. The consensus agrees with my verdict.

I ask if they've found anything out about Henderson's alternative health place. Brattenbury would have gone mental at me if I'd told him about Gary, so I just said Henderson happened to mention the place in passing.

'We'll have a video on the relevant doorway later today. It seems Henderson sees an osteopath most weeks. He doesn't always make it, but pays whether he comes or not. The osteopath seems for real. Getting an interception warrant for the osteopath's room, though. That could be hard.'

An understatement, I would think. Our reasons for suspicion are highly circumstantial and bugging a quasi-medical practice with the attendant 'collateral infringement of privacy' will be a hard sell, even for SOCA.

Brattenbury and Jackson both take calls, receive texts, confer with colleagues. Brattenbury is in charge of the operation overall, but most of the manpower is now coming from Jackson's team and command seems about equally shared to me. Plus Roy Williams is Jackson's man, not Brattenbury's. And it's more than just a chain-of-command issue for Jackson. He was a guest at Roy and Katie's wedding. I saw the pictures.

It's been twenty minutes, or a little more.

'OK,' Rogers says. 'Stand up. There, yes, like that.'

I stand. He places the hockey stick upright, so it touches the bone above and below my right eye socket. Jackson gets into position behind me. Susan Knowles is staring at us, like we're a collection of savages.

'Short, sharp knock,' says Rogers. 'Close your eyes. On three.'

He hits me on *two*. Doesn't move the stick, just slams it hard and sharp with his hand. I feel a fierce blow on my skull, but it's shocking more than actually painful. Like a sudden bolt of blackness, shot through with stars.

I fall over. Jackson catches me. Slides me sideways into a chair.

I put my hand to my face. Feel a lump already starting to rise. Skin and muscles starting to rise and thicken, obedient to a new physiognomy.

'Ow!'

Rogers inspects his handiwork and grins. 'It's coming up lovely.' To Susan Knowles's appalled face, he adds, 'Trained as a sports physio once upon a time. Amazing the things you learn.'

I ask for peppermint tea. Then there's a bit where we all just sit around and drink tea and eat cake.

I say to Brattenbury, 'You'll have to take me to Manchester, of course?'

'Yes.'

To Jackson: 'Is there any way you could arrange—'

'Already done. Your young man will be in Manchester. We'll give you as much time together as we can arrange. Make the most of it.' His face shifts a little and he adds, 'These long assignments. They get to anyone. It can take time to settle back into normal.'

I realise that my apartment would have been under surveillance from the moment that Roy Williams was reported missing. Someone would have seen Henderson kiss his fingers and touch them to my lips. Seen that and reported it, but Jackson is too wise an owl to let the matter go any further.

I also realise that from Jackson's perspective and from Brattenbury's this whole arrest process is a way to get me out from active undercover work. They couldn't simply withdraw me: that would flag me up as a spy to Henderson and his buddies. A big, loud, public arrest is probably the single most common way of withdrawing an undercover officer from duty. From their point of view, Fiona Grey has just about reached the end of her useful life.

I eat more cake, but I'm getting fidgety. I'm not sure that I want to stop being Fiona Grey.

I say, 'The cell I'm in. Can you make it as cold as possible? I want a rough night.'

Rogers goes off to sort something out.

I ask about Quintrell. How her interrogation has gone so far. Jackson pulls in Jane Alexander, who's been leading the interviews. Jane is a friend, sort of, and she stares at my face, the obvious question on her lips.

I tell her that I answered back to DCI Jackson. 'Big mistake,' I say.

My mouth is stiff on the left, because the bruising reaches down to my cheek. When I smile, I smile with one side only.

Alexander darts me a look that's a mixture of things: polite smile, alarm, professionalism and something else. Respect, or something like it. She has an exaggerated view of my abilities and is perhaps a little scared by my oddity.

But she collects herself. Summarises things with swift brevity. Quintrell is so frightened of what Henderson might do to her that she's revealed nothing. She's heard the audio recordings made at her house. She knows she's going to jail. Knows that the only way to reduce her sentence is to cooperate. But she has still said nothing, other than answer a few basic questions about name and identity.

I say, 'Keep going. Make it long. Make it hard.'

Alexander nods. She'll do turn and turn about with a colleague, for most of the evening if necessary.

I stand up, ready to be taken to my cell.

Brattenbury stands too. 'Good luck, Fiona. Anything you can get.'

A custody officer comes to the door. No one has told the staff here that I'm a police officer, but when an interview room is stuffed with senior officers and chocolate cake, it's fairly obvious that I'm not a regular criminal.

The officer looks at my face. Under ordinary circumstances, he'd file a report. Cardiff isn't the sort of place where suspects get beaten up in underground rooms. But these aren't ordinary circumstances. Jackson says to leave it. I say so too. The officer tells Jackson he'll need to report the matter to the custody sergeant – the right response – and escorts me to my cell.

Two beds. Thin blue mattresses laid over concrete. Blankets. An all-in-one metal loo and washbasin, which sounds odd but looks practical. A concrete shelf which doubles as a table.

There's light, but no window. Home Office guidelines require that prisoners can tell the difference between night and day, so the Cardiff suite was built with solar tubes that extend as much as twenty metres down from the roof. A panel in the ceiling releases a weird, luminous glow. Cold air blows from some vent.

The guard says, 'All right,' and closes the door. Steel door, painted blue.

I'm all alone. Somewhere, invisibly, a microphone gathers the silence.

37

Quintrell is brought to the cell when the light is dying.

She looks rough. Not injured and knocked about, like me, but exhausted. Defeated. She's still in her cutesie little summer dress, but someone has given her a grey fleece to wear over the top.

We stare at each other.

She sits on her bed. There are four blankets in the room and I've got them all.

'What happened to you?'

'Resisting arrest,' I say. 'Except some of it happened after arrest.'

She draws her legs up on the bed. 'Can I have my blankets?'

I give her one.

'And another?'

I tell her to fuck off. Say I'm cold.

'So am I.'

I shrug. Not interested.

There's a pause. A pause sealed off by steel doors and concrete walls.

'They bugged my house. My phone. They've got everything.'

I shrug.

Light dies in the ceiling.

She tries to make herself comfortable. Twitches the fleece and blanket, trying to get warm. A losing game.

There's a call button by the door which allows prisoners to ask for help from staff. She presses it, asks for more bedclothes. Someone laughs at her and tells her to go to sleep.

She stands by my bed and says plaintively. 'You've got my blanket.'

I tell her again to fuck off. She's bigger than me, but I'm scarier. She goes back to her bed.

The light fades some more. I try to sleep. The aspirin has worn off and my head hurts. Quintrell starts crying. Quiet sobs, that tumble into the blanket and are smothered. Down the corridor, we can hear more suspects being brought in and processed. Doors slam through the night: church bells calling the hour.

I sleep.

38

Sleep and eventually wake.

Light glows from the ceiling. A prison dawn.

Quintrell doesn't look like she's slept much. She's propped against the wall. Blanket doubled up over her legs. She's staring at me. Her skin looks blue.

I don't have my watch – it was removed at processing – but Quintrell has hers. I ask her the time.

'Coming up to five o'clock.'

'Thanks.'

I rinse my mouth in the little metal basin. Drink a bit.

My headache comes back and I want aspirin. Could ask for some, in fact – the custody staff would bring them – but I don't want the intrusion.

Sit back down on my bed, look at Quintrell.

She says, 'You should report them.' She means the bruising on my face.

'That'd work well.'

Quintrell trusts my legend completely now. Perhaps she did before, I don't know, but my injuries and my presence here have washed away any last trace of suspicion.

I cover up with blankets again. Then relent and throw one over to Quintrell.

'Thanks.'

She pulls the blanket over her shoulders and arranges it over her front. She looks like a disaster relief victim, or would do if disaster relief victims wore pretty little summer dresses with matching loafers.

'I like your dress.'

'Thanks.'

Silence fills the cell.

Silence, and that eerie light which seems unconnected to any sun.

'Is this your first time? You know: in prison.'

I say, 'This isn't prison. Prison's worse.' Then after a bit, I add, 'There was stuff in Manchester. I've never been in for long.'

'The policewoman yesterday told me that I could get ten years.' She starts to cry again.

I watch her with interest. Envy, actually. I've only cried once in my adult life. I want to ask her the secret. What interior handbrake has to be released.

'There was one guy, Somebody O'Brien, who got seventeen years. For fraud. They showed me the reports.'

I say, 'They showed them to me too. I don't think we'll get seventeen years.'

More crying.

Light strengthens in the ceiling. Down the hall, we hear a prisoner – mentally ill, almost certainly – shout and bang in his cell. Down the corridor, a movement of men.

'I've got a daughter, you know.'

'Have you?'

That's news to me. No glimpse of it in Quintrell's life so far. Nothing on the Tinker records. Brattenbury didn't know it. Jackson didn't. Jane Alexander didn't know it when she was interviewing.

'I was very young when I had her. Seventeen. When I was in my twenties, I wasn't coping so well with things and gave her up for adoption. She's eighteen now. We were just starting to get to know each other again.'

275

'What's her name?'

'Julia.'

'That's nice.'

'She's an art student. Lives in Bristol. We were beginning to do OK.'

'She can visit you. It doesn't have to end.'

'She won't visit.'

I let time go by. We've got plenty of time. I was arrested just after eleven. Quintrell would have been taken about the same time. The law permits us to be held for twenty-four hours without charge, thirty-six hours with the authority of a superintendent – something that Jackson can easily obtain – and ninety-six hours if a magistrate agrees. A magistrate probably would agree, given the circumstances, but it would be easier just to charge us. For a serious offence, like ours, and with murder and abduction in the background, we'll almost certainly be remanded into pre-trial custody.

Fear, exhaustion and time: interrogation's holy trinity.

I say, 'Anna, how did you get into all this? Why did you get started?'

And she tells me.

Almost without further prompting. Without thought for where she is or who could be listening. It's a beautiful illustration of the interrogator's oldest maxim: that people *want* to confess. An urge as deep as breathing. The beautiful relief of sharing secrets.

As she tells it, Henderson approached her eighteen months ago with some queries about payroll. That must have been when Henderson discovered what Kureishi was up to. The point at which a little local fraud started to go big time.

'I mean, I'm a *trained* accountant. I'm a *professional*. Vic's just a thug. He knew nothing at all. Didn't know the basics. He didn't even understand the potential. It took me to explain it. I mean, really, that's the silly thing. The whole

276

thing was my idea. They just took it from me. They treated me . . . treated me like . . .'

She isn't able to finish that sentence, because what she means is 'they treated me like *you*'. Quintrell still sees herself as officer class. I'm several rungs below that. Servant class. A skivvy. Her confessional impulse now is given extra urgency by her bitterness at Henderson's treatment of her.

I neither challenge nor support her. Just let her talk and let the hidden microphones record her song.

'Terry – that's not his real name. His real name is Ian Shoesmith. He ran some kind of IT start-up thing in London. Enterprise software. Got loads of money from investors and screwed them over. I think they looked at prosecuting him, but there wasn't enough evidence. But he was shafted anyway. Not a fit and proper person and all that. Couldn't be a company director again, and no one was going to employ him. So when Henderson took *my* idea, and it was *totally* my idea, to him, he took it up. The idea, back then, was that Terry would do the IT stuff. I'd be in charge of designing what the system had to do. James Wyatt was brought in because they thought they needed an accountant. But really! What did he ever add? *You* knew more.'

She's wrong about Wyatt, as it happens. His real expertise was with the offshore plumbing. The network of accounts in Panama, Belize, the Virgin Islands. I don't say so though. Just let her talk.

And talk she does, in sour, extensive detail. She seems affronted that a bunch of gangsters stole her intellectual property. Like she was expecting them to give her share options and a seat on the board.

I ask if Henderson is in charge.

'*No*.' Her *no* is scathing. 'There's some rich guy behind it all. He's got legitimate money, I think, but Vic says he just invests in whatever promises a return. This looks good, so it

277

gets the investment. Vic says they've spent four million already. Obviously got some of that back from' – she waves her hand at me dismissively – '*your* stuff. But still. Four million.'

Your stuff: she means the payroll frauds that I and the other moles enacted.

'That barn. The place we were taken to. Is that where the rich guy lives?'

'I don't know. I've always been blindfolded. I've never left the barn. Nor has anyone else. Ram told me they came in the back of a van without windows.'

I say, 'That guy who had his hands chopped off. Did you know about that?'

She says, dismissively, 'He was stupid. I mean, none of us wanted to do it, but he *was* talking. He was dangerous. If we hadn't done it, he could have messed the whole thing up.'

That sounds like conspiracy to murder to me. It'll sound that way to a court too. Quintrell doesn't yet know it, but she's just upped her maximum sentence from a dozen years or so to life imprisonment. She can hang her pretty blue summer dress up somewhere safe. She won't be needing it for a while.

Shoesmith probably doesn't wear summer dresses, but he's fucked too. Him, Wyatt, Quintrell, Henderson. We have enough on them now to secure convictions for fraud at a minimum, conspiracy to murder at a maximum. If our colleagues in India come through for us, then Ramesh and his buddies are screwed as well. The UK has a decent extradition treaty with India. And we've a decent chance of getting the identifications we need.

We eat breakfast at six thirty. Break open the plastic-wrapped packs we were handed last night. Cereal. Two slices of bread. Jam. Margarine. I eat my cereal, leave the rest.

Quintrell talks about herself until eight thirty. She asks nothing about me. At eight thirty, I pee and wash my hands.

The act interrupts her self-absorption.

'You, you'll be all right,' she tells me. 'I mean . . .' She waves a hand. 'You're used to it.'

I don't reply. A few minutes later, she's taken off for interviewing and she'll learn just how stupid she's been.

I'm alone in an empty room. Invisible microphones close on silence.

39

Manchester. Cheadle Heath.

Another custody suite. More solicitors. Mental-health examiners. More procedures. More searches. But this time I get a cell to myself. I ask for pain relief and get it. I still have a headache, but it's concentrated round my eye. No longer extends to the entire skull.

I sleep for ever.

Morning comes and my first court appearance. I'm charged with fraud and resisting arrest. I plead not guilty.

The magistrate asks, 'How did you come by those injuries?'

I say, 'I slipped in the shower.'

The magistrate orders an investigation and yet another report. I'm remanded to custody, to await trial. Two uniformed officers escort me downstairs to an underground car park, mostly full of police patrol cars. But I'm not going in one of those. Brattenbury is there, at the wheel of a silver Lexus with leather seats and exhausts with a lovely deep growl.

I get in, feeling sore.

Brattenbury watches solicitously. 'Head still hurting?'

'A bit.'

I don't mention it, but my neck has hurt ever since Henderson slapped me. It would be quite nice to go a few days without anyone hitting me. Or chasing, arresting, imprisoning, handcuffing or blindfolding me.

'Where are we going?' I ask.

'A private house. You'll like it.'

We drift into silence.

It's mid-July, but you wouldn't guess it. Rain and wind. Grey skies bolted down over sodden earth. Brattenbury drives impatiently, the way I do. Keeping too close to the car in front. Overtaking with a surge of power when he gets the chance.

Wet tyres on wet roads. Wipers like metronomes. Sidelights on, even though it's broad daylight.

'Will you charge her with conspiracy?' I say.

'Not yet. We want to keep that back as a bargaining chip.'

'Anything more on Roy Williams?'

'No. Nothing.'

'The shop in Ebbw?'

We're stopped at lights and Brattenbury slides me a look. 'Someone came in at opening time. Bought the full list for cash.'

'CCTV?'

'We're looking at it.'

'The telecoms tower?'

He laughs. 'Taking all the bits you've given us, we reckon we can narrow the area to about three or four hundred square miles. The southern part of the Brecon Beacons, most likely. That sounds a lot, but you're only talking about an area twenty miles square. We just need to find a barn and a farmhouse, where the barn has been through some extensive remodelling.'

'Name searches for Nia? Even in Wales, that's not so common.'

Brattenbury sees a gap in the traffic and blitzes through it. The sprayback from a lorry up ahead drenches our windscreen and Brattenbury has to put the wiper on full to clear it.

'Fiona. We're doing everything. We do know how to do this.'

'I know.' There's a brief moment when I see myself through the eyes of a superior. Talented but difficult. Hard to manage. I have a moment of clear vision, a windscreen newly cleared of rain. 'Sorry,' I say. Then the rain comes again. The spray. The splashback. And I don't know what I'm apologising for.

Brattenbury drives to a place in Altrincham, I think. I don't really notice. Edwardian houses. Pretty street. Front gardens that smell of rose blooms in the wet. Philadelphus. A taste of orange blossom.

I feel a sudden surge of emotion. A surge that takes me by surprise and, because I'm unprepared, it takes me a few moments to find any description of it at all. There's a period – a few seconds maybe – where I don't know if I'm feeling, happy, sad, angry, frightened, or anything at all. I just feel that rush of internal movement. See the rain shine on wet streets and fallen petals.

'Are you OK?'

'Where are we?'

'This is a colleague's house. He and his wife are away for a few weeks, I thought it would be nicer for you to stay in a real family home than a hotel.'

'Oh.'

That phrase *family home* gives me the clue. I've spent so long away from all of that – from my house, from Buzz's flat, from my parents' home – that I find myself moved and disconcerted to be here in this wet street, these quiet gardens. As though the kind of life they promise is still a possibility.

'Are you OK?'

'Is Buzz going to be here?'

'Buzz?'

'David Brydon. My fiancé.'

'He's coming this afternoon. We'll have debriefs most days. Long ones to begin with. You and – did you say Buzz? – can have the rest of the time together. We'll still need to process you through the courts, but you're on record as being held at Cheadle Heath. You might have to do some nights there, just to maintain the legend.'

'That's fine. And yes, I'm OK.'

I don't move though.

It's strange to know that I can just walk up and down this street. Go to the shops, eat a meal, chat with a neighbour. I can be Fiona Grey or Fiona Griffiths, it doesn't really matter.

It feels almost like that time outside the hotel. The air bubble. Neither colour nor weight. Only it's different this time. Like it's a good weightlessness, not a bad one. It's as though I feel both my lives walking in front of me and realise I can choose either one.

A sense of potential.

'What about Western Vale? I've been fired, I assume?'

'Just a bit.' He laughs. The laugh says, *You're very fired*.

'What about my cleaning?'

'I don't know. They probably just think you've gone AWOL.'

I nod. Cleaners come and go. The ultimate transient workforce. When I stop turning up for work, my boss will just replace me. I wonder who Lowri is coughing at now. But I'll miss it, the cleaning. I never liked payroll.

'Are you OK to go in?'

'Yes.'

But I don't move. Brattenbury thinks this is the end. Not of the operation, but of my role in it. The public arrest. The criminal charges. The unlamented collapse of my career in payroll.

This, in undercover terms, is the start of my reintegration. The nice house in a pleasant district. Time spent getting to know Buzz again. A gentle reintroduction to my old job, my old commitments. It's everything I'm meant to want.

Please don't be concerned.

I say, 'I can't forget Roy Williams.'

'Nor can any of us.'

'I'd like to see Katie, please. When she's ready. When there's time.'

'Of course. We've already asked her and she's said she wants to see you.'

'He's in that farmhouse, isn't he? I was a hundred feet from him.'

'Probably.'

We do know how to do this.

'Have you arrested James Wyatt?'

'Not yet.'

'Ian Shoesmith?'

'Not yet.'

First intelligence, then arrests. The SOCA way.

'He was nice, Ian, Terry, whatever you want to call him. He helped me at Monopoly.'

'So we shouldn't arrest him?'

'No, we should just arrest him nicely.'

We're doing everything.

Brattenbury thinks that this is the end for Fiona Grey, but I'm not so sure. My cover is now perfect, beyond question. And little Fiona may yet have her uses.

The rain starts to clear. The pavement starts to shine with an apologetic sunlight. The Lexus engine ticks softly as it cools.

Buzz is coming this afternoon and I realise I do want to see him. I'm not sure what that thing with Henderson was – lust? fear? isolation? – but I feel insulated from it now. Seeing Buzz will be strange, but good-strange, I think.

I open my car door.

'OK. Let's do it.'

And we do.

40

Buzz says, 'You've lost weight.'

He says, 'Your hair's longer.'

He says, as he gives me a bunch of yellow roses in a pale blue jug, 'I got these, because I thought you'd prefer something simple.'

He says, as he shows me the suitcase of my own clothes he's brought from my house, 'I didn't know what you'd want, so I asked your sister to help choose.'

He says, as he soaps my back in the large white rolltop bath with claw feet that stands in the prettily decorated upstairs bathroom, 'Your face, babe. It looks terrible.'

He says, as we go through to the bedroom, and the big white bed, and the rose-patterned wallpaper and the sweet peas in a glass on the window sill, 'We can take it slow.'

And I say, as I lie beside him afterwards, staring up at the ceiling and burying my hand in the thickets of his hair, 'Oh Buzz, I would get so lost without you.' And we press up close and I don't talk much and don't let him talk much except that, when we get hungry, he's allowed to walk downstairs naked to the kitchen and come back with brown bread and butter and smoked salmon and (for him) a bottle of beer. And we eat sitting up in bed, telling each other off when we drop crumbs onto the sheets, and we lick each other's fingers clean, and when Buzz settles back with his beer, I sip the foam from the head and start nibbling the hillock of muscle at the top of his arm.

Slowly – because I'm not very alert to these things at times – I realise that there is a feeling spreading outwards from my belly. At first, I thought it had something to do with the bread and salmon: a feeling of being replete. Then, as I belatedly turn my attention to the sensation, I think, *This isn't what I usually feel like after food.* I'm perplexed enough that I start interrogating the feeling the way I used to. The way my doctors used to train me. *Try to name the feeling, Fiona. Just see what fits. Is it fear? Anger? Jealousy? Love? Happiness? Disgust? Yearning? Curiosity?* Most of those feelings, I can quickly discard. The feeling is quieter than most things, so not curiosity, or fear, or anger, or jealousy. Quieter than those, and warmer.

I remember once sitting in a stairwell, bum on a concrete step, wearing a floaty mint-green dress and strappy shoes and thinking, *This is love. Love, plus a good splash of happiness.* I had just starting dating Buzz and he had just kissed me. That feeling then: it was a bit like this.

I say, to myself more than anything, 'I think I might be happy.'

Buzz laughs at me. 'You *think*? You don't know?'

'It's complicated. Or at least, it is for me. I don't know how it is for other people.'

Buzz strokes my hair and the stroke turns into a long rub which ends at my knees, with stops en route to explore sites of particular local interest. I kiss his neck.

'You just feel something and that's it. You *feel* it.'

In philosophical terms, I'd say that Buzz's position makes him a strong non-cognitivist, a reputable position to adopt, even if it isn't mine. But I don't think he's seeking that kind of discussion. I keep a hand on my belly, feeling the warmth. Its settled, confident glow.

Happiness. This is happiness.

I roll over in bed, facing Buzz. Say, 'Can we look at wedding dresses soon?'

'Yes, love, of course we can.'

Love and happiness: the sunshine twins.

41

Long debriefings: Brattenbury wasn't kidding.

I'd hoped that I could stay in the house, but Brattenbury wants me at the SOCA office in Manchester. I don't have my car here, so Buzz drives me in. He's been given some liaison project with the Greater Manchester Police, and goes on there afterwards.

Brattenbury leads the debriefing, but Mervyn Rogers is there, representing our force, and Susan Knowles leads anything to do with IT.

Until you've done one of these things, you can't quite imagine the detail. We start with the people. Who I saw. My impression of their attitudes, expertise, emotional position, relationship with colleagues, and much more. Also identifications. It's easy to confirm that 'Terry' is Ian Shoesmith. Ditto James Wyatt. I make the identification from surveillance photos and sign a statement confirming the match. That's not something we need for investigative purposes, but we need to keep an eye on what a court will expect in due course.

We make progress also with Ram and his colleagues. We have a limited amount of material from India, but we have CCTV from Heathrow, passenger lists, and some immigration data, topped up with various industry magazines and websites from Bangalore. I identify Ramesh and one colleague, Dilip Krishnaswamy, with certainty. Their two colleagues with moderate confidence only.

We get nowhere on Geoff. Nowhere on Allan, Geoff's Glock-wielding colleague. I'm pretty sure that both of them have a military background, but plenty of people do. Allan has that characteristic way of rubbing his beard as he plays Monopoly, but we don't yet have a database that can make use of that insight.

Nowhere also with any of the people involved in the distribution discussions. Nowhere on Nia. And nowhere with any of the people who might have been over in the farmhouse, who might or might not have been present that first evening when I launched myself at Henderson. I work with an e-fit specialist to produce images of Geoff and Allan. I think the one of Geoff is reasonably accurate. Allan, I'm not so sure about. I get a vaguely reasonable picture of Nia, the waitress.

But still, Brattenbury is pleased to have a good, arrestable list of names. The images of Geoff and Allan are circulated to all police forces in the United Kingdom. Shoesmith and Wyatt remain under close observation.

In a regular police operation, surveillance might last as little as twenty-four hours before we made arrests. Classically, we'd want to wait until we had enough evidence to warrant prosecution, then go in hard, fast and nasty, using the evidence we have to secure more. When suspects see how fucked they really are, they start to calculate, correctly, that their best chance of reducing their jail terms is by cooperating. That doesn't always happen, but it happens often enough to make it a game worth playing.

SOCA operates differently. Its close connection to the intelligence services gives it a preference for the long game, the subtle collection of data. I think if we were in a normal situation, that would be Brattenbury's preference too. Play it delicate, play it slow.

But this isn't a normal situation. Roy Williams, a police

officer and our colleague, has been abducted. All of us think of Sajid Kureishi, but I'm the only one who has actually watched that killing. Kureishi's rapid, terrified talking. His arms taut against their bindings. That savage, repeated hacking. That changing face. The anguish and the pain.

I'm OK with dead people but Kureishi isn't really dead, for me. He's just frozen in his dying. Like one of those ancient Greek torments, which the victim is doomed to repeat for ever, unable to escape, even by death.

I want Roy Williams to avoid that fate. Katie too.

We have infinite strategy discussions, but they all come back to a simple conclusion. We can't close down the operation, until we get Williams back. Which means locating the farmhouse. And not merely locating it, but entering with enough speed and force to preserve Roy's life. A big ask.

Brattenbury says, 'And of course we have to be alert to the risk that . . .' No one wants to say it, but Brattenbury has to. 'That they apply pressure. Inflict torture.'

That word. That thought.

It crouches in the room with us, an alien third party, discomfiting us. As though our nostrils were already catching the whiff of electrical burns on skin. Our ears hearing the gasp of breath struggling against wet cloth.

The implications ripple outwards too.

Roy doesn't know much about the broader investigation. Doesn't have many secrets to spill. But he does have one: and I am she.

I feel the looks of my fellow investigators clustering on my face.

I say, carefully, 'It's possible, but I doubt it. Everything points away from it. Evidence obtained by torture is known to be unreliable, and Roy is hardly going to be a soft touch. Plus, if these guys are sophisticated enough to detect an undercover officer, they probably also know a bit about standard operating procedure. If they do, that'll tell them Roy doesn't know too much. And then again, these guys are mostly silkily efficient. They're not thugs. Even with Kureishi, where they knew the guy had been stealing from them, the whole murder was accomplished in a matter of two or three minutes.'

Minutes which I watched, and no one else here did.

People discuss my comments – most people agree with my assessment – and the conversation moves on. But I still get more than my share of looks. And the smell of burned flesh lingers.

In the meantime, those debriefings run on and on. The first day is spent mostly on faces, names and identities. Days two and three focus exclusively on IT. Susan Knowles leads things. She's in her element here and for the first time, I understand the depth of her expertise. Always well dressed and impeccable – dark skirts, businesslike jackets, that gorgeous Venetian hair tied back in a knot – she tries to understand exactly the system design and how far advanced it is. My ignorance is frustratingly extensive. Although I heard endless hours of Ramesh and Ian 'Terry' Shoesmith talking about these things, I understood so little of what I heard that it's hard for Susan to extract what she needs.

But a picture emerges. It seems that Shoesmith has managed to steal or otherwise obtain the program code for an old version of TPS software. He and Ramesh are currently seeking to adapt that code: bringing it up to date and inserting the 'skim'.

At one point, early on, someone asks Susan how hard it would be to have the software skim funds.

'Easy. A few lines of code. The hard part is Fiona's part' – she means getting the payroll part of things up to date and accurate – 'then distributing the software, and getting any stolen money offshore and laundered.'

'And distributing the software. Just how do they do that?'

'They've got a few different options. One, they can seek to take over the software supplier's own systems. That would be the best way: you would actually get a global software company distributing your infected software and you could, theoretically, reach pretty much every one of its customers.

'But it wouldn't be easy. To achieve it you'd either need an accomplice – probably a few accomplices – in the software company, or you'd need to have obtained a backdoor route by some other means. Some kind of sophisticated hacking operation. Trouble is, we've arrested Quintrell and, of course, Fiona. Tinker must be aware that we've penetrated them, at least to some extent. So although their initial objective was probably to attack the supplier, they must be aware that that route is going to be more protected than normal.

'But there is an alternative. It's not as good, but still very viable. If you can't hit the software supplier itself, you could obtain access to the customers themselves, firms like Western Vale. You'd need a way to replace their *legitimate* payroll software with your *infected* copy. That could be quite easy, depending on access, but you'd have to work customer by customer. You'd basically need another Saj Kureishi, planting dodgy software everywhere he went.'

Brattenbury asks, 'So you would need *physical* access to those corporate computer systems?'

Knowles says, 'Ideally, yes. But how would you get physical access to enough corporate systems to make it worth your while? Realistically, you'd probably have to figure out a way to access those systems from outside. A lot of corporates have weaknesses in their computer security, but even so, you'd have to approach every single firm as a different challenge.'

We also talk extensively about timings. Shoesmith's timetable said, 'Specify, program, beta-launch, full launch.' I'm pretty sure we're midway through the beta-launch, with

292

more testing yet to go. But what then? When does full launch happen? And will that be corporate-by-corporate, or in one huge roll-out?

We don't know. Once again, our ignorance is frustratingly great.

We discuss these things endlessly, but keep coming back to two central threats.

The first is Shoesmith's Fuck It button. If Tinker's software gets distributed widely enough, that button could cause tens of millions of pounds to vanish almost literally overnight. However quick the remedial action, the theft would still be colossal. Some large firms could even be bankrupted by the loss.

That line of thinking says, Play safe, don't screw around, make some arrests. Put payroll systems into lockdown. Deploy armed guards in corporate software suites, if you have to.

Except, if we do that, we come to the second horrendous risk: that we lose Roy Williams. Lose him, and fail to catch the big bad guys who are directing Tinker. At the moment, the most senior man in our sights seems to be Vic Henderson, and none of us believe that he's any more than some security ops guy. The brains – and the profits – lie elsewhere.

Briefings and discussions run all week.

Meantime, elsewhere, an inquiry team of more than a hundred officers is chasing every possible lead.

Planning departments have been checked for barn conversions which tally with the measurements I've provided, but nothing appears to tally exactly. Loads of buildings that tally approximately.

We've sent young police officers, out of uniform, into pubs right across the area, south of the Brecon Beacons, where we think the farmhouse is located. They're briefed to look out for any Nias who fit my description. Also to start conversations about brawls at posh cocktail parties and see if they can catch

293

any gossip about my own little presentation. So far, we've achieved nothing at all.

SOCA's spooks did apply for an interception warrant on the osteopath's office. The application was turned down. A SOCA guy made an appointment for osteopathy himself – an old problem with his shoulder – and reports that the osteopath seemed competent and knowledgeable. Interestingly, though, there are two doors into the osteopath's office. One, the door that patients use. The other a locked door, which gives access into the building next door. Brattenbury says, 'The door's left over from when the building was divided down the middle a few years back. The stuff next door is a property management company. Accountants on the top floor. Solicitors on the bottom floor. We've adjusted our video coverage on the front so we can survey both offices. We've photographed the appointments book at the health centre and all the visitor sign-in books at the offices next door. We're going through all that now.'

He shrugs. No one says it, but these things are huge consumers of resources. The inquiry now has three full-time data officers, simply to manage the flow of information.

I also, I think, detected a ripple in Brattenbury's tone when he talked about adjusting the video coverage. If we've got legal authority to monitor a particular doorway, we don't thereby have the right to monitor the entrances to right and left. Knowing Brattenbury as I do, I imagine he'd usually be scrupulous about those things. Adjusting the video coverage might seem *to us* like simple, practical policing. A defence lawyer might argue that we had no legal authority to do any such thing.

A defence lawyer might even be right.

But those aren't my problems, or not really. I do, however, have to maintain the existence of Fiona Grey. I spend some time in custody, making myself just visible enough that other prisoners will be able to attest to my presence. I quite like it in detention. Small rooms, easy meals, time to think.

Interestingly, a lawyer asks to see me. Not a legal aid type. A real solicitor belonging to some fancy Manchester firm. I agree to see him, and am led from my cell to an interview room. He's got that glossy look which money brings. He calls me 'Miss Grey' and shakes my hand with a soft palm. His business card names him Christopher Winterton.

I say, 'Did Vic send you?'

'Does it matter? I'm instructed to take care of you.'

'Well, say thanks to Vic, won't you?'

'I'll pass your regards on to my client.'

'Is it OK to talk in here?'

'Yes.' He talks about client–lawyer confidentiality. His words come out in a smooth, comforting stream. The café latte of verbiage, billed at £250 an hour.

'Anna will tell them everything. She probably already has.'

'We're aware that Ms Quintrell has not protected her interests, or the interests of others, as well as she could have done.'

'She's an idiot.'

Winterton gives me a thin smile and waves a hand, as though to deflect something unappealing. 'Perhaps if we start with your own position. What they've asked, what you've answered.'

'They've asked me lots of stuff. I've mostly told them to fuck off.'

'And what about the part that wasn't mere imprecation?'

I stare at him. *Imprecation?* Who uses words like that these days? It's as though lawyers think they're a nature reserve for endangered words.

'Imprecation,' he says. 'It means swearing.'

'I know what it means. I'm not stupid.'

'No. Sorry.'

'I told them the truth.' Winterton doesn't like that much and his face twitches. But then I continue, 'A man called Vic broke into my room. He asked me to do stuff in my job at Western Vale. I said no. He threatened me. Showed me a video of some guy being chopped to pieces. So I did as he asked. At one point I ran away to London, but he came to find me. I had to do what he said.'

'That's your defence?'

'That's the truth.'

'Did he offer you money?'

'I didn't want the money.'

'Did you give any name other than Vic?'

'I don't have any name other than Vic.'

'Would you be able to identify this person Vic?' Winterton's voice goes funny as he says that.

I don't react to the change in tone. Just say, 'No.'

'But you saw him. You said he threatened you.'

'That's why I couldn't identify him. Because he threatened me. I'd be too scared.'

'So you wouldn't be able to pick him out of a police line-up, say?'

'No.'

'And what did you tell the police about Ms Quintrell's involvement?'

'I told them to fuck off.'

'What did you say about your trip to your conference venue?'

'What conference venue? I don't know what you're talking about.'

Winterton asks what happened to my face.

I say, 'What do you think happened?'

'I think you might be the victim of police violence.'

'Yeah, well, that's what I thought while he was hitting me.'

Winterton wants to know more, so I improvise. 'I told the

cop who was interviewing me that I'd give him a blow-job if they dropped charges.'

'And?'

'He didn't keep his end of the bargain.'

'He hit you?'

'Not immediately.'

'So what did happen?'

'I didn't react particularly well. Then he hit me.'

'The name of the policeman?'

'Mervyn Rogers.'

I grin internally at that. Rogers won't be charged with anything, of course. Jackson and Brattenbury will sort something out. But Rogers will have to appear in court, for the sake of appearances. He'll also get plenty of stick from colleagues. So will I, but what the hell. It's been a while since I've been the principal butt of office banter, and it's time to restore my natural place at the head of the hierarchy of ridicule.

Our interview goes on a while. Mostly Winterton wants to be sure I haven't done a Quintrell and he becomes progressively reassured that I haven't.

His hand makes notes on a yellow legal pad. He writes with an amber fountain pen, trimmed with gold.

At one point, he wants me to give him my details: phone, address, previous address, dates of employment, that sort of thing. I start to write them out, but manage to press too hard and I splay the gold nib out, so it's unusable.

'Oh, I think I just broke your pen.'

He tries to fix it. Can't. Glares at me. Gives me a cheap plastic biro and I use that instead.

After about an hour and a half, he thinks he's done and gets up to go.

I say, 'That stuff with Vic, I'm not really worried about that.'

'Oh?'

'He threatened me. I protected myself. I'm allowed to do that.'

'We can certainly develop that defence.'

'The Manchester fuzz think I stabbed someone.'

'When?'

'Last year.'

'And did you?'

'Yes.'

'Did you mean to?'

'Yes.'

'I'll have to consult my client. I don't have instructions that currently—'

'It was self-defence, OK?'

'If you say so.'

'Tell Vic that if he wants to help, he can help with the stabbing. I'm not worried about the fraud. And you can tell him that Quintrell is a fuckwit.'

Winterton's face moves at that. He murmurs, 'I think my client is well aware that Ms Quintrell has not been entirely helpful.'

Not long after that, I appear in court for a second time. Winterton applies for me to be released from pre-trial detention. He argues that my history of physical abuse means that custody is an excessively punitive sanction.

There is also the matter of my injuries. A police report from Cardiff spoke about my 'resisting arrest violently and continuously'. On Winterton's advice, I wear flat shoes and speak quietly. A court official has to tell me to speak closer to the microphone. The magistrate asks the Crown Prosecution guy if it's correct that I was arrested by four male officers. He looks embarrassed and says yes. The magistrate asks if some of my injuries were received while I was in custody. The CPS admits the possibility. Snappishly, the magistrate demands a further report from the custody sergeant in Cardiff and adjourns the case for another day.

Manchester Police haven't brought charges against me for the stabbing, but they want me to remain in the city to continue assisting with inquiries. Overall, in fact, Fiona Grey's legal affairs are going rather well, and she's pleased about it. During her sessions in the cells, she reads more of her speech therapy books.

And for Fiona Griffiths too, things are flourishing. I spend time with Buzz.

Increasingly, this feels a little like the life I left. One evening, I tell Buzz that I'll cook for him. He says, 'Oh no,' but smiles when he says it. We shop for food together and he remembers the bits I forget. I drop a James Bond DVD into our shopping basket, so he has something to keep him entertained while I'm getting lost in the kitchen. When we go home, I set him up with the movie, some beer and some crisps, then cook a *boeuf en daube*. I thought it would be a good recipe to choose because I'm quite good at things that can be cooked in one pot and because the Waitrose recipe I'm following tells me that total preparation time is fifteen minutes. Now admittedly, fifteen Waitrose minutes equate to about forty or fifty of my kitchen-minutes, but where I really come a cropper is that the recipe calls for an overnight marinade, then three and a half hours in the oven. I ignore the marinade and get the thing in the damn oven at seven, which is good going for me, but then we have to wait till after nine before the stew is even vaguely cooked enough. By that time, Buzz has finished his beer and his movie, and we've eaten all the crisps, have raided the cupboards for some pistachios, have had a bath together, and have sat on the bed trying neither to look at our watches nor get more nibbles, but, as I say brightly, 'That means we enjoy it all the more.'

And we do. We eat by candlelight, and Buzz teases me, and the life which was once ours starts to flow again.

I wear my engagement ring and watch it flash in the yellow light.

Buzz asks about wedding dates and I say, 'Not yet, Buzzling. Not yet, but soon.'

I'm good, too. Well behaved, by my standards. My discovery about Gareth Glyn goes on nagging at me. I can't help feeling he'll lead me to some altogether deeper knowledge of my father and, with luck, of me too. Ordinarily, I'd just give way to obsession. Work all the time. Withdraw a bit. Sleep too little. But I realise Buzz needs me to be more normal than that. To be a better girlfriend. A better fiancée. So I oblige. I work as hard on those Tinker debriefings as Brattenbury desires, but apart from that, Buzz and I just spend time together. Eating, sleeping, watching TV, talking, going for walks. I like it. I think: *This is what Roy and Katie Williams do too. This is what married couples do.* It feels terribly strange but nice-strange, definitely nice.

And one afternoon, at the tail end of July, I go shopping for a wedding dress. To my surprise, however, I realise that it is important Buzz isn't with me. This has to be a private, girl-only thing. I normally rely on my sister for that kind of help, but since she's not available I ask Susan Knowles, shyly, if she'd mind coming with me.

She's surprised to be asked, but is very sweet about it. Says yes. Says she'd be thrilled and might not even be lying.

So we go out together. One Wednesday afternoon. A cold day and windy, but no actual rain. Having lunch before we start, Susan says brightly, 'So. What kind of thing are you after?'

I have to tell her the truth. That I'm completely useless at these things. That I rely almost totally on others. 'I was a bit funny as a teenager,' I say. 'Most bits have come back OK, but I'm still a bit screwy about some things. I find buying clothes difficult.'

When I say that sort of thing to people – and mostly I avoid saying anything remotely like it – I normally get a look which, though often kind, signifies some kind of discomfort. Susan's not like that. She's nice. 'You do OK,' she says. 'You look good.'

'My sister gets stuff for me. I'm lucky.'

The truth is, I found life easier as Fiona Grey. I found most things easier. Sleeping. Shopping. Choosing what to eat and wear. I probably fit in better at the hostel than I ever will at police headquarters. I've got my friends in CID, but plenty of my fellow officers either dislike me or find me weird.

'You could try pushing yourself less hard,' says Susan gently.

'Yes, but police work is the one thing I'm good at. Life: that's the part *I* find hard.'

So Susan guides me through the dresses the way my sister would. Makes me try on different things. Tells me off when I stand frozen and awkward. Cajoles me into expressing an opinion.

I try. I honestly do. But I can't make sense of the person I see in the mirror. This improbable white princess, bathed in a halogen glow. Shop assistants ask me questions about necklines and organza, beading and bodices, trains and lace and underskirts.

I have no opinions at all.

I start to feel very spacey, dangerously so. I sit on a white pouffe holding a long satin glove and I don't know where I am. Where or who. I have that upwardly drifting headiness that so often spells disaster.

I anchor myself by counting breaths and looking mostly at my, now mostly faded, facial injuries, a calming palette of yellow, grey and purple. I press the bruises till I feel their ache. I think of Hayley Morgan's little corpse, the bitemarks in the plaster.

The sweet, ammoniac smell of death.

Susan, I think, sees that I'm not coping and is about to coax me away. In my muddled state, I half imagine that this will be another SOCA-style extraction: all flashing police cars and armed officers. I'm quite close to asking her to see that no one hits me.

Then, by some fluke, a shop girl arrives with a dress that doesn't quite freak me. I don't know how to describe it. It's off-white with some glossy stripe effect. It has a big skirt, a nipped-in waist, and a belt and clutch bag in matching fabric.

I stand under the glare of the lamps, their forensic scrutiny, and study Wedding Girl in the mirror.

And, though I don't see myself exactly, I don't see some impostor either. I can just about see my reflection without diving into the map of my bruises.

I say, 'Susan?', meaning, *Is this OK?*

Meaning, *Help me*.

Susan knows by now not to ask me if I like it. She tells me what *she* thinks. The view from Planet Normal. She says, 'That's really good. It's not too fussy. It's very weddingy. Very fifties. It fits you well and it goes with your look.'

I don't know that I have a look, or ever have had. But I don't feel too weird. That upward draining starts to settle a little. I can't feel my legs at all, but I can feel my arms. Can feel my waist and chest. When Wedding Girl moves, I'm aware that her movements and mine are somehow synchronised. That knowledge doesn't feel ordinary, but it doesn't feel so strange either.

Susan takes a photo. 'So you can remember,' she says.

The shop girl, who has been patient and kind, wants to get payback for her patience and kindness by blitzing me with veils and tiaras and gloves and shoes and stockings and basques and that whole infinite assemblage of things made of white lace and silk *for your special day*. I try to inspect her gifts, but quickly start to lose my bearings again and Susan has to step in to close things down.

We go outside. I haven't made a purchase, but I've got all the details I need.

We sit in her car and she waits for me to tell me what I want to do next. I say, 'Can we just drive somewhere?'

She wants to ask where, but that's a Planet Normal question and I'm not doing well with those at the moment. So, bless her, she just says, 'OK,' and we roll out of central Manchester, aiming for the loops of motorway and dual carriageway that spool round the city.

After a bit, I say, 'Can we go to Sheffield?'

Susan glances sharply at me, but says, 'OK,' and heads for the A628, the Sheffield road.

When we've picked up the route, she says, 'What's in Sheffield?'

'Nothing. Sorry. I just like the mountains.'

The road crosses the Pennines. High moorland and scudding clouds. Grass as tough as wire, hills as old as time.

Susan smiles. 'I like them too. I used to do a lot of fell running.'

She drives.

When we reach some high point, we stop. Walk out into the pale green-gold. Susan pulls on a thick coat from the back of her car. She offers me a blanket, but I say I prefer to get cold. We sit on a rock and look at the universe. Feel the wind penetrate our bones.

She says, 'It's perfectly normal for people to have problems readjusting. There's psychological support if you need it.'

'You're sweet, but these aren't adjustment problems. They're me-problems. I always have them.'

She says, 'You looked nice in that dress. The last one.'

I realise I haven't even asked her if she's married, so I do and she is.

'No kids yet, but we've only just started trying.'

She shows me photos on her phone. Her with hubby. Her at her wedding. I say she looks lovely and she does. Like some Celtic princess, all tumbling copper hair and skin the colour of buttermilk. It's not her looks I most envy, though, it's her comfort. Her easy ability at being human. Her uncomplicated citizenship of Planet Normal.

As we drive back, towards Altrincham and a waiting Buzz, Susan says, 'You know, it will go back to how it was. Once you start to realise that you're not Fiona Grey any more.'

'But I am.'

'I know. The legend will always stay intact, but—'

'That's not what I mean. I mean that as far as Henderson is concerned I'm still Fiona Grey. I'm still potentially useful.'

The road curves over the mountains and demands attention, but even so Susan slips me a look.

'Fiona Grey the payroll clerk was useful. But I don't think you're going to get many offers of employment in payroll now.'

I say, very quietly, 'Yes, but they've got a distribution problem, haven't they? Isn't that what we've been talking about all week?'

Susan falls silent a moment, then says, just as quietly, 'What do you mean?'

'I'm a cleaner. I was a cleaner before I had anything to do with payroll. My firm services most of the big offices in Cardiff. You keep talking as though gaining physical access to these places were difficult. I walk into corporate IT suites every day. Physical access? I'm changing their bins. I'm under the desks giving their computers a good dust.'

There's a lay-by up ahead of us. An unmetalled strip off the main road, with some wooden benches and green litter bins. Susan pulls over. Kills the engine.

She says, 'How long have you thought about this?'

I shrug. I don't really understand the question. When I first uncovered Kureishi's role in that initial small fraud, it struck to me that the critical aspect of his work wasn't that he was a computer expert: any fool can load a program onto a PC. What really mattered was his ability to enter corporate workplaces unchallenged, to sit at a computer without arousing suspicion. And a cleaner can go anywhere at all. That's why I clung to that part of Fiona Grey's legend. Did what I could to embrace and enlarge it.

I mutter something and we look out of the windscreen at low hills and a horizon starting to clot with rain. She says, 'They might not take you back to the farmhouse.'

'No. Not necessarily.' But I think of Shoesmith's slogan: *Specify, program, beta-launch, full launch. And test, test, test, test.* I can't see Shoesmith, Henderson and the gang hitting the start button without one final round of testing. And they need me for that. Need me, if I'm still part of the team.

Susan follows my train of thought. She's an IT type herself. She knows how these things work. She picks up her phone, gingerly, the way an Egyptologist handles papyrus. 'You don't have to go back. These things are always voluntary, you know.'

'I know.'

'Are you OK if I call Adrian?'

'Yes.'

'You're sure?'

'Yes.'

I'm vaguely aware of Susan as she calls Brattenbury. Vaguely aware of what she says. But not really. The green-gold hills melt into a blackening distance and the first glimmer of lights. I'm going to spend the evening with Buzz. And today, perhaps, I found a wedding dress.

42

I have what will be my last court appearance for a while. Greater Manchester Police have completed their investigation into the 'stabbing' and have accepted my self-defence story. South Wales is still charging me with fraud, but are about to accept that I am not a flight-risk and do not need to be held in pre-trial detention.

Winterton tells me that he thinks the CPS will have difficulty overcoming my self-protection defence and may prefer not to even try. 'We'll present you as a victim,' he says. 'Of domestic abuse. Of organised crime. Even the police. Juries don't like convicting women at the best of times. I think we'll be OK. If we can, we'll get them to drop charges completely.'

I still don't like him, but he's a decent barrister.

I phone George Noble, my immigration lawyer. I want to know if my recent legal complications are going to be an issue for the New Zealand authorities.

He says, 'You've been *charged*? What with?'

I tell him.

'And Greater Manchester Police wanted to question you in connection with *what*, exactly?'

I tell him.

'Ah.'

'Is this going to be a problem?' I try to sound like a citizen wearily outraged at small-minded bureaucrats.

'I'll make some calls,' he says and we hang up.

That same day, we get news from the Dyfed Powys Police. A girl's body has been found, tangled in dock leaves and stinging nettles in a wet field margin. Death was by gunshot to the back of the head. Face beaten to a pulp to make identification difficult. But the body was put together with a MisPer report, and DNA comparisons identified the corpse as belonging to Tania Lewis, a student and occasional waitress from Llanybydder, near Lampeter.

Tania: usually shortened to Nia.

Llanybydder: definitely not in the arc of land where we think the barn and farmhouse lies.

The victim: the waitress who sorted out cigarettes and clothes for me. Who was nice to me. Who showed kindness.

The family: said that she was given occasional waitressing gigs by a conferencing firm who did corporate events. The conferencing firm was for real – based in Aberystwyth, does about a million pounds in turnover – but the gigs that came from Tinker were always shrouded in secrecy. The person who made the arrangements, Henderson at a guess, had said that there was a large corporate software deal being arranged. The deal-makers were working in secret because of past attempts to hack the organisations involved. Nia had been made to sign a confidentiality agreement, was picked up by a car with darkened windows. 'A limo, very posh,' the grieving father said. Nia never knew where she was taken, but had heard mutterings about Tregaron. She was paid well and looked after, so never really cared. She liked the thrill of being in on something big, however marginal her role.

Tregaron: another place nowhere close to the arc of land which has drawn our scrutiny.

The corpse: not just been badly beaten. Someone had used a stick to penetrate her, roughly. The girl's vagina and uterus were badly damaged. The pathologist was neutral on whether the harm was done pre- or post-mortem, but our working assumption is that the injuries were added post-mortem to make the assault like a random sex-crime, not a cold-blooded murder. Although no semen was found to be present, it often isn't, even at quite violent rape scenes.

Given the data we have, and a few further guesses, I think what happened was this. Tania Lewis was recruited as a waitress from an area remote from the farmhouse itself. She was given false information about the location. Normally, she did her work, was paid well, was driven back. On this occasion, however, my arrival gave her two things to gossip about. One: my scene with Henderson. Two: when she went for clothes, she found herself driving, or being taken, to Ebbw, which isn't close to Tregaron at all. Both of those things could have been explained away. Neither of them would have sent Lewis to the police. But Henderson – or one of his colleagues – decided that the risk of loose conversation was nevertheless too great and tied off that loose end in his own inimitable way.

In short: my actions at the farmhouse triggered Nia's death. That knowledge plucks at me – it can't not – but I don't feel guilty, or not really. Henderson is the killer. My own role was close to incidental.

But the corpses are stacking up. Hayley Morgan: an accident, almost. Saj Kureishi: a violent punishment. A warning. Nia Lewis: the snipping of a stray thread. The erasure of a minor error.

And Roy Williams? Corpse or prisoner? I don't know. I do see Katie Williams, who comes up to the Altrincham house specially. She cries a lot. Asks questions, most of which I can't answer. I tell her that I'm sure we'll get him back. Tell her that we have the best people on the job. How much Jackson and others respect her husband.

'Oh I know,' Katie interrupts. 'Roy always told me you were special. I mean . . .'

She hesitates, wondering how much truth is acceptable in this context. I spare her the embarrassment.

'You mean, I'm a bit weird, but good at my job. That's OK. I *am* a bit weird.'

'Mr Jackson told me that you were in the place where they've got Roy.'

'Yes. At least we think so.'

'And it wasn't . . . it wasn't . . .?'

'No. It was very nice. Very tidy, very clean. Quite luxurious really. And these people aren't animals. They wouldn't hurt someone for no reason. And we aren't going to give them a reason.'

'Thank you.'

Katie cries again. There's something about her peaches-and-cream complexion to which tears are very suited. Raindrops on roses.

When she's about to leave, she makes a little speech. Pre-prepared, I think. 'If you see him, tell him . . .'

However much preparation went into that speech, her sobs spoiled it. But I get the gist. She loves him. Always has, always will. Admires him so much. He's been such a good dad. Such a good husband. If I weren't almost incapable of tears, I'd be crying too. I rub her back and get kitchen towel for her eyes.

I watch her leave and stand waving till her car vanishes round the bend.

Call Brattenbury. Ask, 'Do you have enough on Henderson to secure a life sentence?'

He starts to bullshit me, but he knows me well enough by now to know that I don't do well with bullshit.

I interpret. 'Basically, we'll press for a conspiracy to murder conviction. We might get it or we might not.'

'That's about right. We'll get him on a humungous fraud charge, though. A twenty-year stretch, minimum.'

I don't say much to that, but I come away with another

item for my to-do list. Secure enough evidence on Henderson that we secure a conviction for murder. The death of Tania Lewis demands nothing less.

And finally, my Manchester visit is due to end. Buzz and I are to go out for our final evening here. Italian food. Candles. Carnations. Waiters with giant pepper grinders. We say all the right things to each other, but the pull of separation is already on us. I'm too much Fiona Grey, too little Fiona Griffiths. I try to unscramble my head, but find it hard.

Buzz as usual is patient. That unfathomable patience.

At the end of the evening, I slip my engagement ring off and give it to him.

'This'll be the last time,' he says.

'Yes.' I don't know if that's true, but I agree anyway. 'Thank you for letting me do all this.'

I wave my hand. A gesture that mostly includes check tablecloths and Mancunian diners, but is intended to mean the entire Fiona Grey adventure.

'That's OK, love. I think you were right. It was something you had to do. Get it out of your system.'

One of those optimistic Buzz beliefs: that doing this is another solid step in my confident progress towards Ms Normal. I try to feel whether I've got anything out of my system, but I get confused between Fiona Grey and Fiona Griffiths and just say yes and look down at my hands and feel muddled.

At ten this evening, a patrol car will take me back to Cheadle Heath. Early tomorrow morning, I'll be released from detention and permitted to return to Cardiff. My passport has been seized and I'll have to report to the police every week, but I'll be a free woman once again.

Free to re-enter the world of Fiona Grey.

But I'm not just going back. I'm going deeper.

43

I find Henderson as he emerges from the osteopath's. There's a flight of stairs coming down. A black painted door facing onto the street. And I'm there, just outside the doorway, sitting on a bit of dirty sleeping bag, folded double. I'm smoking a joint. He doesn't see me as he emerges and he almost kicks me as he tries to stop himself falling.

'Hi, Vic.'

'Fiona.'

He's instantly wary. Doesn't know how I found him. Is worried that there are cops or cameras watching.

'You don't seem very pleased to see me.'

'It's always nice to see you.'

His eyes flick left and right. Checking sightlines. Checking for white vans that might hide surveillance squads.

There's nothing there. Nothing except the video feed which will already have noted his presence, but which he certainly won't be able to detect just by looking. That and two armed officers in plainclothes. I haven't been able to pick them out, so I'm sure Henderson won't be able to.

The armed escort is part of my deal with Brattenbury. Given the risk that Roy Williams may have given up my name under torture, Brattenbury only consented to let me return if I was within reach of police marksmen at all times. Previously, I only got the full treatment when I was meeting Henderson or one of his buddies. Now, it'll be constant. Brattenbury tells me that only the Queen and the Prime Minister are as heavily guarded as I now am.

I'd prefer to travel light than travel this heavy, but I don't make the rules. And either way, and perhaps for the very first time, I think we're one step ahead.

'How did you find me?'

I tell him the truth or close enough: that I was scared of Henderson, that I wanted a friend of mine to know who he was, that I asked Gary to spy on him that day at Quintrell's house.

Henderson searches back to the day in question. 'A homeless guy? Beard, shopping trolley, cider bottle?'

'That's him. Gary. He's not always on the booze.'

'Go on.'

'He sells the *Big Issue*.' I gesture out onto the Hayes, where Gary is probably busy flogging his wares right now. 'He said he'd look out for you.'

'How long have you been here?'

He indicates the doorway with distaste.

'Three days so far.'

Three days: the truth. Three days, twenty-two ciggies, four joints. Five attempts to move me on. Eleven inappropriate sexual advances.

'Did you tell any of this to the police?' He means my knowledge of Gary's researches, not my life on the street.

'What do *you* think, Vic? Have you had the cops up your arse?'

Henderson – lightweight summer jacket, chinos, pale blue shirt – stares at me grimly. He's calculating the security risk of all this. Trying to work out what my reappearance means, whether it holds a threat for him.

I don't know the outcome of those calculations, but his face clears and he says, 'OK. Fiona, have you had lunch? Do you know the Old Radnor Castle?'

He names a gastro-pub a few hundred yards away. I nod. I know it. Never been inside.

'Right. We'll meet there, but let's just make sure it's only the two of us, OK?'

He gives me a complicated route to follow. Tells me to have my phone with me, as he may ask me to change course. I do as he instructs. At one point he does phone, tells me to double back on myself. I do, then after thirty seconds, he repeats the instruction and I double back on my doubling back.

There are people on the street – shoppers, tradesmen, delivery guys, business types – but I avoid their eyes. A big screen under plane trees on the Hayes is showing highlights of what is meant to have been a successful Olympics. Women in lycra doing remarkable things. Men in Union Jacks and tears.

I'm on my hands-free and follow Henderson's instructions. His obedient servant, as ever.

When I get to the pub, a waiter wants to take my coat. He also looks at my bit of sleeping bag and thinks about offering to put that somewhere, but decides against. I fold the material up so it's as small as possible. Try to keep the least dirty bit facing out.

I walk over to where Henderson is waiting for me. I'm about to speak, but he raises a finger to his lips, and starts scanning me with his RF scanner.

'Anyone ever tell you you're paranoid?'

He finishes his sweep, then answers. 'I'm not in jail. You're not in jail. Anna *is* in jail. She wasn't paranoid enough.'

I sit down.

I gesture at the sleeping bag. 'I lost my room.'

'You're sleeping rough?'

'No. I'm back at the hostel. One of the guys lent me this.'

It's true. When my room was searched, my cannabis plants were found and confiscated, and the landlord terminated my let. I miss my studio flat, but I think I prefer the hostel. It's been my favourite thing about this year.

'I'm sorry to hear that.'

'I don't mind.'

A waiter brings us fishcakes and salsa verde and a beet and pea-shoot salad and chips. The whole thing is served on a piece of blue slate.

'I ordered for you,' says Vic.

I start eating chips with my fingers, then think I should probably wash my hands first, so go to the bathroom and clean up a bit.

Vic is on the phone when I return. I stand a few yards back, waiting for him to finish. When Fiona Grey waits, she usually looks at the floor and doesn't fidget much. She seems more peaceful than me. I think she's happier.

When Vic is done, he signals it's OK for me to come over. We resume our meal.

I thank him for the lawyer. He thanks me for keeping my mouth shut while in detention. Thanks me too for wiping my hard drive before leaving Western Vale. 'That was smart thinking.'

I shrug, in a *de-nada*-ish sort of way.

We eat a bit.

We're both, I think, trying to figure out where we stand on the lust front at the moment. After almost four weeks in Manchester, and seeing Buzz almost every day, my body isn't as screamingly hungry for touch as it was. All the same, I think there was more to those dust devils than just missing Buzz. I have the thought, *Fiona Grey wants Vic Henderson. It's Fiona Griffiths who wants Buzz.* There's a neat logic to that thought which appeals. And it has some truth, I can feel it. If I go into my Fiona Griffiths part, I can feel Henderson recede, until he's little more than a pale blue shirt, a summer jacket, thinning hair and intelligent eyes. If I move into my Fiona

314

Grey place, he strengthens again. I become aware of the dark hairs peeping from his open neck, the pattern of blue in his eyes, the quick movement of his fingers. I don't have to be in that place for long, before I feel the tug of something stronger than myself.

I try to damp it down. To stay away from those thoughts.

He eats his fishcake with a fork only. 'I haven't forgotten that I owe you a weekend away.'

I don't respond, so he tries another tack. 'You lost your room. What about your cleaning job . . .?'

'They've given me seventeen and a half hours a week. I'm hoping to go full time again soon.'

'That's city centre stuff, is it? The way it was before?'

'Yes. I'm on early mornings again.'

He wants to know more. Which offices I clean. What access I get. What my shift pattern is.

I answer him, or start to, but then break off. 'Look, Vic, it doesn't matter. I'm OK, all right? I just wanted to . . .'

'Yes?' I think he wants to hear me say something about him. How I can't contain my passion any longer. That sort of thing.

I say, 'My emigration. It's still on. My immigration lawyer, Noble, says that criminal charges aren't necessarily a no-no, just so long as they don't lead to anything.'

'That sounds fair.'

'But he says it's more work. It's a more difficult case.'

'He wants more money?'

I nod. 'And I need to show I can be self-supporting. Money in my bank account.'

'How much?'

'Twelve grand. I've already got some money of my own and it's cheaper in the hostel.' Because he doesn't instantly respond, I add, 'Our original contract said you were going to pay me twenty-two, plus the lawyer. I haven't had nearly that much. Then you said you'd double it.'

Vic's gaze closes on mine. His mouth is slightly parted. Behind his eyes, there is the rapid movement of calculation.

He says – whispers, rather – 'Fiona, can you give me ten minutes?'

I nod.

He tells me to step outside. Onto the street. Indicates the spot where I'm to stand, so he can keep me in view as he talks.

I go and stand there. Smoke.

I can see him, through the window, talking. To whom, to whom? That's the whole riddle right there. Tinker's dirty little secret. But we can't decrypt the phone. Can't always say for certain which handset he's using. Didn't have enough notice to get the pub wired for sound. If we knew who he was speaking to, we could probably close the case in twenty-four hours. But we don't. And we can't.

Henderson stares out at me through the window. There's a window box just outside, planted up with lobelia, I think, and something pink. He knows I've seen him, but holds his gaze. I have the strong sense that the person on the other end of the line is asking about me. Whether I'm to be trusted.

Trusted or killed: that's the choice.

Kureishi: killed.

Tania Lewis: killed.

Anna Quintrell: trusted when she shouldn't have been. I bet her arrest sent memos flying around the Tinker network. Next time, kill the bitch.

I smoke my cigarette and let Henderson appraise me through the lobelia.

Eventually, he beckons me inside. I go back to his table. Wait till he invites me to sit. Then sit.

'Fiona, you want to work for us, right?'

'I want you to pay me what you said.'

'Payment in exchange for work, correct?'

I shrug.

'I've checked with my colleagues and we want to honour our agreement. Honour it, that is, if you agree to honour yours.'

I shrug again. I've done everything they've asked.

'And if we are to go on working with you, we'll need you to be more reliable. No more running off to London. No more tracking down colleagues and sitting on their doorsteps. No attacking me in the middle of a drinks reception. We'll need you to do nothing that you haven't cleared with me first. Do you understand?'

That's his don't-make-me-cross-or-I-might-have-to-murder-you voice.

I say, 'Yes.'

Again that appraising look. Trust her or kill her? The only choices on this particular menu. I don't usually hold his gaze, but this time I do. Sit there and let him scrutinise me. He has two colours of blue in his eye. Something sombre, the colour of deep sea or rain clouds. And flecks of something much brighter. Lobelia. Cobalt blue. Something tropical.

A waiter comes to clear the table and I look away.

Henderson has finished his meal. I've eaten half a fishcake and all of my chips. I don't want to see the colours he has in his eyes. Don't want to imagine the taste of his lips on mine.

When the waiter goes, Henderson says softly, 'OK. Good. You need to mean that "Yes". Now, we *will* pay you what we said. We'll even speed up the payment schedule. Help you get to New Zealand. But the work we'll need from you will be a little different.'

'OK.'

'There'll be some training involved, but nothing you can't handle.'

'OK.'

317

'And a few other changes too.'

He starts to tell me what he means, but I'm pretty sure I know what he has in mind. *Was* pretty sure that I was ready for it.

Only self-knowledge is an unreliable thing. You expect one thing, then – *boom!* – your body delivers something quite else. As I listen to Henderson's calmly decisive explanation of the next steps in Fiona Grey's unfolding criminal career, I find that she – she and I, the two of us together – is as frightened now as we were that time he hooded us up for the journey back into Cardiff. This time, though, the journey is darker and will last for longer.

44

Five in the morning. Fitzalan Place. Dawn proper doesn't come for more than an hour, and my co-workers are once again dark shapes huddled by pale glass.

Fiona Grey isn't here, however.

In her place: Jessica Taylor. I don't know who she is, this Jessica, though I have her papers in my pocket, a bank account in her name. Jessica tells Euan Tanner, Fiona's old boss, that Fiona had to leave town, that she mentioned that there might be a job available. I say – Jessica says – 'I've cleaned before. Loads of times. We can make this a trial day if you want. I'm a grafter.'

Tanner, peering at me in the darkness, agrees to a one-week trial, 'which we'll have to put down as a work experience thing. Just the first week. Then take it from there.' My old battle-buddy, Allergy Lowri, is present but, to my relief, Tanner partners me up with someone else. Stella. Lowri coughs and complains as we're being issued with cleaning stuff, but she doesn't take a second look at me.

To be fair, before finally agreeing to the swap, Tanner had the decency to try reaching Fiona, but without joy. It's not surprising: Henderson took her phone. Pocketed the SIM card, ditched the rest.

Most of Fiona's clothes have gone too. Ditto her friends: Abs, Gary and Clementina, Jason the nice bus driver.

Also gone: her room at the hostel, her Anger and Anxiety

sessions with the much-bebangled Melinda, her visits to the library, her walks in the park.

That's not all Fiona Grey has lost. She's lost her looks, literally. When Fiona and I stare into a mirror now, we see somebody else altogether. Jessica is blonde. Short hair, pixie-cut, feathery and upbeat. Bright red lips. More eye make-up than I ever use. Jewellery.

Jessica has taken over my wardrobe too. Out go Fiona Grey's cost-conscious purchases from eBay and Matalan. Out go her greys and her blacks and her unobtrusive neutrals. In comes – I don't know. Jessica's stuff. Skirts shorter than I'd wear. Leggings. Tops tighter and tartier than I'd ever choose. It's not that Jessica doesn't look perfectly OK in those outfits. Nor that women of her age don't have every right to wear what they want. But still. When Fiona Grey and I look in a mirror, we see the glass occupied by some third party, whom neither of us know or would ever naturally be close too.

The three of us nevertheless brush our teeth in sync. Wash our faces together. When we clean corporate washrooms, Fiona and I scrub mirrors, wipe them clean, then move on to the soap dispensers, taps and sinks and countertops. In theory, Mirror Jessica does the same. The same action, even the same pace of movement. But Fiona and I find it hard to believe in her effort, that she really works to get things clean. There's something smirking in the way she mimics us, a cool girl laughing at the dorky ones.

The simple fact is that we resent her presence, Fiona and I. Resent her blonde, extrovert brightness. The way she is always staring at us. The way she barges into our job, our washrooms, our lives.

But I shouldn't grumble. There are gains too.

One such gain, small but significant, is an ankle bracelet. The sort they use to tag offenders. Jessica's bracelet is fastened on the right leg. It's immovable. I can't get under it even to wash. Henderson, who put it there, told me, 'It's a precaution. The bracelet combines a very sensitive audio recorder with a basic tracking device. It means that we know where you are at all times. Also that we know who speaks to you and what they say.'

Jessica, I think, doesn't mind the bracelet too much. There used to be something of a Cardiff ASBO culture in which such things were worn as a mark of pride. A badge of social distinction. While I dislike the thing intensely, Jessica is half keen to flaunt it. Wants to sit outside, at pavement cafés in the city centre, wearing bare legs and heels, letting people see the thick-strapped bracelet, like a too-chunky watch without a face, watching their expressions as they slowly figure it out.

I don't quite let her do that. I mostly let her have her way with clothes – a leopard-print top, a push-up bra, a pair of wet-look leggings – but I generally insist on slouch boots, loose but concealing around the ankle. My body, my rules.

Of course there are times when Jessica rebels. Does what she wants, dresses as she chooses. Other times when I assert control. Make her dress down. Even force her into a bookshop now and again. The Waterstones on the Hayes. The little bookshop on Wellfield Road, where I search for cheap editions of the classics and Jessica flips through anything with pictures.

We get along. Not friends, but ill-assorted housemates carefully negotiating our shared social space.

I say to Henderson, 'If the police take me in, they'll find the bracelet.'

'Yes.'

'It won't take them long to realise I'm Fiona Grey.'

'No.'

'They have my DNA. And my fingerprints. And . . .'

Henderson says, tautly, 'The bracelet is for our protection, not yours. If they take you into a police station, we'll know that they've done so. If they talk to you, and don't wipe the

321

recording, we'll hear what they've been saying. If they talk to you and *do* wipe the recording, we'll know that they've done so. That's what we'll check for. Every day. Is there twenty-four hours of material there? Does any of it suggest a police approach?'

I don't say anything, but Jessica and my two Fionas share a common view of this approach to our welfare and I expect my face expresses that view.

Henderson says, 'Fiona, if the police approach you, we have a problem. We do. You do. Your job will be to say absolutely nothing and we'll work, as we did before, through a lawyer. There's nothing illegal about changing your look. Nothing illegal about wearing an ankle bracelet, if it comes to that. Stick with us and we'll stick with you.'

I shrug. At this point, in any event, I have no choice at all.

And there are other gains, besides.

Henderson has put me into a one-bedroom flat down on the Bay. It's bland and boxy. Street view not sea-view. First floor not penthouse. But still. It is, by most standards, the smartest accommodation I've had all year. Fiona and I don't really like it, but we recognise that Henderson meant well. He was even nice enough to tell the truth. 'We've got audio and video feeds from the apartment. Audio only in the bathroom, so if you prefer to get changed there, you should feel free.'

I say thank you, but my thanks are not effusive.

The kitchen has nothing in it except an unopened box of cheap crockery from Argos. A box of cutlery. Some glasses. And a salt carton. 'Everyone needs salt,' says Henderson.

Nor is it just my accommodation that gets an upgrade. My education does too.

Henderson takes me to spend a long day with Ian Shoesmith in London, learning how to hack computers: a new skill, another gain.

What's remarkable, really, is how simple it is. You think these things must be complicated, but they're not, they're really not. My first step – Jessica's first step – will be to obtain the necessary passwords. So we simply place a keystroke recorder on the back of the relevant computers, something so easy I did it once myself on another case altogether, and wait for those recorders to collect the user's passwords. Then, the next day or the next week, depending on my cleaning schedule, I use those passwords to place a little bit of software on the relevant computer. The software is, I think, just a classier version of the Trojan horse software that Kureishi once used. You can buy commercial versions of the same thing easily enough, the only real difference being that the commercial versions let you know they're there.

Indeed, although my training day was long – ten hours all told, plus a good six hours of travel – the essence was simple: steal some passwords, load some software. The whole thing only took as long as it did because Shoesmith made me practise on a whole variety of computers, configured with multiple different operating systems, firewalls, and security set-ups. By the time we'd finished, I was as quick and as certain as Shoesmith himself. That's not a boast, or not really. The process just isn't that hard.

At the end of the day, I asked Shoesmith if I could have a copy of the software. He said, 'Why?' I said, 'Just because,' and he said, 'OK.' So I set up a Hotmail account under a false name and emailed myself a copy of the software. I don't really know why I wanted it, even. It's just the sort of thing I prefer to have.

Another gain.

These gains and losses are bewildering at some level, but the Fiona Griffiths me understands it all. Predicted it all, indeed.

Simply put: Tinker needs me, three times over. First, because I'm still the only payroll clerk they have. The only person who knows how a payroll department actually operates.

Secondly, they've lost Quintrell. Her precise accountancy view of payroll isn't quite the perspective I bring, but they still need someone who can look at a payslip and tell them if the National Insurance has been calculated correctly. And then, third, there's my role as cleaner. The role I now share with Jessica. My ability to get into corporate premises. To get up close and personal with the computers that matter.

But I'm not an easy hire. Uppermost in Henderson's mind is the fact that Fiona Grey is now known to the police and dancing round a fraud charge, at that.

And that's their dilemma. Tinker wants Fiona Grey's expertise and access, but they're worried by the risk of contamination. I'm simultaneously essential and potentially lethal.

The solution that Henderson and his buddies came up with was to create a new girl in the mould of the old one. Hence Jessica Taylor's arrival: a clean identity, a woman without a past. Hence also the need for the costume, hair and make-up changes. Henderson coaches me to speak differently, walk differently, act differently. He wants Jessica's new 'clean' identity to belong to someone who isn't even recognisable as the old Fiona Grey. Her polar opposite.

And I think she is. I mean, yes, Buzz would recognise me if 'Jessica' spent time with him, but I'm sure that if I passed him on the street, he'd never notice me in her. Lowri, who I still bump into now and again, is a self-absorbed cow admittedly, the only real hold-over from my old life, but she's not shown the slightest surprise or curiosity when she sees me. Just tells me about her allergies with the same wearisome from-the-top approach she adopted the first time she met Fiona Grey. I try to make Jessica louder, brassier, less pliable with Lowri than I do elsewhere – I try to make her character consistent with her clothes, her look, her make-up – but I genuinely wonder if I need to make the effort. To Lowri, I'm just another girl.

Henderson is right, of course. Given his role and his objectives, he's doing everything right. The way I'd do it, if I were him.

But while I *understand* all this – and had assumed myself ready to accept the new conditions of this undercover life – I find myself taken aback by the reality. I'd found it easy enough to become Fiona Grey. More than that: I enjoyed the change, found it simpler.

But this Jessica Taylor: I don't relate to her. Not to her looks, her confidence, her outward brightness. If my head was less muddled, I'd handle these things better. I'd be brassy, mouthy Jessica when I had to be – with Lowri and the other cleaning girls, or when out in town – and myself the rest of the time. Henderson only cares about the public performance. He doesn't care who I am in private.

But I'm not that fixed, that centred. When my air bubble floats into Jessica's world, I end up becoming her, because I'm not sure who else or how else to be. I bounce between my different identities, trying not to say the wrong thing to the wrong person, and all the time feeling my head degrading. A pellet of uranium 235, spitting alpha particles. Teetering on the brink of collapse or ignition.

It's at home when these things are at their worst. When I'm getting ready for bed, standing in front of the bathroom mirror, I sometimes don't know who I am. I try to remember my name, my real one. Try to remember anything: about Buzz, Jackson, Brattenbury, my family.

I usually get there, sort of. An accumulation of scraps: some names, a few images, a memory of past kindness. But nothing that really joins up. Nothing that lies in a straight line between actual people and me. And whenever I almost get something, the blonde girl in the mirror shakes her head at me and the surface of the pond breaks again and I end up with nothing but confusion and a pocket full of scraps.

And sometimes I get really, properly lost. End up sitting on the bathroom floor to avoid the girl in the mirror. Sometimes go to sleep there, or think I do.

Once, when I think I was very lost, Henderson phoned me. I was lying on the bathroom floor and had been there I don't know how long.

'Are you OK?' he asked.

'I don't know.'

'What's wrong?'

'Nothing.'

'Do you want me to come over?'

'No.'

There's a pause. I have the hallucination that Hayley Morgan is in the bathroom with me. I know she's dead and I think I might be too. I think I was probably asleep when Henderson rang, so this isn't quite like a full-blown psychosis. More like one of those things where it takes time to recover fully into wakefulness.

'You've been in the bathroom two hours.'

'It's the only place you don't spy on me.'

He says something about the need to protect Jessica from police intervention. How my interests are protected by all this.

I don't know what that means. My hips are hurting from lying too long on a tiled floor.

'Can you take the camera out of the bedroom?'

'OK. I'll do that tomorrow.' There's a pause on the line. A softly crackling emptiness. 'No, cancel that. I'll come over now.'

I don't know what I say to that, if anything, but the line goes dead. I sit on the bathroom floor and count my breaths. *In*-two-three-four-five. *Out*-two-three-four-five.

Some time later, it doesn't seem that long, Henderson arrives. He opens the bathroom door, appraises me a moment.

326

Disappears. Comes back in a few minutes. Has a little piece of electronics in his hand.

'This is the video camera from the bedroom.' He drops it by the sink. It's tiny: these things come very small these days.

I think he expects me to stand up, but I don't. He slides down beside me. Takes my hand.

'Finding this hard, eh?' he says.

'Are you alive?'

'Am I *alive*? Yes.'

'And I am? I mean, you *think* I am?'

'Yes. Of course.'

'What's my name?'

'Your real name? Fiona Grey. At the moment, you're pretending to be someone called Jessica Taylor, but that's just a temporary thing. You're still Fiona Grey underneath.'

'Am I getting married?'

'Getting married? No. Not as far as I know.'

'Who's in this bathroom?'

'Right now? You and me.'

'You haven't looked.'

Henderson makes a show of looking. The bathroom is tiny, so I suppose his initial estimate was always likely to be accurate. But he confirms it: 'Just you and me. I've checked.'

His words give me the confidence to look around. And he's right. I can't see Hayley Morgan anywhere on the floor and even she wouldn't be small enough to fit in the cupboards. 'Sorry. I thought there was someone else.'

'No. Just us.'

He starts saying some other things, but it all feels very complicated and I don't listen.

I don't know why he uses so many words.

After a bit, he stops talking and lifts me up and carries me through to the bedroom. The blonde girl, Jessica, stares at me from the bedroom mirror and I want to go back into the bathroom, but when Henderson works out what's bothering me, he lifts the mirror down and places it, glass side inward, against the wall.

I look around cautiously. Say, 'Is she here? The blonde one?'

Henderson starts to say one thing, then sees my face and says, 'No. It's just you. You're Fiona Grey. The only people in this room are you and me. Nobody else.'

'And you're alive?'

'Yes.'

'And I am?'

'Yes.'

'You're sure?'

'Yes. I'm sure.'

I get into bed then. Don't get changed with Henderson there, but do what I need to do. He tucks me in. Helps me with pillows. He rubs my shoulder in a nice way, and I can feel that his hand is definitely warm, which means he *is* alive and, in that case, I probably am too. I almost ask him to kiss me. Not because I want his kisses exactly, just that all that warmth and activity would be the best possible kind of proof.

But I don't ask.

He sits there holding my hand and I start to feel more normal.

'Sorry, Vic. My head. It doesn't always work brilliantly. It goes funny sometimes.'

I point at my head, in case he has trouble locating it.

'You're doing fine. It's not for long.'

At some stage, I go to sleep. At some stage, Henderson leaves.

In the morning, I see him again. Fiona Grey is still on police bail and she has to report every week to the police station down on the bay. This is my first time doing that since I dyed my hair. When Henderson enters my flat, he's worried that I'm still crazy. But I'm not. I'm feeling OK.

He gives me – gives Jessica – a wig that's more or less Fiona Grey-ish. I tuck my blond pixie-locks under the wig, dress soberly in what I have left of my old clothes, and present myself for Henderson's inspection.

'The old Fiona. Welcome back.' He looks me over. 'You're all right, are you?'

'Yes.'

'After last night, I mean?'

'Yes.'

'Bit weird that.'

'For you, maybe. I'm like that sometimes.' I shrug. 'It comes and goes.'

The truth, more or less.

He checks my ankle for the presence of the bracelet, checks the battery level, then drives me down to the station, parking a few hundred yards away.

I put my handle on the car door, but don't yet get out.

'Vic?'

'Yes?'

'Last night. That sort of thing used to happen more. I'm OK now mostly, but I'm under a lot of pressure.'

'I know. You are.' He's about to give me the you're-doing-well speech, but that's not what I want now and I cut him off.

'There's a medication I used to rely on. Amisulpride. It's an anti-psychotic. An anti-nutter drug, basically. It's what they give to schizophrenics.'

'You want some?'

'Not to *take* it, no. But to *have* it, yes. Just in case. A precaution.'

I'm not lying to him. Ever since coming out of hospital, I've carried the drug with me. Haven't used it for years, but I need to know it's there if I need it. And last night was a bad episode for me, as close to the edge as I've been for a long while.

Henderson gives me that stare that sane people give their less-than-stable friends. It's a kind enough look in its way, except there's always that hint of condescension in it. A hint of top-hatted Victorian smugness.

'Do you know what you need?'

'Yes.' I find paper and pen in the seat pocket and write out a prescription. Amisulpride. Normally sold as Solian. I choose the liquid formulation: 100 mg/ml in a 50ml bottle. I prescribe myself 200mg twice a day. Pass the sheet over to Henderson.

'If I get this . . .'

'If you fake a prescription with that on it, I'll go to the pharmacist and pick it up.'

He smiles. I'm his favourite sort of nutter: one who's happy to do his dirty work. 'I'll get onto it now.'

I walk down the road to the police station. The duty sergeant doesn't treat me any differently from the other people in reception. While I'm waiting, I scribble a note to DCI Jackson.

New identity: Jessica Taylor. Am permanently wired for sound. Also permanent location-tracking. Do NOT attempt to make contact. I give my new address, but add, *Flat wired for audio, video. Do NOT enter. Inform Adrian. Infiltration going well. I'm fine. FG.*

I don't give the note to the duty sergeant, because I don't want him to say anything that the ankle bracelet might pick up. So I just fold the note and write on the outside *For DCI Jackson. Urgent and Confidential. Operation Tinker.* I add his work mobile as well, so that anyone seeing the note will realise that whoever's written it knows Jackson well enough to call direct. I leave the note in an out-tray on the front desk.

Then leave. Walk down the block. Get into Henderson's

330

ever-purring BMW. Give him my wig, fluff out my hair. Take off my grey Matalan jumper to reveal a printed top in reds and golds and oranges. Add a leather jacket, waiting for me on the back seat. Dark glasses, worn up, with tortoiseshell frames. Henderson, meantime, comes round my side of the car. Plugs something into my bracelet to download the audio straight into his laptop. He listens to the audio on headphones as I adjust my make-up. By the time Jessica's red lips and black-rimmed eyes are staring back at me, Henderson has heard all he needs. He snaps the laptop shut. Looks over at me. Smiles and shakes his head at the transformation.

'OK?' he asks.

'They didn't beat me up.'

Henderson smiles at that. 'I think we don't pay you enough,' he says. Slips the car into gear. And we drive off, Henderson, Jessica and I. Fiona Grey lies crumpled on the back seat: an old grey jumper and a less-than-flattering wig.

Do NOT attempt to make contact.

Do NOT enter.

Am permanently wired for sound.

This is what I wanted. What I engineered. And for the first time since accepting the assignment, I wonder if I'm crazy to have taken it at all.

45

I don't like Jessica, but she's good at her job. It takes her three weeks to compromise every major computer system in Cardiff.

Henderson helps, of course. He, or one of his colleagues. At any rate, Jessica gets moved around from job to job, office to office, in a way that little Fiona Grey never did. Jessica is a bird of brighter and more glamorous plumage than her discarded predecessor, and she flits through the high-life of commercial office cleaning with the assurance of an A-lister on Oscar night.

In three weeks, Jessica has stolen passwords and planted software on the systems of six nationally important companies plus two major government agencies. It's not even hard. Stealing the passwords is a piece of cake. Planting the software takes a little more time, requires me to dodge around the whereabouts of my cleaning partner, but it's still not hard. Most cleaners dislike doing the bathrooms and I just offer to take over a few of their bathroom chores in exchange for ten minutes alone in whichever corporate systems suite we happen to be in. My colleagues know that I'm up to something – they assume I'm looking for cash to steal – but they don't really care. So Jessica steals passwords, plants software and cleans an almost endless array of corporate bathrooms.

I even, strangely, start to make my peace with this strange blonde girl who cleans with me. For all her loudness and her trashiness, she is more popular than I am, than Fiona Grey was. I don't like her friends much, their sunbed skin and their Marlboro Lights. Don't like the gold jewellery, the high-volume mascara, the rapid conversation and too-loud laughter. But I know my limits. I'm not good at making friends. Jessica somehow does it for me. I stand in her shadow, a gawky sister at the dance, feeling better for the company that I wouldn't otherwise have.

Brattenbury doesn't forget me. Six days after I left my note for Jackson, new neighbours move into the flat two doors down the corridor from me. I don't recognise the young couple, though they seem nice enough, but I do recognise the woman's 'father'. Fifty-four. Divorced. Two kids. The DCI from my training programme.

I help them carry some boxes in. Tell them about how parking works. The woman – 'Karen' – makes tea. The guy – 'Aaron' – shows me his automatic pistol. Shows me that Karen has one too. Shows me a box of electronics and points at my ankle. I slip my boot off, while continuing to chat brightly with Karen about the local shopping.

Aaron does something with his box of tricks. The DCI shows me a piece of paper, on which is written:

Hello Fiona,

Like the new look! To confirm: we will not speak to you unless there is an emergency. We have your flat wired for sound, but we won't insert video. We did not enter the flat and will not do so. Aaron will use your ankle bracelet to monitor your movements. You will be tracked 24/7. The audio recorder in your bracelet does not transmit signal, however, so we cannot listen in – we can only follow your movements.

We have armed police officers on standby at all times. Use the same emergency codes and procedures as before. No word on Roy Williams. No breakthroughs on the farmhouse. Just get yourself there safely. We'll watch you all the way. <u>Then keep your head down</u>. Those SCO19 boys are pissed off at missing the show last time. They won't miss it this time.

One assignment for you, if you can manage it. We need to know when they plan to launch. If you can find out, please do. But your safety comes first. Roy's safety second. Launch timing comes third. <u>Don't place yourself at risk</u>.

Also — I know you'll want to know this — we've got something of interest. Last time Henderson visited the osteopath, he exited via the building neighbouring the health centre. We spoke to the osteopath who confirms Henderson did not receive a treatment, just stepped through the connecting door into the building next door. Osteopath confirms this was not the first time this has happened. We're applying for surveillance warrants for that other building now. Fingers crossed on that. We <u>have</u> looked at visitor sign-in books, etc. Nothing obvious so far, but we've only just started.

Susan sends love. So does Dave Brydon. Jackson wants to know if you're taking care of yourself. I hope you are! Take care, stay safe.

Adrian.

I read the letter twice, then hand it back to the DCI. Aaron raises his thumb and points at my ankle bracelet. Shows me a monitor that indicates he has indeed picked up my signal. Karen shows me some red-spotted tableware that she picked up cheap in Cardiff Market. Asks me what I think.

She's talking a lot to make it easier for me to keep my cover up, but I'm OK anyway.

I take the paper from the DCI and write, *Get me lock picks.*

Disguised, obviously. Hair grips? Make-up stuff? I know how to use them.

The DCI stares at me. It's a 'you know how to use *lock picks*?' sort of stare.

I nod, in a 'doesn't everyone?' sort of way.

He spreads his hands in a 'have it your way' way.

The whole thing with the letter and the guns and the box of electronics and the conversation-by-gesture takes only three or four minutes. I don't stay long. Not long enough for the tea they offer even.

I'd almost have preferred flying completely solo. This silent watching isn't much comfort to me. And no one says it, but if Henderson wants to shoot me, then he will. By the time an armed response unit is on the scene, I'll be as dead as I'm ever going to be.

But still. It's good to know Brattenbury is on the case. And I welcome those snippets of news. No word on Roy. Nothing on the farmhouse. In a strange way, I'd be disappointed now if this case was broken without me. It's my case and I've earned the right to be there at the close.

I don't see Henderson much. He comes by every two or three days to download the audio and replace the batteries on my ankle bracelet. Sometimes he's in a rush. Just does his stuff and goes. Other times, he lingers. Takes me out for a meal or makes tea and paces around my tiny flat, staring out at the street, trying to spot any surveillance vehicles. He brings me that prescription too. An NHS thing. Looking totally kosher. When I take it to the chemist, they give me the drug with little more than a whiff of 'ooh, look at the nutcase'.

A few times I go to the library to check the internet. As always, I have to check my bag at the entrance and, a week or so after meeting Aaron and Karen, I find that the make-up in my bag has changed a little. Experimenting later, in a coffee shop toilet, I discover that I have acquired a couple of raking-tools-cum-hairgrips. Also a tube of mascara: something called Glam'Eyes Lash Flirt, a product which would attract me more had it been less reckless with its apostrophe. I fiddle for a while, then manage to detach two slender lock picks from the shaft of the tube. An eyebrow pencil gives me one more pick. An eyeliner gives me two more, plus a rather weedy-looking torsion wrench.

Five picks, a couple of raking tools and a wrench. It's a pretty feeble set, to be honest – the one I use normally has more than thirty picks – but most locks give way to even quite basic technology. And Brattenbury's buddies have done a superb job of concealing the objects. The mascara looks just like mascara, the eyeliner like eyeliner. They're not fake either: the make-up itself is real enough, as Jessica is quick to prove to herself. And I'm pleased to have the equipment. It's a slim advantage. An edge that Henderson doesn't know I have.

And, though my investigative freedom is acutely limited at the moment, I make use of what little I have.

At work one day, just after I've corrupted another computer and just before I turn my hand to all the bathrooms that Stella has left for my attention, I call up – via a proxy server – all the data that Brattenbury's team have accumulated on the building next door to Henderson's health centre.

Names of staff and visitors. Dates and times. Building ownership. Tenancy agreements. Insurance details. Council tax filings. Planning permission applications. Fire safety records.

I review it all briefly – *very* briefly, I don't have long – then whack out an email from my fake Hotmail account. An email to my father. I write:

Dad,

At Christmas, you said you might be able to help my investigation. I'm hoping so! I've attached a whole lot of

336

info, which doesn't mean much to us – but somewhere here there is (I think!) a lead to a man who is responsible for three deaths already. I'm guessing that man is wealthy, capable and has some legitimate money as well as some extensive criminal interests. We've got nowhere with this and I'd love any help you can offer.

Could we meet up? That's totally not allowed under police procedure, but I'm missing you all so much and I'd love to see you. Friday evening, maybe? At your cocktail bar? One little wrinkle though. I'm wearing an ankle bracelet that contains a very sensitive audio recorder, so we can meet, write but not talk. Oh, and I'm blonde at the moment and called Jessica. I'll tell you more when all this is over. A few more weeks then we're done.

It will be amazing to see you. I'm absolutely fine but really missing you all.

Lots and lots and lots of love.
F.

I attach a set of the most interesting documents to the email and send it. The whole thing took me twelve minutes, which is pushing the limits of what I can get away with safely. Then close up the computer, run to the bathrooms and start to clean and wipe like crazy. Jessica, in the mirror, cleans and wipes like crazy too and, for the first time almost, she looks like she means it.

Later that morning, Henderson drops by my flat. Says, 'We're almost done in Cardiff, but I've got you a placement in Birmingham. Birmingham, then London.'

Jessica is painting her toenails when he says this. The colour on the bottle says Urban Coral, but that makes me think the makers can't know much about coral.

'I'll get caught,' I say. 'I've done what you asked.'

'There's more money. Don't worry about that.'

'I wasn't worried about the money. I was worried about going to jail for seventeen years.'

'We'll put the money offshore. Bank account. Your name. You set the passwords and security info. The British police will never find it. You'll have access to the money, wherever, whenever.'

'Wherever? Literally wherever? Like there's a cashpoint in Drake Hall?'

Drake Hall: the prison where Anna Quintrell is currently considering her future.

'Twenty grand. For two weeks in Birmingham, three weeks in London.'

'Get someone else, Vic.'

He stares at my toenails, as if disconcerted to find them changing colour. I'm wearing Aztec print leggings and a tank top. Sitting on the floor with my feet on a towel. Brush in one hand, bottle in the other.

Poised.

'We've tried.' His voice is hoarse. 'We've made fourteen approaches. Recruited eleven possible candidates. Eight of them were . . . they were just brainless. Terry did what he could, but they had no idea. They didn't even complete the training day.'

'So? Eleven minus eight equals three, Vic. I'm trained in payroll, I spot these things.'

'One of them flaked. She was on drugs. We knew about that before we recruited her, but . . . it didn't work out. The other two were both caught and fired. Instantly, pretty much. Within the first week.'

'Oh well, that's fine then. There's obviously no risk. Silly me to have worried.'

'They were *fired*. They weren't arrested.'

'Really? Perhaps they weren't on police bail at the time.'

'Nor are you. Not Jessica.'

'That waitress. The one at the farmhouse.'

'Yes?'

'You killed her. She was the girl they found in that field.'

I'm not breaching secrets here, not Fiona Griffiths's secrets anyway. The deaths were in the newspapers, photographs of Nia before she had her face smashed in.

'Not necessarily me,' Henderson says automatically.

'You. Geoff. Allan. I don't care which of you did it. And it was because of me. Because I caused a scene.'

'Not really. It turned out she wasn't as discreet as we thought.'

'She was a fucking waitress, Vic. She probably didn't know that having a laugh with a mate was going to get her head beaten to a pulp. I'm guessing you missed that bit off the job description.'

Vic's face turns grim. Not at me, particularly, just that he came to do a job which he thought would be easy – offer me twenty K for five more weeks of computer fraud – and it's turning out hard. He looks at his watch. A chrome and leather aviator thing.

'Look, I've got to be somewhere. Why don't I take you out? Tonight. Somewhere nice. We'll talk about this stuff. If I can persuade you, great. If not, well, we'll just have a nice evening.'

Jessica and I consider that.

Jessica wants to go, whatever. She's already thinking about her dress, shoes, hair, and make-up. Fiona Grey isn't sure. She still has flickers of lust for Henderson, but there's something about his attitude to murder which she finds something of a passion-killer. She's old-fashioned that way. So that leaves me, Fiona Griffiths, the *capo di tutti capi* of our little sisterhood, with the casting vote.

But it's not a choice for me, or not really. Roy Williams is still in captivity. Katie Williams still hollow with shock. The ghosts of Hayley Morgan, Saj Kureishi, and now Nia Lewis still look to me for their rescue.

I shrug. Go back to my toenails. But the shrug was a yes, more than a no, and Henderson accepts it.

He moves to the door, but says, 'Do you like spas? Massage, all that stuff?'

'Yes, Vic. Us minimum wage cleaners, we can't get enough of them.'

He ignores my sarcasm. Makes a call. A luxury hotel on the bay. Books Jessica in for the afternoon. Any treatments I like. Massage, hot stone, aromatherapy, seaweed. Whatever. Books us both in for dinner in the hotel restaurant later.

'Have a nice time. I'll see you there later.'

'Do they have a jacuzzi?' I ask.

'Of course. All these places do.'

'I've never had one. I knew a fell-runner once who said they were amazing.'

'Well, have fun.'

I shrug. Go back to my toes.

The pathologist's report – and this is police information, not public – estimated that Nia Lewis received in excess of fifty blows to the face. She hadn't been sexually assaulted, but her naked body was thrown into a tangle of nettles hard against a wire fence. One arm had been broken, probably prior to death. The gunshot wound was consistent with Geoff's Glock, but I've no doubt Henderson has something similar available to him.

I finish painting my toenails, then stand at the window till I see Henderson exiting to the street. Stay watching till I see his BMW roll silently up the road into town.

I go through to the bedroom and make myself ready for an afternoon at the spa. An evening with a killer.

46

I say yes, of course. Negotiate Henderson from twenty K to fifty. Payable into a bank account on Grand Cayman. My signature. My security questions. My passwords. I say that I won't do the three weeks in London until the Kiwi visa has been approved.

Henderson says yes to all that. Finds it funny, really, that I've learned security paranoia from him. I don't think the fifty K was even close to being a deal-breaker. I could probably have pushed for more.

I also demand to know exactly what my schedule is meant to be.

'It always gets more, what you want,' I point out. 'This needs to be the last time it goes up.'

'We pay you more too.'

'It's never been about money. You know that.'

'OK.' Henderson gets out his phone. Checks the diary pages on it. Gives me my dates for Birmingham. Two weeks there. Three weeks in London.

'Those three weeks in London. You go live after that?'

'Yes. In five weeks' time.'

'OK.'

'And we'll want you for a weekend, as well please.'

'Are you propositioning me?'

He smiles at that, but it's not much of a smile. His mind is on business, not sex.

'The farmhouse. Our final round of testing. It'll be right after Birmingham.' He gives me the dates. September 22 and 23. A year, pretty much, since I first sat in that furniture superstore with Huw Bowen smelling Kevin-from-Swindon's body odour. Calculating forwards, it looks like Tinker is planning to launch its fake software in mid-October. We're five weeks from the biggest theft in history. I hope Brattenbury is listening. Hope he knows I've just ticked off the third of the three objectives he gave me.

'I won't wear the hood again,' I say. 'The eye-mask thing was OK.'

A small hesitation but, 'All right. As you wish.'

'And it'll be an extra ten K.'

'Ten thousand pounds? For a weekend?'

'No. Ten thousand pounds for seventeen years in jail. That's five hundred quid a year, a bit more than one pound a day.'

Henderson looks at me. He's amused more than anything. He has dark hairs peeping from the join in his white shirt and I can see the two colours of blue in his eyes. Rain clouds flecked with the tropics. Cobalt shimmering on a dark Welsh sea.

They don't move me now. Not really. Not me, not Fiona Grey, not Jessica. We catch killers. We don't sleep with them.

But Henderson doesn't know that. He says yes to my ten grand. Pours wine.

I don't sleep with killers, I catch them, but sometimes the two rivers run close. And after dinner, after the light had died on the Bay, after the amuse-bouches and the complimentary champagne and the artisanal breads and the seven-course tasting menu and the coffees and the petits fours, I say, 'Do you have a room?' Henderson doesn't reply directly. Just calls a waiter over. Has the whole thing arranged without leaving table.

He finishes his coffee, I play with my petit four, then we go up. Side by side in the elevator, hardly talking.

He let us into the room. Not a room, even. A suite. Huge glass windows over the sea. No curtains, not meaningfully, because aside from the big ships heading up or down the estuary, there's no one there to gaze at us. There are a couple of side lamps switched on by the bed. Some wall lamps in the sitting room. Henderson stands back, watching to see what I want. Ready to do whatever it is. More lights, less. Music. Champagne.

But I don't want any of that. I like the deadness of the light. The huge grey bay waiting like a boneyard beyond the glass.

I stand at the foot of the bed and shrug slightly.

I'm wearing a dress that I chose, not Jessica. A little black number. Not too tarty. Not too glam. Just a dress.

Date-wear. The sort of dress that might say sex, but doesn't have to.

Henderson comes up close. Kisses me on the lips. A little bite as he finishes.

He's low on the foreplay, though. I think he figures that an afternoon and evening in a luxury spa, plus sixty grand for five weeks' work, has pretty much covered him on the foreplay front. If he isn't pushier now, I think that's only because he knows Miss Grey can be a bit of a wildcat.

I reach behind my shoulder blades. Find the zip and release it. I suddenly feel very naked. Stop the dress falling beyond my waist, then realise that's stupid and let it drop to the floor. Put my hands to Henderson's jacket and shirt. Encourage him to join me in this nakedness.

He does.

There's a brief moment when we're both in our underwear. Black M&S stuff in my case. I think the same in his.

There's something missing, however, and I think even Henderson feels it. When we were kissing through the hood,

343

or even earlier when he came to my room in the barn with the bags of clothes from Gap, we both felt a kind of passion that was as hungry, at least in my case, as anything I've ever known.

It's not like that now. The negotiations over money, the sense of mounting risk, the abduction of Roy Williams and the death of Tania Lewis, those things have all killed what there once was.

A darkened ocean beats time beyond the windows and I sit on the bed. Say, 'Was it you who killed Tania Lewis?'

He looks at me sharply, but says, 'No.'

'Were you there?'

'Yes.'

'And did you . . .? She was really hurt.'

'We didn't hurt her much beforehand. She died from a gunshot. Most of what happened to her happened after that.'

'But you helped. You helped do that?'

'Yes.'

'What about the guy in that video?'

'Yes. That was me. The man concerned had become significantly dangerous. Stole money, started talking. And he *wasn't* a waitress. He *did* know the score.'

'What is it like? Killing someone.'

'You stabbed someone once.'

'That was different.'

'I have my job, Fi. I'm tasked to keep things secure and I do. That's it, really. I don't have big feelings about it.'

My dress lies in a pool of black viscose at my feet. I pick at it. Finding the shoulder straps. Lifting it, until an unfilled torso rises from the pool. A dark shape, waiting for me to enter it.

Vic's shirt lies on the floor next to my dress. A dark blue number, with a bit of shine. He is well-muscled. The kind of body you only get from the gym. Taut biceps curling into

344

well-developed deltoids. A cloud of dark hair wanders across his chest. Bronze light reflects from his skin.

I rub my fingers into his chest. Look into the two colours of his eyes.

It doesn't move me any more. The chest, the eyes, anything.

'I don't think I can do this, Vic. I'm sorry. Not now. Not while everything is still . . .'

He doesn't answer directly. His mouth is a line of grimness, but his eyes are softer. Eventually he says, 'It's OK. It was probably a bad idea.'

'*My* bad idea. I'll pay for the room.'

'No. Don't worry about it.'

He lifts my ankle. I'm still wearing my tights and they bulge over the ankle bracelet. I wriggle out of the tights. He inserts a cable into the output socket, enters a code via a handset, and wipes the past two hours' recording. Checks it twice to make sure it's gone. As he does all that, I pull my dress back on, my tights. Apologise again.

The data is gone. I'm dressed. Henderson gets a cold beer from the minibar. Asks me if I want anything, but I don't.

He grins over his beer at me. He only spoke as freely as he did just now, because this was his choice of hotel, because the room was booked last minute, because he knows that I have not been approached by the police nor, indeed, have I been anywhere except my own flat or the hotel itself since the plan to come here was concocted.

A raft of precautions. A row of green lights.

But even Henderson can fuck up, and he did just now.

I did have my afternoon at the spa. Got a massage, which was nice: I've never had one before. Also booked in for a seaweed wrap, because it sounded like the single stupidest thing on the spa's long list of very stupid things. But I didn't get to the wrap, because the woman on the massage table next to me was Susan Knowles. We smiled at each other, but barely spoke.

Then, after we'd each been rubbed and pounded, we moved through to the jacuzzi. I sat on the edge, dangling my ankle in the foaming water. My ankle bracelet, with its oh-so-sensitive audio recording, listening to the noise of a million bubbles. A surge of water and the beat of a pump.

'Hey, Susan, nice to see you.'

'You too, blonde girl. Good thinking about the jacuzzi.'

'I wasn't sure if anyone would get my fell-runner reference.'

'Adrian knows that I run. But if it hadn't been me, we'd have sent someone else.'

We chatted a bit. How's Adrian. News from the case. Buzz sent his love. But mostly we were quickly down to business.

'I want to get a confession tonight,' I said. 'Can you get the restaurant wired up?'

'We're on it already. The simplest thing is just to put recorders in the salt cellars. Something like that. We'll do every table probably.'

'And a room maybe? If we go upstairs afterwards.' Susan raised her eyebrows, but I was quick to add, 'I don't think he would ever speak in a public place. Even if he felt sure it was secure. A bedroom, maybe. I'm not sure. It's worth a try. I won't go all the way.'

Susan looked hard at me and said, 'You know, your man Brydon, ages ago, he came to us and said that if you had to do something – get intimate, whatever – in order to secure a conviction, then he'd understand. He just said you should never tell him. Never let him know.'

'What did you say?'

'It was Adrian he spoke to. Adrian just said that there was absolutely no question of you becoming intimate with anyone. That that wasn't your role in the case.'

That sounds like Buzz to me. Like Brattenbury too. Both

doing the right thing. The professional thing. But it would kill Buzz, I think. And 'never tell him' is all very well. But if I secured evidence essential to a prosecution, that evidence would have to be aired in court, no matter where I obtained it.

I don't know what my face said, but Susan said, 'He's a good man, your one. Hang on to him.'

I nodded, dumbly. Thinking that for this long year Buzz must have had half a worry that I wasn't just working undercover but working under the covers too. A Welsh Mata Hari.

'Anyway. We'll put a room aside for you. And record the hell out of it.'

'Thank you.'

She looked at me and grinned. Gave me a hug.

'We'd best keep this short,' she said.

I nodded.

'Not long now.'

Nod.

'And make sure you get the bastard.'

By now, I expect, she knows I did.

When I leave the hotel that night, walking back to my flat, still feeling the touch of that almost-intimacy on my skin, I think of how much it has taken us all to get here. Hayley Morgan and her purposeless sacrifice. Saj Kureishi and his anguished astonishment. Nia Lewis, in her tangle of nettles and wire netting. But Buzz too. His honourable waiting. Dennis Jackson and his gruff, senior-officer kindness. Brattenbury's professionalism, Susan's intelligence.

I've got Anna Quintrell in jail. Henderson now on record as confessing to murder. Wyatt and Shoesmith in our crosshairs. Ramesh and his buddies too.

If we get them, we're likely to find enough to get Geoff and Allan too. When we rip into the house searches, the forensics, the interrogations, we're pretty much certain to get the leads we need. Geoff, Allan, plus some of the others involved in finance and distribution.

But that's not enough. The Hendersons, the Wyatts, the Quintrells – they're not enough. I don't just want them: the salarymen and women of this particular crime. I want the person I've never heard mentioned. I want whoever it is that owns the farmhouse. I want whoever has four million pounds of seed capital to fund this venture. When Brattenbury and I have sketched Tinker's hypothetical organisation chart, we've always had a space that just says, *The Boss* – ???. And I want that man. In jail for fraud and murder. A life sentence. Some huge minimum tariff.

So far, we've not had the glimmer of a clue as to that person's identity. We don't, if we're honest, even *know* that the person exists. But Henderson walked from his osteopath's office into the building next door, presumably in order to see someone. You don't do that – find a building with that odd connecting door arrangement, attend a long sequence of osteopathy appointments, then use that cover to skip next door for an hour before returning the same way – unless you are seeking to cover something up.

Something – but what? I don't know, but for the first time I feel we have a tangible clue. I hope Brattenbury feels the same excitement. I guess he would, except that I think he was nudging me to lower my expectations. His letter said, *We're applying for surveillance warrants for that other building now. Fingers crossed on that.*

Fingers crossed: a reminder of the legalities involved. Thus far, there's been little difficulty in getting authority to surveille, bug and tap almost everything we've wanted. Our legal argument has been textbook in its straightforwardness. Roughly speaking: we know, or have a very strong and evidentially based suspicion, that this person (Henderson,

Quintrell, Allan, Shoesmith, Wyatt) is involved in criminal fraud and conspiracy to murder. We want to bug their home/phone/mobile/whatever. Easy.

Amazingly enough, every interception warrant is personally authorised by the Home Secretary herself, and no sane Home Secretary would conceivably reject most of the applications we've made so far. But bugging an entire building full of perfectly innocent people in the hope of catching a single (and very occasional) non-innocent encounter that *probably* takes place somewhere in that building – well, you don't have to be much of a civil libertarian to have anxieties about that approach to policing. I think Brattenbury expects a *no*.

So near, but yet so far.

I've made arrests before. Secured prosecutions, convictions, seen people put away for life. But I've never hit the big guys. The owner-managers of organised crime. The people who are so far above the dirty day-to-day stuff that they run their legitimate enterprises, send their kids to private schools, collect fatuous awards for entrepreneurship, make ostentatious donations to charity, collect trophy wives and pretty mistresses, and no one even thinks to ask if this or that well-connected businessman might actually be a major league arsehole.

Am I bitter? I am. The last big case I worked on had a rich, successful guy as its primary target. A man who, at one stage, ordered me killed and who evaded our intended prosecution with such sweet ease that we might as well have tried to clap handcuffs on the ocean.

In my only big case before that, the same thing, except that the bastard rich guy in question had the good grace to die before my investigation even started.

I'd dearly love to break my duck. Dearly love to get Tinker's Mr Big behind bars. To nail him on a series of charges so long, so inescapable, that he'll grow old and die behind prison bars. I'd like to watch as he finds his comb thicken with grey hairs, as he feels the first loosening of teeth in his gums, as he watches his face slowly break into a river delta of wrinkles, and to know that the only thought which beats in his head is, *This is all remains to me now. This ten foot by six foot cell. This prison food, these clanging doors.*

As I walk home under this northern sky, the stars above ask if I'm ready. If I mean business. If I'm going to get my man.

And I am, I tell them, I really am.

47

Wednesday night. Dad's cocktail bar.

I enter the place not long after its evening opening. We minimum wage cleaners keep early hours, even Jessica. I order a drink – a fruit juice thing that looks alcoholic but isn't – and sit at the bar in a place where the security cameras can easily see me. Turn to the camera and wink. A couple of boys are eyeing Jessica up from their corner booth. Jessica's their sort, I think. She's aware of their gaze and flirts a bit. She's wearing skirt and heels, nothing too trashy, but her ankle bracelet is very visible and I think it may be acting as an extra come-on. But these are Welsh lads still on their first drink and I predict they'll need a second before they make their move. I don't think I'm going to be waiting that long.

I'm right.

I've not been there ten minutes before a guy comes in at the front door and raises a thumb to the barman. The barman slips me a note in Dad's handwriting which just reads, *All clear at the front. Come on upstairs.*

The office: not Dad's corporate headquarters, but the little back room which all his ventures possess. A place where Dad can retreat to with his cronies. Green benches round a wooden table, low lighting, office stuff intermixed with Dad's remarkably eclectic collection of mementoes and knick-knacks.

I go up to the office, but I'm not thrilled about it as a

location. The bracelet will tell Henderson where I am and bars aren't meant to be quiet places.

I needn't have worried. As I swing open the office door, the murmur of a bar greets me. People talking, laughter, footsteps, even the sound of a falling glass. There's no one here though, only Pa, who stands to greet me with a huge bear hug. We just stand and embrace without words, the best way.

Then we do pull apart. Dad points to the speakers which are piping sound up from below. I'm impressed, as ever, at Dad's remarkably neat stage-management. His approach gives us privacy whilst also giving me the perfect auditory cover. I give Dad a pearly-toothed smile, showing him I appreciate his thoughtfulness. He plucks at Jessica's blond locks, looks down at her ankle bracelet and laughs at her.

We sit.

Dad has put out a laptop for us – I type fast and he's no dab hand with a pen.

I write, *Lovely, lovely, lovely to see you, Dad. Been missing you soooo much!*

He's a poor typist. He told me once, I don't know with what truth, that he'd always assumed he was stupid, because he never got on well at school. Struggled in tests, left without qualifications. It was only later, when he was in his thirties and his flourishing criminal career very much established, that someone told him he suffered from dyslexia. Dad even claimed that his switch to legitimate business came about mostly because he realised he could get an accountant and a lawyer to do all the stuff he had never been able to do himself. Register companies, fill out VAT forms, all that side of things. I don't believe him, not entirely. There must have been more to his particular career choices than some dismissive teachers and some crappy schooling.

Anyway. It takes Dad time to answer. Even now, he's

sensitive about his writing skills and his finger hesitates over the keyboard, picking out the letters one by one like an elegant woman selecting chocolates from a box.

He writes, *Lovely to see you too! Your Mam misses you*. He's not all that confident in his use of the shift key. So when he wants a capital letter or an exclamation mark, he secures the shift key with the index finger of his left hand, checks it, then whacks the 'L', the '!', the 'Y' or the 'M' with his other index finger, trying to whip both fingers away at the exact same time. The technique works, however, just as well as mine.

I write, *Can we go straight to business? I can't be here too long. Sorry! The case won't last much longer*.

Dad doesn't type an answer. Just moves two stack of papers in front of me. The documents I sent him, but annotated in his own terrible handwriting.

The first stack is marked *Boring*. Names and faces that Dad doesn't know. Paperwork that didn't strike a note with him. I flip through it, to remind myself what's there and to see if I have any questions. Dad doesn't interrupt me exactly, but silence isn't his forte. As I read, he does a huge yawn, pretends to fall asleep, shoots himself with an imaginary gun. I laugh at him. Punch him in the chest. He leaves the room, comes back with a beer, asks me in mime if I want anything. I mouth 'no thanks', but he leaves again anyway to come back with another fruit thing and some salted nuts.

He can't stay still, my dad. Another big reason for his becoming a criminal, I think. Most regular jobs would have driven him crazy.

Then I turn to the pile marked *Interesting!!!!!!*

A smaller pile this, but he's not wrong about its interest. The building next door to the health centre houses a property management company, a firm of solicitors and a firm of accountants. The data I sent over to Dad – data I've not been able to look at properly myself – contains long lists of clients, both personal and corporate.

Now that I have time to look at them, those lists look fairly classy. There are some names I recognise. Charlotte Rattigan: the widow of a very wealthy, very wicked man whose doings I once had a hand in exposing. Ivor Harris: local MP, immaculate reputation, but too close to Brendan Rattigan for me to trust him. Idris Prothero: an arms dealer who once tried to kill me and was involved in at least one other death, arguably two. David Marr-Phillips: a man who had some minor business dealings with Prothero. Other names too: Galton Evans, Joe Johnson. People I have no real reason to think badly of, except that they were also close to Brendan Rattigan and I don't trust anyone who knew that man well.

Cardiff's not a huge city, of course, and it's not bursting with the upmarket professional advisory types that London is full of. There are probably only a small number of firms that handle the prestige clients so it's no surprise to find many of those names here. It's not even as though there's an obvious pattern in who does what. Ivor Harris, for example, seems to get his annual tax returns done by the accountancy firm, but has no dealings with the other two. Marr-Phillips is, via a couple of his businesses, a client of the property management company, but appears to get his legal and accountancy work done elsewhere. And so on.

But my suspicions aren't allayed. Henderson would not have walked through that connecting door without a reason. Henderson does *nothing* without a reason. And if you wanted to meet someone in the centre of town without anyone knowing the two of you had met – well, what could be a neater arrangement? One man goes to his osteopath. The other goes to his accountant, or solicitor, or property guy. The two men are in different buildings. Enter and leave at different times. Sweet, simple, effective.

Dad's comments are even more interesting than the names themselves. He's been through those client lists with a thick red pen. Against some names – most of them – he's scribbled *Don't know* or, when he got tired of writing that much, just *DK*. A red scrawl that flies from the page with impatience.

Against other names he's written *Legit*, a word that gradually becomes abbreviated to an *L*, and then simply to a flicked flash of the pen, no longer readable as a letter.

But then, on a minority of names, a small minority, he's written more. *Bastard!!! Don't trust,* is the first such comment. Against Marr-Philips he's written *Shark! Very dangerous man*. Against Ivor Harris, he's written *Would do <u>anything</u> for cash. But not a real player*. Against Prothero: *Nasty piece of work, but not big time*.

Not all the names that mean something to me incur a wrathful comment from my pa, but it seems to me there's a more than random overlap between the names that arouse my suspicion and those that arouse his. I'm also struck by some of his judgements. Idris Prothero – who exported at least sixteen million pounds' worth of armaments without an export licence, who ordered me killed, who had one of his own engineers framed for a drugs charge, who almost certainly arranged for the professional murder of a would-be competitor – this person is one whom my father regards as a small-timer. It's not even as though he didn't know Prothero's background. I've told him all of it, except the part about my almost-killing. I'm struck by how little I really know of Dad's past. That, and the depth of his own criminal professionalism. A fund of knowledge that has no bottom.

I'm out of time really. I promised myself I would be here no more than twenty minutes, and I've been here closer to forty. My ankle bracelet transmits my location real-time. Henderson won't be worried to learn that I'm in a bar, but if he or one of his buddies drops by and doesn't find me here, I could be in trouble. Five minutes, or even ten: that could be a toilet visit. Forty minutes, though, that would be harder to explain. Once again, I become aware how narrow is the line that secures my safety. Think of Nia. How she didn't even know that she'd crossed a line. That there *was* a line.

For a moment, I'm lost in that same tangle of nettles. Wire, dock leaves, and blood thinning to water in the rain.

But I struggle back. Dad's presence helps. And, out of time or not, I do flip through the rest of Dad's *Interesting!!!!!!* pile. He's taken a look at the list of visitors: the people who entered the office building the morning of Henderson's incursion. Here, it's mostly DKs, or just a small red dot, marking impatience. But there are exceptions. Three people with red circles round their names and one person – N. Davison – by whose circled name stands the word *Fixer!*

I look at Dad, question marks in my eyes.

Dad types, ignoring the shift key and punctuation, *fixer works for cash dirty jobs guy*. He looks at me, gesturing at his mouth. Meaning, 'I could tell you so much more.'

I type, *Do you know who he works for? Is there anyone he's particularly close to?*

Dad ignores the keyboard. Just picks up the client list and waves his hand. I think he means 'Anyone' but then think maybe he means 'All of them.'

I stare at him. I'm out of time. I want to spend two days interviewing Dad about all this, but I'm not going to get the chance. Not now, certainly, but maybe never. I suspect Dad's current willingness to divulge has been spurred on by the thrill of this clandestine meeting. If I started to come over all police-officery, I think he'd revert to his normal cheerful evasions.

I stand. Hug my father. He wraps both arms around me and crushes me into him. He's never really got the hang of hugging smaller women. It's as though he doesn't notice that my mouth and nose are struggling for oxygen, my feet slightly lifted from the floor, my back finding new shapes as his arms pull my spine towards my sternum. Mostly, since my illness, I've fought shy of these monster crushes. Sought hugs that are more on my terms, that give me a fighting chance of emerging with some dignity. But today this old-fashioned hug – the sort he used to give me when I was ill – feels just right. I lean into Dad's embrace until I can't breathe, then fight my way clear.

I type, *I LOVE YOU. I'M COMING HOME SOON. THANKS A MILLION FOR ALL THIS. YOU ARE THE BEST DAD EVER. LOVE YOU LOADS!!!!* I'm not usually one for all-caps or the multi-exclamation mark, but Dad's earned them.

I go back downstairs. I don't leave the bar immediately, though. The boys who had been making eyes at Jessica are still there. Blood-alcohol levels raised enough for them to call to me as I pass. Jessica spins, banters back, solicits – and gets – a drink. She spends the next hour in their company: mouthy, brassy, popular, loose. At the end of that hour, I go out the back of the bar to smoke a cigarette with Darren, the tallest and least idiotic of the boys. He wears a grey jacket and an ironed shirt, white with a blue flower design on the collar and pocket. Pulling wear.

We have a ciggy, then I throw my stub away and start kissing him. Hard, lustful kisses that he reciprocates. He tastes of cheap cocktails and Starbursts. We spend five or ten minutes like that. Kissing, squeezing, moaning.

This sort of thing doesn't happen to him much, I suspect. He thinks he's pulled because of his handsomeness and wit. Doesn't know that he's my alibi-snog. That I just want there to be a guy who, if Henderson starts poking around, will say, yes, he did have a snog that night with a pixie-haired blonde called Jessica. The timings won't quite make sense –

my absence not quite correlating with the time of the snog – but they don't have to. Darren will say one thing. I'll say something slightly different. Time will have gone by. Alcohol was involved. The audio recording will prove I was always in a bar or had my tongue down somebody's throat. Any investigator – even Henderson, even *me* – would drop things at that point. The nettles and the wire: they may come to me some day, but not tonight, not because of this.

I tell Darren he's cute, give him my number, and go home. I'd like to tell Brattenbury what I've discovered, except that I haven't really discovered anything and what I do have comes from a source that I'd be highly reluctant to disclose.

Ah well. I've never believed in being too open with senior officers. It's bad for their egos. I shower hard, brush the taste of Darren out of my mouth, and go to bed.

48

As with Cardiff, so with Birmingham. Jessica flits through corporate offices. Steals passwords. Sabotages systems.

Her crimes are more or less blatant now. Every two days, I'm in a new office. The first day I steal passwords. The second day I plant software. Then move on. Henderson, or whoever, must be bribing my bosses to put me on this kind of shift pattern. Cleaners are never moved around like this unless there's a one-off absence that needs to be filled.

But I don't care, nor does Jessica. I'm a thief and a saboteur, but the reckoning for my thievery – for Tinker's thefts and murders – won't come here, but in a farmhouse somewhere in South Wales. On the Thursday of my second week in Birmingham, I plant my last keystroke recorder. A big manufacturing firm. Employs forty thousand workers in the UK. An old-fashioned firm. Avoids outsourcing. Protects jobs and skills. Invests locally. Is regularly picked as one of Britain's top employers.

On Friday morning, I find a note from Adrian Brattenbury tucked into my cleaning stuff.

> Fiona,
> Well done! Just get yourself to the farmhouse. We will follow you there. We can track your ankle monitor. We will have multiple vehicles, plus air support. Real-time access to CCTV. We will <u>not</u> lose you. Once you're there, don't do

anything. Don't look for Roy Williams. Don't seek to help us. SCO19 are going to be there in force and they're trained for this. You've done your stuff. Now we'll do ours.

Stay safe!
Adrian

It's not quite 'We shall fight them on the beaches', but it works for me. I rip the note up and add it to my bags of rubbish.

And Jessica performs her last duties too. She gathers the harvest from her recorder. Username, passwords. Enters the firm's computer system and plants the software which will let Ian Shoesmith sabotage it from within. Thefts of the scale we're contemplating could, in theory, bankrupt the firm. Jeopardise jobs, investment, everything.

When I catch sight of Jessica in a mirror, her face looks angrily determined. Vengeful. If I were her target, I'd be scared.

At midday, my working day is done. I go outside. Smoke a cigarette with just a sprinkle of resin.

At quarter past, a black BMW glides up the road towards me. Window down. Henderson at the wheel smiling.

'Ready?' he asks.

I am, I say. I truly am.

49

The drive from Birmingham is easy. Blast down the M5. Onto the M4. Severn Bridge. The wide blue estuary with Amina's shushumow kicking around in the undercurrents. Mud banks and seagulls.

I'm not wearing my eye-mask. Just dandling it on my lap as Henderson drives.

He notices my fidgeting hands and says, 'No need for that now. For the time being, we're just heading home.'

I'm still wearing my ankle bracelet. It feels like a ten pound weight around my leg. A good weight. A protective one. I try not to fidget or draw attention to it.

We reach exit twenty-nine. The A48, Eastern Avenue. My normal route into Cardiff when coming from England. We pass the turn.

Also pass exits thirty and thirty-one.

Thirty-one: the exit that doesn't exist. An interchange for which planning permission was granted twenty years ago but which has never been built.

Exit thirty-two, Northern Avenue. We glide by that as well.

I'm getting jittery. Trying not to show it.

Henderson notices, though. Says, 'We're not going into town. We're meeting Geoff and Allan on the other side.'

Exit thirty-three. Culverhouse Cross and Barry.

We swing off the motorway, head south. Henderson makes

a call as he drives. 'We're almost with you.' At a retail park in Culverhouse, a car swings out behind us. Black BMW. Same model as Henderson's. Geoff at the wheel, Allan next to him on the passenger side. Continue south. The A4050 towards Barry.

To the east of us, over Cardiff, there's a traffic helicopter. Routine, ordinary, doing what traffic helicopters do over cities.

Only, I don't think this is a traffic helicopter. I think it's here for me. Watching, monitoring, passing back data. It's not particularly close to us, but with the right optical equipment, it shouldn't need to be.

Henderson puts his phone onto hands-free.

I start to feel frightened and I don't know why.

Up till now, our route has been logical enough. The sort of route that a person might drive if they were looking to get from A to B. No longer.

Henderson veers off route. Down the St Lytham's Road, then takes a turn to Dyffryn. A real Welsh lane. Hazel hedges on either side, rising to more than head height. The road so narrow, two vehicles meeting head-on can't pass each other, without one reversing to the next field gate or passing place. Steep banks and ash trees.

Where the road allows it, and especially when trees overhead give cover, Henderson and Geoff switch places. Geoff in the lead, and Henderson following.

If we encounter cars, which we don't very often, we hear Allan's voice on the phone, noting make, model, colour and registration.

Soon after taking the Dyffryn turn, Henderson reaches inside his jacket. Takes a Glock from a shoulder holster. Drops it into the side pocket of his door. Easier access.

I don't comment and nor does he.

When we hit Dyffryn, we veer south again. Then twist back

on ourselves. Another tiny lane. Then bury ourselves in the tiny back streets of Pencoedtre Wood.

I swivel in my seat to watch. I can't see very well, but I think Allan is taking photos of the drivers too. Recording everything.

'You're paranoid,' I say. My normal comment about all this.

Henderson doesn't make his normal rejoinder though. Leaves a gap of silence for a few seconds, then, 'You were in police custody a long time. Then they let you go. That's probably fine, but we need to make sure.'

Pull back, Adrian, I think. *Pull back.* I'm worried that Brattenbury's surveillance team will end up burning themselves in the effort not to lose me. And we can't afford that. *I* can't. Nia Lewis died for less.

But I shouldn't worry. We discussed all this in Manchester. Vehicle-based surveillance works if you have plenty of vehicles, and if the bad guys don't have much time or aren't taking precautions. Brattenbury won't be short of manpower, but we know from before that Henderson is tricksy and cautious. So we agreed to play it safe with the cars. As long as my ankle bracelet is still transmitting, they can find me anywhere. And it's pretty much impossible to hide from a helicopter.

Back onto the A4050. Speeding now. Some reckless overtaking. Geoff following us and Allan turned in his seat checking the cars behind.

Then a sudden turn onto a side road. Our BMW pulled tight onto a grassy verge, so tight that it couldn't be seen by someone until they had almost completed the bend.

Henderson watching the road, noting cars. Geoff and Allan sixty yards behind us doing the same. Passing information to and fro. But not many cars now. I have the feeling that we're in the clear, or almost.

I shift my legs, easing the tension.

'You can have that off now, if you want.' Henderson passes me a key, indicates my ankle.

I take my bracelet off, massaging the skin underneath. Drop the thing in the little shelf under the glove compartment.

'Does anyone ever keep gloves in the glove compartment?'

Henderson says, 'I do. Gun, gloves, bullets.'

We laugh, but without mirth. From those lips, that comment is the opposite of funny. It makes me think of that hotel bedroom. That dead light and the huge grey bay open like a boneyard. For some reason, I think Henderson is remembering the same thing.

Now that I'm free of the transmitter, Henderson asks me to step out of the car, so he can sweep me down with his RF scanner. The grass verge has been cut recently and the cut ends prickle against my ankle. The scanner comes up with nothing. I'm clean as I always am. As clean, and as naked. I pick a flower, a yellow one. Bird's-foot trefoil is its proper name. My dad calls it Granny's Toenails. I tuck it behind my ear.

I've got my bag with me. My bag, Jessica's clothes, but including the make-up bits and pieces that Brattenbury sent me. Henderson scans the bag – it's clean – and inspects the clothes minutely for any evidence that they have been tampered with.

'Fuck's sake, Vic. *You* bought me that stuff. You've known where I am every single minute since you gave it to me.'

He laughs. Spends another few moments looking at my stuff – belt buckles, buttons, jewellery, my little bottle of amisulpride – then crams everything back.

I say, 'All this stuff. The scanning. The messing around with cars. Where did you learn it? Can you get an NVQ in that sort of thing?'

Henderson shoots me a glance. 'I have a security background,' which is hardly illuminating. His accent is basically English, but it often has a hint of something else. South African? Aussie? Or perhaps somewhere else in Africa? Kenya or Uganda or somewhere like that. I don't know.

We get back into the car. Move off again towards Barry. The phones still busy between our BMW and the other one, but there's something relaxed in the conversation now.

We've done it, I think. Feel myself relaxing. Henderson couldn't have been more careful to avoid pursuit and clearly thinks he's been successful. That's what we wanted. What we planned for. I'm careful not to look too obtrusively, but I can still glimpse, from time to time, my beautiful helicopter circling over the west side of Cardiff. Penarth. Near enough to watch a pair of BMWs playing tag in the country north of Barry, I reckon. Who needs cars when we've got choppers? I feel like laughing.

'OK,' Henderson says. 'Almost done.'

Out of Barry on the Port Road. Normal speed. Normal everything.

Normal everything, except for that phrase, 'Almost done', which trips a feeling of gathering sickness in the pit of my stomach. I'm not good with feelings always. It can take me a long time to feel them. To know what they are and make sense of them. But I know this one. The clenching in the abdomen. The dry mouth. The spasms in the palms of the hands.

This is fear and I know her well.

From the A4226 to the airport. Cardiff International.

I see my friend the helicopter clearly now. We're moving west all the time and the pilot isn't moving with us. We're driving into the most heavily restricted airspace in Wales and the chopper can't travel a single inch closer. It's five miles from where it needs to be and there's nothing it, or anyone, can do.

We will have multiple vehicles, plus air support. Well, Adrian old son, the vehicles were burned off as soon as Henderson made the effort to lose them. The air support is in the wrong place. And as for that ankle bracelet, I'm betting that Henderson has a plan for that too.

He does.

We drive into a multistorey car park. Henderson in front. Allan and Geoff close behind.

'Quickly now.' Henderson's command.

His voice is terse. I don't mind that. I can handle terse. But he's carrying a loaded gun and he gestures with it as he speaks. Not exactly pointing it at me, but not exactly pointing it away from me either. His voice, his gestures are hardened by the car park's steel and concrete. Every word, every movement has the force of ricochet.

I do as he says.

We bundle out of the BMW, engine still running. Allan runs from the rear car to take the wheel. Henderson directs me to the back of a white Transit van, its rear door hanging open.

My ankle bracelet is in the car that Allan is now driving. As all this is happening, a pickup truck is reversing out of its parking space. The red face of a Welsh builder back from holiday. Him and his fat wife. They're looking at the gap between their wing mirror and a concrete support pillar. Checking to see they can make it out without dinging the mirror.

They can. They definitely can. But they're not looking at the bit which most interests me. The ankle bracelet flipping through the air into the back of their truck. Henderson closing the doors of the Transit. Tossing me an old red cushion to soften the metal floor of the van.

Our van driver – I don't know who it is – drives off. Moving down the exit ramps. A bit of stop-start traffic, then the steady burr of an open road.

An airport car park will be covered by plenty of security cameras, but you never get total coverage from those things.

There are always blind spots in the imaging, or a camera that doesn't work or has been disabled. If Henderson was careful enough to set up this particular manoeuvre, he'll have been careful enough to avoid doing it on TV.

The moving pickup truck was a lucky stroke, but it didn't really matter. They could just have left the bracelet on the ground, or disabled it, or attached it magnetically to any other car in the car park. It would all have worked every bit as well.

We will not lose you.

Don't do anything.

Stay safe!

Henderson listens to the thrum of the road rising through the wheel arches. Moves forward to speak to the van driver, through a little grille-covered hole in the plywood panel. Then leans back, grins and relaxes. The gun that he's been carrying loose in his hands gets holstered again.

'Sweet,' he says. 'Very sweet.'

And it is. It really is. A textbook evasion.

Jessica, the traitor, smiles.

50

We drive to the farmhouse. A two-hour journey, though I can't shake the feeling that we're circling round rather than driving straight there. The three or four hundred square miles of possible territory we identified all lies within forty or fifty minutes of Cardiff. An hour, max.

Hill roads, often enough. One sharp bend on an abrupt slope sends me scooting across the van into Henderson's lap. He helps turn me the right way up. I give him my flower.

We don't talk much. The back of the van is too noisy. The metal walls and floor reverberate constantly. The vibration enters my head, a tremor cased in mild steel. My feet buzz, as though my boots and trousers were acrawl with bees.

Henderson has his fingers twined into the perforations on one of the metal uprights supporting the van roof, and keeps himself from sliding around. I try the same thing, but my fingers get sore, so I give up and just let myself bounce and slide. I end up colliding with Henderson three more times. Hit the rear doors twice, once quite hard with my head.

And eventually we're there.

The same steep ascents. The sharp bends. The transition onto an unmetalled track. The van stops. The driver in front kills the engine. My head is still ringing, but the note has changed. My legs are still buzzing probably, but I can't feel them any more. Can't feel anything below my waist.

I still have the eye-mask with me. Henderson tells me to

put it on. I do. Henderson bangs on the van doors and they're opened from outside. Henderson and another strong male hand guide me up the steps into the barn.

They sit me down, take the eye-mask off.

It's the same as before. Same barn, same decor. Same locks on the door, same padlocks on the windows.

Geoff and Henderson in front of me. Geoff holding out a bottle of water, in case I'm thirsty.

'OK?' says Vic.

'It was better than the Stereophonics,' I say, taking the water.

I get the same room as last time. Same bed, same bathrobe, same little paper-wrapped soap and hotel-style shampoo. No daffodils, though, and no Quintrell.

'It's weird without Anna.'

Henderson gives me the work schedule for the weekend. It was intense last time, but this is worse. Ramesh has a team of five working with him this time. The big downstairs room is full of Ramesh's guys, each with laptops, a server on a table in the corner, and a big beast of a printer on the floor beneath.

The talk now isn't of field selection and filter value resets. All that stuff has been done. What we're doing now is the 'test, test, test and test'.

Ram and his boys run an endless series of payslips for me to examine. Payslips, and a whole menagerie of tax forms: the plain old fare of P14s and P45s and P35s, the vaguely aristocratic P11D, its rarer cousin the P11D(b), those crafty P9(T)s, the plain old P6 and the ugly P7X. We have to deal with the exotica too. The monarchs of the payroll savannah – the P46(pen), the WNU and the P46(expat). Forms which almost never crossed my desk at Western Vale. Form retrieval matters too: we lowly payroll clerks need to be able to call up such things as the SL1 and SL2 from the HRMC system.

There's no Quintrell here, so the burden of testing falls

on me entirely. And in any case, this is more my sphere than hers. I'm the person who's processed a million of these things. I start work on my day of arrival – no one cares that I've already worked an eight hour cleaning shift, or that I've spent seven hours playing car chase with Henderson. I get given a sandwich and a drink, then get sat in front of the first mound of dummy forms.

I work from half past seven to half past nine, under Ramesh's supervision. He tried the 'beautiful lady expert' line once, but it reminded us both that my sister in beautiful expertise is currently behind bars, her plain vanilla fraud charge wittily accessorised by a shiny new conspiracy to murder one.

So Ram drops the effort to charm. Treats me instead like one of his underlings. As brusque and, when I make a mistake, as snappy. And because Ram puts his underlings under pressure, they apply the same pressure to me. They give me long lists of things I have to accomplish. Circle round behind my chair as they're waiting. Because the team is badly lopsided – six of them and only one of me – they get to spend time drinking coffee and talking in their own language, well garnished with English and laughter. I think some of that mirth is aimed at me, I don't know why. At one point, one of the men came to me with a stack of about a thousand payroll forms, dropped them on my desk and said something to his colleagues which made them all howl with laughter. He then moved the forms and patted my shoulder, but didn't for a moment suggest that I could join in the joke.

I have once again, it seems, found my true level, which is to be the most junior element in any hierarchy. The most risible. The element that starts cleaning bathrooms at four in the morning and has its shoulder patted at nine in the evening.

I don't mind, or not really. At half past nine, Henderson comes to rescue me.

He takes me outside for a cigarette and a cup of coffee. I

sip the coffee, but I'm still wary of caffeine. I like the ciggy, though, and have two. We sit on the steps in the darkness, listening to owls hoot in the woodland beyond.

The sky is blanketed in thick cloud. I can't see the moon, or the telecoms mast, or anything at all beyond the little parking area and a glimpse of hawthorn. You can just about sense the change in the seasons, even now, even at night. The air carries a new chill. A sense of the leaves turning. It was this time of year when I found Hayley Morgan.

A weird thought that: a year gone and the case still running.

'Is Ram treating you OK?'

'Yes.'

'What does that mean?'

'It means no, not really, but I don't care. It's not for long.'

'Can you do another hour or so tonight?'

'Yes.'

We smoke a while in silence.

Henderson seems reflective. It's not just my part in all this that's coming to an end. His is too. Once our dodgy software is installed and operative, it either works or it doesn't. The theft either happens or it doesn't. But any problems will be dealt with either by Shoesmith or, remotely, from India. The money exiting the country will be looked after by James Wyatt – a task that can be accomplished from anywhere. Henderson's own particular brand of expertise will no longer be called for.

'What will you do after all this?' I ask.

'Take a bloody holiday.' Henderson laughs, then coughs. Stubs his cigarette on the step, breaking it at the join of the filter.

'What does a Vic Henderson holiday look like? I'm thinking maybe Paris and fancy hotels and lots of beautiful women.'

He looks sideways at me. 'Yes, some of the time. But right now, I think I'd be in the mood for a few months in the Caribbean. Rent a boat. Drift around between the islands. I wouldn't exactly say no to the beautiful women, though.'

Something in that image tugs at me. The way he looks at me as he says it. I realise that his words contain an invitation. That if I want to be the girl on his boat, I can be. Wear a loose cotton tunic and watch my legs turn brown as Spanish cedar. All I'd have to do is share my bed and not mind that my lover has an itsy-bitsy tendency to murder.

I say, 'You're sweet, Vic, you really are. But I think I need to go to New Zealand. I promised myself.'

'Fair enough.'

'You can come and visit me.'

'Any time I need speech therapy.'

We smile. I finish my cigarette. Resist the temptation to take his unsmoked stub. Go back inside.

That extra hour is a long one. It finishes finally at a quarter past midnight, and only then because Henderson speaks angrily to Ram.

I shower, then go to bed.

Don't sleep though.

If Brattenbury knew where I was, I think SCO19 would have been here by now. A dawn raid is still perhaps on the cards, but the intention was always to come in hard, as soon as the target was located.

And if tomorrow dawns without the smash of bullets into woodwork, without the Kevlar jackets and the jabbing guns, what then?

How do I rescue Roy Williams?

How do I rescue myself, if it comes to that?

That fear I felt when I realised Henderson was deliberately driving into restricted airspace is with me again now. Or rather: it's been with me all the time, but only now, in the silence and the dark, do I feel it completely. Like a bronze statue pulled from the ground, but still present in all its parts.

A bronze statue glittering with ice and frozen soil. The hole beneath it shaped like a coffin and the earth still fresh.

How do I rescue Roy Williams? How do I rescue myself?

I think of Jackson's joking comment when I was pulled into custody. *Don't flatter her. She'll cock everything up. Or start shooting people.* He's not wrong. It's true that it was Brattenbury's job to follow me here, a job that he flunked, but the bigger failure is mine. This whole venture was my idea. My idea to reinsert myself into Tinker. My idea to distribute software for them. My idea to lay myself in front of Henderson again.

More blameworthy still, it was me who demanded a level of operational independence so great that it ended up blinding the judgement of my more cautious senior officers.

But perhaps I don't have to stop at proving Jackson right. What if I proved him righter than right by cocking things up *and* shooting people? What if a little carefully considered violence ended up saving Roy's life, and mine? Saving our lives and smashing this gang?

That thought appeals no small amount. But Henderson is armed, as is Geoff, and as is Allan. And we strongly suspect that the security team is more than three strong. And I'll bet that every member of it is armed.

Plus the exits are all locked.

Plus Geoff, Allan or occasionally Henderson are always within sight of the front door.

Shooting people is one thing. Shooting people and surviving quite another.

I wish Lev were here. Or that he was in the woods outside. I'd back Lev's abilities against a barnful of Hendersons. But Lev isn't here and Lev isn't coming. The woods are empty of both him and SCO19. It's me, little me, and nobody else.

How do I rescue Roy Williams? How do I rescue myself?

Some time after two, I fall asleep. The same two questions in my head. The same roaring absence of an answer.

51

Saturday and Sunday: work, more work.

I start at eight. Ramesh's boys, or at least two of them, have been at their desks an hour or two before I arrive. They hurl me straight back in it. Another mountain of tax forms. Error messages and computer screens too. They need me to check that their software looks right and handles right. They want it to feel like the real thing. Once, I come across a page which normally loads instantly but on the fake system is taking as much as twenty seconds to show its face. There's a brief fury of recoding, then I'm asked to check again. For some reason, I don't know why, I've become known not as 'Fiona' but as 'FG'. So when I'm needed at a computer terminal, there are cries of 'Effgee, Effgee, come please!'

Shoesmith talks with Ramesh about program code. Wyatt comes in now and again and annoys everybody. Henderson comes regularly as well, careful to protect me. He insists that I'm worked for no longer than three hours at a stretch. That I get half-hour breaks in between. If Ramesh is naturally patriarchal, used to treating women as servants, Henderson is something more primitive. A he-lion stalking in the long grass, skin hot in the sunshine, and one fierce eye fixed on his harem.

Maid-of-all-work or concubine. Those are my choices.

Again, I don't mind. In a funny way, it's nice to be told what to do and when to do it. Nice to be able to defer the moment at which I have to decide what the hell I'm going to do.

Our first full day, the Saturday, we work till nine p.m. Everyone's keen to keep blasting on – it's dull work and it needs to get finished – but Henderson, Geoff and Allan break things up. They drag a big-screen telly in from somewhere, play a movie, distribute beers and pizza. A party atmosphere prevails. We're not going to be done by tomorrow, the original hope, but we look set fair to have everything complete before the end of the day on Monday. Terry says, 'We should have a big celebration. A giant piss-up.' Geoff catches Henderson's eye, laughs, and says, 'Well, you might just get lucky.'

By ten o'clock, I bail out and go to bed.

Sleep badly. Hayley Morgan, Saj Kureishi and Roy Williams crowd in on me. I keep asking them to leave, and they do, but as my awareness dims again, they always come back. Roy Williams keeps asking me to help him back to Katie and his little girl. I am vaguely aware of Katie too, but she's a long way off. The wrong side of a dark hill, unreachable.

The next day, Sunday, it's back to work. Start early. More tedious, patient work in two- or three-hour blocks. I'm less tired than I was. Have caught up with myself a bit, but I still don't fancy starting work as a cleaner in London tomorrow or the next day. I try to ask Henderson about this, but he's away a lot today. Busy and pressed. He just says, 'Don't worry, we'll sort it,' and gives me the kind of gesture which makes me bide my time.

At five in the afternoon, Henderson orders us all out because they need the room for a while. I can't think why. There are fewer people here than last time. Three people working in Distribution. Two, including Wyatt, in Finance. There are other rooms in this building that would easily accommodate anything that Henderson has to do and by turfing us out, he's simply put back the time by which we might finish. We can't even reassemble in some other room, because all the office equipment is in the main conference area and we can't work without it.

I try to find Geoff to talk crap with him, but he's in with Henderson too. So is Allan. With our armed guards all hidden away for the time being, I think seriously of getting my lock picks to work on the front door. Would probably even try it, in fact, except that Ram and his boys are setting up a game of cricket, played with a cardboard tube and an old tennis ball, and the tennis ball bounces too often into the front hall for me to have any chance of privacy.

So I go to my room and lie on the bed and drink peppermint tea and try to remember what Buzz looks like. Or what *I* do, for that matter: the beast in the mirror is still blonde and pixie-locked.

Strange to say it, but I miss Quintrell.

It's ten to seven before we're allowed back. There's a smell of toner cartridge and the printer output tray is warm to the touch. I tweak out the main paper tray and crunch up the pages on top before returning the thing to its place.

We continue work for forty minutes. The accuracy of our fake system is getting better all the time. Shoesmith sets up a whiteboard with forms and output data to be checked. Each item has to be checked a minimum of ten times, using different combinations of input variables on each occasion. Shoesmith, a bottle of brown ale in hand, says, 'We need ten out of ten scores on every single thing. Or twenty out of twenty. Then one more run of everything for luck. Then we're done.' The whiteboard marks our progress. Still slow, but some niggles with changing tax codes were sorted just before five and our successes are coming faster now.

At half seven, someone tries to print something and the machine jams. The man who tried to print – Dilip Krishnaswamy, the one who got the cricket game started –

jabs impatiently at the green print button, then calls out to me, 'Effgee, printer jam!'

Effgee, aka Jessica Taylor, aka Fiona Grey, aka the woman I once thought I was, goes over to sort things out. The printer's on the floor, so I get down on all fours to attend to it properly. I'm hardly an expert in office machinery, but I understand these things better than my current colleagues. And printers, I happen to know, contain their own computer chips. Their own stored memory. I clear the jam, but stay down on hands and knees flipping through the menu options. The machine does its best to be helpful and, Lord bless its inky little printer head, the thing succeeds. 'Print History' it suggests. I hit OK to see the submenu and it offers me a choice of Print Last and Print All. I choose the latter and replace the paper tray. Pages start pouring from the machine.

When it comes, I give cricketing Krishna his work. Keep everything else.

We work till nine thirty, at which point Henderson comes in to inspect. I've got about fifty reports to inspect and the IT boys are now mostly just goofing around as they wait on me.

Henderson – beer on his breath – asks me how it's going.

'Not well, to be honest. I've got a splitting headache. I might go and lie down for a while.'

Henderson checks his watch. 'No. Let's end it there for tonight. You've done enough. Have you eaten?'

I ask him for a club sandwich and tell him that if he's extra nice he'd get me a mug of peppermint tea. He promises to be extra nice. I pick up my pile of work papers, including the stuff from the printer, and go to my room.

Henderson joins me there in ten minutes with the sandwich, some tea, a bottle of beer for him and a bowl of crisps for us both.

'Can I join you for a while?' he asks, and I nod.

I'm lying on my bed, back against the wall. My stack of

papers down on the floor beside me. He notices them, but it's just work stuff. I've had papers in here all weekend, and there's nothing obviously special about these.

'Your team seems to be making good progress,' he says. 'Terry is happy.'

'Yes. Vic, look, I'm meant to be cleaning in London tomorrow morning. That's obviously not going to happen, but I might need a couple of days off before I do start. I'm knackered.'

One of those micro-pauses, then a nod. 'That's fine. In fact, I've got good news for you. We're ditching those London dates. We're just going to launch everything just as soon as Terry and Ram give the thumbs up.'

I stare at him, wondering if this is a genuine change of plan or if those London dates were all just another blind. A red herring. With a bolt of alarm, I realise that Terry may be planning to push his Fuck It button as soon as Monday evening. If that happens, then Brattenbury won't be ready. He'll be assuming he has another three weeks, and instead he'll be presiding over one of the worst bungles in law enforcement history. One officer kidnapped. Another infiltrated to no good effect. And the biggest theft in history taking place right under SOCA's always-confident noses.

Don't flatter her. She'll cock everything up. And I have done. Brattenbury wanted to know the date of launch and I gave it to him, but the wrong one. The police officer who enabled the biggest crime in history: that's me.

Trying to keep my voice level, I say, 'I thought London was the biggie. I thought the biggest payroll departments were based there.'

'They are. We found . . . other means of access. But we won't be paying you any less. We'll stick to what was agreed.'

I nod. In actual fact, they already *have* paid me. This last week, as it happens. The full amount. Sixty grand. Sitting in a bank account, offshore, in my name. That might seem unusually trusting for a bunch of criminals, but for one thing, they do trust me. For another thing, they'd happily kill me if I crossed them. Trust comes easy when you're the one with the gun.

I say, 'You'll get your holiday early, then.'

'Yes. The offer's still open. If you care to join me . . .?'

This time his question is direct. It wasn't last night.

I shrug apologetically. My answer remains the same. He looks genuinely sad. Runs his finger down the line of my jaw. 'Pity,' he murmurs. I think he means it. I give him sad eyes too. I mean those too, about 50 per cent.

We talk a bit. Eat the crisps. I yawn. He leaves.

He leaves and I turn to my pilfered documents. Documents that were so secret, the likes of Ram, Shoesmith and myself were never meant to see them.

And yet – there's nothing remarkable here at all. There are some work schedules of the sort that have already been distributed. A checklist of things to be done before launch, a document that has been kicking around all weekend. Then too, a menu for Terry's precious 'Leaving Party': a list of canapés and drinks. We've seen that too. Geoff's initials, GK, against a draft shopping list. A draft list of attendees: I appear only as 'FG? – check with VH', which doesn't say much for my overall importance. But Ram and his team aren't there at all, which suggests it wasn't much of a list anyway.

I throw the paper in the bin and go to bed.

Sleep.

And wake, icy with a sudden realisation. I flip the light on and go back to the Leaving Party. The initials that aren't on the list. Vic isn't there. Nor Geoff, nor Alan. Ram isn't there, nor any member of his team. That leaves me and Terry from the Product Design team. James Wyatt isn't there, but his colleague from Finance is. The three people from Distribution.

Not much of a party.

I'm left wondering what kind of 'leaving' Geoff had in mind, and I don't think I'm going to like the answer.

At any rate, the question crystallises things. I need to get out now, tonight. I need to liberate Roy. And I need to let Brattenbury know where the hell we are.

The shock of action sheathes me in something cold, but I recognise, underneath, the beat of a gathering energy. The beat of Fiona Griffiths in hunting mode.

I pull on jeans, T-shirt and a loose floral shirt. Leave my room. Go up the little flight of steps to the hall table, where Geoff is flipping through yesterday's paper. His gun is lying on the table next to a packet of biscuits and a can of Coke.

'You all right, love?' he says, with a note of surprise. It's two thirty in the morning.

'Not really. I'm coming down with something. Do you have paracetamol or codeine? Something like that.'

'Not here, but I can get you some.' He gestures through the wall towards the farmhouse.

I say, 'Yes, please.'

He pockets his gun. There's a keypad on the wall which releases the main door lock, but it's a six digit code and Geoff shelters the pad as he keys it in. He leaves.

I jog back down to my room. Come back with my hairgrips and make-up stuff. The door has an electronic override, but the basic mechanism is still a regular lock. The torsion wrench goes in easily, and it's obvious which way the lock turns, which isn't always the case. I rake out the lock, then start with my picks.

I'm not familiar with these damn picks though and this is a big brute of a lock. Heavy and difficult to work.

Excuses, excuses.

I get a couple of pins free, but I'm working way too slowly. Then my left hand, the one that holds the torsion wrench, slips and the lock pings back to its original position, cancelling my gains.

Sod it.

Plan B.

I shove my tools into a back pocket, go over to Geoff's table and pour a good glug of my amisulpride into his Coke. It's not a particularly dangerous drug in overdose – you wouldn't give it to nutters if it was – but, like everything, it has side-effects, which are all the more prominent for those who aren't used to it.

I asked Henderson for the liquid formulation on the assumption that the taste must be OK. I've always used tablets myself.

I start to make myself peppermint tea in the kitchenette.

Geoff comes back. He gives me the painkillers, which I swallow.

I gesture at my tea and say, 'Thanks. Look, can I sit with you awhile? I'm feeling weird.'

That's no lie. I *am* feeling strange. Shaky from the stress, or shaky, perhaps, because I feel new blood surging back into my system. My blood. Fiona Griffiths's finest.

Geoff says, 'Course you can.' Insists on going to my room and fetching me a jumper.

We sit down, share his biscuits. I clink my tea mug against his Coke and we both drink.

We chat a bit. About work, of course: the damn project looms over us like those mountainsides of colliery spoil. Huge grey slopes hanging over rows of little white cottages. Obliteration in a single slip of rock.

We talk about Ramesh. Timetables. I say it'll be odd when everything's over. Geoff rubs my forearm and says, 'We've all enjoyed having you on the team.. You've been . . . you've been great.'

His eyes want to say something more and his hand is a

little too slow to leave my arm. Half creepy, half motherly. Somewhere in between.

I say, 'Thanks.' Crinkle my eyes at him.

We do a quick crossword together, then I stand up in a going-back-to-bed sort of way.

Geoff stands too. He has that kind of courtesy. Henderson does too. It must be part of the professional killer's training.

But it's hard standing on a bellyful of amisulpride. Big doses make you drowsy and first-time users, even those on a more regular dose, usually complain of faintness on standing.

Taken aback, Geoff starts to say something. His hand reaches blurrily for his Glock.

But I'm there first.

Pick it up by the barrel. Lash the butt into his head. My first blow dazes him. The second one, a smasher, lays him out cold. The floor is stone and his head bounces, once, on impact. A little curl of blood leaks from his left ear.

'You've been great too, Geoff,' I tell him. 'You've been great too.'

I check I know how the gun works – I've made that mistake before – then stuff it into the waistband of my jeans. Go back to the door.

I've got more time now, but more adrenalin too.

Torsion wrench. Raking tool. Then the picks, the delicate picks. The too-delicate picks straining to shift the too-heavy tumblers.

Sod the sodding SOCA idiots, I think. I bet they gave me a girly little lock set. I bet they keep the real tools for the big rough tough guy cops who know how to use them.

A flare of anger.

Stupid. Not helpful.

I try to keep my attention in my fingertips.

One of my picks has, I'm sure, caught one of the pins. But catching is nothing. Turning is all. I apply increasing force to the pick until the damn thing suddenly breaks free in my hand. The pick itself is broken off inside the lock. I can't winkle it out with my fingers. Can't even get a proper hold of the end.

Sod it.

Big sod it, in fact.

Geoff is laid out cold, but he'll come to at some point and will do so knowing that it was me who hit him. And I'm in a stone-built prison with a door I can't open and locks on every window.

I don't know where Henderson or Allan are – or how many highly armed buddies they may have outside – but I do know that this is not now a safe place to be.

I get Geoff's Coke. Pour out what he hasn't drunk. Find some scissors in the stationery cupboard and snip out the top of the can. Then the bottom. Then cut straight down the side, so I have a flat metal rectangle.

Thus far, I'm sure of myself. I'm a bit vaguer about the next bit, but I cut away at the bottom half of the rectangle until I have something that looks like a well-manicured fingernail, pointing down.

Fold over the top of the rectangle to give myself something to work with.

Take my tool into the conference room which has two big windows, shuttered and padlocked.

The manicured fingernail is my best effort at a padlock shim, a little slip of metal that can slip over the shaft of a padlock to release its mechanism.

But I've cut my shim too thick. Can't get the fingernail to fold over the shaft.

Snip away at the metal. Reduce its width.

Try again.

This time the metal fingernail slips down all the way. Only the collar, the top half of the rectangle, remains proud of the shaft. I pull the collar round in a circle, keeping it tight.

Down and turn. That's the action. I know it in theory, but haven't done this in practice, or not for years anyway. There are YouTube videos which remind you what to do, but there's no internet in here. No phones.

I push down and turn. Nothing breaks, but nothing happens.

Damn it. This is starting not to feel like fun.

Then, a gesture of annoyance as much as anything, I test the padlock. As I should have done immediately. Because the mechanism *has* been released. The shank pulls free of the body. A half-inch of empty space, promising freedom.

You beauty, I think. *You little beauty.*

Open the shutters. Open the windows. Gun in my hand. Climb out.

There's wind on my face. A sprinkle of late-summer rain. And Fiona Griffiths has left the building.

52

I head far enough from the open window that I won't be easily identified by anyone looking out. The farmhouse is just fifty yards away. No lights on inside, but an outside lamp glows over a back door. Our barn, the one I've been living and working in, is part of a larger cluster of buildings, some of them converted, some just left as farm buildings.

A sheet of corrugated iron creaks in the wind.

Somewhere in the distance, I hear a helicopter's choppy beat.

Who sends a helicopter aloft at night? Air force training perhaps. Medical evacuation or mountain rescue, just possibly. But helicopters don't often fly at night, not here on the edge of the mountains, when all that lies beneath their blades is dark country lanes and slumbering fields.

Adrian Brattenbury, you beautiful man, I think I love you.

Adrian Brattenbury, for all your plum-coloured jumpers and your girly fits of temper, I think I can do business with you, my friend.

I jog over to the back door of the farmhouse, gun in hand.

The back door has an ordinary lock. The sort a locksmith can open in twenty seconds, the sort I can get through, even fumbling, even with my enfeebled pick set, in under a minute.

I enter, and find myself standing in a stone-flagged corridor. Stairs leading up. Doors off. An understairs cupboard, bolted top and bottom.

I nose around. The corridor opens out into a bigger hallway. A grander front door. One half-open door leads into a large and well-equipped farmhouse kitchen. An oil-fired range cooker, but also a gas-fired hob. Knives and pans. A good stock of drink. Flour and sugar in five-kilo jars. Cooking oil in a ten-litre tin.

It's nice. A good space. The sort of place I'd be happy to cook in, I think, before I remember that I'm a terrible cook and have never been so master of my kitchen as when I lived in a bedsit on the North Road with a single pair of electric rings and one bradawl-battered saucepan.

I decide to leave the cooking for another time. I take a knife, and leave.

Roy, Roy, Roy. Where are you?

No contest really.

You don't have two bolts on an understairs cupboard if all you keep there is a couple of brooms and a wash bucket.

I go back into the kitchen. Pour some of that cooking oil onto a cloth, and use it to soak the bolts and hinges of that cupboard door. When I loose the bolts and open it, it glides noiselessly open, beckoning me silently on like the most expensive sort of servant.

A flight of stairs, leading down.

Cobwebby. Dark.

There's a light switch, though. I flip it on and a couple of wall lights come on, cheap stable-style fittings.

I walk on down.

The cellar is low-ceilinged. I can stand without problem, but any man would need to stoop. The place is full of the kind of rubbish that accumulates in cellars. Old apple boxes. Tables that seem too good to chuck out. Bits of machinery. Floor tiles. A stack of plastic garden chairs. A filthy window high in the wall, an old coal chute possibly.

And Roy. Unshaven and rough-looking. A loop of heavy

chain bolted to the wall. He's lying down, on a mattress and under blankets, so I can't see how he's fastened. But he's in one piece. And snoring. Snoring so loudly, I wonder how Katie puts up with it.

I approach the bed and kick his feet.

He wakes up, a snore still heaving in his throat.

'Morning, Sarge.'

'Fuck! Fiona!'

Neither of us are quite in 'Dr Livingstone, I presume' territory, but we can work on the transcript later.

'I thought maybe you might like to piss off out of here.'

He pulls his blankets away. He's manacled at the wrists and waist. And badly beaten. Legs lying at a bad angle.

The padlocks I can possibly deal with, the injuries I certainly can't.

'I tried to escape three days ago. They gave me a kicking and broke both legs.'

Roy explains this with a touching simplicity, as though describing a clever bit of play in rugby. Now that I see his face more clearly, I see that he's not just looking rough, he's looking injured. In pain.

My plan, such as it was, starts to collapse. 'You can't walk? I've brought lock picks.'

'I can crawl.'

If that's what it has to be, it's what it has to be.

I start work on the smallest of the padlocks. First with my shim – which isn't even close to being strong enough – then with my picks. Get nowhere. These are big locks, agricultural things, and my picks are designed for ordinary household doors.

I'm getting nowhere.

Roy looks at my tools bending in the lock and says, 'Fiona, get out, get help, come back.'

I nod. Not much else to do.

'You better have this.'

I offer him my Glock.

Roy shakes his head. 'There's a gun room somewhere. I've heard them talking about it. When I tried to escape, they came after me with shotguns and rifles. I didn't make it more than thirty yards.'

I nod. 'OK.'

Disappear back upstairs.

No sound from the slumbering house. Just a tick of water somewhere. Guttering loosely jointed. That and the sigh of wind.

Of course a house like this has a gun room. Rabbits and foxes. The occasional escaping copper. And you wouldn't keep weapons upstairs. They're strictly ground-floor items. And not at the front of the house. Somewhere close to the back door. Opposite the steps to the cellar there's another door. A boot room. Boots and waxed jackets. A washing machine and dryer. Beyond that, a further door. Glass cabinets and guns. Shotguns. Rifles. Handguns. Shells and bullets.

The cabinets are all locked, but the keys sit in a little pottery bowl on the window sill.

You don't need much conventional security when you've got Henderson and his buddies on the prowl. They're better security than keys.

I take a rifle and shotgun for Roy, a shotgun for me. Plenty of ammo. Trot downstairs and get Roy tooled up. He looks better that way: sitting up and with an armful of guns.

'Fucking hell, Fi. You're something else, you really are.'

That sentence seems logically weak to me, but I'm not going to quarrel.

'I told Katie I'd get you out. So here I am: getting you out.'

'Thank you very much. I appreciate it.'

'DCI Jackson once told me that you're not allowed to just

388

shoot the fuckers. You have to say "Police" first. Then you can shoot them.'

'OK. Good to know.'

I go to leave, but Roy calls me back with a low whisper.

'Fi, if I don't make it for any reason, tell Katie—'

'I saw Katie. She told me to tell you that she loves you and always will. And that your daughter loves you and always will. And she cried when she said it. And she looked more beautiful than ever. And when she said it, she meant it with every bone in her body. And if you want to say anything to her in return, you can bloody well tell her yourself.'

'All right. I will.' He has tears in his eyes, a catch in his throat. He's a lucky man.

'Roy, I'm going to make a bit of a mess. When stuff goes off, you might want to break that window.' I point at the coal-chute window. 'You'll want the air.'

The stack of roof tiles is within his reach. I'm not sure I'd be much good at breaking a window with them, not while lying down, but I'm sure Roy will do fine.

I realise we need some sort of parting gesture. Don't know why, but it's what the moment calls for.

I say, 'Do men do fist-bumps? Or is that just an American thing?'

'No, we could do that.'

We knock our fists together. His huge one. Dark tattoos circling his wrist. Tattoos and a manacle. My small fist. I'm still wearing Jessica's bracelets and even though Roy hits me gently, I can still feel the power in that arm. I don't know what he finds in mine.

I lope upstairs. Bolt Roy in again. Load my shotgun in the light of the back door.

In that plastery silence, limewashed and old, every click of the gun feels too loud. I probably haven't been in the house for more than ten minutes, but it feels too long.

Entering the kitchen, I move stuff around until I find a pair of red propane cylinders. There's no mains gas out here, so a gas-fired range needs the bottled stuff. I pour cooking oil round the cylinders. Sugar. A bottle of brandy. A couple of wooden chairs that are easy to move.

I'd do a better job if I had longer, but I'm getting nervous now.

Leave a little trail of flammable stuff leading out of the kitchen, then light it with a box of cooking matches. The long ones, designed not to burn your fingers.

The trail was a nice idea in theory, but stupid in practice. For one thing, flame just woofs along the brandy in a single breath of fire. For another, I have to hang around in the kitchen door to make sure that I've got a good blaze going around the propane.

I have.

A smoke alarm starts to shriek.

I run for the back door. I've got the shotgun in my right hand and can't easily turn the handle with my left. Try it a couple of times, shaking, then switch hands. Roy would probably just have opened the door with a single kick.

I run out into the darkness.

Lights are coming on in the farmhouse upstairs. There's an orange glow coming from the kitchen, like someone opened the wrong door and found the lick of hellfires within.

I can still hear, or think I can, the blades of a helicopter.

Hope you're watching, Mr Pilot Man.

Then the kitchen explodes. A double explosion, in fact, but so close together it sounds almost like one. A huge plume of yellow fire.

The fire's held within the farmhouse walls, however, and once propane is gone, it's gone. There's still a fire burning, but not necessarily a come-and-get-me-one, as viewed from a distant helicopter.

I jog around looking for the oil tank. Find it. A big thing. Two and a half thousand litres, something like that. I fire into it with the Glock.

Nothing.

Not even the splash of oil.

I have a spasm of anxiety, then realise that the tank might not be full and I was shooting high. Aim lower, and a plume of beautiful oil jets forth. My friend Lev once blew up an oil tank with no more than a couple of bullets. It takes me five, but I get there in the end.

More fire.

The human eye can, I believe, see a single candle-flame from a distance of three miles and more. The helicopter pilot will be more than three miles away, but I'm sending up a thousand odd litres of kerosene, plus a farmhouse that's already half ablaze.

How long before SCO19 arrive?

Not long, I'm guessing. Ten minutes? Fifteen?

I can't see Roy failing to hold out that long.

As for me, I'm not quite certain what to do next. Assuming that Henderson and friends were first alerted by the smoke alarm, it'll take them time to figure out what's happened and who's behind it. What's more, I'm well concealed by darkness. I'm no longer in immediate danger.

So I stick around. I take precautions, of course. I move away from the farmhouse. Move into the trees, stay clear of the farm track. Keep an eye on the buildings behind me.

A whirl of activity.

Figures come streaming out of the farmhouse. It's impossible to be precise about numbers, because the only light comes from my two fires and it's hard to see anything beyond their orange hearts.

There's also the sound of vehicles. A van – probably the one that brought me here – reverses swiftly towards the barn.

The front door opens. Someone is there – Henderson? Geoff? – ushering people out. Light spills into the yard. The gleam of wet stone, trout-brown.

I can see Ram in his pyjamas. Another man, protesting, being almost thrown into the van. But only dark skins, dark faces.

Wyatt doesn't come out. Nor Terry. Nor the other Brits.

There are gunshots from inside the barn. Not the sounds of a firefight, but the orderly sounds of execution. The pace of the shooting is considered, almost stately.

I think Terry's leaving party has come a day early.

Ram and his colleagues weren't invited, but I was. I had a question mark by my name, but I was still on the list.

The six Indians are all out now. Inside the van. One of them, I couldn't see which, was wearing underpants, nothing else.

The gunshots keep coming. I try to keep my imagination pulled back from what's happening in there, but I can't do it. A tide of blood. Wyatt's arrogant face. Shoesmith's more human one. Each obliterated because the project no longer requires them. Obliterated because Henderson's security rulebook calls for the elimination of every risk, no matter how small.

What did I really think? That an organisation which would kill Tania Lewis for almost no reason would leave me free to live? Would leave Terry and Wyatt and the others?

I think we've always underestimated Tinker. That *I* have. That we've never fully appreciated its rigour or its ruthlessness.

But I also remember those conversations with Henderson. Those conversations about the boat. I think if I'd said yes, if I'd agreed to be his brown-legged Caribbean boat-girl, I'd have been spared the massacre. His regret was genuine. Regret not merely that we wouldn't become lovers, but that he'd have to slaughter me with the rest. No wonder he gave me sad eyes.

Even Geoff, a lesser man than Henderson, was the same. His 'you've been great' comment and that creepily lingering touch on my forearm: those were his way of saying, 'So sorry I'm going to have to shoot you.'

The shooting inside the barn comes to an end. The van, with its cargo of Bangalore knowhow, has already vanished, screaming down the track. I didn't get its number plate, but this mess is no longer mine to clean up. I hope to God that SCO19 manage to pick up the van as it escapes. Still, as Brattenbury would probably tell me, 'Fiona, we *have* done this before. We *do* know how to do this.'

And he does. He really does. He's never come across a Tinker before, though. I doubt if any law enforcement body has. This last year, it's been a privilege. An honour, really. An honour and a privilege.

As I'm thinking these thoughts, I see what I expect to see next. A glow of fire from the barn itself. The simplest way to destroy evidence. Kill everyone you don't want to talk, then burn the place down. It's hardly going to stop our investigation, but it's a pretty good delaying device. The flames grow big enough, fast enough, that they must have used petrol. They presumably had cars ready for just such a contingency.

More cars leaving the farmhouse.

Or no, I realise, not cars, but a pair of those four-wheel-drive mud-buggies that farmers use. *Crap*. They're intending to avoid roads altogether. Will Brattenbury be ready for that move? I doubt it. SCO19 will have road vehicles aplenty and no shortage of air support, but that's not quite the same thing as having vehicles which can cross field and mountain, no matter what the conditions.

The buggies avoid the farm track, avoid the road. There's a

gate above the farmhouse. I can just see its weather-whitened timbers gleaming like bone in the dying firelight. The two buggies make for the opening. They're not speeding. Just moving purposefully and without a single wasted moment.

Lower in the valley, I can see the orange glow of street lighting. The buggies are heading away from all that, into an area where there are no lights, no sodium glow.

As I thought, we're in the mountains, or on their very edge. The ragged line between man and mountain.

Once again, Tinker is ahead of us. I see it as clearly as I see the last of the fires licking out the remains of the oil tank. A column of smoke, inky and foul, is lit in orange from below. A slow rain, quietly falling, murmurs regret.

Brattenbury will be coming, and coming fast, but I'm the officer in charge and on the scene. These are my decisions and I will make them.

Shotgun in hand, Glock in waistband, knife in pocket, I start to pursue.

53

The night is dark. The moon is full enough, I think, but the sky is wadded in great rolls of cloud, unspooling from across the Irish Sea. As I move away from the farmhouse, my eyes grow used to the night, but even so visibility is very poor. I run up towards the gate, pass through to the fields beyond.

The buggies are unlit, but they're diesel-engined and hardly quiet. I hear the thump of the motors. There's a track, of sorts, cut into the field. Red mud and jutting stone. Coarse mountain grasses growing freely in between. A rising path, and moorland beyond.

My shoes are Jessica's shoes. Ballet pumps. Black and white polka dots. Quite nice actually, and comfortable enough. But not well suited to running, or even walking, on this terrain. I lose one shoe almost straight away, and fall as I lose it. The other I discard on purpose, because the effort of trying to keep it was slowing me down.

No shoes, no problem.

I'll do this barefoot.

I can't see enough to be confident of running fast, but move at a pace I think I'll be able to sustain. Far down in the valley, I hear the first wail of sirens. Blue lights on hedgerows.

I think about going back to the farm. Simply reporting to Brattenbury, or whoever is to be in charge of the assault. But as I'm debating this, I catch a momentary flash of lights up ahead. Not headlights. Just the quick dart of a torch, furtive and brief.

There's a change in the sound too. Up till now, the two vehicles have driven fairly steadily, moving with a steady, puttering rumble. What I'm hearing now is different. A sudden revving. A low-gear yowl. Perhaps the sound of a wheel slippage.

Then headlights. Again only brief, but angled sharply upwards, at right angles to the track I'm on. An abrupt lurch forward, then the lights are killed.

They're turning, I realise. Fighting to turn up the slope and double back on themselves.

They can't want to return to the farmhouse. The sirens are close now, a minute away at most. *So why double back?*

I've answered my question almost as soon as I've framed it. The track they've taken gives them the quickest, easiest access to the open hill. Once there, they have, in effect, the freedom of the Brecon Beacons. No hedges, no walls, no boundaries.

But that freedom comes at a price. The hills themselves are very open: bare and windswept. Henderson's security brain will be keenly aware of the risk of pursuit from above. So the escapees have to get back to the broken ground of a valley floor as soon as they can. *But not the valley of the original farmhouse.* That's their plan. Get out onto the hills. Skirt the base of the ridge until they can drop down into the adjoining valley. Then lose themselves in the woods. Or hide out in an outbuilding till dawn. Or switch vehicles and just drive calmly away.

That's what *they're* doing. But what is Brattenbury doing? What is his countermove?

And again: no sooner have I framed my question than I've answered it.

Priority one: find Roy Williams. Find me.

Priority two: secure the property. Put out the fires. Check

396

on victims. Save those that can be saved. Secure any evidence that has escaped the flames.

Priority three: pursue and capture any suspects that have left the property *by road*: the type of pursuit that any police service handles as a matter of routine.

Nowhere on Brattenbury's list will there be a memo item *Check to see if there are any all-terrain farm utility vehicles creeping, without headlights, on the margins of the hillside above.* Even if, in theory, Brattenbury had considered the possibility of such an escape, he couldn't, given the tiny gap of time, have prepared a response. He'd need all-terrain vehicles of his own. Night vision equipment. A mass deployment of officers in this valley and the neighbouring one. None of which could, realistically, be assembled in the time available.

I see all this, with the same clarity as I see the yard in front of the farmhouse now filling with blue lights and armed officers. See it and think, *We've blown it. After all this. They're getting away.*

Only my feet are moving faster than my thoughts.

I'm scrambling directly uphill. There's no track here, just roughly thistled grass. This isn't a place where you want to be barefoot but then Ernest Shackleton probably didn't want his ship to sink under him in the Antarctic. Those guys in Apollo 13 probably weren't best pleased when they found themselves in a crippled ship two hundred thousand miles from Earth.

Shoes, schmoes. We don't always get what we want.

I go on jogging upwards.

Jogging up, until I see a hedge looming black against the skyline. Hawthorns, stunted by the wind. Barbed wire. Blackthorn and maple. A couple of fenceposts, softly lichenous and rotten at the base. The sigh of open moorland.

It's too dark to tackle the hedge with any strategy, so I just shove myself into what looks like a weak spot. I flail around for a few moments, struggling for a foothold in the jumble of black branches and wet leaves, but I push through somehow. Emerge into the sudden wideness of the mountain proper.

As I do so – face flat on the muddy ground, legs still thrutching free of the hedge – the beat of a diesel engine draws near. So near, I can feel the stones in the ground shaking under my cheek. I'm half lying on my shotgun and can't get the Glock out from my wet jeans.

I heave forward on my elbows. Heave and roll. Get the shotgun free.

Fire.

Not *at* anything. The gun is still half under my body and I can feel the blast of shot and escape gases warm beneath my face. I just want to cause havoc. Disrupt the smooth ease of this escape.

Want to, and do.

I think the buggy must be a few yards from me when I pull the trigger, no more. The detonation – its sight and sound – acts like a stun grenade discharged at point-blank range.

I don't know if I've hit the driver. I don't think so. But the buggy veers from the blast, lurching uphill. A hard right-angled turn at speed and on a nastily climbing slope. I hear, and half see, the buggy's engine shriek as its left-sided wheels lose contact with the ground, as it bucks up on its side.

There's a moment of astonished equilibrium. The vehicle held in temporary balance, a mountain trapeze.

I'm urging it to overturn. Urging it to continue its toppling curve.

But it stands steady against the night, then lurches back. Jounces hard on its springs. Hits mud and stone, slithers down a small bank, and ends, still pointing up the mountain, perpendicular to its original direction. It took a hard knock or two, for sure, but the engine is still running and those damn things are made for rough ground, rough use.

I seize the moment. Fire the shotgun flat and low into the

nearest tyre. I'm not much of a markswoman, but at this range it's impossible to miss. Fire a second shot to be sure. The gun takes five cartridges and I want the last two available if I need them. Wrestle the Glock out of my waistband – cursing Jessica for the needless skinniness of her skinny jeans – and fire that too. Into the air. I'm not trying to hit anyone. I just want the confusion. The confusion and the noise.

Down at the farmhouse, they will hear the shooting and be starting to respond.

As all this is happening, I can hear people clambering out of the buggy. The driver – Allan, maybe? Vic? – is swearing as he tries to get the thing into gear and back onto the level. Whoever it is, he can't do it. Not with one tyre blown out, the slope and mud against him.

But I'm not the only one who can play at this brutal, muddy, rain-blunted game.

A shotgun blast, not mine, roars out into the night. A second shot follows, then a third and a fourth. An arc of fire, splitting the air. An arc that would threaten to saw me in half, except that I'm lying face down in the mud and whoever's shooting will be seeking a chest shot. The lethal stroke.

I try to wriggle forward and sideways, but my leg is caught in something. A twist of wire, a loop of root. I'm not sure. Either way, I'm stuck and lying flat, when another voice – male, rough, not one I recognise – shouts, 'Leave it! Leave it! Just run!'

Two men – perhaps three or four – stampede past me. They pass so close in the darkness that one of them hits my head a glancing blow with his boot. The blow makes me drop my guns momentarily. When I recover myself, I fire low with the Glock, hoping to hit a foot or a leg. Don't know if I succeed. Blaze off the shotgun at the same flat angle, the muzzle flash so bright that I have to close my eyes against the glare.

Only one shot comes back out of the night. I see it more

than hear it, but feel a sudden burning in my right foot and calf. The sensation is so hot, so fiery, that it takes me a moment to realise I've been hit. I try to kick free of whatever is holding me back and this time, my movement is unimpeded, as though the shot unhooked me from whatever held me back.

Shove more cartridges into my gun.

Two buggies left the farmhouse and I've only disabled one.

I try standing. I feel slightly vertiginous with shock, but more OK than not. My ankle is stiff and a strange state – simultaneously hot and numb – but when I take a trial step or two, I don't fall over.

Fuck you, and fuck you, and fuck you, I say to myself. Out loud or in my head, I'm not sure.

I start limp-jogging back up the valley in the direction that the first buggy came from. In the direction where I assume the second buggy still lurks. I don't have a plan, don't have a strategy. Just can't bear the thought that these bastards might be getting away.

Fuck you, and fuck you, and fuck you.

I limp-jog for four minutes, maybe five.

My injured ankle feels hot to begin with, then feels nothing at all. I've lost all sensation in my feet, but when I look down I see them still there. Ghostly white, mud-splattered, still attached to my legs.

Good enough.

Behind me, police vehicles, Land Rovers at a guess, approach the spot where the shooting took place. They'll have found the injured buggy. Be searching for runaways.

I don't know if any of my shots found their target, but at least I directed our resources to the right spot and deprived the first batch of fugitives of their getaway vehicle.

The second batch I'll handle alone.

And ahead of me, not far away, I can still hear the puttering beat of that other buggy. It's not moving fast, not on this terrain, not in this light. I try to figure out what they're trying to do. We're moving up the valley, into the mountains. These are glacial valleys, scooped out by the last Ice Age. The sides of the valleys are steep – too steep for any farm buggy – and the headwall itself is only fifteen or twenty degrees off being perfectly vertical.

At some point, surely not far off, the buggy will find itself in a dead end. A cul-de-sac of the mountains.

I'm just starting to doubt myself. Question the whole pursuit, when I realise – with stupid slowness – that I can no longer hear the buggy ahead of me. Taken aback, I move forwards with extreme caution. My limp, I notice, has become more exaggerated, and even my good foot seems clumsily reluctant to obey my brain.

Shoes, schmoes, and feet will heal.

Shotgun levelled, and Glock easily accessible in the front waistband of my jeans, I creep on. Watching, listening – hearing nothing.

Then I hear something. The tick of an engine cooling. A fan. A drip of water.

See the gleam of light, curved over metal.

The buggy, empty, no humans present.

I do what I can to search the landscape round me for possible threats. It's not yet dawn, not yet close. But the clouds have thinned. There's more moonlight than there was, and over towards England there's a hint of brightening, a vinegary silver, a first glimpse of the coming day.

The track that we've been following leads on to the head of the valley. A track for farmers and ramblers and nobody else.

A track without exit.

Above me, there's a spur of rising ground leading up to the main ridge high above my head. The incline is as much as forty-five degrees and the slope is tussocky and uneven.

A car won't cope with that, not even a four-by-four, but

human legs will cope just fine. The fugitives will even now be climbing up to the ridge, and from there, they'll be able to scatter wherever they want. Brattenbury won't be able to throw a cordon round these mountains. There aren't enough police officers in the country to do it.

I can't follow. Not sensibly, not realistically. Not with my poor fitness, my injured ankle, my bare and increasingly tattered feet. Plus I don't fancy the thought of creeping up the slope above me into Tinker's waiting guns.

We've lost, I think again, *we've lost*.

Reason says: fire your guns. Set fire to the buggy. Summon help. Do what can be done. At least play out a losing hand. Stay in the game to the last hopeless shake of the dice.

Reason, my old buddy. Reason, the only friend I never quite lose.

But even friends need a good kick from time to time, and this is one of those moments.

For some reason, I can't quite bear the thought of encountering my colleagues just now. Not under these circumstances. Just can't bear to watch the police machine clanking energetically into action on this losing cause. Like watching some industrial automaton, mighty but blind. A King Kong of the Cambrian mountains. Raging, brave, defeated.

For no real reason except tiredness, wanting to sit down, I ease myself into the buggy's driver's seat.

Ease myself in, and catch a glimpse of something moving. Keys swinging from the ignition. A little cluster of metal and hope.

A stupid oversight that, to leave the buggy still driveable – except that the buggy can't make any ground on the slope above and the runaways can't have known I was only a few hundred yards behind. Can't have known, come to that, that they were even being pursued. A regular police pursuit involves light, machinery, and noise. My pursuit involved next to nothing. A girl with bare feet and skinny jeans. One blonde Jessica, two vengeful Fionas.

They don't know that they're being pursued, I think.

Swinging keys, sighing wind. Those things, and empty air. A smell of peat.

We've lost, I think, *except just possibly not*.

The fugitives will work slowly upwards to meet the ridge at the top. Then logic will tell them to put as many miles between themselves and the farmhouse as they can. The high ridges of these mountains all bear footpaths, good ones, well maintained and even paved in places. The getaways might scatter left or right once they hit the top, but either option would be better than working their way down the difficult opposite slope in bad light.

I put my hand to the ignition and start the buggy.

A poor chance is still a chance.

54

I ride the buggy up to the head of the valley. My feet, no longer forced to carry my weight, are sending a long, slow swell of pain up to my brain, which listens gravely to their complaints. Then tells them to fuck off.

Has my language got worse since all this started? I think it has. I like riding the buggy though. It has a tough but easy power, like the best sort of men.

Like Buzz, actually. I wish he were here. Or would wish it, except that he would definitely want to stop me doing what I'm about to do and I would definitely want to do it anyway.

I drive on. A bouncy, jouncy, tussocky ride. A puttering growl trotting alongside, like a dog.

The mountains gather me in and encircle me, a huge bowl of silence.

A glassy silver starts to lift the rim of night.

I don't know these mountains well. My father has never been the outdoorsy type, and when we did leave the city, we usually headed for my Aunt Gwyn's farm in the Black Mountains. All the same, we did make excursions now and again. Often led by Gwyn herself, my mother in slightly frightened but acquiescent support. We visited the ruined monastery at Llanthony. Paddled rubber dinghies on the Monmouthshire and Brecon canal. Explored the disused tunnel at Torpantau, once the highest train tunnel in Britain. And we went for walks in the Brecon Beacons. For all I know, we used to walk and picnic in this very valley.

So though I don't know these mountains well, I perhaps know them well enough. The valley headwalls look vertical from some angles, but they're not quite. They're twenty degrees off, even more in places. And there are lines of weakness. Gullies that break these clean lines, the dirty drainage pipes of geology.

Once, in a valley like this, my father dared me to climb one of these gullies. The sort of dare my father couldn't help but invent, then couldn't help but try to meet. So we did. Him and me. Panting our way up the weakness in the headwall. Strips of rock and near-vertical grass to right and left. The gully itself a torrent of clay, peat, rock and streaming water. We emerged from the top of that damn thing slathered in mud. Head to toe. Creatures of earth and bogwater. Aching, frightened, incredulous, elated.

That day, we climbed in broad daylight, properly shod, without a wounded ankle, and without a fistful of guns. But phooey to that. I'm here to catch bad guys. I drive the buggy up to the headwall, till it looms above me like the fall of a dam. Drive it, till the wheels spin on the rising slope and the sodden moorgrass.

Fuck you, and fuck you, and fuck you.

I kill the engine and the silence swells around me.

There are two main gullies piercing the cliffs above. One spiking up and to the right, the other up and to the left.

Eeny-meeny-miny-mo.

I choose the left-hand one. No particular reason, except that it will drop me out onto the ridge closer to where I think the fugitives themselves are headed.

My route to that point is shorter than theirs. More direct, no wasted miles. Also, up till now, I've been doing a steady six or seven miles an hour on the buggy. A speed that I doubt they'll be able to match themselves.

I start to climb.

Quite quickly, I find that my ankle is not happy with my decision making. It's arguing in favour of doctors, hospitals, painkillers and clean linen. My feet are sending memos that make mention of clean water, soap, medical care, bandages.

The numbness that has gripped my lower half is beginning to pale into some low throb of pain. A beat I'm now struggling to ignore. I find myself falling, when I now, more than ever, need to move.

At one point I see a rock which is well-positioned for where my right foot needs to be. I put my foot onto it – watch it into position – then shift my weight over. And simply fall. Sideways and painfully. I think, *How can I even climb what lies ahead when I can't even stand on a stupid rock?*

I actually hit my thighs in frustration. Stupid, useless things. Not good.

Not good at all, and I'm aware of a kind of anger at this situation. In a way, my whole life has been an exercise in cutting off from my feelings. I'm a world-class dissociator. Numbness is my forte. I'm the empress of numb. Most of the time, somehow, I still manage to get on with my life.

So why not now?

For a moment, I struggle to get a grip of myself, to wrestle the pain into oblivion. To force it away with simple mind power. That doesn't work, but when I withdraw my attention, with a silent *pop*, the pain vanishes. Not just the pain, but almost all physical sensation. I can hear the wind, feel the rain gentle on my face, but that's more or less it. I can't feel the barrel of the Glock jabbing against the top of my leg. Can't feel the shotgun, cold in my hand. Can't feel tiredness or pain or even fear. It's like I'm walking alone in the universe, the only person here.

A strange state of mind, but useful.

Fuck you, and fuck you, and fuck you.

Somehow, I manage to keep climbing.

The slope increases. To start with, I was using my hands and arms only occasionally for balance. Now, I'm using them all the time. Hands, elbows. The stock of my gun. Whatever works.

I still can't see much, but I can see enough. And strangely, there's some sort of upside in having no boots. My toes clutch at stones. Stab themselves into mud. Twist into whatever wiry grass that survives at these heights.

I inch higher.

Or more than inch. The valley starts to level beneath me. Tracking sideways with my gaze, I estimate I'm a quarter of the way above the valley floor. Then halfway. Then even more.

Left foot, right foot, hand, hand.

Left foot, right foot, hand, hand.

I sing, chant and swear myself upwards as the wind chatters at my clothes and hair. It's not wet, not really, but there's still enough rain that I'm properly soaked. Jessica's pretty floral shirt – £9.99 at H&M, a bargain we were both happy with at the time – is a thing of rags. Her loose jumper – some acrylic thing in red, bought at a price and from a store I no longer recall – is near useless. Freely letting in the wind and rain and yet managing somehow to impede my movements.

Up and up.

The slope to either side of me is some good fraction off vertical. Perhaps twenty degrees at its steepest. The wall itself is made of bands of rock, mingled with sodden moorgrass and slopes of tumbling scree. It's steep enough – high and exposed – that you find arctic alpine flora here. I don't know enough to name the species, but these mountains were sculpted by the Ice Age and you feel its blast in these lines, these screes.

My gully, lying at an angle, is a little shallower than the wall itself, but best of all, it's like a notch carved into the slope. I can use the left hand wall to brace myself as I move up on the right, and vice versa. One muddy hand steadying me, as the opposite muddy foot claws to find support.

Everything hurts, but in some other land. The empress of numb waves a vague hello to that land of sensation. She'll make contact when she's ready.

The wind snickers, waiting for a fall.

Once, out to my left, I see a couple of sheep placidly munching, an extraordinary sight in this luminous pre-dawn. White smudges grazing the edge of the impossible.

I test everything before trusting my weight to it. A few times, too often to count, I feel myself slipping. But I never slip more than a few inches. The holds that don't give way make up for those that do. One time, the worst time, three-quarters of the way up the wall, both handholds give simultaneously with a wet ripping of grass and root, and my right foot flails to find a hold that will keep me in balance. I manage to save myself by biting down on the knot of vegetation in front of me. I survive the moment, but realise that if I slip more than a foot or two, nothing would stop me. And if I tumbled out of my gully onto the headwall proper, the momentum of a fall would be irreversible. I'm sheeted with mud and water. A human toboggan.

And every further yard is a yard further to fall.

Left foot, right foot, hand, hand.

A low dawn burns on some far-off horizon. My mouth tastes of red sandstone. My hair is moorgrass and peatwater. My nails date back to the Old Devonian. My feet are rags of shoe leather, pulled from a Celtic bog.

And then – I'm there. The sky seems suddenly closer. The summit line lies fierce and low above my head. The wind gives out a low whistle as it breaks over the bowl of the ridge.

All that, and a cigarette end. A broken V, split where the filter meets the tobacco.

The cigarette is wet, but not sodden. Not pulped. In this weather, it can't have been lying here long. Any real time up here and the damn thing would have almost melted into the mountain.

I look up, see nothing, but there's nowhere to go but up.

The ridge is closer than I'd understood. Indeed, I only really become aware of how close it is when I look up and see a knot of dim whiteness huddled close above me. I don't understand what I'm seeing and am peering for a better view when I dislodge a rock and the huddled white resolves itself into a little trio of sheep, nestled against the wind but now startled by my presence.

The leading sheep, frightened, breaks out onto the summit edge with a clatter of hooves and a small avalanche of tumbling stone and scree. A second sheep follows.

I'm about to follow when I realise there's a dark figure on the skyline. A figure summoned by the noise of the first sheep. A figure that is upright, armed and watchful.

Henderson.

He has a rifle levelled at the head of the gully. Night vision glasses round his neck. But, as the final sheep heaves its way out of the gully, in another explosion of kicking hooves and scattering stones, he smiles. Lowers his gun. Puts a cigarette in his mouth and tries to get it lit. One hand working the lighter as the other hand cups the flame.

Bad move, Vic. You never were a capable smoker.

Two hands occupied and my turn for the exit.

I pull my way out, levelling my gun as I do so.

'Morning, Vic.'

His eyes jump to his rifle but he can see I'll fire if he moves for it.

'Back off, Vic. Back away.'

409

He does so.

I get level with his gun and kick it over the cliff. It disappears into the wind, soundlessly.

'Walk up to the edge.'

He doesn't do that. He thinks I'm going to shoot him and leave him to fall, but that's not my intention. I just know he'll have other weapons and I want him in a place where he won't be tempted to fool around. I explain this and he complies. Standing on a rock at the lip of the cliff. He takes off his scarf and down coat as I watch. He's got a shoulder holster with the Glock. A spare magazine for the rifle and the handgun. A radio. He throws his goodies over the cliff, at my instruction. Puts the coat back on. Leaves the scarf.

My gun never deviates. He watches me continuously, disarms slowly, but he's not in a good place to try anything stupid, his face to the wind and his back facing emptiness.

'Can I smoke?' he asks when he's done.

I nod.

He lights up. Throws me cigarette packet and lighter.

I put a ciggy in my mouth. It's hard lighting it one-handed. Hard lighting it when my eyes never flicker from the man with his back to the cliff. But I'm a resourceful girl. Tobacco and I go way back. I get the damn thing lit and we smoke.

'You came up the valley?' Henderson asks, trying to work things out.

I nod.

'Up there? The cliff?'

I nod.

It isn't a cliff, not really, but I'm not about to argue. Every twenty seconds or so, I glance behind me. I don't know who else was on that buggy, but don't want someone sneaking up behind me.

Fortunately, the mountain here is wide, bare and open. No men. No guns.

On a far ridge, I do see a couple of figures hurrying away towards the west.

Henderson sees my glance and says, 'That's them. You won't get them.'

'They left you?'

'No. I stationed myself here. To ward off pursuit. Security: it's what I do.'

Not quite well enough, in this instance, but I don't press the point. Up on this ridge, he'd have detected pursuit from any direction, except the one I came in.

Henderson has never quite been explicit, but I'm certain that he's the head of security, the boss of Allan and Geoff and those other guys. And if that's right, then the two men I see hurrying away are the ones that matter. Mr Big and some close associate. The ones we've been so anxious to catch. Henderson, I know, wouldn't have entrusted their safety to any lesser hands.

I think, *Henderson has sort of lost, but sort of won.* He's lost, because here he is at the point of a gun, his chance of Caribbean freedom dwindled down to two shakes of nothing at all. But he's won, because his job was to save Mr Big and that's just what he's succeeded in doing.

I think these thoughts, but keep glancing behind me, unsure if Henderson is truly alone.

He says, 'It's just me. There were only the three of us.' He gestures down to the valley, to the four-by-four he left behind.

I believe him, but stay watchful.

There's a pause for a moment. Not silent. Just wind in the moorgrass, a low and turbulent moan.

Henderson: 'You're police.'

It's not a question, except that it is, a bit.

'No, Vic. Not now. Never was.'

'You rescued the copper.'

'Really, Vic? Really?'

I'm not sure whether to grace him with an answer, but I do. Angrily.

'You get me involved in all this.' I wave my hand, down the valley. There's no fire down at the farmhouse any more, but a thread of smoke still winds up from the fields and trees far below us. 'You invite me to come with you on your boat and, by the way, I was really tempted, I really wanted to come, but I was being good, trying to get my life together, so I said no, but kind of hoping you would come out to New Zealand, kind of hoping we could finally get it together, properly, away from all the bollocks. But instead, you boys arrange for me to come to your leaving party. A party I don't think I would ever have left alive. What the *fuck* would you do if you were me?'

'How do you know about the leaving party?'

He asks the question, but it's hardly relevant, and I don't answer it. He continues anyway.

'OK, so you find out somehow. And you think, you need to switch sides. Give the cops something in exchange for immunity.'

'Yes.'

'How did you even know we had a guy in the basement?'

'I didn't. I just entered the farmhouse to see if there was anything – data, proof, I don't know – just something I could take to the police. I heard a guy moaning. I went downstairs.'

I'm not quite sure why I'm still pushing the Fiona Grey story. I mean: what I'm doing is perfectly in line with undercover procedure. Wherever possible, our legends are maintained into eternity. For my protection, for tactical interrogation reasons, for possible reuse on another case. But it's not procedure that's driving things right now. It's Fiona herself, the other Fiona, Fiona Grey. It's her angry and alone on this mountaintop, confronting the man she once sort-of loved and yet sort-of hated.

I leave the two of them to get on with it. A guy and a girl, sorting through their issues. But it's me, Fiona Griffiths, with her hand on a gun and her finger on the trigger.

Henderson: 'He told you he was a cop?'

'Yes. I told him I wanted immunity. He said he couldn't promise it, but told me to fuck things up as much as I could. So here I am. Fucking things up.'

'Fairly effectively too.'

He smiles.

I smile.

Two Japanese combatants, bowing over tatami mats and little brass bowls.

'You could let me go,' says Henderson. 'I'd pay.'

'Yeah, you could pay. Or possibly kill me.'

Henderson nods. Not saying, Yes, he'd kill me, just acknowledging the validity of my concern.

'And,' I add, 'I still need to give the police something. So far, I've just spoken to one man who claimed to be a copper and who might or might not be alive to confirm my story.'

'Yes.' Henderson nods, agreeing with the logic. 'Thing is, though, I don't want to go to jail. Not even to help you out.' He pauses. There's tactics here, but also emotion, blowing through this thin mountain air. 'For what it's worth, I didn't want you to come to that leaving party. Yes, I wanted you to come to the Caribbean, but . . . If I'd had my way, Fiona, we'd have left you free to go to New Zealand. I wanted you to.' His mouth wrinkles. 'Unfortunately, we had a house rule. About emotional entanglements. I made the rule. And when it came to the point, I lost the argument. I'm sorry.'

I shrug. A *de-nada*-ish sort of shrug.

Silence falls. There's a long conversation we could have, but now isn't necessarily the best time for it. Perhaps the best time lies far back in the past. And in any case, Henderson has other things on his mind.

'What's your plan?' he asks. 'You're going to take me down into Brecon?'

It's a good play. A sensible one. But I'm not buying it. I'm barefoot. Wounded. Tired. A creature of mud and stone and water.

Perhaps I could get Henderson down to Brecon at the point of a gun. But perhaps not. One stumble, one misplaced step, and I'd soon find out whether I was escorting Nice Vic or Nasty Mr Henderson. And I'm pretty sure that neither of them has romance on his mind right now.

'Sorry,' I say.

I jab my shotgun towards his lower legs. A couple of shotgun blasts down there and he won't be leaving this hill, except by stretcher.

'Yes, fair enough.' His tone is casual, as though confirming a dinner date. 'Just . . . just, I can't go to jail. I always promised myself.'

He darts a half glance behind him. The arrival of dawn is touching the sky with a swelling grey light, but the light hasn't properly reached the valley below, which is a brimming well of darkness. A bird of prey swings out from the gloom beneath us, hits the air streaming over the ridge, and the uplift sends it shooting above us, out of sight.

Henderson swallows. He chucks his cigarette away, gropes for another, but I have the packet and the lighter. It's as close as I've seen him come to a show of fear.

A show that doesn't last for long. Something else is there now, I don't know what.

His face wrinkles again.

'We still on for that dirty weekend?'

'You bet. Just as long as you promise to do a little less murdering. I never quite got to grips with that side of you, Vic. You were very sweet in other ways.'

'You think you'll really do it? The speech therapy, I mean?'

'That's the plan.'

'Pity. You have some wonderful criminal talents.'

I smile. Fiona Grey does, or I do, or we both do, I don't know. One of us says, 'Thanks for the books, Vic. I will remember you.'

'Enjoy New Zealand. I'm sure you will. They're good people, the Kiwis.'

I'd say something to that. Express my respect for New Zealanders in general, their country, outlook and landscapes. I'd discourse on speech therapy. My hopes and plans for a new life.

I'd say something to continue this conversation, because I don't want to watch what happens next.

And what happens is this. Henderson touches his fingers to his lips. Nods once. And leaps backwards. Arcing backwards, a backwards flip, an attempt to bring his head down and his feet up.

I hear one sound only. Not a scream. Just the collision of something hard against something rocky. The night vision glasses, perhaps. His skull? I don't know. What impresses more is the silence. The way a human can vanish into it so completely, leaving not a trace behind.

I stay with the silence for a while. The silence and the wind.

He *was* sweet, Vic. A multiple murderer who bought me books on speech therapy and once searched my bathroom for corpses that he knew could not be there. Searched for them, because I asked him to.

And that leap, that final, silent leap. I think that was the bravest thing I've ever seen. That movement of his fingers to his lips – regretful, tender, so much unsaid – and that leap backwards into night.

I want never to see something like that again.

There's enough light now for the search-and-rescue boys to get active and, sure enough, down the valley, a couple of choppers start to circle the land over the farmhouse.

Better late than never, boys, better late than never.

I don't need to do anything now. Just wait. Someone else can think about how to get me off this mountain. Someone else can figure out what to do with my feet, my ankle, my identities, with whatever's left of Vic Henderson, with all the rest of this the whole damn complicated shemozzle.

I stick my shotgun, barrel down, into the ground. Tie Henderson's scarf to it. An improvised flag. And lie down. Fiona, Jessica and I, on the cold ground together. A red acrylic jumper and the skinniest of skinny jeans.

We're too tired to bicker now. And in any case, our little sisterhood has done well tonight.

The ground smells of wet clay and moorgrass. We can hear the thin sigh of wind moving in the bilberries. Sheep champing. And somewhere, a movement of water over rock.

55

Homecomings. Real life in all its sweet complexity.

The easiest bit is my family. Dad's uproarious desire for reunion. My mother's fussing delight. My sisters' unfeigned pleasure at seeing me again. It's all that I could have wanted, and more. I've missed them.

My sister Ant, who has always for some reason wanted to be blonde, loves my new look and my mother, I think, is secretly curious. But my sister, Kay, who I always trust on these things, tells me it's no good at all and, with my encouragement, does stuff with hair dye and scissors that turns me back, more or less, into the person I was. She takes three of Jessica's tops and two of her skirts by way of payment.

It is a relief to be able to look into a mirror and not see that blonde self peering out at me. I never got on with Jessica, the poor, temporary creature. I'm pleased she's gone.

The next easiest bit is work. I don't go back into Cathays straight away. Partly Jackson and Brattenbury both want me to spend a couple of days reacquainting myself with my nearest and dearest. But also, I end up spending a night in hospital. My injuries aren't particularly profound. I was taken off the mountain by helicopter and brought straight back to Cardiff. The shot which hit my leg was fired blind and I was hit only by a perimeter scatter. The skin around my ankle looks angry and red, with pimples rising where the pellets entered. Of more concern to the doctors was the damage done to my feet, which were raw and cut all over, with half a hillside worth of mud and sheepmuck trodden into every wound.

They cleaned my feet, using a few stitches where the cuts were notably bad. As for my calf and ankle, they simply extracted as many pellets as they could and left the rest. Hooked me up to an IV antibiotic for twenty-four hours, more as a precaution than anything else. They tell me that the flesh will simply close over the pellets that remain, forming little fibroids under the skin. I'm given a letter confirming the existence of metal shot in my body: I may need it, in case I bleep in airport metal detectors.

I like that thought. Like the idea that I'll carry this encounter on the mountain with me wherever I go. Some women, I know, have favourite bits of jewellery that they can't bear to be without. I'm not like that. I do have some bits and pieces – necklaces mostly, some earrings and a silver bracelet – that do me good service. But they don't feel essential. They're not core me.

These gunshot spheres – about a dozen, the doctor guessed – feel right. Precious and personal. I even like it that they're hidden. Spoils of war. The doctor said, 'You may not feel them at all, but experiences vary. You could get a bit of soreness in some weathers, or feel some coldness.' My leg is bandaged now, so I can't see it, but I'm looking forward to the removal of the dressings. I hope there'll be something to see. Small white freckles and lumps beneath the skin.

And for all that I want to get into the office, catch up with the investigation, I enjoy the hospital. Its cluttered quiet. This fresh, medicinal linen and the chatter of nurses.

One of them, a student nurse, sits on my bed for forty minutes and tells me about her degree course. I ask to check my chart and she passes it to me, putting a blood pressure cuff on me as she does so. But it's not my blood pressure I care about, but my name. FIONA GRIFFITHS. Block capitals and computer printed.

The nurse says, when she sees my gaze refusing to detach from the chart, 'It looks all OK. It's all fine.'

I nod and hand back the chart. She's right.

After a long sleep, at the hospital and a second one, the following night, at home, I'm ready for work again, or sort of. Buzz comes to get me. He says, am I strong enough to go into work. 'Jackson wants you for a debriefing if you're up to it.'

I say I'm fine. It'll be weird going into the office again after so long, but nice-weird, not bad. We drive there in Buzz's car and, for once, I'm allowed to put my hand on his leg and keep it there, even when he's changing gear. I'm on oral antibiotics and aspirin, and I've been given special orthopaedic boots and crutches, which I don't really need. My feet are sore, but not atrocious.

At Cathays, I hobble into a lift and up to Jackson's floor. Go to his office.

He's there with Brattenbury. He and I sit side by side on the squeaky fake leather sofa. Jackson leans back on a matching chair. The shadow line of dust under Jackson's sofa is still there. Mr Conway, the strictest of my various bosses, would have reprimanded me for that.

I pluck my jacket into some sort of shape. Try to look professional. Try not to notice the brown leaves curling on the carpet.

Jackson sends someone to get hot drinks and brings me up to speed with the case itself. Some of it I already know, but it's nice to have the whole thing from the top.

'Roy's fine. Legs smashed to buggery. They need to be reset. A whole lot of surgery. Don't even ask, but . . . compared with what might have been, he's fine.'

Jackson's face moves. I already know that a man was sent

419

down to the cellar to kill Roy. Part of the clean-up. Roy shot the man with a triple blast from his shotgun, killing him outright from close range. I don't know if he shouted 'Police!' first.

Jackson tosses me a photo of the dead man. It's not a face I recognise, but there were no innocents in that farmhouse.

I say this to Jackson, or something like it, but he shrugs. 'There'll be an IPCC investigation, of course, but they're very sympathetic. We won't have any problems with them.'

The IPCC is the Independent Police Complaints Commission, and they're obliged to mount a full inquiry whenever a police officer discharges a weapon. That inquiry will certainly include me in its scope. I think, though, strangely enough, I didn't operate outside the law at any stage. It'll be odd to be the subject of an inquiry and not have to lie. I'm getting old.

Then I remember that I have sixty thousand pounds of Tinker's money in an offshore account so secure that only I can access it and which is untraceable by any British law enforcement agency. Money which I have no intention of declaring. I also remember that, after spending a day learning computer hacking at the hands of a master, I emailed myself a copy of the Trojan horse software in question. It occurs to me that while the IPCC would be quite interested in these things, I am most unlikely to tell them.

I feel faintly relieved, like finding that my lost youth isn't actually lost at all.

'What about Tinker?' I ask. I want to know if they ever pressed Terry's Fuck It button.

Not unexpectedly, the answer is yes.

Brattenbury says, 'The fake software went live from about the time you started blowing things up. We got alerts out to everyone we could. Sent officers to the IT departments of every corporate which we knew to be compromised. Notified banks. Notified the software supplier. HMRC. Got some accounts frozen.'

'And?' I ask.

'They took thirty-four million pounds. From twelve different corporates, ones we didn't even know were in danger. Even there, I have to say, the firms concerned were not . . . they were not as security-aware as you'd think they would be. None of the firms in question will be endangered by the loss. It's a maximum of a week's payroll in most cases. They can think of it as a small reminder to tighten up their act.'

'Thirty-four *million*?'

Jackson doesn't let Brattenbury answer. He says, 'We were expecting a further three weeks before that button was pressed. Given the circumstances, and the fact that liberating Roy, and you, and securing the farmhouse were our top operational priorities, I think it's remarkable how well we did. Tribute to Adrian's professionalism. His and that of his colleagues.'

I don't doubt Brattenbury's professionalism. Never have done. But *thirty-four million quid*?

'Who have we got?' I ask in a low voice. 'That first farm buggy, did we get any of those?'

'Three. Allan Wiley. The man you call Geoff. One other.'

He throws some photos on the table. Sure enough: Allan, Geoff, one other I don't recognise. Brattenbury tells me that his men heard the shooting up on the hill, where the fields met mountain, and responded instantly. They saw the damaged buggy, saw that any fugitives would now be escaping on foot and poured search teams into the area to pick them up. It took until two hours after dawn to get the three men – all scattered, all located in different spots. At one point, there were a hundred and fifty police officers engaged in the hunt.

'This man,' I say, indicating the photo of the man I've not seen before. 'Is he . . .?'

'No. He's a thug, basically. A hired hand. Michael Edwards. Did a tour in the army. Conviction for affray. Involved with a unlicensed boxing gym in Llanrumney. He doesn't seem any too bright. Plus he wants a legal aid lawyer, because he claims not to have the cash for one of his own.'

So Mr Big *has* got away. I think of that black figure hurrying away from me and Vic, on that distant ridge. Him and whoever else was with him. Anna Quintrell's 'rich guy' with 'legitimate money' is thirty-four million pounds up and laughing.

'Henderson?' I ask in a low voice.

'Alive. But in a very bad way. Broken neck, broken back. Bad head injuries. Last I heard, he might survive.' He shakes his hand in a toss-up sort of way. '*Might.*'

I don't know what I feel about that.

Part of me wants the full police experience. I want to be there behind the one-way mirror as I watch the interrogation. Watch as they play the audio of his and my little session in that hotel bedroom. Watch his face change, as he realises how complete, how inescapable, is the case against him.

But not all of me. Fiona Grey, I think, wants him to complete his act of escape. Wants that leap into night to be rewarded by death. A dark almost-love-affair finding its dark almost-resolution.

Me too, I think. I usually want my criminals to encounter their justice at the hands of a court, behind the bars of a jail. But Vic, I think, might be an exception. Faced with the choice of death or jail, he chose the former and I'm not too sure I'd want to challenge or alter his decision.

'Four?' I ask. 'We got four?'

'Five, if you count the man that Roy shot,' says Jackson. 'Plus five dead in the barn. Plus the whole of the Indian IT team. The Metropolitan Police arrested the lot of them at Heathrow. They were flying to Dubai. We're charging them not just with fraud but with conspiracy to murder. We're telling them to expect life in prison. I'm told they're absolutely terrified. Giving us very full cooperation.'

His face moves. One of those Jacksonian faces I can't interpret. Boulders in an empty river bed. Grey stones beneath a grey cliff.

'And look, at some stage, you're going to get a lecture from me about making appropriate judgements of risk in fast-moving situations. There's absolutely no way you should have pursued those vehicles on your own. You had absolutely no right to place yourself at risk in the way that you did. But if you hadn't broken up that escape route, the men involved would have got away. All of them, not just some. I'm still going to give you that lecture, but not right now. Speaking not as a police officer now, but just man to man, you did a bloody good job.'

I stare at him.

He says, 'Man to woman, then.'

'Women. Fiona was there, Fiona Grey. And Jessica.'

Jackson doesn't share my passion for exactitude, and in any case Brattenbury is saying something now. 'And remember, we're still working. We've got a lot of leads.'

'Ownership of the farmhouse?'

'A Jersey registered company. Beneficial owners in Bermuda.'

'Forensics? DNA?'

'Well, between you and Henderson, we weren't left with quite as much as we'd have liked, but the farmhouse was only partially damaged. We've got a lot of traces, including a laundry room which our forensic boys are absolutely loving. We're working through it all now.'

'Vehicle movements to and from the farmhouse? Where's the nearest camera?'

My two bosses exchange a look, but indulge me for a change.

Brattenbury says, 'The nearest camera is two miles away on the far side of the village. If they chose a route to avoid the location, they could easily drive fifteen, twenty miles without passing anything.'

That's not helpful, obviously, but ANPR doesn't just rely on fixed roadside cameras. Filling stations and police cars are also linked in to the system. And although you *can* get from Cardiff to the Brecon Beacons without using the A470, you'll waste a lot of time doing anything else. A rich man, in a hurry, believing himself to be beyond police scrutiny – might he not use the A470 before starting to wiggle around on back roads? Not in the past year perhaps, but before then, well before, when the whole of Tinker was just a gleam in the eye? And indeed, I don't think the barn was constructed just to service Tinker. I think other criminal enterprises have been conceived there too. Legitimate ones as well, maybe.

It'll be a massive exercise. Massive beyond massive. Tracking every car on the A470. Homing in on those owners who boast a few million in assets, quite likely a lot more. Trying to determine how many of those have legitimate business up in Brecon or deeper into Powys. Cross-tabulating that data against users of the business centre neighbouring Henderson's osteopathy place.

As I'm thinking this through, I mutter, 'That health centre. Henderson was meeting a guy called Davison.'

Brattenbury and Jackson both look at me sharply.

I add, 'He's some kind of fixer. Does dirty jobs for cash. He's been Henderson's go-between. Henderson meets Davison. Davison liaises with Mr Big.'

There's a pause and a micro-nod from Brattenbury, indicating that he'll leave this one to Jackson.

Jackson says, 'Fiona, the source for this is . . .?'

'Henderson.'

'He *told* you this?'

424

'No, of course not.' I make something up. An overheard phone message. A strange reaction from Henderson. Blah, blah.

Normally I try to make my lies convincing – or I do when I'm speaking to my superiors. It's a mark of respect, the least I can do. On this occasion, though, my heart's not quite in it and I peter out before I should.

I try to scratch my foot, which is itchy, but the boot prevents much scratching action.

'We'll mark that down as unconfirmed intelligence, shall we?' says Jackson.

'You can call it conspiracy hearsay bollocks if you like, sir. But I believe it.'

Jackson once told me that if I ever found myself believing a piece of 'conspiracy hearsay bollocks' then I was to tell him so, and he would treat it as true, no matter how dubious the source. It was part of a pact between him and me, a pact whose purpose was to stop me ending up in places where bad guys were trying to shoot me. Obviously the arrangement hasn't worked out too cleverly, but a promise is still a promise.

'OK. Then so do we.' He nods at Brattenbury to tell him that he's included in the deal too. Brattenbury is perplexed, but accepting.

There's a pause.

Grey light enters through a grey window. I have a strange feeling. I think, *This is my life. My ordinary life. No one is trying to kill me. This is the ordinary life I always wanted.*

The thought doesn't make me feel good, particularly. More accurately, I suppose, I just don't know what I feel beyond a certain giddiness. It's as though, in some ways, I've learned to live on Planet Normal. Breathe its atmosphere, cope with its gravity. But that doesn't mean I'm at home here. Perhaps this soil will always be alien, and its people strangers.

Brattenbury starts to say how pleased he is. Not just with

425

my safe return: all that has already been said. He starts to say how well the operation has gone down in London. 'We have disrupted the largest theft ever to have been attempted in the UK. Most of its perpetrators are dead or in custody. Those in custody can expect very significant sentences, life in most cases. As you know, because you've been working undercover, we're prohibited from making any public recognition of your work, but I want to you know that our DG, the Director General, has told me that he's written to the Home Secretary herself to express—'

He means well, I recognise that, but Adrian doesn't know me the way Jackson does.

I interrupt. In my opinion, an operation which allows its primary perpetrator to escape uncaught – his identity not even guessed at – is a near-total failure. An operation which enriches the primary villain by thirty-four million quid is nothing short of a catastrophe. I state these things in an English which is pithy, expressive, and makes generous use of terms drawn from the Anglo-Saxon and Old High Dutch. I use the mature and respectful tone I usually adopt when expressing disagreement with a superior officer.

Brattenbury sits back, so Jackson can yell at me better. But he doesn't yell. Just shakes me into silence with his empty coffee mug.

'Fiona, shut up. Just for a change, shut up. Yes, this is a partial success, not a full one. But the case isn't closed and we're not going to close it until we have the main man. If you want to remain associated with the operation, that's fine with me and I'm sure . . .?'

'Of course,' Brattenbury says. 'Same here, of course.'

'Thank you,' I say sulkily.

Then I have one of those clear windscreen moments and add, 'Sorry. I'm sorry.'

Brattenbury says, 'The fact is that, and I'm speaking for

426

SOCA here, we are very good at disrupting major criminal activity. We are good at securing convictions for the lower-level criminals. But we often just don't have the tools to arrest the top-level operators. If the money goes offshore, we can't follow it. If we don't get a confession or some unusual breakthrough, it's relatively rare for us to get the guys at the very top. But we go on trying. And we know that the better we are at disrupting crime, the more we raise the costs of criminal activity.' He smiles ruefully. 'SOCA top brass: they regard this case as the biggest success they've had in years.'

I glower. Not at them – I have no complaints with their handling of the operation, none whatever – but at a world where enriching some rich fuckwit by thirty-four million stolen pounds is regarded as a success.

I say, 'Arresting Henderson, killing and arresting all those other people – you realise that's only increased Mr Big's profit? If Henderson and the others had been around, the money would have had to be shared out somehow. I don't know how, but it would have been parcelled out. As it is, our bad guy has no one to share it with. He's made thirty-four million pounds, in a single night's work. How is that raising the cost of criminal activity?'

My question doesn't have an answer. It's not that Jackson and Brattenbury don't share the same objectives as me. More that, with time, they've grown accustomed to outcomes that fall short of what they once wanted. It's not a skill I've yet learned. Not one I want to learn.

Brattenbury says, 'You're OK, are you? Your feet and everything, I mean.'

'Yes.'

He pauses a moment. I notice for the first time a graveness in his face. A remorse.

He looks at his coffee cup, finds it empty and puts it down. He swivels to face me.

'Look, Fiona, I need to say sorry. I promised I wouldn't lose you. I promised to get SCO19 to the farmhouse and I failed. I allowed you to enter a situation which was unacceptably dangerous and I apologise. I've asked the IPCC to include that failure in their investigation and they'll have their process. But quite separately from that, from me to you, I'm sorry. I shouldn't have let that happen. Or allowed you to enter a situation where it could have happened.'

I say the right things, or think I do. But the truth is, I think I knew SOCA would lose me. I think I knew Henderson's subtlety would defeat Brattenbury's. For all SOCA's efficiently deployed resources, it is easier to shake surveillance than to maintain it. I think that, when I stepped into Henderson's car, the day he came to pick me up from Birmingham, I knew I would be entering the farmhouse alone. Trusted my own wits to do whatever needed to be done. I don't say that exactly, but I don't want Brattenbury to feel bad.

Jackson looks at his watch. Brattenbury too. Says he has to catch a train to London. Has a cab waiting downstairs. Jackson and I walk him to the lift. Or Jackson walks him, and I hobble him. I use my crutches, but only just need them.

'You'll come and see us in London sometime? Let Susan and I take you out to lunch?'

I nod. Make a promise.

The lifts open and close.

One phase of my life finishes. Another, presumably, starts.

Jackson says, 'They'll offer you a job. You know that?'

I look at him. Probably do something with my face that implies a question.

'They'll give you lunch somewhere nice. Little tour of SOCA HQ. Get you to meet the DG. Flatter you a bit. Tell you how important their work is, how *sexy* it is. They may not even offer you a job directly, just encourage you to ask for it.

That way, the theory is, I don't get pissed off when they nick my best officers.'

This is news to me. I hadn't even thought about working for SOCA.

'They'll have bigger cases to offer you. More resources. More opportunity.'

'Oh.' I can't imagine leaving Cardiff, and say so. 'I think I like it here, sir.'

'Good.'

He starts steering me towards the stairs, then remembers my crutches and goes back to the lifts. Punches the down button.

'Sir, when I'm like that.' I point back at his office and my stream of Old High Dutch. 'I'm sorry. I can't always help it. And sometimes I can help it, but I do it anyway.' I'm about to end that little speech with another 'sorry', but I seem to be all out of apology juice, so I just shrug instead. Jackson looked at me as I was speaking, but his face doesn't do or say much afterwards.

When the lift arrives, he hits the button for the basement. The canteen.

'Fiona, I've been talking with some of my colleagues. Senior ones, including the Chief Constable and including Rhiannon Watkins.'

I nod. That sort of intro normally spells trouble, but I don't think it can on this occasion.

The giddy feeling I had before is stronger now. I have to lean against the wall of the lift to keep my balance.

'And we agree, all of us, that it's ridiculous you still being a detective constable. An officer of your abilities needs to climb the ladder. I know Rhiannon has already spoken to you about this. We want you to take the exams for detective sergeant.'

I start to object, but Jackson says, 'Fiona, I'm trying to do things nicely, but I'm not really asking a question. I am telling

429

you what you *are* going to do. We call it giving an order.'

'Oh.'

'You remember those?'

'Yes. I mean, yes, sir'.

We're at the canteen now. Double doors, opening in. There's a noise from inside. The rolling buzz of conversation. A conversation that self-silences as we enter.

The room – the biggest in the building – is a jam of people. The whole of CID. A spatter of uniforms.

I shrink back. My giddiness is now out of control. I'm a marionette without the strings. Just for a moment I don't know who or where I am.

Somehow, though, my feet know to follow Jackson. If I'm clumsy, my crutches excuse me.

I feel very strange.

There's a podium of some sort. Roy Williams on it in some weird form of wheelchair that allows his legs to lie flat in front of him. Katie is there in the front row, next to the chief constable.

Jackson says something. A speech. I can't hear much of it. Or rather: I hear it all, but don't make much sense of it. I see Buzz sitting next to Katie. His face seems like the most familiar thing in the world and the strangest, both at once.

Jackson's oration concludes.

'We did everything we could. Every resource, every database, every lead, every officer, every bit of fancy technology at our disposal. And we failed. We did our best to get Roy back and we failed. But our police service has never just been about technology and fancy databases. It's about guts and brains and sheer damn determination. And I'm telling you that Roy here owes his safety and well-being entirely to the actions, courage and resourcefulness of this young officer. And if—'

He doesn't finish.

The room stands. There's a roar of applause, of clapping. A

wall of sound: that phrase which doesn't quite mean anything until you encounter something like this. A physical sensation, of being pushed back almost. Something dense pressing to occupy a once empty space.

Roy is a popular officer and there's a way that this is Roy's show more than mine, his harvest of approval. But it's my show too. Jackson pumps my hand. Roy Williams gets his arms round my waist – the only place he can reach from his wheelchair – and hugs me in a way that still somehow manages to lift me off the ground. Katie – dewier, tearier and prettier than ever – joins in too. Buzz hugs me and says something in my ear that I can't really hear because of the noise, but it was a nice thing, whatever, and I make nice in return.

I do what I think I'm meant to do, but I find it hard. The noise of the applause – the din, that sense of mental concussion – is like the shooting up on the hill, only I was more comfortable there. More at ease. Since I can't reasonably start shooting anyone now, I just shrink into myself and wait for it all to stop.

For a moment, I don't know where to look or what to do. I talk to Katie, because it means I don't have to face my colleagues. Then the chief constable sorts out my social awkwardness by making a short speech that manages to deflate the mood and send everyone into a coma of talked-at, semi-official boredom.

Then some catering folk start serving beer and wine and nibbles and I hide out in a corner with Katie and my friend Bev and try to avoid people coming up to me. The strategy doesn't work tremendously well, but in the end it's Jackson who rescues me. He's with Buzz. Jackson has a full bottle of beer in his hand, and it's not his first. Buzz has a glass of wine, and it's not his first.

'I think you two little lovebirds ought to bugger off now,' says Jackson.

I say, 'Is that you doing it again? Saying something nicely, but really—'

'Yes. Bugger off. That's an order.'

I polish up one of my gay-man-waving salutes and hand it over. 'Yes, sir.'

Buzz salutes the military way, crisp and correct.

We leave.

As the canteen doors swing shut behind us, and we walk down the corridor, I ask Buzz if we can stop a moment.

We do, and there is a look of enquiry on his face, but all I want is to listen to the sound of the room behind us. The rolling sound of conversation, drink and laughter.

I realise this is the sound of happiness. Of a collection of human beings who, more than not, like and respect each other. Who like their work in life. Who form a community, a mutually supportive community, that shares its troubles and its triumphs. That welcomes back its own.

I realise too that, for all my odd awkwardness, I am an accepted member of that community, today more than ever. I feel moved, more than when I was shrinking from attention up on the dais earlier.

Buzz is looking at my face. Gesturing at the lifts.

'OK to go on?'

I nod. I surely am.

56

Homecomings and sadness. The sweet and the sour.

That evening, I go back home with Buzz. We go to bed together, eat together, renew our acquaintance, like a couple of blind people each tracing hands over the other's once-familiar face.

I had intended to do this tomorrow, but when Buzz starts talking about dates for the wedding, I have to tell him. Have to say the truth.

'Dearest Buzz, I have something to tell you. Something difficult. And I'm so sorry. I always wanted to be the best girlfriend in the world for you, because you deserve nothing less. But I'm not that person. I'm not . . .'

I don't quite know how to say the things I need to tell him. Buzz is so intact, so sure of himself, of who he is, what he wants, the things he likes, that it's hard communicating with him sometimes. I'm his opposite in too many ways.

I say, 'I'm a mess, Buzz. More of a mess than you understand. I'm not very good at knowing anything about myself. I'm not very good at being a human being, it just isn't one of my strengths.'

I say more than that too.

I tell him that being Buzz's girlfriend and then fiancée have been just about the best things in my life. My highest accomplishment.

I tell him that I love him and respect him and have depended utterly on his love and straightness.

Tell him that I wouldn't be as much of a human as I am had it not been for him. It was Buzz, more than anyone else, that first helped me tread the soil of Planet Normal.

But there are things I don't tell him. Don't, because I can't, because he wouldn't understand if I did.

I don't tell him that Fiona Grey was mostly happier than I am. That her milieu of homeless shelters and divorced bus drivers and single-parent Somali immigrants and richly bangled mental-health workers was easier for her to navigate than the one I live in. That Buzz's remarkable strength, patience and simplicity are almost problematic for me. He's too good for the person I am.

I say, 'I think I need to find myself more before I can commit to anyone. Even to you, my best and dearest Buzz. And I'm so sorry, because I owe you so much more than this. I will always love you and always want your happiness. But I'm not the woman who will make you happy. I can't marry you. I'm incredibly sorry.'

It's not as simple as that, of course. Buzz cries. I don't because, apart from one time, I've never cried in my adult life. But I feel the emotion. Keep telling Buzz he's the best of men, and yes I'm sure, and yes, this feels like the ultimate, 'it's not you, it's me'.

As we talk all this out, Buzz understands what I'm saying, or almost. Understands it in a Buzzian way, which is all I can hope for. He's not happy. Not reconciled. He looks broken-hearted, in truth, and the worst thing about all this is that I'm the one doing the breaking. But I don't have any doubts, not even now.

I had wanted to spend the night with Buzz, this night of reunion. Spend one last night with Buzz and tell him tomorrow of my decision. But it doesn't work like that and we both realise it's impossible for me to stay under his roof tonight. To share a bed together.

So I leave. I don't have my car with me – it's at home – so Buzz calls a taxi for me instead. We wait, cuddling, till we get a call telling us it's arrived.

I say, 'Buzz, promise me you'll seek your own happiness. Don't let this be more than a road-bump. You deserve the best.'

He nods, but that isn't good enough.

'Buzz, I need you to *promise*. Get over me. Find someone else. Not straight away, but do it. Please. Promise me.'

He nods and this time it counts. We kiss each other lightly on the lips. My giddiness is so great now, I have problems with ordinary movements.

'You're OK, are you?' says Buzz. 'Sometimes those painkillers . . .'

'I'm on aspirin, nothing else. And my feet are fine. It's my head. It's – not well. But it's my problem. I should never have tried to make it yours.'

He walks me downstairs, an awful sadness in his step.

'I'm so sorry,' I whisper. 'I'm so, so sorry.'

I give the taxi driver my home address. He drives up into the town centre then out on the Newport Road towards Eastern Avenue and Pentwyn.

My house, my life.

A world without Buzz.

I've got too many things in my head and I don't know how to sort them out.

When we're no more than a minute from home, I ask the driver to turn around. Ask him to head back in towards Cathays, to the office. The driver does as I ask. It's been a good fare from his perspective.

I pay him and he goes.

Roll myself a cigarette and smoke it, a dark shape against the pale glass.

Then go inside and sign in. The desk officer doesn't know who I am, doesn't care. It's not so usual for detectives to work through the night, but it's not so unusual either. I left my crutches with Buzz. They'd been annoying me, a hindrance more than a help.

I take the lift up to Jackson's floor.

Go to the cleaning cupboard opposite the lift. It's not locked. There's a trolley there, a good one. Different cleaning products from the ones I'm used to, but good enough. A vacuum cleaner. I drag everything out. Look for a tabard. I like those, when they fit. But there's nothing there, so I do without. Hoover the carpets first. Long sweeps of grey, changing colour slightly as I work. Do Jackson's room with care. Move the sofa and hoover underneath. The skirting board hasn't been touched for ages, so I sponge-wash it, scrubbing till I bring out the white. Dust the window sill. Squeegee the window. Do a careful job on the pot plant, picking off all the bits that are brown or heading that way. His keyboard is disgusting really. Needs a proper clean with the right sort of fluid, but I don't find any in my trolley, so Jackson will just have to suffer.

I normally do a room like this in eight minutes, but because of the sofa and the skirting board, and because I took extra care with the other bits, and because my hobbled gait and painful feet make everything slower, it takes me sixteen. I do two other offices, and one set of bathrooms, the women's ones. The longer I work, the more I relax. I would do more, but my feet won't let me.

It's only when I'm just about done on the bathroom that I dare to look at myself in the mirror. Look properly, I mean.

Jessica's gone. It's only me and my sister Fiona here now. We're relieved to be left alone.

I can't quite tell what I see in our face, but it's OK, I think. It's scary letting go of Buzz. I know it's the right thing to do, but it's still a very big deal for me. Trusting that I'll be OK on my own.

Anchored enough. Sane enough.

I give the sinks a final wipe. I like the shine of ceramics under halogen.

Put the cleaning stuff away. Call a taxi.

I've cleaned three offices this evening. One of those belongs to a superintendent, the recently promoted Gethin Matthews.

Before I go downstairs, I re-enter Matthews's office. Turn on his computer. I can't log in as him without stealing his password, and since I can't be bothered to wait that long, I just log on using the default login details, the one any copper can use to access the basic databases. Then I go to my fake Hotmail account. Download the Trojan horse software that poor, dead Ian Shoesmith gave me. Load it onto Matthews's computer. Close down. I feel a little ripple of Jessica-ishness rise in me as I do all that. I didn't get on with her, but I liked her coolness. Her brassy don't-give-a-damn quality. Enough to forgive her the odd push-up bra and questionable top.

Gareth Glyn went missing in 2002. There are, broadly speaking, three possible explanations for that. One, he just got tired of his wife and wanted to make a clean break. You don't usually do that by simply vanishing, but still: stranger things have happened.

Two, he was indeed murdered, as his wife alleges, albeit for a crime of whistle-blowing which he committed some fifteen years earlier. Again, not obviously likely, but you can't rule it out.

Or three, that request for information from the security services could have related to something, some current inquiry, which was threatening to resurrect the ghosts of the past. Ghosts that might have called for Glyn to have entered a witness protection service.

There isn't, as of 2012, a single systematic witness protection service covering the whole of Britain, but there have always been local programmes, administered by each regional police force. As superintendent, Gethin Matthews will have access to all that information. He'll be able to request further data without arousing suspicion. And now, thanks to the software I've planted, *I'll* be able to send that request on his behalf. I'll be able to monitor the reply, delete it once I've read it, and will be able to do all that remotely, from my own computer. From home, or anywhere else.

If it comes to that, I'll be able to access any information that a superintendent can command. Which is a lot.

It's a nice feeling.

I won't rush into anything. I need to get my own head straightened out before I plunge into all that again. But that sense of gathering excitement which came to me that day in Hayley Morgan's cottage is here again with me now. Here, amongst these neatly hoovered floors, these tidily dusted surfaces.

Fiona Grey came to be a pretty damn good cleaner, I reflect, but her partner, Miss Griffiths, is a pretty useful investigator. Somewhere down that Gareth Glynian road lies a clue which will take me closer to my biggest and most urgent mystery. The mystery of me.

A different taxi takes me home.

Magnolia paint. Stainless steel kitchen. A garden that is a blank strip of nothing. A living room without decoration.

My house. My home. Even Fiona Grey had more care for her interiors than this.

I walk around my living room and kitchen. Feeling things. Opening doors and closing them. Feeling the presence of what used to be my life. A castaway on the shores of normal.

I don't feel sleepy, though it's now very late. But I act as though I am. Brush my teeth. Take off my clothes. Look at the dressings still oozing blood on my feet. Put on a nightie, a scoop-necked thing with a blue bow and a pattern of tiny blue flowers. Like bilberry flowers, I think. Tiny bells.

I'm intensely aware of the lack of surveillance. No video, no audio. I walk past power sockets in my underwear weirded out by the realisation that no one is watching.

And I realise that Fiona Grey is not dead. An undercover identity is never ended. It survives the operation, ready to be used again. I don't need her now and she doesn't need me, but if life gets challenging for me, Fiona Griffiths, I can always walk into the hostel again. Play table football with Clementina, stand outside and smoke ciggies with Gary.

I think too of the wedding dress I almost bought. Glossy stripes and a nipped-in waist. I wanted to be that person. The one who could have worn that wedding dress with authenticity. With a sense of belonging. I wanted that more than almost anything.

I hope Buzz finds happiness.

I hope I do too.

I make a cup of peppermint tea, plump up my pillows, and turn out the light.

Afterword

This book is a fiction, of course, but one which rests on some firmly factual footings.

The life of the undercover police officer is often as remarkable – and as dangerous – as I've portrayed it. It's true, for example, that the national undercover training course is the hardest offered by the police service. True too that the vast majority of applicants fail. Also true that undercover officers receive no huge overtime payments, no vast bonuses to make up for the fact that their old life disappears, that their family ties are severed, almost completely. It's also not my invention that a legend is for ever: the bad guys don't go away just because you happen to have completed an assignment. The fear lives on.

As for the technology in this book – all that audio and video bugging, the transmitters and the RF scanners – they're all real too, and not just real, but very cheap. If you want to buy a voice-activated bugging device that looks like (and is) an ordinary power socket, it'll set you back about fifty quid. Pens that record, little magnetic gizmos that track cars, RF scanners that find them – you'll find all these things sold by the bigger online stores, and at prices that are scarily affordable. In this new dawn of surveillance, no one ever knows if they're safe.

Furthermore, many of the incidents in the book were informed by my conversations with former undercover officers or those that managed them. When, for example,

Brattenbury decides to 'arrest' Fiona as a way of removing her from the enquiry, he was simply doing what countless other police officers have done in real life. When Anna Quintrell makes a long and detailed confession to her cellmate, her mistake is one that countless other criminals have made in the past. Even that final journey to the farmhouse: the way that Henderson eliminated aerial pursuit came straight from an account given to me by a recently serving police officer. If it seems ungenerous of me not to name those people who have helped me – well, they would prefer to remain in the shadows. My thanks to them anyway. This book owes them, big time.

Oh, and one last thing. The press has been rightly critical of certain recent undercover operations, which were poorly targeted and slackly managed. But those operations are not, I think, typical. Most undercover enquiries are aimed at infiltrating and breaking some deeply unpleasant organisations: criminal gangs who use intimidation and violence as a routine part of their trade. Those gangs need to be destroyed and their senior officers arrested and convicted. The burden of achieving that – and achieving that by lawful means – falls, to a disproportionate extent, on a small group of astonishingly brave officers whose exploits will never, and can never, gain public recognition. We all owe them, however. Our streets are safer because of their commitment and courage.

HB

We've attempted to track down the copyright holder for the dedication quote, but without luck. We invite that person to get in touch with us directly.

A Note on Cotard's Syndrome

Cotard's syndrome is a rare but perfectly genuine condition, and an exceptionally serious one besides. Its core ingredients are depression and psychosis, which together bring about an extreme form of depersonalisation. Or, to put the same thing in plainer language: sufferers believe themselves to be dead. Patients frequently report 'seeing' their flesh decompose and crawl with maggots. Early childhood trauma is implicated in pretty much every well-documented case of the syndrome. Full recovery is uncommon, death by suicide all too frequent.

Fiona Griffiths's own state of mind is, of course, a fictional representation of a complex illness and I have not sought to achieve clinical precision. Nevertheless, the broad strokes of her condition would be familiar to anyone unfortunate enough to be acquainted with it.

*The Strange Death
of Fiona Griffiths*

Reader's Notes

About the Author

The twenty-five word biog:

Forty-something.
Married. British. Kids.
Living in Oxfordshire.
Runs The Writers' Workshop (www.writersworkshop.co.uk).
Used to be a banker.
Now a full-time writer.
Likes rock climbing, walking, swimming.
Done.

The Story Behind *The Strange Death of Fiona Griffiths*

The hardest challenge for any author of series fiction is to keep each new book the same but different. It has to be the same, because the central character marches on from book to book, and because many of her challenges, colleagues and objectives remain identical. But it has to feel fresh, too. Different settings, different rhythms, new discoveries.

After I was done with the last book (*Love Story, with Murders*), I had no idea where to go next. I cast around in the way I usually do: reading widely, wild swimming in the Thames, daydreaming a *lot*. Then I came across a comment in an excellent book on police procedure to the effect that the old tricks are still the best. Tricks, for example, such as having a police officer pose as a prisoner so that they can share a cell – and confidences – with the prisoner who is the real target of investigation. That was a real lightbulb moment for me. I knew instantly that I wanted to have Fiona imprisoned in the same cell as one of her key suspects. But a one-off, single night's adventure felt too small, too safe – so that led me to the idea of making her work undercover throughout the inquiry. And I loved the idea of her gaining the trust of the criminals by entering their lives at the lowest possible level: a homeless woman with an unhappy past. Who could possibly be afraid of little Fiona Grey, after all?

I cast around and found a former undercover officer willing to talk to me. More lightbulb moments, many of them. To take just one example, my contact was explaining to me how the police tended to extricate officers who they thought might be in danger. We were eating in a pleasant pub by the side of a river. 'Let's just say that you were the undercover officer,' said my contact, 'and let's say that I was the DI in charge of the operation. We'd probably place bugs in this salt cellar, but because we wouldn't know which table you'd be sitting at, we'd just bug every single table. Then, if we wanted to pull you out, we'd do that very visibly. Four or five squad cars. Armed officers. We'd arrest you with plenty of force, hurting you if need be. Get the handcuffs on you and get you out of there.'

Wow! It wasn't hard to see Fiona revelling in that kind of situation, and it was also pretty obvious that I'd have a lot of fun messing around with her various identities. So all I needed was a crime, a corpse and I was off and running.

I loved writing *Strange Death*, but I did worry about it at times. Was it just too grim? Too relentlessly hard on poor old Fiona? In my first draft, I took things just a little easy, because I was scared of making things too intense. Then I showed that draft to my editor, who basically said, 'Great, Harry, but can you make it more intense, please? Just ramp it up.' So I did. What you've read is that ramped-up version: for my money, the best book I've ever written. I loved writing it, and I hope you enjoyed the ride as much as I did.

Harry Bingham, 2015

For Discussion

- How important is the landscape in *The Strange Death of Fiona Griffiths*?

- Are Buzz's expectations of Fiona fair? Has she been fair to him? Did you want their relationship to last?

- 'The braveries and stupidities. The two things, hand in hand.' Do you think they are hand in hand?

- 'More than half the time, we ask questions whose answers we think we know. Often enough, you ask the question *because* . . . you want to force the other person to acknowledge that fact.' Do you agree with Fiona, or does this tell us something about her – or the police?

- 'I often like the bad guys.' Why do you think Fiona feels this way?

- 'You know when you're excited? That's quite like being scared, isn't it? I mean, it's like they're next-door feelings, almost the same thing.' Do you agree with Fiona? And what does it tell you about her that she feels the need to ask?

- Why is Fiona Grey happier than Fiona Griffiths?

- 'People *want* to confess. An urge as deep as breathing. The beautiful relief of sharing secrets.' Is this your experience?

- Why does Fiona like the thought that there will always be shotgun pellets in her leg?

- Which Fiona do you like most?

Q&A

Q Why did you choose Wales as a setting?

A Lots of reasons, but the main one is simple: I love the place. I spent much of my childhood (and all the best bits) not far from the hills where Fiona and Henderson enjoy their final intimate moment. The valley where that farm-house is located is one of my absolute favourite places in the world – and I'm not telling you where it is.

Q 'I don't do well with careful.' How important is Fiona's recklessness?

A Very. It's one of the keys to her character – although I'm not sure if 'reckless' is quite the right word.

For one thing, her don't-give-a-damn quality extends to everything, large or small. So if one of her bosses is yelling at her, for example, she simply doesn't care: she just notes that Brattenbury's rollickings are a bit more Oxbridgey than Jackson's, and lets him go on doing his stuff until he's ready to finish. That's not reckless, not really – she just doesn't care.

Also, recklessness normally implies something like stupidity. But you have to remember that Fiona has acute problems feeling her own feelings. The sensation she gets at times of extreme peril is actually calming to her. Yes, she's scared . . . but then, that must mean she's alive, she's human. She's *feeling* things, which is great: the outcome that Fiona wants more than anything else in the world. That's not a logic which makes sense to the rest of us, but to Fiona, it's compelling.

Q 'I find it easier to deal with her appearance than my own.' Why is Fiona Griffiths more comfortable with Fiona Grey than with herself?

A Interesting question. I think the reason is that Fiona Griffiths knows that she's meant to be a *real* human being, with a solid footing on Planet Normal, yet she has a pretty ropey understanding of who she is, what she likes, what she feels, what music she likes, what clothes she prefers, and so on. Simply put: she has huge problems being herself. Maybe we all have those problems to some extent, but Fiona's challenges are on a much bigger scale.

As for Fiona Grey – phooey. She's just an artificial construct, a creation of the police service. She doesn't have to be 'authentic': there's no such thing. I think Fiona Griffiths finds that restful. And then, too, it's OK for Fiona Grey to bump along at the very bottom of the social order. She doesn't face any expectations that she should be anything other than a put-upon skivvy. Fiona Griffiths, I think, finds that lack of pressure very calming.

Q 'You can't be a police officer and not admire criminality at its most talented and audacious.' Do you admire the proposed crime?

A Hmm. Let me reverse the question. Do *you* admire – to pick a real-life crime – the guys who ran Lehman Brothers? Or the people who drove the Royal Bank of Scotland into the ground? On the one hand, what they did was epic. It was heroic in scale, almost Shakespearean. But what they did was really, really destructive, and the perpetrators have walked away scot-free. There's certainly something

452

striking about that kind of behaviour. But admirable? I don't think so. I think it stinks.

Q How important is Fiona's intelligence?

A Yes, it matters. Personally, I think any decent mystery novel needs a super-intelligent sleuth at its heart. The novel needs to display the evidence, in a reasonably fair way, to reader and police alike. The reader and the police can come up with whatever conclusions seem logical . . . but then (ta-daaa!) the detective reveals what's *really* been going on. So in that sense, I don't think I'm doing anything unusual in making my detective preternaturally intelligent. I think it's my job.

On the other hand, Fiona's intelligence extends well beyond mere matters of criminal detection. So, for example, when she goes tootling down into Roy's cellar with an armful of weaponry, he says what most readers are surely thinking: 'You're something else, you really are.' Fiona being Fiona, she can't help but notice that his statement is logically weak (because he hasn't defined what the something is that she isn't). That's a weird excess of intellect to have at a time like that, and perhaps one of the things that keep her floating above Planet Normal.

But then, as well, Fiona can be a complete idiot. She's a useless cook. Her grasp of popular culture is dismal. And some of her remarks ('Do men do fist-bumps? Or is that just an American thing?') reveal how clumsily she sometimes navigates the world she finds herself in. It makes her wonderful to write about, though.

Q Do you know how Fiona's life will progress, or do you work on a book-by-book basis?

A I know the broad outline of the series. I know who her biological father is. I know if she will be successful in finding him, and what she'll do with that knowledge. I know what happened to her in those first two mysterious years. I know whether she'll have a successful long-term relationship and, if she does, who the lucky individual will be. I also know that the crimes of books one, two and three are a little more interconnected than most readers will have guessed. Indeed, I know that those crimes and Fiona's strange past are more connected than they appear. The book after *Strange Death* will take a big step forward on some of these issues, but there'll be plenty of mysteries yet to uncover.

Q Why doesn't Fiona like Jessica Taylor?

A I'm not sure. I think it's two things. The first is that we all have a range of personalities inside us, ones that express themselves differently in different circumstances. The Fiona Grey personality wasn't a bad fit for Fiona Griffiths – and indeed, Fiona got some unexpected benefits from her little Grey sister (those self-help books, that Anger and Anxiety course). The blonde and brassy Jessica, however, didn't really work for either Fiona. There was just too little overlap. My Fiona isn't a creature of push-up bras and mouthy popularity, so she found that character stressful and hard to maintain.

In addition, I think Fiona simply overestimated her ability to handle the fakery. She was good at slipping from one identity into another, and did it so well she hardly missed her real self. But then she was asked to do it again, and now had to keep *three* identities going, each carefully presented to three different groups of people, with hideous consequences arising should she mess things up. I think she started to crumble under that load. I don't blame her!

Q 'I have once again, it seems, found my true level, which is to be the most junior element in any hierarchy.' How important is this for your writing of Fiona?

A Oh, good question, very good. That sentence holds the key to the book, in a way. I mean, Fiona Griffiths herself already looks like a fairly powerless individual. (She's small, young and female. She works at a junior level for a provincial police force and is often treated as somewhat marginal by her own employers.) But then the shift into Fiona Grey takes Fiona's unimportance to a whole new level.

In the course of this book, Fiona becomes homeless. She works for the minimum wage and sometimes less. That first time at the farmhouse, she is slapped around and laughed at. She's arrested and imprisoned and is hit again. Her friends are homeless people and immigrant cleaners. When she spends time with Amina, she starts out as her friend, then her 'wife' and 'helpmeet', then (when Amina slaps her) she actually becomes Amina's battered wife. And that would seem to be as low as you can get in our society: to be the homeless battered wife of a minimum wage, single-parent illegal immigrant.

But no! At the end of the book, it turns out that she can go lower still. In that final section, Fiona loses her name. She's now just 'Effgee', the skivvy that everyone orders about. And when she climbs that headwall in the Brecon Beacons, her humanness seems to dissolve completely as she becomes a 'creature of mud and stone and water . . . My hair is moorgrass and peatwater. My nails date back to the Old Devonian. My feet are rags of shoe leather, pulled from a Celtic bog.'

Yet that homeless, battered, put-upon creature-without-a-name goes on to smash the criminal ring which has, for so long, seemed like the most powerful thing in her universe. She burns the farmhouse, releases Roy, destroys the gang's escape route and, finally, causes the gang's chief enforcer to hurl himself off a mountain top. And she does all this armed to the teeth – shotgun, Glock, knife – and utterly confident in her own ability to do what she needs to do.

There's something personally impressive in all that, of course. It's one hell of a woman who can do what Fiona does. But more than that, I hope there's a whiff of something broader. Some message to us – the FoFs, the Fans of Fiona – about what we could achieve, some glimpse of the world that could be ours, if we had a bit more of her strength and courage.

Q Do you like Fiona?
A I've said it before and I'll say it again: I love that girl. I adore writing her. I feel more alive in her company. If I ever met her in real life, I'd probably go all pink and tongue-tied, like a teenage boy introduced to some supermodel.

Some readers have (quite rightly) challenged me on this. I mean, Fiona is a police officer but, in this book, she takes £60,000 that isn't hers and she sabotages a senior police officer's computer. In previous books, she's helped herself to illegal firearms and raced off on vigilante-style expeditions to defeat bad guys. This is *not* how police officers should behave, to put it mildly. And the truth is that if Dennis Jackson ever found out what Fiona was up to, he'd fire her on the spot, and probably launch criminal proceedings, too. Personally, I think Jackson would be right to do so.

Q **Do you have a way for readers to stay in touch with you?**

A I do indeed. On the contact page of my website, HarryBingham.com, you can sign up to a mailing list which will let me tell you whenever I have a new book out. You'll get, at most, one or two emails a year, and it'll be easy to unsubscribe if you want to. But I do hope that there'll be plenty of people who want to follow Fiona's journey all the way: she and I are lucky to have such committed readers.

Suggested Further Reading

Faceless Killers by Henning Mankell
The Neon Rain by James Lee Burke
The Field of Blood by Denise Mina
Let it Bleed by Ian Rankin
The Millennium Trilogy by Stieg Larsson
Rogue Male by Geoffrey Household
The Spy Who Came in from the Cold by John le Carré
Emotion: A Very Short Introduction by Dylan Evans